BLAME IT ON THE PAIN

ASHLEY JADE

Attribution

A special thank you to the photographers listed here as we greatly appreciate their work and artistry.

Picture Acknowledgments
Some photos use are used via creative commons and built upon the originals.
https://creativecommons.org/licenses/by-sa/2.0/

Blame It on the Pain

"Only after disaster can we be resurrected. It's only after you've lost everything that you're free to do anything."
—Chuck Palahniuk, Fight Club

Prologue (Jackson)

P ain. It hurts us. It pushes us. It punishes us.

Or, for the few poor souls out there like me...it defines us.

I'm not a good person.

There are no redeeming qualities about me...not anymore.

Any that I had, I'd given to the devil on the night that changed everything.

The night my baby sister died.

The night I murdered her killer.

Yes, I've taken a life...and I would do it again in a heartbeat.

I grew up in Boston. For the most part, I was just an average hard working kid trying to make it into the professional world of MMA fighting.

My mom kicked the bucket when I was 18 from a heroin overdose, and if you know where my father is...well then, give that asshole sperm donor a big *'fuck you'* for me.

It's safe to say that Lilly was the only family I had.

She was four years younger than me, and I spent most of my life either looking out for her or bitching about how annoying she was.

After our mom died, it was just her and I.

Who am I kidding...it was her and I since day one.

My mother's death changed nothing. In fact, Lilly's high school didn't even question when I was the one who stepped up and filled in for all the parental duties.

Here's where I fucked up.

I let my best friend date my little sister.

Mike was training to become a professional MMA fighter as well. We all grew up together, and one day, I caught him making eyes at Lilly...or rather, her making eyes at him.

Obviously, I put an end to that shit as soon as it started.

When she was 14.

The next four years were filled with them making constant googly eyes at one another, but other than that- we were like the three musketeers.

Lilly would even watch us train...she was like our own personal cheerleader.

I'd see her innocent blue eyes and strawberry blonde curls routing for us at every single session.

On her 18 birthday...I caved.

"I'm in love with your sister and I swear to god, I'm going to marry her one day," Mike said as I choked on my beer.

Before I even had time to knock him out or protest...Lilly's 5'1, lanky frame bounced into the room and landed beside Mike.

She grabbed his hand and looked up at me. "I love him, Jackson."

I grunted and downed the rest of my beer before I reached over and grabbed Mike by his shoulders. "Outside...*now*."

He let go of Lilly's hand and followed me out to the porch.

The old wooden swing seat creaked under our weight when we sat down. "You're 22...she's 18."

He laughed. "I know. But it's really not that much of an age difference anymore, especially now that she's legal." He looked down at his feet. "Besides, I've loved her since she was 14."

My stomach knotted and I balled my fists. "That's disgusting."

He rolled his eyes. "Obviously, I didn't do anything about it, asshole," he said. "It's not like that. It's more than sex."

My entire body tensed at those words and I stood up.

I was about two seconds away from knocking his lights out when he shouted, "Which we still haven't had, I swear!"

We both breathed a sigh of relief then. "Look, I know I'm going to spend the rest of my life with her. Now the only question is whether you're going to be happy and support us, or if it's going to come to blows and we're going to ruin a friendship over it. Not to mention, possibly ruining your relationship with your sister."

I shook my head. "You're a fucking prick."

He gave me a wry smile. "No, I'm not, Jackson. If I was, you would have knocked my ass out already. You know I'm a good guy. You know I'll take care of her. I'm *your* best friend for crying out loud."

I crossed my arms over my chest. "You hurt her, I'll kill you. You knock her up before she's 30, I'll kill you. If you cheat on her, I'll kill you. If you ever make her cry...I'll kill you."

He looked me in the eyes. "If I ever do any of those things; then, I wouldn't want to live anyway." He paused. "So, does this mean we have your blessing?" I halfheartedly gave a nod as I heard Lilly come bouncing out the front door.

Her smile was infectious and her eyes were gleaming.

She wrapped her arms around me tighter than she ever had before.

"I love you, big brother...this is the best birthday ever!"

I sighed and returned her hug.

F or two years Mike kept his promise.

He treated her like gold and I'd never seen Lilly happier.

Both Mike and I continued to train hard, trying to make it big in the MMA world.

We trained at one of the best gyms and had a coach who swore our big break was right around the corner.

He was right.

Mike was closing in on a deal with a big time sponsor, and I was about to sign a pretty big endorsement deal with a sponsor myself.

My first professional fight was scheduled for one week away.

At almost 24, my dreams were finally coming true.

I was so wrapped up in my own world...I never noticed the signs.

I never noticed when my sister's innocent blue eyes lost their sparkle.

I never noticed when her bubbly personality changed.

I *almost* didn't notice when she stopped showing up to watch us train.

"What's up with my sister? I haven't talked to her in like two weeks. She hasn't shown up here lately...why is that?" I asked Mike as we headed to the locker room after a training session.

Mike shrugged. "I don't know, she's been studying really hard. I think she wanted to go shopping today. She said something about wanting to get a new outfit for the big fight next week."

I laughed. "Yeah, I guess that makes sense. Her boyfriend and big brother are having their first professional fight on the very same night."

I knew that no matter how hard Lilly's intense course load at Harvard was, she wouldn't miss the fight for the world.

He looked down and I watched as he shifted his weight from foot to foot. "Yeah..."

Something was off. I put my hand on his shoulder. "What's going on?"

He shrugged me off and walked toward the showers. "Just a little nervous is all," he called out.

I finished showering before he did.

I walked over to our lockers and proceeded to get dressed. He stupidly left his locker half open...and that's when I noticed it.

A tiny bottle of something that wasn't labeled...along with a needle.

It didn't take a genius to figure out what it was.

Steroids.

I swiped it from his locker and waited for him to come out. "What the fuck are you doing, Mike? Are you trying to ruin your career before it even starts?" I screamed.

He looked around the locker room. "Keep your fucking voice down. What if coach hears you?" he hissed as he reached for the bottle.

I pulled back. "Over my dead body. No way am I letting you ruin everything you've worked so hard for. What the fuck is the matter with you? I never thought you would do something like this!"

He punched the locker beside him. "Everybody in the sports industry uses, Jackson. I'm going to stop after I win the next few fights...it's just enough to put me on the map."

"You're an idiot. You're about to sign a deal with a big sponsor! You don't think they're going to test you for roids? Even more than that, you're ruining the integrity of the sport. *All* sports. Passion is what should be flowing through your body...*not* this shit."

"Look, some of us don't have it like you do. Some of us need a little help from time to time. And I'm not the only athlete to ever try it, most have. It's just a little pick me up."

I shook my head and glared at him. "This isn't a 'pick me up', this shit will send you straight to hell in a hand-basket. Train better, work harder...*don't* do this shit."

He sighed and slumped down on the bench. "You're right. I fucked up, I've just been so nervous and I'm second guessing myself. I don't want to lose."

I sat down next to him. "I understand. What makes you think

I'm not feeling the same way? This is a huge deal for us, and it's normal to be nervous. Use that nervous energy as positive fuel. This shit will ruin your life."

He nodded. "Don't tell Lilly about this, please."

"I won't. Besides, if she knew, the fight next week would be the least of your worries. I'm pretty sure she'd kick your ass so bad you wouldn't be able to train for weeks."

He grinned and began changing into his street clothes. "Yup, you're right about that. God, I love that woman."

Blood.
        So much blood. Everywhere.

That's one of the things that I remember most about that fateful night.

To this day, I can still close my eyes and recall every single surface marked by blood. The metallic smell of it permeating my nostrils, the way it smeared the walls, the way it pooled on the floor —the large bloody hand print on the wall.

The night my entire world changed, was also the night of the big fight.

I had won. It was a close match and I was definitely swinging for the fences like my life depended on it. My opponent ended up tapping out after a hard uppercut to his jaw that sent him staggering, followed by an axe kick which finished him off.

I looked out into the crowd expecting to see Lilly's smiling face...but I didn't.

Even more alarming...Mike never showed up for his own fight.

Some guy named Tyrone ended up taking his place and won after 3 minutes of conducting an intense ground and pound on his opponent that was brutal enough to make me wince.

Something was definitely wrong...I felt it in my bones. I high-tailed it out of the arena while dialing their numbers repeatedly.

I hopped in my truck and headed straight for their apartment.

When I walked in I had to take a step back.

My worst nightmare couldn't have conjured up what was waiting for me on the other side of the door.

Everything seemed to play out in slow motion while I tried to take in and process what I was seeing.

The first thing I noticed was the large bloody hand print against the stark white wall of their small kitchen. My eyes dropped down and my heart squeezed for dear life when I saw the large pool of blood on the floor. It expanded and rounded a corner leading up to the living room.

I didn't want to know where it was coming from...but I knew I had no choice but to find out.

I closed my eyes and took a few tentative steps forward until I rounded the corner.

There on the floor beside the couch...was where my heart turned into dust and my world as I knew it, would cease to exist.

My small, fragile, baby sister's pale, cold, lifeless body was laid out before me.

Her shirt was torn and bruises covered most of her limp, frail, body.

The image still haunts me in my darkest moments.

I dropped down beside her and willed her to wake up.

How could someone do this to her? My innocent baby sister. The greatest person I'd ever known.

I shook her, I shouted her name. I begged and I pleaded harder than I ever had in my life.

"Who would do this to *you*, Lilly?" I whispered, as I held her. "Come on baby sis, wake up. Please," I continued to beg as I felt the first few tears start rolling down.

My thoughts went wild. I thought up dozens of different scenarios in that moment. Everything from a burglar, a secret stalker at the college she attended, to a drug dealer who had the wrong house looking for his money.

Mike. Where the hell was he?

Shit, maybe whoever did this was holding Mike hostage somewhere?

I looked back down at Lilly and my chest felt like it caved in. Something deep within me had severed in that moment. Nothing would ever be the same again.

I looked up to the ceiling and screamed with tears streaming down my face.

I heard some kind of rustling in the distance, near the bedroom down the hallway before a tall shadow loomed before me.

I knew that shadow well. *Almost* as well as I knew my own.

I gently let go of Lilly's body and rose from the ground.

He had the makings of what looked like was going to be a black eye. He also had a fairly large scratch across his cheek.

I quickly looked down at Lilly's pink nails and noticed some dried blood caked under them.

She fought like hell.

I lifted my head and glared at him. I looked him right in the eyes...and I *knew*.

He did this.

He killed her.

He murdered my baby sister...the girl he swore he would love and protect.

Suddenly everything made sense...like why she never showed up to watch us at practice anymore. Why she seemed so distant. Why she didn't seem as happy anymore when I talked to her.

He was abusing her...and *I* ignored all the signs.

I didn't protect my sister...the only person in the world that I loved more than anything.

He bowed his head and teetered back as I advanced toward him. He held up his hands. "Just let me explain. It was an accident. It was her fau—"

Rage filled my blood, and it burned through my veins. I punched him hard. Hard enough that I heard the satisfying snap of his jaw dislocating. "Don't you *dare* try to blame her. Did you give Lilly a chance to talk before you beat the shit out of her and killed her!" I screamed as I punched him again, even harder. This time, sending him to the floor.

He tried to get up but I sent a sharp kick to his ribs. "I told you what I would do to you if you ever hurt her," I sneered before I picked him up by his hair and bashed his head into the nearest wall.

He tried to fight me off, but he didn't stand a chance in hell.

I punched him again and relished when I saw a few teeth fall out. Blood filled his mouth as I dragged him into the kitchen, purposely knocking his head into every hard surface I could find along the way.

We grappled for a few more minutes before I landed on top of him. I continued to punch him letting my rage take over.

"It was the steroids, Jackson. It turned me into a different person. I don't know who I am anymore. Lilly pissed me off and—" he started to sputter through the blood in his mouth.

The fact that he was even attempting to defend himself and still blame Lilly after what he had done only fueled my anger and pain.

"You're a fucking killer," I growled before I dealt another blow to his head.

It was something we were going to have in common real soon.

His eyes opened wide. "Stop. You're really gonna kill me, Jackson."

My fist went flying straight for his chest, effectively silencing him.

His eyes rolled back in his head and a low gurgling sound filled the room.

I reached down and fisted his hair while meeting his stare. "Did *you* listen when my baby sister begged *you* to stop?" I questioned before I sent a karate chop straight to his neck.

Adrenaline mixed with guilt, grief and wrath like I'd never felt before coursed through me as I continued to pummel him.

At some point, I saw life leave his traitorous eyes and heard sirens looming in the distance.

"His blood was *literally* found on your hands, Mr. Reid. You don't stand a chance in hell of walking away from this without doing some serious prison time." My good for nothing attorney informed me.

I glanced down at the cuffs around my wrists. "Did they test his blood for steroids like I told you to have them do?" I asked.

"Yeah. He came back clean."

Fuck. How was that even possible?

That meant that he was in his right state of mind when he murdered her after all.

Rage bubbled in my chest at the thought.

I leaned back in my chair and sighed. "He *killed* my baby sister. It was self-defense."

He matched my sigh. "His attorney is saying otherwise, son."

"*His* attorney. What the fuck are you talking about? He's dead- as he *should* be. Why the fuck does he have an attorney?"

He fixed his tie before he looked at me. "I didn't want to be the one to break it to you, but there's no point in keeping it from you any longer. The big-time sponsor and agent that Mike signed with are going after *you*, Jackson. Not to mention his *very* wealthy parents. They're working with the prosecution and blaming it all on you. They're doing everything that they can to protect their brand. And his parents are doing everything *they* can to protect their family's reputation. They're fighting your story tooth and nail. They're a huge sponsor and combined with Mike's family they have lots of connections and resources. They have the means to take you down."

He paused and looked down. "And the fact is- there were only three people there that night...and two of them are now dead. It's your word against theirs...and it doesn't look good. Especially because you basically admitted to killing him."

He reached into his briefcase and pulled out a folder. "Also, this showed up at my office today. I'm really sorry, Jackson."

I skimmed the letter and pounded my fist on the table. My own sponsor and agent had officially dropped me.

I would no longer be welcomed in the professional MMA world ever again.

"So what are my options?"

He ran a hand over his bald head. "Well, I talked to the prosecutor. I got Man-one off the table." He pulled another stack of papers out and moved his glasses up his nose. "The best they will offer you at this point is Manslaughter-two. 15-25 years. However, here's the clincher- if you *don't* take the deal. Mike's team *will* be teaming up with the prosecution against you." He sighed. "I hate to say it—but this is the only shot you've got."

I pinched the bridge of my nose and snorted. "15-25 years, for killing a piece of shit abuser?"

He visibly swallowed. "And Lilly," he whispered.

I stood up to my full height of 6'3 and got in his face, my shackles straining against me. "What the fuck do you mean *and* Lilly? I didn't kill my sister!" I screamed.

If I wasn't shackled to the heavy metal desk, I would have beat the crap out of him for spewing some shit like that.

He took a step back. "I told you, Mike's team is working with the prosecution. They're not putting the blame on Mike for this, Jackson. They're twisting some horrid tale about you and your sister being super *close* after growing up the way you did...if you catch my drift."

Bile ascended my throat as he continued. "They're going to say that you were jealous of Mike and your sister's relationship. Combined with the fact that he came from wealth and landed a much better sponsor than you did...it all leads to jealousy being the motive."

"But, I was at the fight that night. Hell, I *won* my fight that night. Hundreds of people saw me with their own eyes. Mike and Lilly never even showed up!"

"They're saying that you killed them before the fight because you didn't want him to compete in the first place." He made air quotes with his hands. "Because your jealousy got the best of you and finally came to a head."

I threw up my hands. "And then what? I just decided to attend my fight with his blood on my hands and *then* return to the scene of the crime instead of getting the hell out of dodge? That's insane."

"According to the prosecution's story, you returned to find a way to get rid of the bodies."

"This is bullshit."

"It is," he agreed.

I shook my head. "I'm *not* taking that deal. I'll take my chances in court. I didn't kill Lilly. If they were just accusing me of killing Mike, I would consider folding- because I *did* kill him. But I will not go down for committing the heinous act that *he* did."

He rubbed his scalp again and sat back down in the chair. "Look, I've got to level with you. We won't win this." He motioned toward the papers on the desk. "I'm good at my job. And I fully believe you didn't kill Lilly, even more- I understand what you did to Mike...but I *can't* win this. The system is corrupt as fuck, and we've got everything going against us right now. You're not walking away from this. The only option left is to plead insanity and spend the rest of your life in a straight jacket and a padded room."

I got up and motioned for the guard on the opposite side of the door.

"No," I said gruffly.

Ten days before my trial was supposed to begin, I was informed I had a visitor. Since my lawyer had pretty much all but given up on the case, I was a little surprised.

Maybe he had finally come to his senses and decided to fight for me the way he was supposed to.

I looked around the dreary gray room while I took a seat beside the metal desk. My attention soon focused on the sound of the door opening.

In walked a man wearing an impeccable suit, holding a fairly large briefcase.

He tipped his hat at me before he sat down in front of me.

"Who the hell are you?" I asked.

He gave me a smirk and pulled a pack of cigarettes out of his pocket. "I'm your new lawyer," he said.

I stood up and tilted my head in the direction of the guard, signaling him to let me out so I could go back to my cell. "I think there's been some mistake. I don't recall asking for a new lawyer." I eyed his expensive suit and snorted. "Besides, I'm positive I can't afford you anyway. I have legal aid for crying out loud."

"Sit down, Jackson." His voice boomed throughout the room.

Looking back—I wouldn't say I was scared of him...it was more like intrigued about what he was doing there in the first place.

I begrudgingly sat back down and stared at him. "Okay, let's just cut to the chase then. What's this about? Who are you?"

He cracked his knuckles and leaned back in his seat. "You can just call me your guardian angel, boy," he said smirking.

I had recently turned 24 at that point, and I was practically on death row for killing a man. I was far from a boy and didn't appreciate being told otherwise.

I narrowed my eyes at him. "You have 1 minute before I walk the fuck out of here. I don't give a shit who you are."

He studied me for a beat before he rubbed his chin and laughed. "Alright. Let's just say that I have a proposition for you." He cracked his knuckles again. "Something like a get out of jail free card. You interested?'

I raised an eyebrow at him. "From what I'm told...not even God, himself can get me out of this shithole."

He leaned forward and proceeded to light a cigarette, his eyes gleaming. "No, you're right. God can't..." He flashed me a smile. "But the devil can."

Chills ran up my spine with those words. "I would ask what the catch is, but I'm not sure I want to know," I mumbled.

I heard the click of his briefcase and he handed me what looked to be a contract of some sort.

The first thing that stood out was the name.

"Who's Bruno DeLuca? That you?" I questioned.

He laughed. "No, that is not me. However, I work for him. He's the one who sent me here."

I skimmed the rest of the contract, but I didn't understand it. It just said that I would agree to work for Bruno DeLuca for the next ten years, and failure to uphold my end of the agreement would result in disciplinary action. "What kind of work? And why the fuck would he want me? Who is this guy? And more importantly, what the fuck makes him think he can get me out of serving time for murder?"

He winked and gave me another smirk. "Let's just say that Bruno DeLuca knows a thing or two about murder, kid."

I stood up. "Okay, I've had it with the games. I have a trial in 10 days that I need to prepare for and I really don't need this bullshit." I looked at the guard through the plexiglass and signaled for him but he ignored me. I got up and proceeded to bang on the glass when the man's voice halted me.

"Sign that contract and you won't even have to prepare for trial. You'll be out of here within the next 48 hours. You won't go down for your sister's murder, Jackson. And more importantly, no one will be making disgusting and untrue accusations about your relationship with her in a court of law and tarnishing her memory."

Needless to say, that got my attention. "What does he want from me?"

"He wants you to do the thing you love the most. Compete and fight."

I spun around and faced him. "That's not going to happen...I'm pretty sure I've been canned from the professional world of MMA fighting. No sponsors or agents will touch me with a 10-foot pole."

He barked out a laugh before his expression turned serious. "This isn't professional fighting. This is underground fighting."

I said the first thing that popped into my head. "That's illegal."

He blew a puff of smoke out and shrugged. "Last time I checked, so was *murder*."

Well, he had me there. Even though I still didn't feel a single ounce of remorse for it.

I sat back down at the table and took a cigarette out of the pack. "Okay, explain to me how he has the means to do this and why he wants me...and I'll consider it."

He smiled and lit my cigarette. "I realize you're from Boston, kid, but Bruno DeLuca is the biggest mob boss to hit New York City since the five families."

I took another drag off my cigarette...I definitely needed it.

"And he runs an underground fighting ring?"

He wiggled his eyebrows. "Amongst other endeavors, yes."

"And he wants *me* because..."

"Because you showed real potential before you got locked up. Not to mention, you beat the shit out of and *murdered* a fellow professional fighter- one who our sources say was even *more* talented than you."

"It was only because of the roids he was on," I muttered.

He waved me off. "Personally, I don't give a shit. The point is that DeLuca wants you, kid. And you're not really in a position to say no to him. You're up shits creek without a paddle."

At least on that fact, I could wholeheartedly agree with him.

"I just don't get how I would be able to walk out of here, though. Look around, I'm in *jail* for Christ's sake. I'm pretty sure the judicial system would have something to say about my release."

He stared at me hard before he rubbed his fingers together. "Money and power, kid. It makes the world go round'." His expression turned serious. "For starters, he's going to buy off the judge. He's also having evidence planted that will end up proving your innocence as we speak."

I held up my hands. "Whoa, I'm *not* okay with having an innocent man go down for murders that he didn't commit."

"That's not for you to decide, kid. Let's just say that this guy crossed DeLuca, so he's only getting what's coming to him. You just get to reap the benefits."

I put out my cigarette and went to stand again. "No. I won't do it."

"You don't really have a choice, Jackson."

"What's *that* supposed to mean?"

"If you don't take the deal and work for DeLuca...you will be attacked in your cell, later on, tonight." He looked me in the eyes. "And, kid. I gotta tell ya...the odds aren't in your favor in regards to making it out alive."

I glared at him. Anger pulsing through me. "So, I never had a choice in the first place, did I?"

He shrugged and handed me a pen. "Afraid not, kid. Welcome to the family."

Three years later...

Chapter 1 (Alyssa)

"Yeah, you like that, you slut?" he says as he continues to plow into me from behind.

His words reverberate through my head and I fight back the tears.

Nope. Not even a little bit.

"Yeah," I say, hoping it will all be over soon.

"Who's a little slut?" he asks before I feel his entire body spasm against me.

"I am," I whisper. All while, secretly hating myself for how true it is and for putting myself through this goddamn scenario, yet again.

All in the name of punishment.

That's what I do, though...that's how I cope. If you could even call it that.

A few more slut shaming insults and a loud grunt later...my penance is over.

I leap off the bed and make a beeline for the bathroom.

I force myself to look in the mirror. "You only did it to yourself, Alyssa," I remind myself.

I close my eyes as I run a washcloth under the warm water and proceed to clean myself up.

A moment later the door opens and arms wrap around me like tentacles.

I move my head from side to side, looking for a way out.

"That was great, babe. Huh?" he asks while adjusting his large framed glasses on his face.

I roll my eyes against his preppy, polo shirt and give him a smile that's about as fake as a two dollar bill. "Yup."

I shimmy past him and nod my head toward the front door. "You can go now," I remind him.

He looks puzzled, which only serves to annoy me further.

I swear, every time we have sex...he gets even more attached. I'm going to have to cut him off soon.

I decide to try the nice approach with him one more time. "Look, I have a job interview today and I really need to get ready for it."

He laughs nervously. "Oh, okay. I was getting a little worried there for a second. Thought you were getting sick of me." He takes a step forward. "When can I see you again? I really want to take you out on a date. I was thinking about taking you to the science..."

Ugh...the walls are officially closing in on me.

I cut him off before he has a chance to finish that sentence. "Look, Brock...I think we need to go over the rules of our arrangement again. This..." I gesture between us. "Is just sex. That's it. Once a week—maximum." I walk toward him and cup his face in my hands. "You are a great guy...but I think this needs to end."

Before he has a chance to argue, I continue on with my spiel. "It's not you, it's *totally* me. I just don't think we're looking for the same things anymore." I give him a kiss on the cheek and walk him to the front door. I unlock the door and give him a little nudge. "I'll see you around. Have a safe drive home. Buh-bye."

I slam the door shut and chain lock it behind me.

He's gone...crisis averted.

I fall back against the door...another innocent, harmless nerd prototype bites the dust before he reached stage 5 clinger status.

With a sigh, I walk back into the bathroom and turn on the shower.

I finish the rest of my shower, and study the clothes I laid out for the interview I have later on tonight.

I pull up my favorite tight pair of jeans over my hips and reach for my low-cut white top...made all that more pronounced by my black push-up bra. Then I blow dry my hair and apply a quick coat of lip gloss and mascara.

I shake out my long blonde hair and run my fingers through it a few times.

I glance at the clock and let out a curse.

Given the fact that the city's about two hours away in rush hour traffic, I'm running dangerously close to being late.

And lord knows, I *desperately* need this job.

After throwing on my favorite leather crop jacket, I give myself a once over in the mirror again and decide I'm ready to go.

I can't afford to blow this opportunity.

His dirt brown eyes skim over my body before landing on my chest. He rubs his chin and nods. "Very nice. Now, turn around and bend over for me, sweetheart."

Somewhere very deep inside, my inner feminist wants to claw his eyes out. But then I remind myself that all I've got in the fridge is a container of moldy milk...and cheese that looks like it will make good penicillin soon.

But that fails in comparison to the real reason I need this job.

I turn around and do what he says while he lets out a whistle. After a few moments have passed, I assume it's safe to turn back around and my inspection is over.

He considers me for another minute or so and gives me another nod. "You're easy on the eyes, that's for sure. And you got a rockin' body." He holds up a cue card with a giant number on it. "Think you'll be able to manage holding these up in the cage?" he asks hesitantly.

Seriously...is he kidding?

I maintained a 4.0 for 3 years while studying journalism and news-casting at NYU for crying out loud.

I flash him a strained smile. "Gee, I don't know, Mister. It looks awfully hard."

He cocks an eyebrow at me.

*Shit...*I really need to learn to tone the sarcasm down every once in a while.

He clears his throat. "You and another girl will be trading off. You'll be in the green outfit and she'll be in the red."

Awe, just like Christmas, I think before he continues with his sermon.

"And when you're not working the ring. You'll be eye candy for the elite members. You are to serve them beers, whiskey, whatever their hearts desire in between rounds. Got it?"

I nod my head. "Yes, sir."

He gives me another hard look. "And if you do anything to draw attention to this little operation we got going on here, it will take them a week to clean your brains off the pavement."

I shudder at his choice of words.

"Got it. The first rule of fight club is that you don't talk about fight club."

He shoots me a look of annoyance and mumbles something under his breath that I don't catch.

"So when do I start?' I ask eagerly.

He reaches into his desk drawer and pulls out two scraps of shiny green material. "In two hours. Get ready," he says before throwing them at me.

My mouth hangs open. "You mean, I start tonight?'

He leans his elbows against the desk. "That gonna be a problem for you?"

I quickly shake my head. "No. I would have just come more prepared if I had known is all."

He extends his thumb in the direction of the hallway. "Down the hall and to the left there's a dressing room for the ring girls. There is makeup and all that other girly shit in there." He glances at his watch. "In fact, Lou-Lou should be in there getting ready right now. I suggest you make nice with her. The only fights we like around here are the ones that bring in money. Not no prissy cat fights. Last girl got fired for that," he warns.

"You won't have a problem," I assure him. I make for the door when I abruptly turn around. "Um. So how much does this gig pay anyway?"

He chuckles. "Well, you'll only be working one weekend night, every two weeks," he says. My excitement sinks with those words. "But, you'll be making $800 for the night...plus tips."

I give him a genuine smile this time before I begin walking down the hallway.

L ou-Lou turned out to be nicer than I thought she would be. With her honey-kissed skin, full lips, small stature, and big brown eyes...it was easy to see why she'd been hired.

She flips her long dark hair over her shoulder and studies our reflection in the mirror before she ruffles my hair and winks. "We're like totally salt and peppa," she squeaks. "The guys are totally gonna love us."

Rein in your inner bitch and be nice, Alyssa. I remind myself.

I suck in my stomach and add a bit more bronzer to my mostly pale cheeks.

She gives me another smile before she takes a few steps toward the door. I look at the clock on the wall. "Shit, is it time already?"

She pops her gum and giggles. "No, silly. We need to take care of the fighters before the match."

Say what, now?

"Take care of them...how?" She gives me a wink. "Use your imagination, girlfriend."

Jesus Christ, I knew there was a catch.

Obviously, unfazed by my horrified expression she continues. "You're lucky. You're wearing green. That means you have Jackson...he's like *mega* hot. I mean, I've never been given the chance to try him out, but God, what I'd give to one day." She playfully fans herself. "I'm stuck with some guy who's good looking, but dumb as a box of rocks." She twists her hair around her finger. "See ya in a half hour, babes," she calls out before she leaves.

I spin my chair around to face the mirror again.

Could I actually do...*this?*

I mean...what I do on my own time, is pretty much the same thing. Except I do it with safe nerdy guys. Guys who are into *anime*, and play *dungeons and dragons* in their mother's basements.

Guys who *I* can control. Guys who will say and do whatever I want them to.

Guys who know about my past, but are just so happy to have a real girl to play with, they couldn't care less.

Guys who are really good at hacking computers and taking down certain things that *always* tend to pop up from time to time since that horrible day over two years ago.

I take a deep breath and calm the tremors running through my stomach.

"You only did it to yourself, Alyssa," I remind myself, yet again before I stand up and begin walking down the hallway.

I open the door.

What I'm greeted with, is a sight I'm sure I'll never forget.

Tanned, muscular, flesh- encompassed by the body of an Adonis.

My eyes can't help but stare at the finest ass I have ever seen in my entire life. Two perfect globes...so ripe, I want to bite them.

I bite my lip instead as my gaze spans over his gorgeous back. Broad, sturdy, *powerful.*

I want to scratch my nails down that back, is my last thought...before he starts to turn around.

He briskly runs the towel through his short, dark, hair. "Jesus, Ricardo. Don't you knock anymore?" he barks until he looks at me.

I can't help but look down, but he quickly shifts the towel from his head, over to his package. Doesn't stop me from taking in his large, toned, thighs, though.

Confusion is splashed all over his face. "You're *not* Ricardo," he says in a deep and raspy voice.

I shake my head. Still too transfixed by his body to speak.

My God. His abs. His abs must be made of pure granite. I silently count them in my head. *Yup, he's got an 8-pack.*

He clears his throat, and it's only then that I finally make my way up his body, but not before noticing the name scrawled over his left pectoral muscle in black ink- '*Lilly*.'

Yup, must be the girlfriend...or *wife*.

I swallow my distaste over the fact that he obviously cheats on her, as I lift my gaze and take in his eyes. Wow, they're something else. Mesmerizing, stormy gray swirls that- I'm betting, would almost look dark blue in the right light.

The rest of his face is just as striking. Full, yet masculine lips combined with a strong jawline. Lou-Lou was wrong- '*mega hot*' doesn't even begin to describe how truly handsome he is.

My gaze turns from one of appreciation to annoyance. "So, I'm guessing Ricardo is who you choose to cheat on your wife with then?"

He opens his mouth in either shock, or in an attempt to defend himself, but I don't give him the chance. "Men like you, *disgust* me. There's *no* way in hell, I'm sleeping with you now, asshole. You can forget it."

He takes a step toward me. "*What?*" He looks dumbfounded as I back away from him. "Christ, there are so many things about that statement that's wrong, I don't even know where to start."

I hold up my hands. "Whatever, I don't fuck married men."

"Good thing I'm not married then," he says.

I stare at him wide-eyed.

"Shit, that didn't come out the way it was supposed to. All I meant was that I'm not married. And if I was, I *certainly* wouldn't cheat on her. And furthermore, I wouldn't cheat on her with *Ricardo*- of all people." He smirks. "Let's just say, he's not my type." He looks me up and down, taking in my scantily clad uniform- which only consists of a shiny green bra top and matching booty shorts. "And I don't know who the hell you've been talking to, but you're not expected to fuck the fighters."

"But, Lou-Lou made it seem like—"

He shakes his head. "Whatever you do, don't listen to Lou- Lou. She's very territorial, and likes to steer the new girls in the wrong direction. Just because *she* makes it her mission to fuck the fighters, doesn't mean that *you* have to." He scratches his head. "Besides, if that was the case—*why* would you ever agree to do that anyway? Don't you value yourself at all?" he asks, his tone dripping with both disdain and curiosity.

"I—" I start. I'm at a loss for words. On one hand, I'm appalled at how judgmental he is - but on the other...he's touched on something so personal.

I open my mouth and attempt to answer him again, but instead...I reach for the doorknob behind me and book it the hell out of the room.

I run back down the hall and enter the dressing room. I lock myself inside the small toilet stall and fight back the tears for the second time that day.

His words echo in my head as I look in the mirror. *"Don't you value yourself at all?"*

I draw in a shaky breath and reapply my makeup expertly while I look myself in the eye.

"No, Jackson. Not anymore."

Chapter 2 (Jackson)

"A nd in this corner- weighing in at 235lbs of pure steel. Ladies and Gentlemen, I present to you- 'Jack the Ripper-rrrrr,' " the announcer yells, while I inwardly cringe.

There are no words to describe how much I truly hate my stage name.

Needless to say, I didn't choose it.

Just like every other decision for the last 3 years, it was made for me.

I have no control over my own life anymore. And I fucking hate it.

Ricardo, my mob appointed coach; taps my back and whispers words of encouragement. I nod my head as he walks off to sit in the far corner.

I look up at the camera positioned directly above the ring and give another nod. This one's for the devil himself, Bruno DeLuca.

I'd only met him once, but I know for a fact that he watches every single match, without fail.

I search the crowd for Tyrone, yes—*that* Tyrone who fought in Mike's place that horrible night. Funny how the world works.

Shortly after I joined the 'DeLuca family', Tyrone ended up joining as well.

Obviously, *not* of his own free will. He got involved with the wrong crowd, in his hometown of Alabama; and ended up going down for some shit that really wasn't his fault, but got put on him anyway.

That's, of course, when DeLuca came in to save the day.

Not only is Tyrone one hell of a fighter, but he's also my good friend and roommate. He's also the only person I talk to about Lilly in my darkest times.

He's not scheduled to fight tonight, but we always show up to support one another.

I lock eyes with him briefly. He gives me a big smile and fist pumps the air. "Give em' hell, J-man! Break bad on em'," he shouts in his thick Southern accent.

I try not to smirk, and study my opponent instead.

I've got about an inch on him, but he's got a good 10-15lbs on me. From what Ricardo told me about him, he's more of a boxer, rather than an MMA fighter.

This should be an interesting match.

That's the other thing about DeLuca's fight club. It's pretty much anything goes. Even dirty style fighting.

Especially dirty style fighting.

My opponent rolls his shoulders and snorts.

The announcer walks off and I hear the sound of the cage being locked around us.

I assume my stance and the bell rings.

Adrenaline pulses through me as he advances toward me and attempts a right jab to my face.

I deflect and cock my arm at a 90-degree angle and get him with a right hook instead. He grunts and comes at me with another jab and quickly attempts to grab me. He almost had me for a second, but I get him with a sharp uppercut to his jaw.

Blood spews out and he begins to stumble backward.

Then I see it.

Out in the crowd, I can't help but notice her in the second row.

The same girl who entered my dressing room earlier.

Only, it's not her long blonde hair, smokin' body, or beautiful hazel eyes that grab my attention this time.

It's the utter fear I see in them.

I look down and see that some asshole has his fingers wrapped tightly around her wrist...and he's not letting up. It looks like she was trying to serve him a drink, but instead, he's forcing her to sit on his lap.

His movements are only getting more aggressive, and no one's doing a damn thing about it. He then reaches up with his other hand and palms one of her breasts.

That's when I lose my shit.

I run over to the side of the cage. "Let her go! *Now!*"

Both he and the crowd ignore me and begin to chant my name instead. I cock my head to the side and look at Ricardo. "Help her! Get her out of here!" I scream.

He points to his ear and shakes his head.

Fuck, he can't hear me.

I scan the crowd for that asshole, Luke, who's supposed to be in charge of the ring girls. He looks over at her, but instead of helping her, he only shrugs and smiles at me.

I growl and flip him the bird.

I look out into the crowd for Tyrone and begin rattling the cage. The crowd cheers even louder then.

Bastards.

I begin scaling the cage, and finally; Tyrone looks at me. I point in her direction. "Get her out of here, now..." I start to say until I'm quickly yanked back.

Something solid hits my eye with enough force to turn my head and knock my mouth guard out.

I can hear the crowd collectively gasp.

I've never been hit dead on before. I've always been able to deflect it.

My opponent smiles from ear to ear...but little does he know that he just unleashed hell.

Out of the corner of my good eye, I see Tyrone heading in her direction.

At least, she'll be safe now. This is no place for a girl like her, that's for sure.

Visions of Lilly flash through my mind. The pain flows through me and I let my opponent have it.

We start to grapple, but it's a lost cause for him. I'm hitting him with numerous elbow strikes, uppercuts, and jabs. I don't even realize I've already knocked him out until someone bombards the cage and pulls me off of him.

I almost take a swing at them, before I hear Ricardo's voice. "You got him, man. He's out. You did it," he says.

I stare down at my opponent and all I see is Mike...all I see is that night.

Despite the crowds frantic cheers, I run out of there.

After a shower and a brisk visit with one of the mob doc's, it's declared that, although extremely swollen, there's no permanent damage to my eye.

All the fights scheduled for the night are now over, so I grab my bag and head out into the cool late September night air.

As soon as I step out...I'm immediately struck by a tiny fist to the face.

What the hell?

"Thanks a lot, *dick*," a woman's voice yells.

I look down and can hardly believe my eyes. It's the same blonde from earlier. Except this time, she looks beyond pissed.

Not something I was expecting.

I pull my bag up higher over my shoulder and stare at her. "You know, usually, damsel's in distress say 'thank you' after being saved."

She lifts her chin. "Fuck you," she spews. "I really needed this job and now I'm fired." She jabs a finger into my chest. "All because of *you*. Didn't anyone ever teach you how to mind your own business? I was fine in there."

I shake my head and begin walking. "You weren't fine. You were being *assaulted*." I stop walking and look at her. "What the hell is *wrong* with you?"

She tightens her leather jacket around her and crosses her arms over her chest. "I just *told* you. I got fired and I *really* needed that job."

I shrug. "Trust me, you're better off. This is no place for a girl like you."

"You don't even *know* me," she whispers.

Well, she has me there.

I reach into my pocket and pull out a wad of cash. She begins to protest, but I give her no choice. "Here. Sorry for the inconvenience I caused you. Obviously, you really need the money or you wouldn't have punched *me* in the face over it. Word to the wise...not all men would react the same way I would to being punched, so be careful out there."

I continue walking, even though I can hear her footsteps following behind me. "Thanks, but I can't accept this. I like to earn my money."

She tries handing it back to me, but I decline. "Look, Luke owed you money for the night anyway. Consider this your payment from the club."

She begins walking beside me. "How's your eye?"

"Fine. No permanent damage." I cross the street with her still in toe beside me. "Do you live around here or something?" I ask.

She looks at me curiously and I see the corner of her lips twitch. "Well, unlike *you*. Yes, *I'm* a New Yorker."

"What gave it away?"

She smiles and I see the hint of a dimple on the left side of her cheek peek out. "I don't know, but that's a *wicked* cool accent you got there, Boston."

I can't help but smile myself. She's good, I'll give her that much. "So, damsel, what's your name?"

She shoots me an icy cold stare. "I'm not a damsel. And I'll tell you, *if* you promise to never call me that again."

"Deal, but that deals only in effect until the next time I see you." I give her a wink. "Then all bet's are off," I tease.

"Alyssa."

I give her a smirk. "So does that mean you're planning on seeing me again in the future?"

She shakes her head as we cross another street and walk down another block. "No offense, Jackson. But you're not really *my* type."

Not gonna lie, that stung a little. Then, I think about the reality of the situation and know she's right. I already know that this girl deserves a lot better than someone like me. Not to mention the fact that dating isn't exactly my thing. "Yeah, you're probably right. Take care," I say before I begin walking ahead of her.

"Jackson," she calls out and I can't help but turn around. "Thank you," she says before she opens a car door.

I nod my head, but can't help but wonder. "You drive?"

"Yeah, I live on Long Island. Nassau County to be exact," she says.

"I thought you said before that you were a real New Yorker?"

She snorts and her eyes shoot daggers at me. She lets out a slew of curses finally ending with, "I *am* a New Yorker, you Boston prick."

Then she slams her car door and guns the engine.

That's when I notice it. It's a few years old...but she's definitely driving a BMW.

She's obviously not *that* hard up for money after all. And I just gave her everything in my wallet.

Shit, I guess it's true what they say. There really is a sucker born every minute.

Chapter 3 (Alyssa)

Most women go to bars when they're looking to pick up men for a quick hookup...not me.

I prefer to pick up my men at libraries, bookstores, and the nearest Starbucks.

I glance at the clock on my dashboard. It's just after 11 pm. Luckily, since I'm still in the city everything is open late, especially on the weekends.

I parallel park into the nearest spot outside the coffee shop and turn my engine off.

The nerve of that bastard. Long Island *is* in New York.

But it's not that statement of his causing me to be in need of seeking out a distraction. It's his *other* statement from earlier still running through my head. *"Don't you value yourself at all?"*

I almost wanted to laugh when he said that the club was no place for a girl like me.

He obviously has no idea who I am. Either that, or he's putting on a really good show.

I walk into the almost empty Starbucks and look around before I spot my target.

Glasses-check. Button-up shirt paired with khakis-check. Not overly attractive by conventional standards, but relatively pleasing to the eye- check. Fingers working furiously on a laptop- check.

I order my favorite- a vanilla chai latte with whipped cream and pull up a seat next to him. "Hey there, handsome. Come here often?" I ask as I lean across the table, giving him a nice view of my cleavage.

He gives me a shy smile and takes a sip of his drink. "Lately, yes. I have a thesis I'm working on."

"Sounds exciting," I say.

He then goes on and *on* for the next fifteen minutes about his thesis which has something to do with acid rain, before I decide I've had enough and interrupt him. I reach across the table for his hand. "It sounds like you're under a lot of stress," I say sympathetically.

He nods his head. "Yes, It's tremendous. I feel like I'm going out of my mind."

I swipe the whipped cream from my drink with my finger and lick."You know what helps with that?"

He blushes. "Just so you know—I've never, ever, done this before...but I live 15 minutes away from here."

Oh, he's a virgin...that's even better. Perfect even.

"I have a car. We'll be there in five," I say before I stand up and head for the door.

I park in the lot across from his apartment building. I don't usually go to guy's houses and I'm feeling apprehensive about it.

I take a look around the parking lot. It's empty and pretty dark. "You know, I have to be up early. Maybe we can just do it right here?" I offer.

He looks surprised but doesn't protest as we climb in the backseat.

I begin straddling him and grinding against him until I feel his entire body tense. Poor guys nervous. *First-time jitters.*

I cup his face in my hands. "Relax. You don't have to be nervous with me. I'm gonna make this good for you."

I tilt my head to the side and begin kissing him. At first, the kiss is tender...until he bites my lower lip...enough to draw blood.

I pull back. "Whoa, not so hard, sweetie."

In the blink of an eye, he grabs both my wrists in one hand, before he pulls them around my back and secures them with something metal.

My first thought—is that I'm being arrested for prostitution. But the thing is. I'm *not* a prostitute. This is all just some horrible misunderstanding.

Way to go, Alyssa.

"Look, I know what you think. But I assure you, I'm not a prostitute," I begin yelling.

He flips me over so that I'm lying on my stomach. Then he slams a piece of duct tape across my mouth.

This isn't typical police procedure. *Oh, fuck.*

"You may not be charging me for sex, sweetie. But we both know what a slut you really are. I *knew* you looked real familiar. Let's just say that I've seen you before," he sneers against my ear before he begins unbuttoning my pants.

Oh, God.

It's obvious he's not some safe, nerdy virgin after all. Nor is he an undercover cop trying to arrest me.

It's so much worse than that.

And the worst part is...this is *all* my fault.

I struggle against him, but it's no use.

I bash my head against my window in hopes that someone will hear my muffled screams. Or that I'll pass out before the unthinkable happens.

I close my eyes and whimper against the window before the door is ripped open and I feel myself begin to move forward.

I open my eyes and can tell I'm about to hit the concrete, but I'm hauled up just in the nick of time. I'm then shoved out of the way as some massive creature reaches inside the car and yanks my attacker out.

*Wait a minute...*I recognize that broad back.

I open my mouth to scream, but can't due to the tape.

For the next few minutes, Jackson unleashes a plethora of

punches and kicks. Blood is dripping from the guy's face, lip, and nose down onto the concrete.

I begin jumping up and down in hopes to get him to stop.

I don't want to be the cause of him murdering some guy...even if a part of me thinks he deserves it.

Finally, he stops punching the guy and looks at me. His features change from concern to disbelief. "Alyssa?"

He quickly rips the tape off my mouth. "He handcuffed me, Jackson."

He looks at my bound hands behind my back. "Yeah, I can see that," he says before he picks the guy up by his collar and searches his pockets. "I can't find the key."

The guy lifts his head and spits blood at him. "That's because there isn't one. Whore's like her don't deserve to be free," he says, before Jackson delivers one final punch and the guy passes out cold.

"Um, is he?' I ask.

"No. Should be, though."

With a grunt, he lifts the guy's body over his head and throws him in the nearest dumpster. "I think it's safe to say that he won't be bothering you anymore."

"Thanks, but it was my fault."

He shakes his head. "Why do most victims feel the need to blame themselves?"

"You don't understand. I was the one who propositioned *him* for sex. I mean, I thought he was a nice, normal guy. Then things got out of hand, but *before* that, I knew exactly what I was getting into."

He gives me an odd look, almost as if he's seeing who I am for the first time. "Still wasn't your fault," he mumbles. "I saw you fighting against him, you clearly didn't want it anymore."

That's when it dawns on me. "What the hell are you doing here, Jackson?"

He points to the apartment building across the street. "I live there."

I blow out a puff of air. "So does he."

"Then you really don't have to worry about him anymore." He looks down appearing uncomfortable. "Alyssa?"

"Yeah?"

"Your pants. I don't know the proper way to say this, but they're way past where they should be."

I look down and curse when I notice my jeans around my knees and I realize that I'm standing there wearing nothing but a bright pink thong. "Well, seeing as I'm a little tied up, you think you can help me out with that, chief?"

"Yeah, no problem."

He bends down and his hands softly brush against my thighs, his touch lighting every nerve ending along the way. He looks up at me from underneath his impossibly long and dark lashes while he gently slides my jeans up past my hips. I let out a breath I wasn't aware I was holding when his fingers graze my lower abdomen before he fastens the button. He swallows hard and my temperature skyrockets when his fingers dip lower and he ever-so-slowly drags my zipper up.

So not the time to be turned on, Alyssa, I remind myself.

He quickly backs away, putting a few feet of distance between us. "I think I have something in my apartment, like a saw or something that should be able to get those off."

I bite my lip. I really do have a thing about going back to guy's places. But Jackson's two for two now. In a single night, no less. And call me crazy, but there's just something about him that makes me feel like I'd be safe with him.

We begin walking across the street to the apartment complex. "I have a roommate. But he shouldn't be home now."

I narrow my eyes at him. "Are you expecting something for your services?"

He looks insulted, which of course, makes me feel like shit. "No. God no. Of course, not. I was just saying that in case you were embarrassed. You know, due to your current situation and all."

No, not embarrassed, but *definitely* feeling like shit now.

Chapter 4 (Jackson)

"If you want to go to the police after this, I'll go with you," I say when I open the door to my apartment building.

Hesitation, discomfort, and finally what looks like resolve flash in her eyes all in the five seconds it takes her to answer. "No."

I say a silent prayer that Tyrone's not home as we ascend the stairs to my apartment. Lord knows, he'll have a lot of questions about this.

Especially since for the last 3 years he's known me, I've never brought a girl back to our apartment before.

Let alone, one who's already in handcuffs. I'd be lying if I said the vision of her bound and standing there in her hot pink thong didn't make my cock twitch.

Until I reminded myself how she ended up that way.

With a sigh I continue leading her to my front door ...then I hear it.

Fuck me...this is not good.

"Look, I'm sorry. It turns out my roommate's home after all," I say while trying not to stare into those piercing hazel eyes of hers.

"How do you know? I mean, we're not even inside yet."

"I'm surprised you can't hear it," I mutter as I pull out my key and open the door.

When we walk in, it's even worse than I imagined it would be. He's parading around the living room, *Risky Business* style...in nothing but a pair of green *Hulk* boxers, while Nelly's- *Country Grammar* blasts from the stereo.

Alyssa's mouth drops open and I can't tell if it's because she's impressed by his dance moves, or him in general.

Truth be told, most women are impressed with him.

It's probably the combination of his Southern accent and the fact that he's built like a brick shit house. That, and Tyrone himself has been known to turn on the charm and be a bit of a player when the time calls for it.

And since I've had the liberty of not only being his roommate, but sharing a locker room with the guy for 3 years...I can, *unfortunately*, attest to the fact—that yes—it *is* true what they say about black guys and their equipment.

"From Texas back up to Indiana, Chi-Town, K.C., Motown to Alabamaaaa!" he screams before he spins around and faces us.

Beside me, Alyssa lets out a little giggle.

"Shit, Jackson. I'm sorry. I thought you were still at the club," he says. He flashes Alyssa a coy smile. "And who is this lovely lady?" Before Alyssa can answer, confusion sweeps across his features. "Wait, you're the ring girl. Aren't you?"

Alyssa nods her head while Tyrone holds out his hand to her. "I'm sorry ma'am, where are my manners? We didn't really have a chance to exchange pleasantries at the club, I'm Tyrone."

She clearly can't shake *his* hand, though, seeing as she's still handcuffed and all. She looks down and backs away while uttering a curse. Tyrone immediately and understandably, looks offended, which just makes this whole situation that much worse.

He cocks an eyebrow at me. I know what he's implying and since I'm almost positive that it's not true, I really need to run interference. "She can't shake your hand because she's handcuffed, Tyrone," I offer.

Alyssa begrudgingly turns around to show him.

"Shiiiit, girl. You on the lamb?" he asks.

"No. There was a misunderstanding and I somehow ended up getting handcuffed while in the backseat of my car. But we can't find the key." she says.

She shoots me a glance that I can only interpret as 'please, don't say any more about what happened.'

I nod my head, while Tyrone looks at me, grins, and shakes his head while muttering, "Crazy ass, white boy," under his breath. I take a step behind Alyssa and give him the finger before asking, "Do we have a saw or something around here?"

He rubs his chin and grins. "No Jackson, we're not all freaks like you. But you know who might have one?"

"Fuck," I mumble.

"What? What's the matter?" Alyssa asks.

Tyrone rubs his hands together. "This is gonna be awesome," he says before he opens the front door.

Alyssa quickly follows him even though I try stopping her.

I follow them both out into the hallway. Tyrone pounds on his front door. "Yoo-hoo. Ricky Ricardoooo, I know you're in there. Open up," he says in his mock Spanish accent.

Alyssa nudges me with her elbow. "Ricardo? You mean—"

"My coach," I finish for her.

The door swiftly opens and out comes a shirtless Ricardo...along with a barely dressed Lou-Lou close behind him. Lou-Lou props a hand on her hip. "Peppa? I thought you got canned?" she sneers.

Tyrone and I exchange a glance, but it's quickly interrupted when Alyssa lunges toward Lou-Lou. "Number one, I have blonde hair, you idiot. Number two- you're a *bitch*. Thanks a lot for lying to me about our '*job description*'. I can't believe I almost slept with *him*!" she screams.

I don't have time to be offended by her statement because Lou-Lou cackles, which only infuriates Alyssa that much more. "I didn't tell you to do anything you didn't want to do in the first place. I know a slut when I see one. Not my fault you fell for the trap and showed your true colors." She motions to the handcuffs and her lips turn up in a snarl. "*Puttana.*"

I instinctively stand in front of Alyssa while Ricardo reaches for his shirt. "Whoa, ladies. That's enough," he snaps.

Alyssa proceeds to ignore him, and instead, steps to the side and head-butts Lou-Lou.

Lou-Lou lets out a yelp while I pull Alyssa back to me. "Go home, Lou-Lou," I bark.

Ricardo whispers something in her ear and with a sniffle, she finally, walks down the hallway and into her own apartment.

"You *all* live in the same apartment building?" Alyssa asks when we walk back inside my apartment.

"Yeah," is my only reply because I'm more worried about the red spot forming on her forehead at the moment.

I usher her into the kitchen, pull out an ice pack from the freezer and hold it to her head. She winces, but mumbles a quick "Thanks."

"So, why exactly, do you have the same girl from earlier tonight standing in your apartment, Jackson?" Ricardo asks. His gaze shifts behind her back. "Handcuffed, no less."

He takes a step closer to Alyssa and something flashes across his face.

Alyssa's expression changes from one of annoyance to what I can only interpret as shame...which I'm guessing is due to the handcuffs.

"I've seen you before," Ricardo whispers.

That's odd.

"Yeah," Alyssa says softly while looking down at her feet.

I don't know what the hell's going on, but they exchange another glance and Ricardo clears his throat. "I have a blow torch, I'll be right back."

Alyssa sprouts up from her chair. "A *blow torch.* No. Fuck, no!" she screams.

I run my hand along her cheek in an attempt to calm her down.

She shivers at first before she leans into my touch. "Look, I promise, I won't let him hurt you. It's the only way to get those off, though."

"It's gonna hurt, Jackson. What if he ends up burning me?"

I trace my finger down her jaw and she closes her eyes. "He won't. I won't let that happen," I whisper while she nods her head.

Tyrone clears his throat, shakes *his* head, and pulls a bottle of Jack Daniels out of the cabinet.

He pours a glass and walks over to Alyssa. "This should help calm your nerves."

She gives him a smile as he lifts the glass to her lips and she takes a sip.

A moment later Ricardo walks back into the apartment wearing a welder's helmet and a pair of gloves. He's also holding what looks to be a miniature sized blow torch in his hand.

Tyrone tilts the glass to her lips again, but Alyssa declines. "No thank you. I really *don't* like to drink," she says sharply.

She's trying not to show it, but I can see her begin to tremble.

Ricardo pulls out another pair of gloves. "Jackson, see if you can put these on her hands so I don't end up burning her."

I take the gloves from him and make quick work of slipping them on underneath the cuffs.

Alyssa's eyes connect with mine and she swallows hard. "There's going to be sparks," she whispers.

"I'll protect you," I assure her.

Ricardo walks behind her. "Hold still," he says before he pulls the face part to his mask down.

Alyssa glances over her shoulder. "Um, do you have any experience with this?"

"With a blow torch or getting people out of handcuffs?"

"Both."

He jerks a shoulder up. "I'm a Puerto Rican from the Bronx," he says, as if that answers her question.

Her entire body tenses, until I move closer. "Keep your head against my chest," I whisper. "The sparks will hit me, not you."

She shakes her head, her expression turning solemn. "No, I don't want you to get hurt either."

"It's fine," I say as she tucks her head against my chest and I fold my arms around her.

I try not to breathe in the hint of coconut in her silky hair as I continue to hold her.

Tyrone looks at me and makes a "tsk, tsk" sound under his breath. Ricardo starts the blow torch and less than a minute later, Alyssa's hands are free.

"Thank you," she murmurs to both me and Ricardo.

Ricardo nods and heads for the front door. "Training is at 3pm tomorrow, guys," he reminds us before he leaves.

Alyssa stands up and brushes her hands over her pants. "Where's the bathroom?"

I point over my shoulder. "Second door on the right. If you need anything, let me know."

She gives me a smile before she begins walking.

I walk over to the fridge and grab a bottle of water.

Tyrone, who's still in his hulk boxer shorts drums his fingers on the countertop and stares at me. "That girl is trouble with a capital F," he starts.

I roll my eyes. "Last time I checked, trouble begins with a *T*, Tyrone."

"Well, in her case it's F, because she will *fuck* you over and I don't mean in the bedroom. I know you don't date much, but seriously. Take my word for it, that girl is all kinds of trouble that you don't need."

"She's a nice girl..." I start to say.

"I'm not judging, lord knows I've brought home my fair share of crazies...but last time I checked. *Nice girls* don't show up on people's doorsteps in handcuffs. Nor, do they go around headbutting other chicks."

I run a hand through my hair. "She was in trouble. It wasn't her fault."

He gives me a pointed look. "Yeah, it never is." He sighs.

"Please, just tell me that she didn't ask you for money already."
Apparently my expression must give me away because he lets out
another sigh. "In her defense, she didn't ask. I basically gave her no
choice but to take what I made from the fight tonight."

He spits out his drink. "You mean to tell me that you handed
that girl over *5 grand*!"

"*What?*" a voice shrieks behind me.

In a flash, Alyssa reaches inside her purse. "What the *hell* is the
matter with you? Take your money back, now. I had no idea it was
that much."

I begin to protest, but she slams the wad of cash down on the
countertop while looking at Tyrone. "You should listen to your
friend, Jackson. I'm not a good girl. You don't want to get mixed up
with someone like me," she says before she makes her way to the
front door.

I instinctively reach for her hand. "Stop. First off, you didn't ask
me for the money, I gave it to you. Secondly, you've been drinking-
you shouldn't be driving right now. And finally, I can make my own
decisions regarding the people I hang out with. So, sit your ass
down on the couch...*now*."

She raises an eyebrow at me before she takes a few tentative
steps toward the couch in the living room and sits.

Tyrone glances at the money on the counter and shrugs.
"Maybe I misjudged you after all," he says in Alyssa's direction
before he heads to his bedroom.

I walk out to the living room. "Anything *else* you want me to
do?" she asks.

"Yeah, tell me a little bit about yourself, for starters."

She smirks. "Please, like I'm sure you don't already know."

I have no idea what's she talking about, but I'm getting sick of
her evasive answers. "You know what? Forget it," I huff before I
stand up.

A few moments later I walk back out and hand her a fresh t-
shirt and a pair of boxers.

"What's this?"

"What does it look like?"

She shakes her head. "I had like one sip of alcohol. I'm fine to drive, really. I don't need to spend the night."

"You live over an hour away. It's already 2:30 in the morning. I'll take the couch, you can take my bedroom."

She stands up. "No, Jackson. You've already helped me way more than I deserve for one night. I can't keep taking advantage of you."

Her entire expression softens, and I can't help but think that maybe, she's finally going to let her guard down with me.

"It's not taking advantage if I offer," I insist.

With a sigh, she holds out her hand and accepts the clothes. "Why are you being so nice to me?" she whispers.

"Why not?" I counter.

Then, to my complete surprise. She stands up on her tiptoes and plants a kiss on my cheek. "Thank you, Jackson."

I watch as she closes the door to the bedroom...and I can't help but think that maybe, Tyrone's right after all.

This girl is trouble...but I still can't help but want to know what her demons are.

A few hours later, I hear the sound of the balcony door close and I'm on my feet.

I scrub a hand down my face and walk outside. The sunrise is coming up over the horizon and Alyssa's curled up on a chair with a blanket draped over her.

"I'm sorry. I didn't mean to wake you," she says.

I take a seat on the chair next to her. "It's fine. Are you okay?"

She twirls her hair into some kind of knot on top of her head. "Yeah, I just kind of have a *thing* when it comes to being at other people's houses. I really don't like it."

Hmm, that's interesting.

"I won't hurt you, Alyssa."

She grips the edge of the chair. "Then what do you want from me, Jackson?"

I decide to be honest with her. "That's the thing. I don't want anything from you." I look at her. "Actually, that's kind of a lie. I would really like to get to know you. Maybe even...if you *let* me. Be your friend."

"My friend? Yeah, right. That's new," she scoffs. "Look, you already know I'll put out...if that's what you're after."

I place my hand on her shoulder. "It's not. Please, don't take offense to this, you're beautiful...but something tells me that you need a real friend much more than you need another guy to fuck right now."

"I don't even know what to say to that," she whispers.

"Say you'll have lunch with me today."

"Lunch?"

"Yeah, lunch. That's all, I swear."

She seems to contemplate this as she stretches out in the chair. "I don't even know your last name. Or anything else about you."

I extend my hand out to her and grin. "I'm Jackson Reid. I turned 27 in August and I'm formerly of Boston, Ma- which gives me my *wicked* cool accent...but now I reside here. "

She takes my hand and smiles. "Alyssa Tanner...I'll be 24 at the end of next month and consider yourself lucky. New York City is the best place in the whole entire world."

"So why do you live just outside the city limits then?"

She closes her eyes. "My parent's house is there."

"Oh, so you still live with your parents?"

She gets up from the chair and walks over to the balcony door. "No, I don't."

I open my mouth to find out more about her, but she interrupts me.

"I'm going to try and get some more sleep. But, I'll join you for lunch, Jackson."

Chapter 5 (Jackson)

To my astonishment, Alyssa stayed true to her word and ended up going out to lunch with me.

Since I let her pick the place, we're currently sitting at some hole in the wall diner...seated in a corner booth in the far back.

She looks around the restaurant before she tugs her sunglasses off her face and sticks them in her purse.

I can't help but wonder why she's even wearing them in the first place...given that it's raining out and all.

"Being in public bothers you," I say, making it a statement and not a question.

She folds her hands in front of her before she looks me right in the eye. "How long are you going to go on pretending, Jackson?"

I tilt my head to the side. "I have no idea what you're talking about. I really wish you would just tell me, though."

She studies my face for a few moments. "Tell me, Jackson. Do you have a computer?"

I take a sip of my drink. "Yeah, why?"

"Do you watch porn on your computer?"

I nearly choke on my drink. That was certainly the last thing I was expecting to come out of her mouth.I open my mouth to say something, but luckily, the waitress comes to our table to take our order.

After she's gone, I decide to attempt to break up the now awkward silence between us. "So, you're a porn star. That's the big secret?"

She shoots me an icy cold stare. "Not by choice," she mumbles.

"I don't understand," I say, my confusion growing with every moment that passes between us.

She rubs her temples. "Fine. You really want to know me, Jackson? You really want to know everything?"

"Yes. I won't judge you, I promise."

She leans back against the booth. "I went to NYU a few years ago. If you can believe it, I was on track to become a newscaster. It was my dream, ever since I was a little girl." She closes her eyes for a second before she clears her throat and continues. "Anyway, I was a year away from graduating when my mother decided to get remarried. She ended up marrying a Politician. You've probably heard of him before, John Travine."

The name mildly rings a bell. "Yeah, I've heard of him. I don't remember what he ran for, but the name sounds familiar."

"He ran for mayor of New York City 3 years ago," she tells me.

"So, what happened at NYU?"

She looks down nervously before she begins. "Well, like I said. My mother ended up marrying that piece of shit politician." Her jaw hardens and her entire body becomes rigid. "I hate him, Jackson. The way he exploited my family's tragedy in front of the media. The way he turned my own mother against me. He could drop dead tomorrow, and I honestly don't think I would be able to feel one ounce of sympathy for him."

I reach across the table for her hand. "Family tragedy?"

She pulls back her hand with abrupt force, like my hand is made of lava and I'm about to singe her. There's so much pain in her eyes it almost hurts to look at her. "I can't talk about that. Please."

"I won't force you to tell me anything you don't want to, Alyssa."

She pinches the bridge of her nose. "I was doing really well at

NYU. I maintained a 4.0 and everything. I was focused on my goals and kept myself out of trouble. Anyway, my stepfather ran for mayor and my mother and I were thrust into the political spotlight and all that comes with it. Like I said, he exploited my family, he used my mother, and..." She pauses and looks at me. "Just trust me when I say that he's not a good guy, Jackson."

Her expression is filled with so much sorrow, it practically sears me straight to the bone.

"I believe you," I tell her.

She gives me a small smile that fades just as quickly as it appears.

"I wanted to get back at him. It was so unbelievably fucked up, but I decided to do something horrible. Something that I knew would piss him off when he found out. Looking back it was absolutely stupid, and it ended up backfiring big time." She shrugs. "But I had just turned 21 at the time and I was still naive in regards to certain things. Not that it excuses what I did, but..."

I lean forward, my curiosity coming to a peak. "What did you do?"

"Well, my roommate was dating Dean Gaffney, Jr at the time," she starts to say before I interrupt her.

"Wait a minute. You don't mean Mayor Gaffney's son, do you?"

"Yes. That's exactly who I'm referring to."

I know whatever she's about to tell me is going to be bad, real bad.

"Fuck, Alyssa. What happened?"

"I decided that I was going to flirt with him. Maybe even hook up with him. I wanted it to get back to my stepdad. And I thought-what better way to make him upset than having him hear that I was involved with his opponents son." Her eyes become glassy. "I know I broke the girl code. I know, I'm the worst kind of female in the world, but I just wanted to make him angry. I didn't care about the repercussions at the time. I wasn't thinking straight, Jackson. I just wanted him out of our lives. I wanted him to leave my mother and me alone and find another family to terrorize."

"No judgment here, Alyssa. We've all done things we never thought we would in the heat of the moment."

Like murdering your best friend for killing your sister.

"So, one night—he showed up at my dorm room. Melody, my roommate wasn't there at the time. She was busy with her study group. He asked me if I wanted to grab dinner. I thought it was the perfect opportunity. During dinner he said all the right things...and we bonded over our mutual dislike of my stepdad. He also thought it was disgusting how he was using what happened to my fath..." she starts to say before she stops herself.

"Anyway, after dinner, we went back to his dorm. His roommate was out for the evening. We had a few drinks and..."

That's when I decide to stop her. "So he got you drunk?"

She shakes her head. "No. I mean, not exactly. It's hard to explain. I was somewhere between being buzzed but not drunk. It was just enough alcohol to lower my inhibitions, but not to the point where I didn't know what I was doing."

Shit. I really hate where this story's going, but I can't bring myself to stop her.

"So, one thing led to another and we started hooking up." She squeezes her eyes shut. "I was still a virgin, Jackson."

I swallow against the lump forming in my throat. "Did he rape you?"

"No." She takes a deep breath. "He only filmed me having sex without my knowledge and put it out on the Internet for the whole entire world to see."

She scrunches up her nose. "The best part was when Melody burst into the room at the exact moment I lost my virginity. I'll never forget what she said. 'Alyssa, you slut.' Which is conveniently the name of the video."

"Jesus, I'm so sorry, Alyssa."

She shrugs. "Don't be. I only did it to myself. I deserved it. I broke the girl code and hooked up with my roommate's boyfriend. I hurt my mother to the point where she disowns me." She snorts. " The only good thing that came out of it was that my stepdad ended up losing the election...most likely because of me. Besides, milking my family's tragedy...his campaign was built around promoting abstinence for the youth and other Christian family values. Needless to say, my sex tape made quite a mockery of his entire campaign."

Damn.

"I can't believe your mom disowned you after that, though. That's horrible."

"Yeah, well my stepdad didn't really give her much of a choice. After he lost, they moved someplace down south. He became mayor of a really small town down there. She's obviously happy, so again...it is what it is."

"Why didn't you press charges against him?" I ask.

She bites her lip. "I couldn't afford a lawyer. My stepfather's campaign was going down the tubes at that point and he was pissed. He refused to help me in any way. Besides, apparently there's some kind of law in New York that basically states that as long as one party knows about it being filmed it's not illegal. And just to cover his tracks, Dean also told authorities that I knew we were filming it. The asshole even said it was my idea in the first place to make a porno, but it wasn't. Also, he and his father had one of the best defense attorneys lined up to represent them in case I pressed charges and went through with the lawsuit. And technically, Dean didn't distribute the tape for money."

She holds up her hands and makes air quotes. "It got leaked somehow." She rubs her forehead and sighs. "But mostly, I just didn't want to be in the spotlight anymore, Jackson. That tape ruined my life...I didn't have the strength to stand up in court and have my every move scrutinized."

We both stare at one another for a few moments. "So, what happened to your father?" I ask at the same time she asks, "Who's Lilly?"

I stare down at my uneaten food. "Lilly was my sister," I whisper.

Sadness sweeps across her face. "Was?"

"Yeah. She's...um. She's dead."

"God, Jackson. I'm so sorry. What happened?"

I look at her. "What happened to your dad?"

"He's...dead."

"Do you wanna talk about it?"

She chews on her thumbnail. "No, I really, really don't."

"Me either."

She smiles. "Okay, deal. I won't ask you about Lilly and you won't ask me about my dad."

I breathe a sigh of relief. "Deal."

She takes a bite of her bagel. "So, you should probably know the reason I hate spending the night at places other than my own house is because of what happened. It's made me a little paranoid. I always feel like there's a hidden video camera waiting for me in the shadows somewhere."

I take a bite of my now cold burger. "That's understandable."

"And the reason why I go out and have lots of sex with whole-some 'nerdy guys' is because—" She pauses. "Well, originally it was because they're usually good at hacking computers and making the videos disappear." She sighs. "However, it always pops back up. It's gotten to the point where I've stopped trying to track it down. The Internet really is forever."

"I'm sorry," is all I can manage to say because in all honesty her situation sucks.

She looks down. "And since I'm being so candid with you. I guess I have sex with them as a way of punishing myself."

That's...disturbing.

"Why?"

"Do you have any idea what it's like to have millions of people think of you as nothing but a slut, Jackson?"

"No, I can't say that I do."

"Do you have any idea what it's like to know that millions of people saw you at your most vulnerable moment? Completely exposed, raw, naked. And millions of people are judging you...everywhere you go. I can't go to the supermarket without breaking out in a full on panic attack over the fact that the guy at the checkout counter stares at me for a second too long. I can't get a normal job because everyone knows who I am and knows exactly what I look like giving a freakin' blowjob. Hell, I couldn't even finish school because not only did my stepdad stop paying for my tuition after my little stunt, but I just couldn't take the constant scrutiny from everyone."

She then stares at me with those big, hazel eyes of hers...there's so much agony swirling in them it makes my own heart constrict.

"I don't understand why you punish yourself, though, Alyssa. Haven't you already been through enough?"

"Don't you get it? If I didn't put myself in that position it would have never happened. I have no one to blame my pain on but myself. It's not like I enjoy having sex with all the guys that I do. Trust me, I don't. But, I do it to remind myself of everything that I caused."

Tears threaten to spill down her face, but she lifts her chin instead. "Besides, after enough people call you a worthless slut...you can't help but start to believe it."

"I think what you're doing is wrong," I whisper.

"I thought you weren't going to judge me."

"About your past. I just hate the thought of you continuing to punish yourself for something that you've clearly already suffered the consequences from...and then some. It's no way to go through life."

She takes a sip of her drink. "Noted, now can we change the subject, please."

"Sure. What do you want to talk about?"

She gives me a smug smile. "Let's talk about you."

"I thought we made a deal that you wouldn't talk about your dad and I wouldn't talk about Lilly?"

She hikes a shoulder up and takes another bite of her bagel. "Yeah. And that deal is still in full effect. However, I know for a fact that there's got to be more to you than a dead sister."

I narrow my eyes at her. "Sorry," she whispers.

"What do you want to know?" I grit through my teeth.

She appears lost in thought for a second before she answers. "Well, do you have a girlfriend? Or are you just like every other macho fighter and some super male-whore?"

I can't help but laugh. "Wow, look who's judging now."

She purses her lips at me and for a single moment she looks so carefree, it's beautiful. "Hey, the world does nothing but judge me all the time. You have a point, though. I'll try and refrain from making and using judgmental stereotypes in the future."

I give her a smirk. "For your information, I'm not a male-whore."

"So you're in a committed relationship?" She chews on her thumbnail again. "I mean, I didn't see any signs of a female living in your apartment. Is it long distance? What's her name? Will she be mad that I spent the night?"

I roll my eyes. Yeah, news reporter. I can see it clearly now.

"I don't have a girlfriend."

She leans forward. "Oh. So, what about sex?"

Nope...not going there. I can't even imagine what she would think of me if she knew how I got my rocks off.

I remain silent while she continues probing. "You have seen yourself, right? There's no way you're still a virgin."

So she does find me attractive after all. I polish off the rest of my plate and can't help but grin. "I'm not a virgin. Trisha Summer's took care of that when I was 15."

"So, what do you do about sex then?" she whisper-yells.

Since she stopped eating her food and I'm looking for a diversion from this horrible conversation. I reach over her plate and plop one of her grapes in my mouth. "I have it." I pause. "On occasion. But that's as much as you're getting out of me on the subject."

Her nostrils begin flaring, her gaze intense. "Jackson," she says. "I've just admitted the most honest, vulnerable, and embarrassing thing about myself to you. Hell, you can even watch it if you're really curious."

I hold up my hand. "I wouldn't. You have my word."

And I mean it, I have absolutely no desire to watch a video that ruined her life. Something that only added to the emotional scars she's already endured. Something that forced her to put her walls up high, in order to protect herself from the world. So high, she's ensured that no one will be able to get through them.

Why do I suddenly find myself wanting to be the one who makes them come tumbling down?

The intensity in her eyes softens. "That's not the point. The point is, that if we're supposed to be friends...I expect the same amount of truthfulness from you that you expect from me. Now, tell me something heartbreakingly honest about yourself before I reconsider this whole entire friendship for good."

I'm a killer. I murdered my best friend. I don't regret it and I never will.

Instead, what comes out of my mouth is something that not even Tyrone knows about. "About once every 3 months I go to a bdsm club and have sex."

Jesus Christ...I'm a fucking idiot for admitting that to her.

She stares at me wide-eyed. "Like cat-o-nine's and dog collars?"

"No. To be honest—I'm not even into any of the hardcore stuff. I just like having all the control during sex."

Since it's the only aspect of my life that I can still control.

"I'm not a 'Dom' or anything like that. However, for this partic-ular club membership, which is both really exclusive and expensive. They're good about keeping your identity hidden and you get to wear a mask if you want to...which I do."

She crinkles her forehead. "I have a question."

"Shoot."

"Why go through all that? Why not just fuck Lou-Lou or some other girl who offer themselves to you?"

I decide to be honest with her about my other reason for using the club. "Shit like that gets messy. First off, I don't do relationships. Secondly, women in particular; have a really hard time separating feelings from sex. If I hooked up with some girl like Lou-Lou or another ring girl...well, over time they would start to get attached. Shit, poor Ricardo's having a hell of a time keeping her in line as it is. I also know from watching Tyrone go through the gauntlet with various girls over the years...that it never ends well. The girl always gets hurt...and I don't want to be responsible for doing that if I can help it. This way, I just go in. No names or faces are exchanged. We have our moment...and it's done."

I expect her to yell at me. To tell me I'm a pig and a horrible human being. Instead, she nods her head in understanding. "Why every 3 months?"

That's an easy question to answer at least.

"If you don't show up at the club, once every 3 months your membership gets canceled. And once every 3 months is just enough to scratch the itch so to speak. After, I go back to focusing on training and fighting full-time."

"That makes sense, I guess. How long has it been since you've last gone there?"

I look up at the ceiling, hating how this conversation has shifted focus to me. "A little over a month."

She regards me with another nod. "I don't do relationships either."

I feel a twinge of uneasiness with her statement and I have no idea why.

"So, how did you get involved with an underground fight club anyway?" she asks. "Granted, I didn't see much, but from what I did manage to see you're really good. Why not go legit?"

Oh, fuck. I have no idea how to answer this without lying to her.

"Just sort of fell into it," I mumble. "I love MMA fighting, I've studied the craft since I was a kid." I swallow hard purposely dodging her question the best that I can. "Besides, it pays the bills."

She leans forward and presses her palms together, studying my face for a beat. "Who owns the club?"

Her question completely catches me off guard and causes me to pause. The seconds blending into minutes.

Why does she want to know?

And technically, shouldn't she already know that it's DeLuca's club? From what I'm told- not just anyone can work at one of his establishments, even the fight club. You either have to know someone or he specifically scouts you out.

But then again, it might be different for the ring girls. Maybe all it takes is good looks and a nice body to get you in the door.

My expression must be one of concern because she coughs and says, "Never mind. Stupid question. Look at me...already breaking rule number one."

I run a hand along my jaw, focusing on her eyes. Even after today, I don't know much about the girl sitting in front of me, but her magnetic eyes are her tell. I can practically feel every emotion she's experiencing when I look into them.

And right now...she looks nervous. "Are you in some kind of trouble, Alyssa?"

She quickly shakes her head. "No. I mean, why would I be?"

I shrug and lean back against the booth. Her response should put me at ease, but it doesn't. "I have no idea. But if you were, you know you could tell me. Right?"

Fear crosses over her face and before I can stop her...she's hopping out of her seat and running toward the exit.

I quickly track the waitress down and pay the bill before running after her.

When I finally step outside, I find her leaning against the side of the brick building facing the alleyway. She's rubbing her temples and breathing frantically. My chest tightens and I'm struck with the overwhelming feeling of wanting to wrap her in my arms and protect her from the world.

Instead, I gently reach for her arm. "Hey," I say. "It's okay. I won't let anything hurt you, Alyssa."

Her eyes spring open in both surprise and fear and she immediately pulls away from my touch. It's almost like she's a frightened animal and can't comprehend that someone would show her an ounce of kindness.

It's utterly heartbreaking.

She pushes off the building and begins walking down the alley. "I'm sorry, but I have to go. I have to go home, now," she calls out.

I stay a few strides behind her. I'm close enough that I can watch her make it to her car safely, but not so close to cause her to freak out again.

After she reaches her car, she pauses briefly. "Thank you for lunch. I'll find a way to pay you back for it."

I shake my head. "Absolutely not. In fact, I'm going to make sure you get paid from Luke. He should have never let that happen to you in the first place."

She worries her bottom lip between her teeth. "That's not necessary," she whispers. "I don't want you getting into any fights on my behalf, but thank you anyway."

She slips inside her car and puts her key in the ignition.

I jog up to her. "When can I see you again?"

She looks down at the steering wheel. "I don't do relationships, Jackson." I open my mouth to protest but she stops me. "That includes friendships. I've already let you in so much more than anyone else and I haven't even known you for 24 hours."

I stuff my hands in my pockets. "Maybe there's a reason for that, Alyssa."

And there is...I just have no idea what it is yet.

All I know is that I'm so drawn to her.

And it's not just because she's incredibly attractive, either. It's so much more than that. I have this urge to just want to take care of her, and be there for her.

But most of all...I recognize the pain in her soul...because I live with it every day.

She puts the car in reverse and begins backing up. "I'll call you, Jackson," she says before she rolls up her window.

It's only after she's more than halfway down the block that I realize she never gave me her number...and she doesn't have mine.

Chapter 6 (Alyssa)

I grip the steering wheel and fight back the wave of nausea. I feel my pulse pounding in my ears and I swallow another big gulp of air.

What the hell is the matter with me?

I mean, besides the obvious panic attack of epic proportions that I'm going through at the moment.

Why in the world did I just tell a guy I hardly know such personal things about myself?

Granted, it was nothing he wouldn't have found out about me sooner or later, but still.

Another round of tremors plague my body and with a curse, I pull over to the side of the expressway. The rain is coming down hard and big droplets splash against my windshield. I close my eyes and listen to the steady rhythm as it continues to fall.

After I'm certain that the worst of the episode is over, I start the car and resume driving.

I wasn't always like this.

Once upon a time, I used to be normal, happy, even.

And up until a few years ago, I had never experienced a true panic attack. In fact, I used to thrive and work best under pressure- something I must have inherited from my father.

My father.

I used to wonder if there was a specific number of tears I could shed that would bring back a missing piece of my heart.

Now, I know, there isn't- because I'm almost positive I must have cried them all during the entire year I was 10. Not a day went by where I didn't wake up to a soggy pillow or fall asleep to one.

Then I turned 11. That's when I learned to stop crying...because tears wouldn't bring him back. Tears were nothing but a complete waste of an emotion and they never solved anything.

I also learned, that sometimes; children are actually the ones to take care of their parents.

Needless to say- My mother didn't handle my father's death well.

Not that there really is a "way" to handle the sudden death of the man you've loved since you turned 16...but I'm certain that becoming an alcoholic isn't the best way to cope.

Especially when you have a child to raise.

However, we made the best of it.

She made sure to put a few bucks aside for food and bills before she blew it all on booze...and I learned to effectively lie to the concerned neighbors and teachers; like when she didn't show up to my recitals, or parent-teacher conferences.

Or even worse- when she *did* show up. Looking like a million bucks, slurring her words, and making an over dramatic spectacle of herself.

Those were the worst. Then after we went home she would apologize profusely for being a horrible mother while crying on my shoulder.

I, of course, being a good daughter- would assure her that she wasn't horrible and that I wasn't angry with her. Then I would fix her something to eat and snuggle up with her on the couch while watching the news.

For whatever reason, it was her favorite thing to watch and the only thing to calm her down when she became really out of sorts. Probably because she didn't have to feel so horrible about the reality of her own fucked up life while she watched other people's lives falling apart every night.

As crazy as it sounds. I think subconsciously- the reason I wanted to become a newscaster was so that I could find a way to reach her and connect with her, in my own way.

The day my father died destroyed our happy life.

But the day John Travine entered our lives...demolished our shitty one.

I was 15 when he began dating my mother. I have no idea how they met. I can only assume that it must have been at her favorite corner liquor store.

At first, he would only come around in the middle of the night and he was always gone by early morning. It didn't take a genius to figure out the nature of their relationship.

That went on for 2 years.

One day when I was 17—I came home from school to find that he had moved in. Apparently, he was a married man, but he and his wife had just come to a mutual agreement to get a divorce. Either that- or his wife had finally kicked his sorry, cheating ass to the curb.

I didn't know that he was a hotshot attorney or involved in politics when they first started seeing each other, but I soon found out when he began showering my mother with lavish gifts and taking care of all the bills around the house.

Unfortunately, it came at a price. But I'm getting ahead of myself.

Before my mother had to pay the piper...he made sure to get her into rehab first.

For the briefest of moments, John Travine and I had managed to see eye to eye. I was actually grateful to him for coming into our lives back then. I thought he was the answer to all our prayers.

I'd never seen my mother happier than during those first few months when she got out of rehab. Long before my mother became an alcoholic, she had quite expensive tastes and shopping was one of her favorite pastimes. Being with John helped fulfill her desire to live in constant luxury again, not to mention her need for constant attention.

I'll never forget the night that all ended, though.

I was 18 years old and I had just come home from a date with my high school boyfriend, Toby.

There at the kitchen table, clutching a bottle of vodka was my mother.

With a busted lip and a black eye.

At first, I thought that maybe she had gotten drunk and had taken a bad fall.

But then he entered the room.

He glared at the bottle in her hand before he fixed his hard eyes on me.

And I knew.

She had obviously relapsed...and he had obviously felt the need to punish her brutally for it. Or, for all I know, it was the other way around.

My stomach dropped to the floor and the first thing I did was try and get my mother to leave him...but she wouldn't.

A huge screaming match ensued between John and I while my mother sat in that damn chair, clutching the bottle of vodka for dear life.

I threatened to call the cops and he laughed in my face and said they wouldn't believe a whore and a drunk. Especially when my mother would never admit to it.

The next day, when she was sober-ish, I tried again to get her to leave. She adamantly refused, in addition to issuing her own threat that made me back down.

Then she said something I would never forget. She said that if I didn't support their relationship, that *I* was free to leave.

Yup, my very own mother had made it clear that she would choose a man who hit her...over her own daughter.

So I did the only thing I could do. I stayed.

My mother was the only person I had left in my life then and I couldn't bear to lose her.

I stayed....he continued to beat her behind closed doors...and she continued to drink her pain away.

Any time I tried to bring up leaving him to her, she would yell at me and threaten to kick me out.

After hours of non-stop arguing, I would eventually break down and apologize, tell her I loved her, and agree to stop interfering in their relationship.

Then the next day I would have some kind of gift from John waiting for me.

It was a fucked up cycle that I didn't know how to stop because that would mean giving up on my mother...and I couldn't do that.

John's biggest blackmail gift came when he agreed to pay for my tuition for NYU. I had gotten a partial scholarship but was having a hard time figuring out how to pay for my dorm room and other expenses on my part time after school job.

At first, I declined. Unlike my mother, I didn't want any part of his money. Not to mention, I was still undecided about dorming at NYU because I didn't know what would happen to my mother if I wasn't there.

It was when my mom literally broke down and begged me to accept his money and told me that I deserved to live my dream...that I finally caved.

Walking out of that house was one of the hardest things I'd ever done. The pain was excruciating.

The only exception being my father's death and the last time, I saw my mother.

The very last time I saw my mother was after John's campaign for mayor was well underway and my sex tape had just hit the world.

She asked me to come home that weekend. So, of course, I did.

The first thing she did when she saw me was pull me into her arms. She said that we would figure out a way to get through this.

I believed her.

But in the middle of the night...everything changed.

I woke up to the most heart-wrenching scream I had ever heard come out of my mother's mouth. I rushed out of my childhood bed, grabbed a bat from my closet, and ran into the basement where I heard the scream come from.

I ran down the stairs two at a time and came face to face with a sight that sickened me and made my stomach curdle.

There was John...facing a computer screen.

His pants were down around his ankles, and his erect penis was in his hand.

And he was watching the sex tape.

Before I even had time to process everything that was happening...my mother stalked toward me.

John quickly pulled up his pants...and tried to explain himself...but the war raging inside my mother wasn't with him.

It was with me.

She raised her hand and white spots formed in front of my eyes when she struck me, hard. My face stung so bad I had to close my eyes. "You worthless slut! You stupid whore!" she screamed before she dealt another blow to my face.

This one was so bad, blood dripped down my nose.

I tried to protest, tried to stick up for myself...but she wouldn't have it.

"I never want to see you again," she sneered before she ran upstairs.

I turned to go upstairs to collect my things and return to my dorm at NYU, but not before I noticed the sly smile touching the corners of John's lips.

It was a smile that told me that even though he was now in jeopardy of losing the election...he had won the battle when it came to my mother.

She chose him over me.

He found a way to make her hate me.

"I hope you die," I whispered before I continued upstairs, gathered my things, and walked out of my parent's house.

Two months later, John lost the race for mayor...and I was about to be kicked out of school because I couldn't afford to stay- in part, because I stopped attending class and lost my scholarship.

Soon after, I received an e-mail from my mother. She said that her and John were moving away to some small town in the south. She also said that I would be able to keep my father's house...provided that I promise to never speak to her or John again.

I happily agreed.

With a sigh, I open the door to the house, plop down on the sofa and open my laptop.

My head begins throbbing when I pull up the latest search results. Even though the video is a few years old, there are about 20 uploads on various sites in the last three weeks alone.

I quickly press the pause button on one of the video's and immediately scroll down to the comments section of the well-known website.

I scan over the slew of comments containing things like- '*she's hot, I'd do her*', '*nice tit's*', '*girl sure knows how to suck dick*', and '*whoever the guy is, he sure is lucky.*'

Instead, I focus my attention on the more personal comments.

-*Poor John Travine. Too bad his daughter was so much of a slut it ended up ruining his career. If I was her, I'd never show my face in public again.*

-*I went to school with that girl. Her name is Alyssa Tanner. Always knew she was a whore. I even heard she blew half the football team.*

-*Bet her snatch is the equivalent of throwing a hot dog down a hallway. If you know what I mean ;)*

-*Wow, seriously? Could she be any more of a slut!*

It's like being trapped on a hamster wheel in the seventh circle of hell. I know I shouldn't, but I just can't help myself.

Finally, I look at the last comment that was posted, this one a mere few hours ago.

-*The whore should just do everyone a favor and kill herself.*

Little do they know...I'm already dying inside a little bit every day.

Chapter 7 (Jackson)

"You should get rejected more often. It really makes you train better," Tyrone says while I slam my fist into the punching bag again.

It's been a little over three weeks since I've last seen or talked to Alyssa, and true to form, I've been taking my frustration out during training.

Ricardo's lips twitch as he holds the punching bag. "That's enough for today, guys. Hit the showers."

I'm about to leave, but I notice movement out of the corner of my eye.

It's that snake, Luke waltzing through the gym; appearing to be without a care in the world.

I'm about to change that real quick.

I hip check him into the wall and enjoy the look of utter shock splashed across his face.

"Can I *help* you?" he sputters.

My 6'3 frame easily towers over him and I relish the way his entire body begins to shake from fear.

I don't give into my anger very often. I tend to bottle everything up and save it for the fights in the cage, but when I do let my fury escape—it sure as fuck makes one hell of an impact. "I believe you still owe money to a certain ring girl," I snarl.

He puffs up his chest. "What are you? Her keeper or something? I don't owe that girl shit. Not my fault she couldn't handle the job."

I launch my fist into his rib cage. "Last time I checked, asshole. Being groped against your will wasn't part of the job description. *You're* supposed to make sure shit like that doesn't happen to the ring girls."

He lets out a big whoosh of air before he collapses against the wall.

I ball my fist again, but he finally reaches into his pocket and pulls out a wad of cash wrapped around a rubber band. "Fine, here. This should cover it. But mark my words, Jackson. If you make a habit of attacking me over the girls I hire, instead of focusing on the fights like *you're* supposed to- Bruno will be hearing about it."

I grab him by the collar. "I really don't give a fuck," I sneer before I let him go.

He fixes his collar and glares at me. "Yeah, we'll see about that," he says before he limps away.

When I turn around Ricardo's eyes are narrowed into tiny slits and Tyrone is shaking his head profusely.

"Locker room, *now*," Ricardo barks.

Shit.

The thing about Ricardo is, he's a great coach- and I'm close enough with him to consider him a friend of sorts...but you never want to piss him off.

He's only 5 years older than Tyrone and I, but rumor has it that he has strong ties to Bruno...hence why it's not only his job to train us, but to look after two of his biggest money making fighters.

It's Ricardo's priority to make sure we stay in top physical form as well as stay out of trouble...in every kind of form it comes in.

The fact that I just went off on one of Bruno's men...doesn't bode well for me.

"What the fuck *was* that?" he snaps when we reach the locker room.

I decide to tell him the truth. "He let Alyssa get attacked during the fight and didn't try to stop it...and if that wasn't bad enough he then fired her for causing trouble. He also didn't pay her."

He rubs his chin, appearing to be lost in thought for a moment. "Alyssa. That's the girl in handcuffs you brought home? Correct?"

I nod. "Look, Jackson. Do yourself a favor and bark up another tree. The only thing that girl's going to do is get you in a shitload of trouble. Trust me. You'll be getting into fights out of the ring left and right the longer you hang around her. If Bruno questions me about you going after Luke, I'll defend you and tell him you were just trying to do the right thing." He pauses. "But you and I both know it's never a good thing to be on Bruno's radar. Don't make a habit out of it."

"Yeah," I agree before he leaves.

After I step out of the shower I find Tyrone standing there waiting for me. "In the last 3 years I've known you; I've never seen you strung out over a girl. What is it about her, man?"

I shrug as I continue getting dressed. "I don't know. She's been dealt a really shitty hand, though. She's not at all what you think, Ty."

"So, she's a lost soul, huh?"

"Something like that," I mumble.

He rubs a hand over his face. "Saving her won't bring back Lilly, Jackson," he says before he heads for the showers.

I instinctively put my hand on the tattoo over my heart.

"I know," I whisper.

"I'm tired as fuck," Tyrone says after we leave the gym. "Training really did a number on me today. I'm gonna grab some coffee."

I look at him and smirk as we continue walking down the street.

"Yeah, if that's what you like to call those pumpkin spice froo-froo girly drinks you dig so much."

He turns his head from side to side and grins. "Hey, man. Don't knock it til' you try it."

I roll my eyes and laugh when we approach the Starbucks at the end of the block.

Until I see her.

Looking through the large glass window of the coffee shop, I can't help but notice Alyssa.

She's leaning over the table, her cleavage spilling out of her low-cut top, and flashing a seductive 'come hither' smile to some guy wearing khakis whose typing on a laptop.

How he's still typing with her right in front of him looking like *that* is anyone's guess, but that's beside the point.

I know exactly what she's doing...and it makes me sick.

Sick and pissed.

Tyrone follows my gaze and shakes his head. "Awe, hell. And so it begins," he mutters.

Without taking my eyes off of her, I open the door and walk inside.

Chapter 8 (Alyssa)

I'm at Starbucks, flirting up a storm with my next conquest...when a large figure approaches the table and clears their throat.

I glance up and internally wince when I notice Jackson standing there...his eyes never leaving my face. His expression hard and unyielding.

Before I can even say a word, he crosses his arms over his broad chest. "There you are, babe. I was wondering where you wandered off to," his deep voice growls.

Babe? Has he lost his damn mind?

I open my mouth to tell him off, but the guy next to me bolts up from the table like he's been electrocuted. "Crap, man. Sorry. I don't want any trouble," he sputters before he grabs his laptop and literally runs out the door.

I stand up and head for the door, but not before I feel his hand reach for my elbow and pull me back to him. I try not to let his close proximity or his touch effect me, but I fail miserably. My stomach knots up and my mouth goes dry when I get the faintest whiff of his earthy, damn near mouth watering scent.

"Have you learned nothing from the last time you did this shit, damsel?" he asks, momentarily zapping me out of my haze.

I shoot him a look that hopefully conveys how annoyed I am with him using that term and twist out of his grasp.

I run out the door, with his footsteps following close behind me.

I know he's not going to let up, so there's only one thing left to do. Something I've become really good at. I'm going to push him away, for good.

I spin around and face him. "Christ, stop following me, Jackson. Stop showing up when you're not wanted or needed. And stop acting like you actually give a damn. And most of all, stop trying to save me because I'll only end up taking you down with me." I draw in a ragged breath. "Just leave me alone. I want nothing to do with you."

I know my words aren't kind, but I need him out of my life for once and for all.

It's only then that I notice his friend Tyrone is standing there. He narrows his eyes at me before he looks at the ground.

Jackson's nostrils flare and he takes a step toward me. He reaches for my hand and puts something in it. "Take care of yourself, Damsel," he says dismissively before he turns around and begins walking down the street.

I close my eyes and swallow against the lump forming in my throat.

This is what I wanted. So, why does it feel like I just made a huge mistake?

My eyes are glassy when I finally open them and come face to face with Tyrone.

"Wow, you're kind of a bitch," he says.

I shrug because it's not a lie...especially after that encounter. "Yeah well, it had to be done."

I turn to leave but his voice stops me. "Word of advice...the world becomes a dark and cold place after you push everyone who cares about you away. And it really sucks when you have to face your demons all alone."

"I wasn't lying, Tyrone. I'll only end up hurting him in the end. Everything I touch, I wreck somehow."

He laughs. "Have you seen him? Trust me, the man can take a few hits, Alyssa. And believe me when I say that Jackson is a great friend. Just give him a chance to be yours."

"Why is this so important to you? I mean, not for nothing but you weren't exactly rooting for me the last time we saw one another."

He considers my statement for a moment before he answers, "Because he's the greatest guy I've ever met and he deserves to get what he wants...for *once* in his life."

I'm taken back by his statement, but before I have a chance to question him about it, Tyrone turns on his heels and starts walking down the street. My chest squeezes and everything in my body is telling me not to let Jackson walk away.

Before I can stop myself, I call out, "Tell him to meet me for lunch tomorrow around 12. The same diner we went to last time."

Tyrone fist pumps the air and gives me a giant smile. "He'll be there."

I'm walking to my car when I suddenly remember what day tomorrow is.

There's no way I can meet Jackson...I already have a date.

Chapter 9 (Jackson)

The last thing I should be doing right now is showing up to meet a girl who's made it clear that she wants nothing to do with me.

I shouldn't be pursuing this. I shouldn't be hopeful that she'll finally let me in.

I shouldn't be trying to save her from herself. Lord knows, I'm the furthest thing from a hero and there's a good chance I'll only hurt her in the end if she ever finds out the truth about me.

No, I shouldn't be doing any of those things...but...I just can't stop myself.

Another hour goes by and I glance at my watch. Tyrone told me she said 12. Maybe he got the time wrong and she meant 2?

If she meant 2, I'll be cutting it close to training time, but the gyms not that far from here.

I order another water and look out the window. There's no sign of her. I look at my watch again. 2:25pm. It's obvious that she's not coming and I've been stood up.

With a sigh, I stand up and throw some money on the table before I leave.

M y muscles ache like no one's business after a grueling workout, all I want to do is go home and fall into bed.

Tyrone's at the bar across from the gym, hoping to strike it lucky with his latest conquest. I considered joining him, but decided against it.

I haven't exactly been in the greatest of moods today. I stick my key in the door and feel a hand tap my shoulder. The touch is light and the hand is soft.

I pinch the bridge of my nose, feeling even more annoyed now that I have to deal with her. "Never gonna happen, Lou-Lou. Try Ricardo's door," I growl.

My statement comes out much harsher than I intended. I briefly consider apologizing but think better of it. Better to just let her think I'm a dick, maybe she'll finally get the picture.

I hear the sound of a throat clearing and I spin around.

A pair of red and puffy hazel eyes meet mine.

"I'm sorry about not showing today, Jackson. I forgot I made other plans and I couldn't get out of them," Alyssa's now raspy voice greets me.

I force myself to ignore the current state she's in. I force myself to look right past the sadness in her eyes, and the fact that she's obviously upset.

I force myself not to think about what those other plans she had may have entailed and the pang of jealousy that snags me.

But mostly, I force myself not to care anymore, because every time I do; she only ends up pushing me away and making me feel like an asshole for wanting to be her friend.

Her friend, right- my inner voice taunts.

"You came a long way for something that could have been done over the phone."

"You know I don't have your number," she whispers when I turn back around and open the door.

"Yeah, well, who's fault is that," I say before I shut the door behind me, with her on the other side of it.

A small knock follows. I pull off my sweatshirt and ignore it.

The knocks increase in both sound and speed. Going from cautious and unsure to impatient and angry now.

And for some reason, *that's* what really sets me off.

I swing the door open so hard the walls vibrate.

She pushes past me with an angry scowl on her face, finally stopping in the living room.

I inhale sharply and continue after her until she does something that entices me, confuses me, and unleashes a fury inside me.

She takes off her shirt.

She's about to start undoing her pants when I reach over and halt her. "What the hell are you doing, Alyssa?"

She looks down and gives me a small shrug. "Well, I tried apologizing to you and you slammed the door in my face," she says, her arms hanging loose in defeat.

I raise an eyebrow, not understanding her thought process. "And you thought stripping for me would accomplish what exactly?"

Her cheeks flush. "I'm not sure. I figured I'd just give you what every other guy always wants from me." She looks down. "Go ahead, Jackson. Take me, use me. Be as rough as you want, just try not to destroy me when it's over."

I don't know what irks me more. The fact that she thinks she's nothing more than a pack of gum to be passed around and enjoyed by all, despite *never* actually enjoying it herself. Or the fact that she just grouped me with every other guy she deals with.

I take a step closer to her and lift her chin. "You're too busy destroying *yourself*, Alyssa. How could anyone else?"

I reach for her arms and lift them above her head. Her chest heaves and I can't help but take in the purple lace of her bra, barely covering her nipples, straining against her breasts and just begging to be released. She sucks in a breath and closes her eyes when my thumb brushes her cheekbone before dipping lower, skimming over that adorable dimple on her left cheek. Which seldom makes an appearance.

She probably thinks I'm about to have my way with her. The goosebumps grazing her delicate flesh and the way her pulse is beating erratically against the pad of my thumb lead me to believe that's what she wants me to do.

And *fuck* if that doesn't make my own heart speed up. *But then I would be like all the others*, I remind myself.

Instead, I pick up her shirt and pull it over her head. Her eyes open, uncertainty etched in her features. "Why?" she asks, her voice barely above a whisper. "Why didn't you?"

I lead her to the couch and drape a blanket over her. "Because I'm not gonna be another notch on your bedpost who takes advantage of your self- destruction." My voice drops down to a whisper, "And because one day I failed to notice when someone else I cared about was in pain ...and not a day goes by that I don't regret it."

My hand instinctively lands on my chest and I sigh.

"So, where did you end up going today?" I ask.

I turn my head to look at her when I don't hear a response. Her mouth is parted slightly, her eyelashes fluttering against closed lids, the rise and fall of her chest falling in sync with my own breathing.

I glance at the clock. Tyrone will be home soon...and he might be bringing company.

She looks so peaceful, I don't have the heart to wake her. I gently lift her up, being as careful as I can and carry her into my bedroom. I remove her shoes, flick off the light on the nightstand, and turn to leave.

Her hand reaches for mine. "Stay. Please stay," she whispers before drifting off again.

I crawl into bed and curl up beside her, my hand never leaving hers.

"No! Daddy! Please, no!"

Her screams are the equivalent of waking up to a shotgun going off. She's trembling so hard, I'm convinced she must be having a seizure.

I jump up and flick on the light beside the bed, her screams quickly turning into muffled cries. I gently nudge her, but she doesn't wake. "Alyssa, you're okay. It's just a bad dream," I say. I hold her by the shoulders and try a little harder this time, and finally the shaking stops and her eyes open wide.

She looks around the room, confusion marring her face briefly before she realizes where she is. "Oh god. I'm so sorry." She sits up in the bed. "This is beyond embarrassing."

Her eyes dart to the door and she makes to stand but I gently pull her back to me. I'm all too aware of how much of a flight risk she is and she's not running away from me this time. Especially in this state.

"This happen often?" I ask.

Her head falls against my chest and she lets out a deep breath before whispering, "Not really. Only when I'm exhausted. Usually, I don't allow myself to sleep that soundly because I know what the end result will be."

That's when it sinks in that it wasn't just a random bad dream, but a reoccurring nightmare. I tip her chin up to look at me. "What happened, Alyssa? Trust me enough to let me in." I kiss her forehead. "Please."

She fidgets and squirms out of my arms. Just when I think she's about to bolt, she looks at me and does the one thing I've been waiting for since I met her.

She drops her armor and opens up to me.

Chapter 10 (Alyssa)

"Really, cupcakes for breakfast, Graham?" my mother cried. "That is not an appropriate breakfast for a 9-year-old."

I grinned around a mouth full of my heavily laden chocolate frosted cupcake. "But I'll be 10 in two days, Mommy," I argued. Before my mother could protest further, I added, "And look, Daddy put goblins on them!"

Since my birthday fell on Halloween, my father's nickname for me had always been 'goblin.' Most little girls would have hated it and wished for a nickname more feminine like 'Princess' or 'Pumpkin', but I loved it.

My mother shook her head and looked at my father. A soft smile spread across his face when he walked over to her and held a cupcake up to her lips. "Come on, honey. Take a bite. No one can resist little goblins." He looked at me and winked. "Isn't that right?"

I nodded my head in excitement. "Do it, Mommy. Please."

She let out a frustrated sigh before she took a haphazard bite. She pursed her lips and looked at me, her expression much softer than it was a moment ago. "Okay," she conceded. "Finish your cupcake, but no more. You need to get ready for school."

My father pulled my mother closer. "You have some frosting right here," he whispered before he kissed her.

I scrunched my nose and made a face. "But it's my *birthday*," I whined, effectively interrupting their moment. "Why can't I stay home with you? Or go to work with Daddy?"

My mother put her hands on her hips and gave me 'the look.' I knew that look well. "Alyssa Ford Tanner. It's not your birthday yet. Now finish the rest of your cupcake and get ready for school."

Yup, she called me by my full name. She meant business.

I scrambled off the counter top and let out a giggle when my father swooped down and picked me up. "I'll tell you what, little goblin. How about I drive you to school today?"

My face lit up. "You mean it?" I asked incredulously.

All my dad did was work non-stop, especially as of late. Sometimes an entire week or two would pass without me ever seeing him.

This time, it had been almost *three* whole weeks. I hated it, but he promised me he would be around for my birthday weekend.

I overheard him telling my mother that him and Ford, his best friend, and partner, were working on their most important case and trying to gather intel, but they were encountering some unforeseen problems.

I didn't really understand it, but I knew my father had a very important job.

He caught the bad guys.

However, he never wore a uniform like some of the other officers I saw. Instead, he mostly wore suits to work and participated in things called 'stakeouts' or 'going undercover.' People at work also referred to him as 'Special Agent.' Whatever that meant.

I knew he traveled to the city a lot. That's where his headquarters and most of his cases were located. It was also his favorite place in the whole entire world.

He only moved to the suburbs because it was what my mother

wanted, she thought there was too much crime in the city and it was no place to raise a child.

I, however, loved the city and would beg my dad to take me with him when he left, but he never did.

My dad put me down. "Of course, I mean it. Now go get ready."

I ran up the stairs to my bedroom.

After I was done getting dressed I walked out to the hallway.

That's when I heard it.

"Fuck," my father huffed. "*Now?* This wasn't scheduled to happen for another two weeks." He paused. "The *entire* weekend? You gotta be shitting me."

My stomach dropped. I already knew what was about to happen.

He sighed. "No, it won't be a problem." He cleared his throat. "Yeah, alright. Tell him I'm on my way. I'll be there as soon as I can."

I heard some ruffling and a few more curses erupt from his mouth as I stood outside his bedroom door with tears in my eyes.

He opened the door and glanced down at me. I briefly registered that he wasn't in a suit but wearing black jeans and a t-shirt, which was odd since he was on his way to work.

Hope flickered in my heart.

"Goblin," he began as he kneeled down in front of me.

I lifted my chin, preparing myself for what was to come. "Yes, Daddy?"

His hand reached up and brushed away the few tears that had started to fall. "I'm so sorry, sweetheart. But Daddy has to go to work. I won't be able to take you to school this morning after all."

Disappointment settled in my chest, but that tiny ray of hope refused to leave. "It's okay. I understand," I said. "You'll be here for my actual birthday though, right?"

His hand dropped, the same pain reflecting back at me through his own hazel eyes. "No, baby. Daddy has to take care of something very important at work."

"More important than me?"

"Goblin—" he started, before I cut him off.

I steeled myself, it was the angriest I'd ever been in all of my almost 10 years. "No. I'm *not* your goblin anymore," I said before I turned around and headed for the staircase.

Large arms wrapped around me and held me tight. "*Nothing* is more important to me than you. And you will always be my little goblin."

I turned around and buried my face against his chest.

"I love you so much, Alyssa," he whispered.

"Then stay, Daddy. Please."

"I wish I could. But I can't."

"But you *promised* me!" I shouted through tears.

He closed his eyes and kissed my forehead. "I know. I'm so sorry. I'll make it up to you somehow. I swear I will."

I looked up at him, my resolve firm. "Take me with you."

He gave me another kiss on my forehead and shook his head. "I can't." He pulled something out of his pocket. "I was going to give this to you on Sunday, but I want you to have it now."

I looked down at the white gold chain in wonder. A white gold and diamond encrusted goblin along with a small replica of a police badge containing my father's badge number hung from it.

"But mommy said I'm not old enough to wear real jewelry like hers yet," I whispered as he fiddled with the clasp around my neck.

He smiled and brushed a lock of blond hair from his eyes. "I think we can make an exception for very special birthdays and very special little girls."

I flung my arms around him. "I love the necklace, but I'd still much rather have you for my birthday. I miss you, so much. You're *always* gone, now. I never get to see you anymore. I get so jealous when I see my friends from school with their dad's."

"Jesus, you're ripping my heart out over here, kid," he mumbled.

"Then take me with you. We don't have to tell Mommy."

He chuckled and ruffled my hair. "I can't. I'm sorry. Please try and understand." he said before standing up and walking down the staircase.

Anger burst through me again. Only this time...I had a plan.

I crept down the staircase, being careful to not make any noise as I passed the kitchen and overheard their conversation.

"I have to go to work. We're about to make some major headway. I just got a call from one of his associates that he's doing the drop today. With the way things are going now it looks like we'll be able to nail him for good this weekend," he told my mother.

Her mouth opened in shock. "Really? This soon? That's incredible."

He rubbed the back of his neck. "Yeah, but I won't be back until Monday night, the earliest."

My mother bit her lip and a crease formed between her eyebrows. "But it's her birthday, Graham. Her 10th birthday. This is going to break her heart. You *know* how much she loves you. You're all she ever talks about."

"I know, honey. I know. I don't really have a choice right now, though. Maybe after this case I can take some time off, we'll take a family vacation or something. I'll make it up to her." He bent down and kissed her. "To the both of you." His hand landed on her tummy. "Take care of my girls." He winked. "All three of them."

Three? He always said his *two girls*. What the heck?

She looked down at his hand. "Speaking of which, when are we going to tell her? I'm a little over 3 months already. We can't wait forever."

"Well, I figured we could tell her that she was going to be a big sister on her birthday." He paused. "But, maybe it's for the best that we wait a little longer and let her have this one last birthday as the only child. I don't want to ruin her birthday any more than I already have. She's really upset with me and feels like my job is more important than she is. This certainly won't help matters. We'll tell her when we go on vacation, after I've spent some quality time with her and she's not so angry with me anymore."

Oh no, no, *no*. This couldn't be happening. *Another* kid? A *girl*? I was *never* going to be special to him now. He didn't even have time to spend with *me* anymore...if there's a new baby it will be like I won't even exist.

I recalled what happened to my classmate, Margaret Weiss. She was the only child and her parents showered her in attention, but she said that all stopped after her brother was born.

Now, her parents were always grumpy from being up all hours of the night and they didn't care about her anymore. Which was stupid, she said; because all her new brother did was sleep and cry all the time.

My mother nodded and gave him a kiss. "Sounds like a plan. I guess that means I'll be taking her to school this morning."

"Yeah, I should have left already." He turned to leave and I scrambled to make it to the garage and out to his car before he did.

"Oh and honey," he called out. "Don't make a fuss over the necklace I got her. I know it's a bit much for a 10-year-old, but I wanted to give her something special this year."

My mother huffed before she smiled. "Okay, but you'll have to deal with the fallout if she loses it. She's still upstairs getting ready, right?"

"Yeah. I'll see you on Monday. Love you."

"Love you."

I made my way out to the garage before he did. His SUV was large, shiny, and all black. It even had tinted windows and came equipped with a phone, and special locks.

Problem was...I didn't know how to get inside without him noticing.

I hid underneath the vehicle and watched his feet move as he lifted the hatch in the back and maneuvered some things around, appearing to be looking for something.

He cursed under his breath before his footsteps disappeared and I heard the garage door shut.

Luckily, he left the hatch open granting me the perfect opportunity to climb in and hide under a blanket on the floor in the back seat.

My heart raced when he came back out and climbed in the driver's seat. I thought for sure he would notice me, but he didn't.

We drove for well over two hours at that point and my legs were starting to cramp up.

The vehicle began to slow down and he cursed when his phone rang.

What I didn't count on happening was my mother calling his phone.

"I can't talk right now, honey. I forgot to shut this phone off. I'm just pulling up to the location now."

I heard shouting on the other line before my father's raised voice startled me. "What the hell do you mean she's *missing*, Debra? She was still upstairs when I left. Are you sure you looked everywhere?"

There was some more shouting on the other line.

"Shit. Keep looking. Call the neighbors and check the entire perimeter of the house. I'll put a call into the station. I'm sure she's just hiding somewhere." He paused. "Don't cry, honey. Stay strong. I'm sure she's okay," he said, his own voice beginning to crack. "We will find her. I'm calling the station now. Keep your phone on you."

Oh no. This wasn't supposed to happen. I never wanted to make my mother cry or my dad upset. I just wanted to spend some more time with him and make a point.

He hung up his cell phone and picked up his car phone. "Yeah, Hannah, it's Special Agent Tanner. My wife just reported that our 9-year-old daughter's gone missing. She was last seen inside the house." He paused. "A little over an hour. I want an amber alert issued right away. Blonde hair, hazel eyes..." he started to rattle off.

Panic gripped me. I remembered my father telling me that it was wrong to prank call the police. He told me that it took away from helping actual people who were having real emergencies.

I sprung up from the backseat. "Daddy, stop. I'm here. I'm okay. I'm so sorry."

He clutched his chest and glared at me. "Never mind. I just

located her. Please call my wife and let her know. Thank you and I'm sorry for the trouble," he said before hanging up.

He stared at me for another second or so before he reached over and hugged me. "I'm so, *so* angry with you right now." Relief flashed across his face. "But I'm so happy you're okay. Do you have any idea what it would do to me if I ever lost you, goblin?"

I shook my head, tears welling up in my eyes. "You would be fine. You have a replacement on its way anyway," I grumbled.

He looked confused before he sighed. "No one could *ever* replace you, Alyssa. But, how did you find out?"

"I overheard you talking to mommy about it. You're going to have a new little girl and forget all about me."

He moved his seat back and sat me on his lap. "No, baby. That's not going to happen. I promise."

I sniffled and leaned my head against his chest. "I don't believe your promises anymore."

He held up my necklace. "You see this? You're the only girl in the world who will ever have it. I had it made just for you. That's how special you are to me."

"Then why are you having another baby? Am I not enough for you?"

He leaned down and kissed my cheek. "I love you more than all the stars in the sky and water in the oceans. From the very first second I laid eyes on you, that was it, kid. I was a goner." He looked lost in thought as he continued, "I was only 18 when you were born. Your mother and I were barely even out of high school. I was terrified of becoming a father, especially so young. Do you know who gave me strength to overcome that fear?" he asked.

"Who?"

"You did. I will never forget that moment. Your mother was recovering from labor and the nurses left you all alone with me. I started freaking out because I had no idea what I was supposed to do with you and I was sure I was going to screw something up and leave you scarred for life." He paused and smiled. "I remember talking to you and telling you how scared I was. I was about to have a panic attack, but then your little hand wrapped around one of my fingers and held on. You looked up at me with these beautiful eyes full of wonder and a sense of calm washed over me...and I knew I could do it. I knew we were going to be a team for life."

He brushed a strand of hair behind my ear. "That's why I call you goblin. It's not just because you were born on Halloween. It's because goblins are scary and frightening. And you were the scariest thing I'd ever come in contact with...but the best thing that ever happened to me. No one could ever take your place."

He reached for my hand and held it up to his heart. "We have a special bond that can never be broken, goblin. I will love you for all of eternity. You and your mother are the very best parts of my life."

I let out a hiccup. "I'm sorry I made you worry. I'm sorry for upsetting you. I love you."

"It's alright. Let me just make a quick call to Ford and I'll drive you back home."

He picked up the phone. "Hey, Ford. Look, something's come up. It's a long story. But I need you to distract him for an hour or two and buy me some time if he asks about me. I have to drive back home."

He lifted me off his lap and gripped the steering wheel. "What do you mean, what am I talking about? It's happening today. In the next hour to be exact. I heard it from one of his men myself. I tried calling you on your work phone but you didn't answer. I figured you got the same phone call and you were already here." He looked ahead and turned the key in the ignition. "Fuck," he said. "I've just been spotted."

He glanced back at me through the rear-view mirror and gritted his teeth. "No, I can't just drive off. That will only raise their suspicions further. Not to mention, I can't exactly start a high-speed chase with DeLuca's mobsters while my daughter's in the goddamn car!"

"What the fuck is Alyssa doing in the car with you right now? Fuck this. I'm on my way and I'm sending backup." I heard Ford's voice scream on the other line before it went silent.

He swallowed hard and continued to look straight ahead. Nervousness crept up my spine, signaling that something was very wrong.

"Goblin. I really need you to listen to me right now." My father took a deep breath before he continued. "I need you to go back under that blanket and hide. No matter what you see or hear, understand?"

"Wh-why...what's going...on?" I stuttered.

"Remember how Daddy helps to put away the bad guys?"

I gulped. "Y-yeah."

"Well, the bad guys are outside right now. And something very bad will happen if they see you. So, I need you to go back under that blanket and don't come out until I say you can. Okay?"

"Okay. I will. I'm so sorry, Daddy."

"It's okay, Alyssa. I'm not mad at you anymore. Everything will be fine. Ford and some other officers are on their way to come help us. Just do as I say, right now please."

I went back under the blanket in the backseat, my body shaking worse than a tree in the middle of a hurricane.

"Remember what I said. I need you to be quiet and stay under there. No matter what you see or hear."

"Okay. I love you."

"I love you, goblin. Never forget that," he whispered, right before someone tapped on the door.

He got out of the car and slammed the door shut behind him.

"Nice of you to join us, Graham," some deep voice sneered. "Or should I say, Special Agent Tanner."

I heard a few loud bangs and a few more muffled voices in the background.

It wasn't until I heard my father scream in pain, that I lifted my head out from under the blanket.

I scrunched down behind the driver seat but raised my head enough to partially take in my surroundings.

We were at a dock of some sort. There were a few dark SUV's around and big men wearing all black suits.

Then I saw something I would never forget.

My father chained up against a wall. His lip was bleeding, and someone had taken a pair of pliers to one of his fingers. My stomach heaved when I saw the blood dripping down.

I jimmied the door handle in order to go outside to help him, but it was locked.

I crawled over to the console and reached for the phone. I pressed the same button I'd seen my father press many times before.

"Hello Agent Tanner, this is Hannah. Agent Ford Baker has already made me aware of your situation and he's on his way with backup."

"H-hello," I whispered.

"Who is this?" Hannah asked.

"My Daddy's in trouble. The bad men are hurting him. Tell Ford to come, quick."

"Is this Agent Tanner's daughter?" she asked.

"Yes, this is Alyssa. Come quick. He's bleeding and they're doing something to his fingers."

"Alright sweetheart, please hang tight. Help is on the way. Where are you right now?"

"He told me to stay inside the car. I tried to go outside but all the doors are locked."

"Does anyone besides your dad know you're inside the car?"

"No. They can't see me. Their backs are all turned away from me. And the windows are tinted."

"Okay. Listen, I need you to stay away from the big windshield, Alyssa. It's not tinted like the other windows are. You can stay on the phone with me, but I need you to go to the backseat and stay down."

"But then I won't be able to see them," I protested.

Just then another car pulled up. My hopes were soon dashed when the door opened and out walked one of the biggest men I'd ever seen. Even bigger than my own father.

He wore an all black suit, dark sunglasses, and he had on shiny leather shoes with metal tips. There was also a fairly large scar on his face that stretched from his ear to his jaw.

His lips turned up in a snarl, and all the other men around him straightened their spines and lifted their heads.

He circled the men and stopped to narrow his eyes in my father's direction while he took his sunglasses off his face.

His eyes were dark as coal. The scariest eyes I'd ever seen in my life.

And I knew that something very bad was about to happen.

"Hurry. Another man just showed up. He looks big and scary. He has metal tips on his shoes. And his eyes are really dark and there's a scar on his face."

I heard her mumble, "Shit, DeLuca himself just showed up. Where the hell is backup?"

"Wh-who's DeLuca?" I asked.

"Make sure you stay down, sweetheart. Don't let him see you, please."

Tears pooled in my eyes. "Where's Ford?"

"He's on his way, sweetie."

I sniffled and let out a tiny scream when I saw the man take out some kind of metal object and aim it in my father's direction.

"Don't scream, Alyssa," she warned.

"He's about to hurt my Daddy. I want to talk to Ford. Please. I'm begging you. If you don't, I'll scream as loud as I can."

"I'll transfer you over to him right now."

The line went silent for a moment before I heard the sound of his voice. "Agent Baker."

"Ford, help."

"Alyssa?"

The man took another step toward my father. My father had remained strong, but for a single moment, I could see the desperation in his eyes when he saw what was in his hand. And it absolutely terrified me.

"Yeah. He's about to hurt my Daddy. He's wearing all black and he has metal tips on his leather shoes. He has a scar and he's scary and big, like a wrestler. And I'm pretty sure his name is DeLuca something. You need to get here and arrest him."

"Fuck. How do *you* know that?" He paused. "Wait, are you *witnessing* everything that's happening right now?"

"Uh-huh. Where are you?"

"I'm about 5 minutes away. I'll be there shortly. Stay down and do *not* get out of the car."

Three of DeLuca's men approached my father then.

I breathed a sigh of relief when they unchained him.

"They unchained him. I think they're going to let him go."

"Alyssa, listen to me. I need you to put your head down and stop looking at them. Please, sweetheart."

"I don't understand. Wait, another car just pulled up. Is that you?"

"No, that's not me, Alyssa. Now, stop looking."

I ignored his request. "If it's not you then who is it?"

I watched in confusion as four more of DeLuca's men went over to the car and opened the door. They quickly yanked out two males with dark skin. Both men, if you could even call them that- because they looked more like teenagers; wore baggy clothes and had quite a few tattoos. One boy had a blue shirt on, along with a blue bandanna hanging from his back pocket. The other boy was wearing a red shirt and had a red bandanna hanging from his back pocket. They both looked tired and groggy and had bruises and gashes along their faces and arms.

I didn't understand what they were doing there, or what their involvement was.

I held back a gasp when DeLuca stretched a black glove over his large hand and proceeded to wipe down the metal crowbar.

His men then turned both boys to face one another before they shoved what looked to be guns in their hands. However, both boys appeared to be too out of it to be aware of what was happening to them.

Maybe Ford was right. Maybe it was best that I didn't see what was about to happen. I gasped loudly into the phone when I heard two gunshots go off.

My head jerked up and I let out a cry when I saw the two boys slumped over and bleeding.

My father yelled something at DeLuca then, something about them only being teenagers, I think. But I wasn't sure because my ears were still ringing from the shots.

DeLuca backhanded my father and my father, in turn, spit blood at him.

Then he raised the metal crowbar high above his head.

Everything around me stopped when he took the first swing against my father's skull.

"No! Daddy! Please, no!" I screamed out at the top of my lungs while hitting the windshield as hard as I could.

"Stop screaming, Alyssa," Ford pleaded.

But I couldn't.

I watched as DeLuca continued to bash my father's skull in with that crowbar, deforming his once handsome face.

I watched as my father's body went limp, his blood pooling around the pavement.

I watched as DeLuca smirked and relished every second of killing the man I loved most in the world.

Until his eyes connected with mine.

I screamed even louder...and his smirk grew wider.

Finally, I heard the faint sound of sirens in the distance.

DeLuca took one final look at me before he and his men disappeared into their cars and took off quick as lightning.

I was still screaming when Ford pulled me out of the car and I clung to him for dear life, refusing to be anywhere else.

I was still screaming when Ford barked orders to cover my father's body because my eyes couldn't look away.

I was still screaming when the ambulance pulled up and took out three body bags, instead of stretchers.

I was still screaming when Ford pulled up to headquarters and took me inside an interrogation room.

Whenever I close my eyes...I'm still screaming.

"I t wasn't those boys, Ford. It was DeLuca. I know it was."
I'd spent almost 48 hours in the same interrogation room at that point. I fell asleep in Ford's arms for a few short hours, only to wake up screaming.

They tried bringing in a child psychiatrist. They tried feeding me.

They tried doing everything they could to get me to believe something that I refused to.

I knew the truth. I saw it with my very own eyes.

I just didn't understand why *they* wanted me to believe otherwise.

Ford dragged a hand through his dark hair. His 5 o'clock shadow looked even more scruffy than usual, not that it dulled his movie star good looks.

Like my father, he was young. Both he and my father were the youngest members of the FBI, still in their late 20's.

I sat up in my seat, my legs swinging because they didn't quite reach the floor yet. "Where's my mom? Why isn't she here with me? Especially when I'm being interrogated. Where's my lawyer?"

Ford threw up his hands in frustration. "I'm not interrogating you, Alyssa. I just need you to understand certain things. And you don't need a lawyer because you're not in any kind of trouble."

"Then why am I still stuck here? Where's my mother!" I screamed.

Fords expression changed from one of frustration to sheer sadness.

He reached for my hand. "She's in the hospital," he said softly.
"Why?"

He rubbed his eyes. "She's not in good shape right now, kiddo. And the doctor's need to look after her for another day or so. She knows you're here, safe with me."

"What happened to her? Give it to me straight, Ford. I'm a big girl now. I'm officially 10 years old today."

A look of pity flashed across his face. "After she found out what happened, she collapsed." He paused, appearing to choose his next words carefully, but I cut right to the chase.

"What happened to the baby?"

"She lost the baby," he whispered.

I pulled my knees up to my chest and began rocking myself. "It's my fault. I didn't want a little sister and now she's dead. Just like it's all my fault that my Daddy died."

Ford immediately stood up, walked over to me and sat me on his lap. "No, sweetheart. None of this is your fault."

I sunk against him and put my arms around his neck. "You're only saying that because I'm a kid."

"Have I ever treated you like a kid, Alyssa?"

I thought about his question for a moment before I answered, "No."

He was right. He never treated me like I was a child. He always talked to me like I was his equal. So much so, that he and my mother got into it a few times. Especially after he let it slip that Santa and the Easter Bunny weren't real, back when I was 8 years old.

I liked that about Ford, though. In a world full of adults trying mold me into what they wanted me to be, he let me decide things for myself. He let me draw my own conclusions after giving me the cold-hard facts.

He never told me I shouldn't do something, or told me I was wrong for feeling a certain way...until now.

"And you trust me, right?" he asked.

"You're the only one I have left now. Of course, I trust you."

He turned us in the seat and hoisted me up on the table. "Then I need you to repeat after me- I saw those two boys kill my father after he broke up a fight brewing between them and a few others."

"But I didn't, Ford. I know exactly who killed my father. I'll never forget his face. I see it every time I close my eyes. It was him.

That DeLuca, man. I don't know why you don't believe me. Ask Hannah, she'll tell you."

"Goddammit," he barked. "Listen to me, Alyssa. DeLuca didn't kill your dad. It was two members of rival gangs. He tried to break it up and he got caught in the crossfire. He was at the wrong place at the wrong time."

I shook my head adamantly. "No, it *wasn't*. Ask Hannah! Why won't you believe me?"

He stood up and kicked a chair across the room.

I began trembling. "Ask Hannah," I repeated.

He ran back over to me and grabbed my face between his large hands. "I can't ask Hannah."

I was even more confused by his statement. "Why?"

"Because Hannah's dead. She was found by her car after leaving the station with two bullets in her head."

"W-what?"

His grip tightened around my cheeks. "You heard me. They got to her. I don't know how, but they traced everything. There must have been a mole working for us. A few of them."

He sighed. "And now DeLuca's got all of New York eating out of his pocket. He controls the politician's, the news. Hell, he's about to have *my* department eating out of the palm of his hand soon. Your dad and I were trying to prevent it. We went undercover, without the FBI's knowledge, on our own. Hannah was in on it with us. We were trying to snag him on something and put him away before he became too powerful...but we failed."

His face fell. "We fucked up big time and your father paid the ultimate price for it."

"But he's a bad guy. How is that possible?"

Ford looked at me hard. "Because sometimes in life, sweetheart. The bad guys win."

His grip eased up and I rubbed my cheek. "So put him away for killing my father."

Ford groaned and took a step back. "In order to do that, we

need to have something called motive. Not to mention all the evidence points to those two gang members being responsible."

"What's motive?"

"A logical reason behind doing something. Usually in regards to committing a crime."

"So tell them that you and my dad were trying to catch him doing something bad and he got angry."

"I can't do that," he mumbled.

"Why not?"

He leaned his forehead against mine and put my hands on his cheeks. My breathing became uneven and I didn't know why.

Actually, I did.

It was because I always thought Ford was the most handsome man I'd ever seen. Every time my mom would read me a fairytale, I would picture myself as the princess and Ford as my prince.

I never told anyone about that, though. I didn't think my parents would have liked that very much, for some reason I didn't really comprehend.

"Do you think I'm a good guy, Alyssa?" he whispered.

"Yes," I answered without hesitation. "You're one of my favorite people in the whole wide world."

He smiled at me, showcasing his perfectly straight and white teeth.

"You wouldn't ever want to see me behind bars, right?"

My hand flew to my face. "Never. That would kill me."

"Then you can't ever tell anyone about what your father and I did, okay?"

I bit my lip and looked down. "I won't say anything. Ever. I promise."

He tilted my chin up to look at him. "And you'll tell everyone that it was those two gang members who killed your dad, right?"

I shook my head. "No. Because it wasn't them. DeLuca deserves to pay for what he did."

His nostrils flared and he grunted. "If you say it was DeLuca- do you know what will happen, sweetheart?"

"Yeah. He'll go to jail for a very long time. Maybe even forever."

He grabbed my face again and stared into my eyes. "No, he won't. He knows you saw him, Alyssa. And he'll come after you. Along with me, and your mother. And he won't stop until we're all dead." One hand wrapped around the back of my neck. "He'll bash my skull in and spread my brains all over the concrete."

He lowered his voice and whispered in my ear, "And then he'll do it to your mom. And he'll make you watch every single second of it before he does it to you. Just like with your dad."

I couldn't stop myself from dry heaving with those words. Ford reached for a garbage pail and held it out in front of me while he stroked my hair.

After a few moments, my stomach settled and I was able to breathe again. "But that would make me a l-liar. Being a liar is bad. Those two boys were innocent."

He sat on the chair in front of the table I was still sitting on and put my feet on top of his thighs. "I know your mom reads to you a lot. What's your favorite fairy tale?"

I was put off by the change of subject, but I answered anyway. "Beauty and the Beast."

He smiled and tilted his head toward me. "Do you think the beast was bad?"

"No. I mean, at first, maybe. But he changed his ways for Belle."

"And the beast rescued Belle in the end, right?"

"Well, yes...and no. It's complicated, Ford. The beast loved her and Belle loved him. Despite how mean he was in the beginning. She saw past all that."

He lifted my hand to his lips. "Can you see past the wrong I've done?"

I didn't understand what he meant by that. "Of course. I already told you, you're not a bad guy. You're my favorite person."

"I was only trying to put the bad guy away," he whispered.

"I know. I'm not mad at you."

"Will you let me rescue you then?" His thumb grazed my cheek. "Will you let me be your Prince, Alyssa?"

My cheeks flushed and a swarm of butterflies entered my tummy. "I-um." My breathing became shaky. "I'm feeling nervous and weird right now and I don't understand why," I blurted out.

"You never have to be nervous around me. I would do anything in the world for you. You trust me, right?"

"Yeah-yes."

"I would never, ever hurt you."

"I know."

"Who killed your father?"

"You already know."

The pad of his thumb brushed my cheek again and he moved closer. "Who killed your father, Alyssa?"

I stayed silent.

"Better, sweetheart." He planted a kiss on my cheek and I blushed. "Now I'll ask you again. Who did it? Who killed your father?"

He kissed my other cheek right before I answered, "They did. Those...boys. My father tried to stop the fight between them and they attacked him before they shot each other."

He let out a deep breath. "I'm so proud of you."

He kissed the corner of my mouth. "Thank you for letting me rescue and protect you."

———

"And that's my story, Jackson. You know things that I've never told another soul."

His brows furrow. "Do you still talk to your dad's old partner?"

"Out of everything I just told you, *that's* what you're choosing to focus on?"

I get up off the bed. "Ford protected me from my father's killer."

He runs a hand through his short hair. "Yeah, I know. I get it," he says before mumbling something under his breath that I don't catch. He appears lost in thought before asking, "Is that why you were grilling me about the owner of the fight club? You thought it was this DeLuca guy, didn't you?"

I nod and he stands up. "It's not by the way. He's not the owner. But you realize how dangerous it would be for you if it was, right?"

"Yeah." I stare at him. "I mean, no. If DeLuca wanted me, he would have gotten me by now. Trust me, after the sex tape my identity isn't exactly an issue anymore. Everyone knows who I am now. Besides, the media went with the story about two rival gangs killing a cop. No one knows the truth besides Ford and I...and now you."

"You never answered my question."

"What question?"

"Do you still talk to him?"

"No," I lie.

I might have told Jackson things I've never told another person. But there's no way I can tell him about the exact nature of me and Ford's relationship throughout the years.

Or the moment, or rather, *moments*; it changed.

And the way it broke me.

Chapter 11 (Alyssa)

Past...

After that day in the interrogation room, Ford remained an integral part of my childhood.

He came around every other weekend and whisked me away for a few hours during another one of my mother's drunken binges.

He tried persuading her to go to rehab, so many times I lost count; but as usual, she insisted that she didn't have a problem and that if he wanted to continue spending time with me he needed to mind his own business.

He attended every recital, every sporting event, and even a few parent- teacher conferences.

At least, he did until I turned 15.

After that, he seldom came around and I didn't understand why.

One time, he mumbled something about it no longer being appropriate for us to spend so much time with one another, and I thought my heart was going to shatter into a million pieces.

Before he drove away from my tear stained face that day, he promised me that he would always be in my life.

I hated that he was purposely distancing himself from me, but to his credit, he did text me a few times a week. And he still made it a point to see me in person during the two days leading up to my birthday.

Those were always the hardest for me for obvious reasons.

———

I 'll never forget the night of my 17th birthday.

I had gotten into another horrible fight with my mother and John. One of the worst ones to date. I found out that he officially moved in with us.

After hours of persuading and guilting Ford into coming to see me, he finally relented.

He pulled up in a shiny new BMW. The color matching his dark blue eyes perfectly.

I let out a whistle when I saw it and those perfect teeth of his flashed me a movie star grin. "You like?"

"I do. It's gorgeous."

He opened the driver side door and threw the keys at me. "Let's go. You drive."

I stared at him, too stunned to speak. "What's with the look? You are 17 now." He winked. "I trust you not to crash my baby. Now get over here."

I bit my lip and walked over to his side of the car.

He got out and stood before me, his large frame towering over me. His eyes briefly scanned over my body before he looked away. "Jesus, what the hell are they putting in the milk these days," he muttered.

"What are you talking about?"

He coughed before looking at me again. "It's just...you look so grown up compared to when I last saw you. I can't believe your mother lets you out of the house looking like that."

I smoothed over the micro denim mini skirt that I wore especially for him.

I didn't usually wear suggestive clothing, but I wanted to look different.

I wanted Ford to see me as a woman, instead of some silly teenager. "Looking like what, Ford? It's been an entire year since I last saw you, of course, I grew up."

His gaze lingered over my legs. "Yeah, I guess you did."

He walked over to the passenger side door. "You gonna be able to drive in those heels, killer?"

I smirked. "I'll manage."

Since I was the driver, and the destination was my choice—I knew exactly where I wanted to take him.

"Out of all the places to go to. You chose *this* place. On your birthday."

The stars lit up the night time sky and the sound of water crashing against the docks hovered in the distance as I parked the car.

I chewed on my thumbnail. "I haven't been back here since it happened. And there's no one in the world I trust to come here with but you."

"I haven't been here since that day either," he confessed.

I leaned against the headrest and pushed my seat back. "Do you think he would be proud of me?"

Ford reached for my hand. "Of course, he would. Why would you think otherwise?"

"Sometimes I think he would be mad that I didn't stop my mother from turning into an alcoholic. That I should have prevented it."

Before Ford could interject I added, "Sometimes I think he blames me for causing his death. All because I pulled that stupid stunt. God, I was such a brat. What the hell was I thinking?"

His fingers linked with mine. "You were a child, Alyssa. It wasn't your fault and he would never blame you. He loved you."

I squeezed my eyes shut and tuned out his words. "She still cries over him. Usually, it's after John has gone to bed and she thinks no one can hear her. But I can. I always can. Hell, sometimes I cry with her."

"Sweetheart—" he started.

I cleared my throat and opened my eyes. "So, anyway. What's new with you?"

He drew back his hand and ran it along his jaw. "Well, I met someone."

"Oh?" I said, hoping my true feelings over his statement wouldn't show.

It felt like he tossed my heart in a blender and pressed 'puree.' Twice.

"Yeah. She's a doll, too. She's a nurse in the ER over at Columbia."

I gritted my teeth. "A nurse, how sweet."

Obviously not picking up on my sarcasm, he continued, "Yeah. She is. Better than the last relationship I had. What a disaster that was. I'm thinking it's time for this old dog to settle down. Make an honest woman out of someone."

"You're not old," I muttered. He laughed. "I'm 35. That's like ancient to most teenagers."

I played with a strand of my hair. "I'm not like most teenagers, Ford."

He stared at me for a beat and swallowed. "No. No, you're not. You've been through more shit than most adults have in an entire lifetime."

"So what's this nurse's name?" I interrupted.

"Penelope."

"That's a stupid name," I said through clenched teeth.

In all honesty, it wouldn't have mattered what her name was, I still would have hated it.

He chuckled. "It's a bit of a mouthful, I suppose."

I glared at him. "Does she put out?"

He looked taken back. "I don't think that's any of your business. You don't hear me asking if you've given it up to Tony, now do you?"

I spun around in my seat. "His name's *Toby*." I crossed my arms. "And for your information- No, I haven't given it up yet. I want it to be special."

He nodded, relief flashing across his face. "That's good. It should be special—" he started to say before I cut him off.

"But I've given him one hell of a blowjob."

"Christ, Alyssa. What the *hell* is the matter with you?"

"You!" I shouted. "You left me, Ford. I needed you and you weren't there. You were all I had to depend on after mom went off the deep end. You were the only good thing I had left. Especially after John entered our lives."

He sat up straight. "Has that prick touched you? I swear to God, I'll kill him."

I rolled my eyes. "No. I just don't trust him is all. He's not a good guy. Especially now that he's living with us and controlling mom's every move."

"Shit, she let him move in? You know you can tell me if he steps out of line with you or your mother. Right?"

"Yeah."

We stayed silent for what felt like hours before I finally gathered enough strength to ask him. "Why did you leave me? Why did you go away?"

"I told you. Our relationship wasn't appropriate. People were going to talk and assume things about us, about *me*."

I slammed the steering wheel with my hand. "So let them. Who the fuck cares what other people say."

"It's not that simple, Alyssa."

"I don't buy it. We weren't doing anything wrong. And I don't think people would say shit if they knew the way you saved me. If they knew the way you stepped in when no one else did."

He stayed silent, but I continued probing. "What's the real reason, Ford? You've always been honest with me."

He looked down, avoiding my gaze. "I already told you. It wasn't appropriate."

I smacked the steering wheel again. "Bullshit."

"Would you quit doing that!" he shouted. "You're gonna hurt yourself."

"Stop avoiding my question, Ford."

"I already answered the goddamned question," he ground out.

I slammed the steering wheel again, harder this time.

"Stop it!"

"Make me."

He grabbed my wrists. "Stop acting like a child."

"Stop treating me like one then. And tell me the truth!"

"How many times do I have to say it? It wasn't appropriate, Alyssa."

I struggled against him. "Why? You never did anything wrong. So what *exactly* was it about our relationship that wasn't appropriate?"

"Goddammit, Alyssa. *Me.* My thoughts. The way I was starting to look at you, *think* about you. *Feel* about you. Nothing about it was appropriate."

And just like that, the smoke screen was lifted and my heart soared into orbit.

"How could it not be appropriate when I thought the same things?"

"Because you're a child. I'm an adult. I should know better."

"I'm not a child."

"Yeah, well. You're not an adult, either."

"I'm in love with you, Ford. I always have been. I always will be."

He closed his eyes. "Don't say stuff like that."

"Why not? It's the truth."

"You're my best friend's little girl. I was there at the hospital the day you were born for crying out loud. Do you know how *disgusting* that makes me feel? I want to wash my mind out with bleach every single time I think about you. Do you know how *wrong* everything about this is?"

"Then I'll wait." I swallowed hard. "I'll wait until it's not wrong anymore. Hell, I'll wait for you forever."

"That's the thing, Alyssa. I don't know when it would *ever* be right between us."

"Then I might as well do this," I said before I leaned over the center console and kissed him.

I expected him to push me away, to start yelling about how it wasn't appropriate again. Instead, he groaned and pulled me closer to him as his tongue skated over mine.

Heat coursed through me and I reached for his belt buckle.

That's when he stopped me.

"No. You're not ready for that, yet. You deserve more than some cheap fuck in a car with some old man for your first time."

I reached for his belt again. "Okay, so let me take care of you then."

He pulled away. "No." He sighed. "Listen to me and listen good. You are beautiful and special. You're not some *whore*. You're a good girl, you understand me?"

I shrugged. "I thought I'd do something to make you happy. I thought you wanted me."

He tucked a strand of hair behind my ear. "I do." He looked down. "Clearly that isn't the issue here."

"So what's the problem?"

"Gee, I don't know. Where do I begin? Oh, that's right. How about the fact that what we're doing is *illegal*. Use your head. You got accepted into NYU, didn't you?"

"Okay, so when can we take the next step then?" He muttered something under his breath. "How about when you're old enough."

"Can we still do other stuff?"

He raised an eyebrow. "Like what?"

"Like what we were doing before? You know, kissing."

His lips twitched. "Well you can't un-ring a bell, now can you?"

He leaned in so that I was pressed against my seat. "So fucking beautiful," he whispered before his lips landed on mine.

"So does this mean you and Penelope are over?" I asked between kisses. "I'll break up with Toby first thing tomorrow."

His hand stopped moving midway up my thigh. "I can't just

break up with her," he said. "I asked her to marry me. The wedding's this summer."

I pushed him off me. "You *what?* How could you? I thought you were in love with *me?*"

He exhaled sharply and adjusted himself. "I am. I just never thought this—" He gestured between us. "Would ever happen."

"Okay, and now that it has you can let her down easy."

He looked at me like I sprouted another head. "And say what? That I'm in love with my deceased partner's daughter? Who by the fucking way isn't even 18 yet."

"Maybe not in those exact words, but yeah. Something along those lines."

He shook his head. "You don't get it, do you?"

"Evidently not. Why don't you catch me up to speed, special agent," I bit out.

"No one can *ever* know about us. It will always be wrong, no matter how we feel about one another. I have a reputation to protect. I'm a trusted *officer* of the law for Pete's sake."

"But, I thought..."

"You thought wrong, sweetheart." He grabbed my face between both of his hands. "Look, if you can't handle this. Then it's best we stop right here, right now."

I swiped at the tears on my face. "I can't stand the thought of you with someone else, Ford."

"That's the way it has to be."

"I don't know if I can deal with that."

"Then after tonight, forget about us. I'll always be there if you ever really need me, but I have to separate myself from you. It's too hard to be around you. You invade my senses until the only thing I see is you."

"But I love you."

He kissed me tenderly. "And I love you. That's why it's so difficult."

I pulled him into another kiss. Our mouths coming together in a rough and needy mess. His hand slipped back down to my thigh.

"Goddammit. You have *no* idea how much I want you. How much I've dreamed about this moment. How much I've jerked off to visions of you writhing underneath me."

"Then marry me. Not her."

His hand moved higher, raising the denim of my skirt to the level of my underwear. "I wish I could, sweetheart. Trust me."

"You can. Who cares what other people think and say. We can live in our own little bubble."

"That's not the way the world works," he grumbled.

"So let's make our own world."

"We can't. Now you can either learn to accept it or not. But I'm marrying Penelope. It's happening. Me and *her* make sense together."

I tried to push him off me again but he didn't budge. "Well, I don't accept it. It should be me. She'll never love you the way I do."

I didn't even realize how hard the tears were falling until Ford had stopped kissing me. "Don't you get it now? We can't be together. You can't even handle kissing me without getting hysterical."

His words lit a fury in me and before I could stop myself, I slapped him across the cheek. "Asshole."

He looked as surprised as I felt. He bit my lip and kissed me harder. "That's right. I *am* an asshole. And innocent little girls like you need to stay far away and stop provoking the beast."

"What if I love the beast? What if I accept him for all that he is?"

His fingers grazed over my panties. "Who does this belong to?"

I trailed kisses up his neck. "I think you know the answer to that."

"Say it, Alyssa."

"It's yours."

"Is it?"

I nodded. "You know it is."

"Even after I marry Penelope? Is it still mine then?"

"I don't want to think about that, Ford."

"Well think about it, because it's happening." He slipped a finger inside the material. "Will you still wait for me then? Will you still allow me to be the first? The *only*? No matter how much time has passed between us?"

I held my breath as his finger continued to stroke me. "Answer me."

"Yes. I'll wait for you."

"Promise me."

"I promise."

———————

By the time Ford had dropped me off it was almost 3 in the morning.

I tip-toed inside the house, being as quiet as I could.

Until a voice stopped me in my tracks. "Who was that man that just dropped you off?" John's voice boomed.

I turned to face him. "None of your business. Don't worry about it."

The corner of his lips curled up. "Don't give me any sass, girl. I asked you a question and I expect an answer."

"That controlling tone might work with my mother, for reasons I fail to comprehend; but you're surely mistaken if you think it'll have the same effect on me. I don't answer to you."

I headed in the direction of my room when I was suddenly slammed against the wall. I rubbed the back of my head, trying to thwart off a headache that would be starting soon, thanks to him. "Touch me again and it will be the last thing you ever do, you son of a bitch," I warned.

"Young lady, that is no way to talk to your father."

I saw red at that moment. "You might be screwing my mother, but you are *not* my father."

He looked me up and down, disgust in his eyes. "Yeah, well, maybe if you actually *had* a father you wouldn't be walking in the house at 3 in the morning looking like a tramp."

I was so angry I started shaking. "Yeah, well, maybe if you were half the man *my* father was, you wouldn't have to buy my mother off with gifts to get her to fuck you."

The slap across my face seemed to echo throughout the entire house.

A light turned on in the hallway and my mother stood there in shock.

I took a step forward. "You can try and cover up manure...but at the end of the day, it still reeks like shit."

"What the hell is that supposed to mean?" he barked.

I looked at my mother briefly before focusing my attention back to him. "You might be in her bed now, but trust me when I say that when the booze leaves her system and reality sets in, it's not you that she wants next to her. It will always be him."

My mother gasped but I ignored her and held up my cell phone instead. "And you just made a big mistake by touching me."

I ran out of the house and dialed Ford's number.

A woman's voice picked up on the third ring.

"Hello," she answered.

"Can I speak to Ford?" I heard some shuffling in the background. "It's 3:30 in the morning. Who is this?"

Aggravation coursed through me as it dawned on me. "Why are you picking up his cell phone?"

A giggle erupted, followed by the sound of his low groan. "Because he's a little preoccupied at the moment."

I let out a shaky breath, the impact of her words sinking in.

"Tell him it's important," I whispered.

With a huff, I heard her faintly murmur what I said to him.

"There's nothing more important than you, sweetheart. Just hang up on her," Ford's voice commanded before the line went dead.

I shoved my phone into my pocket and turned back around. I was startled to find John outside on the porch smoking a cigarette.

"Look, I'm sorry about before," he began.

I continued walking, my heart breaking with every step. "Whatever."

"Who was that you were on the phone with?" he asked.

That's when the tears erupted. John stomped out his cigarette, appearing daunted.

"It doesn't matter," I sniffed. "What we had is over, for good. He made that perfectly clear."

He looked pleased. "Listen, I've been thinking, I want your mother to go to rehab."

I laughed and walked past him. "Yeah, good luck with that."

"I'm gonna make it happen, Alyssa. But I'm going to need your help."

He held out his hand. "Truce?"

"Fine," I muttered before heading inside.

An hour later, my phone rang. Ford's name flashed on the screen.

"Leave me alone," I answered.

"Don't be like that, Alyssa."

"Be like what, Ford? Be like you?"

"Stop acting like a child. I told you the way it had to be."

I stayed silent.

"I told you I'll always be there for you when you need me," he said.

"Yeah, except when you're too busy being *there* for her. I won't be the other woman."

He chuckled. "You'd actually have to be a woman for that to happen."

His words stung. There was only one way to make the pain go away. "Have a nice life, Ford."

"Look, I'm sorry. I didn't mean to hurt you like that. You know I love you. I will always love you. But maybe it's best that we don't talk for a while," he said before he hung up.

It was the last time I would speak to Ford for 4 years.

The next time...he would shatter the rest of me.

H e stared at me for what felt like forever, finally standing up from his desk after a full 5 minutes had passed.

His gray suit was immaculate, and even though a few lines creased his forehead with age, it only made him better looking.

"You cut your hair," were the first words he uttered. "It suits you. I like it. Makes you look more mature."

I gave him half a smile. "Most newscasters have shoulder length hair. I figured it was time to conform."

He nodded. "Did you get here okay?"

I held up the keys to the BMW. "Yeah. Thanks to a certain special agent I know."

Nothing shocked me more than when I had received the title and a set of keys to his BMW in the mail, along with directions telling me where I could pick it up.

On his wedding day, no less.

Not wanting to acknowledge that statement with words, he gave me another nod.

I wrung my hands and looked around. "I like your office."

"Yeah, I have the promotion to thank for that. It seems the higher up the chain I go, the less field work I do."

I smiled, until I spotted a picture of him and my father on his desk. His eyes followed mine and he looked away.

Figuring this moment couldn't get any more awkward, I decided, to go for the gold. "How's Penelope?"

"Fine," he responded curtly.

He seemed different now. Colder. "Is everything okay?" I asked.

He cleared his throat and walked out from around his desk. "I guess I'm just trying to figure out exactly why you're here, Alyssa."

I stepped back as though I'd been punched. "You really have no idea why I'm here right now?"

The sex tape had gone viral, my stepfather had lost the election, and my mother had officially disowned me.

I had no one else to turn to. All roads led back to him.

"I guess you haven't been on the internet in a while but—"

"I saw the fucking sex tape!" he screamed loud enough to make me jump.

Not waiting for a response, he continued. "Like I said, I'm having trouble figuring out why you're here."

I swallowed hard. "John won't help me and my mother's turned her back on me."

"Okay?"

"Okay?" I scoffed before my voice started cracking. "You're all I have left, Ford."

I took a step toward him and he lifted his chin. "What exactly is it that you want from me, Alyssa?"

"It happened without my consent—"

He cut me off. "Are you insinuating that he raped you? Because it looked like you were a willing participant."

"No. What I meant was that I had no idea he was filming it. I never agreed to that."

He narrowed his eyes. "But you agreed to spread your legs for him?"

Before I could interject he added, "Like some kind of whore."

I heard that word from a lot of people after the sex tape leaked, including my own mother. But hearing it from his mouth made something inside of me snap.

He held me against him. "Shh." He took out a tissue and wiped my face. "Stop crying."

"I c-can't. You promised you would always be there f-for me." I took a deep breath. "I need your help, Ford."

He kissed my forehead. "What are you willing to do for it?" he whispered.

He put a hand on my shoulder and pushed. I backed away from him, closing my eyes in disbelief.

I looked up at him when I heard the sound of a belt buckle being undone. "No." I shook my head. "You can't be serious."

I had always thought about being intimate with Ford, but not this way. Never like this.

He smirked. "What's the matter, Alyssa? You can fuck some guy on video but not me? The man you claimed to love. The one you promised to wait for?"

"I-I. You got married. You chose her. *You* said we shouldn't talk anymore," I stammered.

He leaned into me until I fell against the wall. "I was *trying* to do the right thing," he whispered before he kissed me.

Our mouths tangled and his hands pulled at my clothing. "What are we doing, Ford?" I panted as he kissed my neck.

He pulled back. "You were supposed to be *mine*."

I reached for the buttons on his shirt and he lifted my skirt. "I am yours."

Before I knew it, my legs were wrapped around his waist and he was entering me with a loud grunt as I moaned.

"Yeah, you like that?" he asked before pulling out and slamming into me hard.

I could only nod, my body too far gone to form actual words.

Until his next statement. "Of course, you do. You little slut."

My eyes opened wide and I stopped moving. "Wha—"

His hand slammed over my mouth and his eyes darkened. "You heard me. You lost all your value and appeal the day you became nothing but a worthless slut. You only did it to yourself, Alyssa."

Tears sprung to my eyes with his cruel words as he continued thrusting and taunting me. "I loved you. I was supposed to be your first, your only. Now you're *tainted*...ruined."

He grunted his release and threw me to the ground. "Turns out you weren't that good of a fuck after all. Figure your own way out of this mess, Alyssa. I suggest you continue to whore yourself around because that's all you're good for. Now, get out of my office."

His hands remained clenched at his sides and he took one final look at me. "Your father would be ashamed of you."

I quickly gathered my clothes off the ground and left.

After making my way out to the hallway, I reached up and felt for my necklace. With shaky hands, I tugged on it until it ripped free and fell.

It was then that I realized.

There are a thousand ways to break a girl...but it only takes one to kill her.

Chapter 12 (Alyssa)

I wake up to a pair of strong arms rocking me.

I look up as Jackson peers down at me, concern written all over his striking face.

I don't even realize that I fell asleep again until I glance at the clock, and it reads 3:45am.

For a moment, I'm nervous that I've said something about Ford in my dream state.

I expect him to start questioning me, or ask what I was dreaming about but he doesn't. Instead, his hand drops down to my cheek and brushes across the wetness gathered there. He looks at his fingers, which are now damp with my tears.

Then he pulls me off of his lap and crushes me against him in one of the most powerful embraces I've ever experienced in my life.

My breath leaves my lungs with a big whoosh, and all I can do is breathe him in and succumb to the warmth I feel.

It's been so long since I've been touched like this, I almost recoil.

He must sense this because he pulls back slightly, his thumbs graze over my cheekbones again and for a second; I think he's about to do something crazy- like kiss me.

I find myself wanting him to do just that. I want him to fix me, make me whole again. I want him to erase the past with his purity and kindness.

I wish our circumstances were different, I wish I was the girl he first thought I was. The girl he briefly flirted with on that walk from the fight club. The girl who isn't so damaged she barely even knows how to function anymore.

His lips move closer and my heart stutters in my chest as I close my eyes.

Disappointment hits hard when I feel his lips land on my forehead instead of my mouth.

"Look at me," he whispers. "I won't hurt you."

I've heard those words before...by the one person who swore they never would.

"You don't know that, Jackson. You can't promise me something like that."

His eyes bore into mine before he hugs me again. "You're right. I can't make that promise." He holds my chin between his thumb and his fingers. "But I *can* promise you that I will never intentionally hurt you. No matter what happens between us, just know that I'll always have your best interest at heart."

I stay silent taking in his words, wanting so badly to believe them. I'm so lost in my own thoughts, I almost don't register when he stands up and walks over to his closet.

"Here," Jackson says. He hands me a clean white t-shirt and a pair of flannel boxers. "Change into these. You'll be more comfortable."

I look down at my skin tight jeans and my constricting leopard print tank top and give him a smile. "Thanks."

He returns my smile before he closes the door behind him.

After I change he walks back into his bedroom, this time; carrying a mug. I look down in confusion when I see its contents.

"Hot chocolate with cinnamon and whipped cream?" I question. It's not that I'm not grateful for it, I'm just curious; especially because I never asked for it.

He looks uneasy before he clears his throat and sits on the bed beside me.

"I used to make it for Lilly whenever she was upset." He shrugs. "It was her favorite. It always made her feel better."

I'm touched that he's sharing this part of himself with me.

I take a sip of the chocolate goodness before putting the mug down on the nightstand beside the bed.

Before I can talk myself out of it, I reach for his hand. His hand dwarfs mine in size, but I lay it on top of mine anyway and begin tracing the lines of his palm.

He looks away but continues talking. "My mom was a heroin addict. We barely even survived living in that trailer on her check from government assistance. She made a lot of wrong choices due to her addiction, one of them including the men she brought home." He swallows. "One night, when I was 11, I came home late. I was out playing ball in the park with my friends and lost track of time. My mother was passed out on the couch. She didn't hear Lilly's screams, but I did."

I grip his hand tighter, hoping to give him the strength to continue. He turns his head and finally looks at me. "I ran into her bedroom and saw my mother's poor excuse for a one night stand with his pants around his ankles while he was standing over her bed."

"Oh my god." My hand flies to my mouth. "Please tell me he didn't."

He shakes his head. "He didn't. With strength I didn't even know I possessed, I charged at him. I threw him right out the door and beat the shit out of him. Then I told him if I ever saw his face again I would finish him. When I went back into Lilly's room, she was shaking and refused to speak. Finally, after an hour or so had passed, she told me she was thirsty. It was around Christmas time and we didn't have much."

I look at the mug. "But you had hot chocolate, cinnamon, and whipped cream," I finish for him.

He nods. "Yeah. After that day, it became her favorite. We were all each other had and I promised her that I would always protect her. In addition to taking up mixed martial arts, I slept on the floor in her bedroom at night, every night." He pauses. "Well, up until my mom died and she didn't have to fear her dirtbag boyfriends anymore."

I rest my head against his shoulder, tears prickling my eyes for all that he's endured. "You were an amazing big brother."

"I tried to be. I wanted to be. She deserved that. She was an amazing person. She was brilliant, sweet, compassionate- everything that was right in the world. She was going places. She got into Harvard, she wanted to make a difference." He draws in a shaky breath. "I didn't tell her often, but I was so proud of her."

I grab his hand tighter, mustering up the courage to ask the question that I don't want to ask, but I have to. "What happened to her, Jackson?"

He leans back against the headboard, his face portraying so much grief and agony, I'm about to tell him that he doesn't have to answer.

"She was murdered."

His words hang in the silence between us.

"Did her killer pay?"

He looks at me and his eyes darken. "Not nearly enough."

I fight the involuntary shiver that crawls up my spine.

It's clear that he's not up to talking about this anymore because he turns and flicks off the light.

I lie on the bed beside him, both of us flat on our backs, not saying a word- our fingertips almost touching.

I never knew how comfortable silence could be until now. But as comfortable as it is between us, I need something else.

I turn and position myself on top of him, my legs on either side of him. His eyes open wide at first, but he visibly relaxes when I slide down until my head is flat against his chest.

I can feel every defined muscle his body encompasses. Every ripple of his abs, how hard and broad his chest is. And I'd be lying to myself if I didn't admit that it causes a physical reaction to stir in me, but this closeness is different than any other I've experienced.

"I hate murderers," I mumble with a yawn. "I'll never understand how cruel and inhumane someone's soul must be in order to take another life. It's unforgivable."

His body tenses beneath me and I know it's because he probably feels the same. "I wish everyone could be good like you, Jackson," I whisper before I close my eyes.

His hand skims up the length of my back, hesitantly at first, until I nuzzle against him and he begins drawing slow circles along my spine, lulling me to sleep.

I have no more bad dreams that night.

I do, however, dream about Jackson.

S unlight peeks in from the corner of the curtain covering the window in his bedroom.

I look down. One heavy and muscular leg is tangled between two of mine.

We must have dislodged ourselves from one another in the middle of the night.

Well, somewhat.

His back is partially turned away from me and my eyes practically pop from their sockets when I notice that he's shirtless, wearing nothing but a pair of boxers.

His broad back is a sight to behold and my breathing hitches in my throat.

When my eyes travel further down, lust crashes into me like a damn tsunami.

A portion of the comforter is draped and bunched up just under that mouthwatering, sculpted V of his, which unfortunately for me...happens to be hiding something that I'm *very* interested in seeing at the moment.

I fight back and forth with my conscience before deciding that if the roles were reversed, I might not like it if he tore back the covers in order to get a better look at my goods.

But then again, I don't look like him.

His body is a work of art. When I look at him, I see the hours of training and discipline, I see the strength he possesses, the well-oiled machine he's molded himself into.

Jesus. Who am I kidding? I definitely wouldn't mind Jackson getting a better look at me. I wouldn't mind Jackson showing any kind of sexual interest in me at all.

The thought surprises me, because although I use sex as a way of coping and punishing myself...the one thing I *don't* use sex for is my desire.

It hits me and I realize how much I've been missing out on.

The question is...does Jackson want me even half as much as I want him?

Like the saying goes, there's only one way to find out.

Since his front isn't facing my back, I'm unable to grind myself against him and feign innocence when he catches on, leaving the ball in his court.

That means I have no choice but to take the initiative and put myself out there.

It's something I've done more times than I care to think about, but for some reason, I've never been so nervous about it before.

And that includes that night in the car with Ford, because I knew deep down that he wanted me.

But with Jackson, I really have no idea. He's so controlled and good at keeping his emotions in check.

I bite my lip and prop myself up on one elbow, my front now pressed up flush against his back. I lift one hand and slowly trail my fingers down his chest. Seeing all those muscles is *nothing* compared to feeling them.

I expect him to wake then, but when I look up his eyes are still closed, his mouth parted slightly.

My fingers find the waistband of his boxers and hover there for a moment. I plant a gentle open-mouthed kiss on his shoulder while I continue tracing the outline of his waistband.

His brows furrow and I think I'm doing something wrong...but then he releases a low and husky groan that goes straight to my core.

Just when I'm about to move the comforter and slip my hand inside the opening of his boxers...I find myself facing the ceiling, with a ginormous weight on top of me.

My wrists are pinned and I'm gasping for air when he settles between my thighs.

The only thought going through my mind is-

Holy. Shit.

When I feel his hardness pressed against my thigh.

"What are you doing, Alyssa?" he asks, his voice raspy with sleep and what I'm hoping is arousal.

I don't answer him because my brain just isn't capable of forming complete sentences right now. Instead, I shift myself so he's exactly where I want him to be and I swear, I die a thousand deaths.

He releases my wrists, grabs a handful of my hair and inhales deeply. "Coconut," he rasps. I don't understand why he's talking about coconuts when all I want to do is lick him from head to toe, but then he groans and flattens his palms against mine. "I fucking love the way you smell." He closes his eyes, appearing to be fighting a war within himself. "I bet you taste as good as you smell."

"Jackson," I whisper. My shorts are bunched up so they resemble underwear and I'm certain that he can feel the wetness between my legs seeping through the material.

And then he thrusts and I feel every single inch of him. Including something I never expected. Something that pushes my own arousal into overdrive.

He lifts his hips and just when I think he's about to end the slow torture and fuck me, he rolls off of me.

I climb on top of him and straddle him, but his hands press down on my thighs rendering me unable to move. "No," he says firmly.

"Why not?"

Then it hits me. Why the hell would Jackson want a girl like me? I'm used up, washed up and *fucked* up.

"Hey." He lifts my chin to look at him. "Whatever you're thinking right now, cut it out. It's not you, it's me."

"Wow," I scoff. "You won't even fuck me but you're already hitting me with the old 'it's not you, it's me.'"

I move my face away from his touch. "I'd rather you just be honest and tell me you'd rather not stick your dick in a dirty whore." I laugh. "Trust me, I understand."

I raise my thighs and attempt to get off him but he clamps down harder, holding me in place. "And that right there is why this can't happen, Alyssa."

I roll my eyes. "Whatever. Don't bother letting me down easy. I don't blame you for not wanting a slut." He groans and lifts his hips pushing his thick erection into me. "Does this feel like I don't want you?"

He shifts and pulls us into a sitting position. "But the thing is, you're not a whore. That's *not* your identity, no matter what others may say. You're *Alyssa*." His voice drops to a whisper, "But you need to believe it yourself. And I'll only add to your pain if I let you use me as some kind of weapon in order to punish yourself. I don't want to be used by you. I don't want you to put me in the same category as the others. That's why this *can't* happen and I can only offer you friendship."

I nod my head in understanding. I have absolutely no argument for that. He has every right to think that I would only be using him. And I don't want to take advantage of him, no matter how much my own heart, mind, and body are in disagreement when it comes to him.

I need to sort out my feelings and make some serious decisions before I pursue anything with him again.

I climb off of him, wishing the disappointment that fills my chest would stop. I wish that everything was different and that I was a normal almost 24-year-old.

We turn in bed and face one another, studying each other's faces, not sure what to say next.

"Can I ask you something?"

"Sure."

I flush when the thought invades my brain, and before I can stop myself, I utter, "Jackson, do you have a cock piercing?"

He opens his mouth to answer me but starts laughing. My heart constricts because he looks even hotter now. "Wow, that was seriously the *last* thing I expected you to ask me," he says between bouts of laughter.

I hit him with a pillow. "Stop laughing and answer the question, jackass."

"Yes, I have an apadravya."

"How did that happen?"

He raises an eyebrow. "Well, it wasn't some freak accident if that's what you're asking."

I groan. "No. I mean, what made you want to get your dick pierced."

He shrugs. "Tyrone."

It's my turn to raise an eyebrow at him. "Really? Wow, you turning me down makes even more sense now."

I swear he flushes when he catches on to what he said. "Fuck. That didn't come out right."

"Hey, Tyrone's sexy. I can't say that I blame you."

His nostrils flare and for a moment, I see jealousy flash across his face. "What I meant," he says through clenched teeth. "Is that Tyrone was the reason *behind* the piercing."

I give him a wink. "I bet he was."

He groans in frustration and pulls me into his arms. "Do you want to hear the story or not?"

I put my finger to my lips. "Hmm, do I want to hear the story about two hot guys getting their cock's pierced? Yes, please."

He rolls his gorgeous eyes and playfully swats my behind. "Now, you're only getting the cliff notes version. It happened after we both won our first fight at the club. We were at the bar and Tyrone ended up getting drunk when he suddenly announced that he needed to celebrate."

I can't stop myself from giggling. "And he thought getting an apadravya would be the way to go about that?"

He gives me a lopsided grin. "It gets better. He leaped on top of the bar and declared that he was going to do something very alpha male. He ended it with a giant 'I am man, hear me roar, fuckers.' "

I put my hand to my forehead. "Oh god. He didn't."

He shakes his head. "No, he didn't. Because when we got to the shop, he chickened out on the apadravya. He only has a Prince Albert." Jackson laughs so hard he begins shaking. "He kept telling the poor piercer to make it look pretty. Crazy thing is, he doesn't even remember getting it done. He screamed like a girl when he took a piss the next morning."

I can't stop myself from joining in his laughter. "That is an awesome story."

"It is. I'll never forget the look on Ricardo's face when he walked into the tattoo shop and saw what we were doing. He was mad that we fell off the grid on our first night, but he ended up getting his own piercing as a sign of solidarity."

I wipe my eyes and scrunch my face. "Fell off the grid? What is he, your keeper or something?"

Jackson's face falls, but our moment is quickly interrupted when some woman yells, "Tyrone Isaac Davis. That is no way to greet Momma. Now put some damn clothes on and tell your lady friend good luck and Godspeed," in a thick Southern accent.

"Shit. Momma's here."

"Momma?" I question.

He nods before he throws my jeans at me. "Quick, put these on."

I do as he says, but can't help but think- What the hell is going on and who the heck is Momma?

Chapter 13 (Jackson)

One second I'm having one of the best mornings I've ever had...and the next I'm hearing the sounds of Tyrone's mother yelling at him from the next room.

I love Momma, I really, really do. The woman is the closest thing to a real mother I've ever had...but her timing couldn't have been worse.

I was enjoying seeing Alyssa laugh, her smile lighting up the entire room...and that dimple.

That fucking dimple.

It gets me—Every. Single. Time.

I would move mountains for that dimple.

I watch as she slides the tight denim over her hips and tucks my t-shirt, which is at least 2 sizes too big on her small frame into the waistband of her jeans.

Fuck, I love seeing her in *my* clothes. I have to bite my tongue when she turns around and I get an eye full of that perfect heart shaped ass.

God, the things I want to do to that ass of hers. The things I *almost* let myself do to that ass of hers.

Fucking hell. Who the fuck was I kidding, thinking that friendship would be enough?

With a grunt, I walk over to my closet and toss on a pair of basketball shorts and a wife beater tank.

Alyssa stands at the door and appears nervous for a moment, but I take her hand in mine and we walk out together.

I'm glad I told her to get dressed. Not that I care what other people think about who I spend my time with...but Momma's opinion has always mattered to me and I don't want her to get the wrong impression of Alyssa.

Lord knows there are enough people in the world who have the wrong impression of her already.

The smell of homemade pancakes, grits, eggs, and bacon make me salivate. There is nothing in the world that beats Momma's cooking.

Alyssa and I are the last to arrive in the kitchen, and when we do...the stares we receive are interesting...to say the least.

Tyrone looks up from his plate and grins at Alyssa before devouring the rest of his biscuit.

Ricardo looks uneasy and a bit angry, until I lift my chin and give him a look. It's a look that lets him know that I'm not ashamed of Alyssa and he should get used to seeing her around. He gives a small nod in my direction before smiling at Alyssa.

And that's when I notice Lou-Lou's expression. She obviously feels threatened by Alyssa's presence. The snarl on her face reminds me of a chihuahua. It's sad because she would be pretty if she wasn't so fucking bitter and miserable all the time.

I guide Alyssa to a stool over at the large oval counter where everyone is gathered.

I hear Momma's throat clear and I look up. Her normally bright ebony eyes are squinted. Her normally smooth, dark and flawless skin wrinkles between her eyebrows and her full lips are in a tight line. She looks like a lion protecting her baby cub, who's about to strike any minute. The spatula in her hand shakes when she glares at Alyssa.

Oh, shit.

Momma's the type who only respects certain people. She's a strong, sassy, Southern woman who takes no crap and expects none to be given. She's also fiercely protective when it comes to her boys...me included. She can be overwhelming at first, but once you get to know her, you end up falling head over heels in love with her.

I make my way to Momma and open my arms wide to give her a hug, but am shocked when I'm lightly pushed to the side instead.

Alyssa raises her chin, holds out her hand and looks Momma right in the eyes. "Hello, Mrs. Davis. I'm Alyssa Tanner and it's a pleasure to meet you, ma'am."

Lou-Lou lets out a small gasp. I look over at her and there's practically smoke coming out of her ears. To this day, I still don't think Lou-Lou's ever greeted Momma properly or looked her in the eye.

The first time she met Momma she cowered behind Ricardo while Momma proceeded to tell her to stop acting like the town cow and givin' the milk away for free. She eased up a little after Ricardo explained that they weren't serious.

The fact that Alyssa just womaned up and didn't let fear hold her back sends a surge of pride through me.

I don't think she realizes how strong she really is.

Momma purses her lips for a moment and looks Alyssa up and down, finally stopping to study her face. Then I see the twinkle in those beautiful ebony eyes of hers. Momma approves, she passed the first test.

She wipes her hand on her apron before shaking Alyssa's hand. "It's nice to meet you too, and please; call me Momma."

I hear the sound of Lou-Lou's glass falling to the floor in the background.

This is fucking great.

Alyssa gives her a smile before stepping to the side. I immediately wrap Momma up in a tight hug. "Hey, Momma. Thanks for making breakfast." She squeezes me tighter. "Nonsense. You know I like to keep my boys fed. How you doin', sugar?" She nods her head in Alyssa's direction. "By the looks of things, I'd say you might have found yourself a keeper over there."

Alyssa returns to her seat, but I don't miss the fact that she smiles at that statement.

I lean into Momma's ear and whisper, "She's definitely a keeper."

"Does that mean you'll settle down and give me some grand babies soon? Because we all know my son, the dip-shit, obviously can't keep it in his pants lately."

I start coughing and Alyssa spits out her drink.

Momma ignores us and continues, "You don't even want to know what I just caught him in bed with. The woman had half her head shaved and tattoo's on her *face* for crying out loud! Not to mention, she was carrying some kind of riding crop when she moseyed on out of the bedroom. And I know she ain't been riding no horse."

Tyrone opens his mouth to say something, but she points a finger at him and shakes her head. "I swear, my boy ain't got the good sense God gave em' sometimes."

I look at Tyrone. I'm not judging, but this is different from his usual modus operandi when it comes to women. But I know he's out screwing anything and everything lately in order to forget the fact that Shelby's wedding is this weekend.

Shelby was his high school sweetheart. Her father was the sheriff in their small town in Alabama, and after Tyrone was hauled off to jail for something that falsely got pinned on him; she was forbidden from ever talking to him again.

He'll always carry a torch for that girl.

He gives me a small shrug and I sit down on the stool next to Alyssa. "Alright Momma, enough," he says.

"Go easy on him, Momma," I say. "He's going through a lot right now."

She flips a pancake and points the spatula at me. "Which is exactly why I'm here right now."

Tyrone shoves another bite of food in his mouth. "I told you, Momma. I'm fine."

She gives him a pensive look. "So, you're saying that you're completely over Shelby, then?"

Ricardo and I groan in unison. Here we go.

"I'm happy for her," he starts before he takes another bite of food. "I wish her all the best with her rich, stuck up, stupid—" He takes a drink. "Ugly, no fun, small dick, stupid—"

"You said stupid already," Ricardo reminds him.

Tyrone tips his drink at him. "Lousy, good for nothing, wanna be cowboy, lying, cheating, mullet haircut, dumb ass, man-boy, soon to be husband." He grips his fork and knife. "Really, guys...I'm *fine*. I hope they have a happy life and have a million mullet-haircut wearing babies."

That went better than expected.

Momma looks at him. "And nothings gonna change your mind about that, buttercup?"

He stabs his eggs. "You got that right."

Momma daintily wipes her mouth with her napkin. "I guess it won't matter then."

Tyrone takes the bait. "What won't matter?"

She smiles from ear to ear. "The fact that last night, our very own Shelby ran right out of her wedding rehearsal in tears. Screaming up a storm about how it should be *you* who should be standing up at that altar waiting for her."

"Fucking shit, man," Ricardo says.

"Well, I'll be damned. Girl's finally come to her senses," I say.

Tyrone shakes his head. "No. There's too much water under the bridge. Too much devastation in our wake."

"Don't be stupid. You better go after her," Alyssa says, much to everyone's surprise.

We all look at her while she looks at Tyrone and continues, "I'm just saying that when you love someone. You don't give up on them. You fight for them. It doesn't matter what obstacles are standing in the way." She takes a breath. "When you love someone, you hold their hand when they're too scared to move forward because all they've ever known is a past that's full of despair and emptiness. When you love someone, you realize that every bit of pain you ever endured is worth it because you found the person who's the very best part of your life." She shrugs. "Or at least, that's how *I* imagine love is supposed to be. Despite whatever bullshit might have happened between you two."

I look at her in awe, but the moment is ruined when Lou-Lou snorts and makes a face at her.

Momma points the spatula in Alyssa's direction. "I knew I had a good feeling about her. She's right, baby. You cain't never could. Which is why I bought you a plane ticket. We leave in a few hours." She pauses and looks at Ricardo. "Don't worry. He'll be back by Monday." She grimaces. "And if he's a little late you tell that no good, son-of-a-bitch De—"

"That's great," I say loudly, cutting Momma off before she says DeLuca's name. "I think you should go," I tell Tyrone.

Momma smiles and Tyrone looks at me. "Yeah, alright. But you know what will happen if it doesn't work out, right?"

"Don't worry. I'll have a bottle of Jack Daniel's ready to go and a copy of Nelly's greatest hits in the CD player. Along with a few Hulk dvd's."

He smiles and reaches over to give me a pound. "My man."

Ricardo laughs. "You better lock that up quick, Alyssa. Looks like you might have some competition on your hands."

She leans forward and crinkles her nose. "I'm not afraid of a little competition." She hikes a thumb in Tyrone's direction. "However, I don't think I can possibly compare to this alpha male with his pretty piercing over here."

The room erupts in laughter...with the exception of Lou-Lou who just crosses her arms and sucks her teeth.

"So," Lou-Lou says while narrowing her eyes at Alyssa. "I take it you spent the night in Jackson's bed? Really giving it the old *college* try with him, huh? Tell me, how was it at NYU?"

Everyone goes silent and Alyssa blinks and looks down, shame all across her face.

I've never wanted to take my temper out on a woman before, until this moment. I absolutely hate that she just did that to her.

Alyssa glances in the direction of the door but I grip her hand under the table and glare at Lou-Lou. "At least she was actually invited to spend the night in my bed. Not just sniffing around me like some dog wanting to get their paws on some scraps." My pupils constrict as I stare down at her. "And despite what you may think, staying up all night and having a meaningful conversation with someone you care about is so much better than being used for sex. But we *all* know *you* wouldn't know about that, Lou-Lou. Now would you?"

Momma claps her hands. "Okay. Who wants seconds?"

Alyssa looks up at me in wonder. "Me. I want more. I would love more."

I search her eyes, feeling the impact of her words hit me right in the center of my chest. I bring her hand to my lips and kiss it. "Me too."

I don't know what I'm doing, but I can't stop myself.

There are a million reasons why I shouldn't be pursuing this. Reasons like the fact that DeLuca basically owns my ass for the next 7 years. Reasons...like what he *did* to her.

There aren't enough words to express how I feel about what he took away from Alyssa.

Not to mention, the fact that I, myself am technically a murderer. And given her own past, I'm sure she won't be so understanding about that.

If I tell her, I could lose her.

And I think I might just be the one person in her life who would be good for her. I would *never* use her.

Which leads me to my next thought.

Something hasn't been sitting well with me since she told me about what happened to her father.

Her strange relationship with her dad's old partner, Ford.

I mean, what the hell *was* that in the interrogation room? That was the very definition of coercion if there ever was one. And on a 10-year-old? I get that he was trying to protect her, but there's a small part of me that feels like he was also out to save his own skin and maybe his intentions weren't as pure as she thinks they were.

However, I *can't* tell her that. When she talks about Ford, it's clear she still holds him in very high regard, even to this day-although she told me that he's no longer in her life.

And if I'm being honest with myself, I'm glad about that.

I've got all these reasons swirling around in my head, but through it all...one thought keeps breaking through the fog.

I want her.

My God, do I *want* her.

But, if I don't slow this thing down...I could lose her.

I meant what I said to her earlier. I *don't* want to be used by her...and I don't want to rock the boat and make things worse for her. I also don't want to stir things up with my *own* sexual desires.

I *have* to slow this down. I have to proceed with caution...not that I should even be proceeding at all. I let go of her hand and move my plate away. "But, I shouldn't. Sometimes too much, too fast can leave you in a lot of pain."

She gives me an inquisitive look before holding her plate out to Momma. "Or sometimes you have to say to hell with it and indulge a little. You might miss out on a good thing and by the time you decide you want it, it's all gone."

Tou-fucking-ché.

Momma fills up her plate with more food. "A girl after my own heart." Her eyes land on Lou-Lou and her barely eaten food. "Men like a little something to hold onto. Can't be all skin and bones with no derriere." She scans the room. "Ain't that right, boys?"

It doesn't take a rocket scientist to figure out that Momma definitely likes Alyssa much more than she does Lou-Lou.

"Yes, Ma'am," we all say in unison while Lou-Lou rolls her eyes and tosses her napkin in her dish.

"I just realized something," Tyrone says in my direction. "If I hop on that plane...I'll miss your fight tomorrow night."

"You have a fight tomorrow night?" Alyssa interjects.

I look down at my plate, hoping with everything that Alyssa doesn't want to come...because she won't like my response.

"Yeah." I rub the back of my neck. "Tyrone. It's okay if you miss my fight. It's not a big deal. There will be *others*."

Shit, I didn't mean for the last part of that sentence to come out so tense.

"I'll come," Alyssa says, excitement in her tone. "Tomorrow is my birthday and I don't have any other plans. I'd love to watch."

How the hell did I overlook that? Fucking hell.

Momma leaps up from the table. "Oh, sugar. I wish I would have known your birthday was tomorrow. I would have whipped you up something special."

"You *can't* come," I whisper.

Alyssa laughs and pats her tummy. "It's okay, Momma. This breakfast was more than enough." She continues talking, obviously not hearing me. "So, do I need to purchase tickets for this thing, or what?"

"No, because you're *not* coming," I grind out softly, hoping she hears me this time.

Momma looks contemplative. "No. I'll admit, I haven't seen many of their fights. I don't much care for the violence, but every time I've ever gone...I just show up with Ricardo and they let me right in the door." She winks. "If that doesn't work, you can always tell them you're Jackson's girl. They'll let you right in."

Motherfucking shit.

Alyssa looks at Ricardo. "Is it okay if I tag along with you?"

Ricardo opens his mouth to answer.

I slam my hand down on the table, startling everyone. "God-dammit, *No.* You're not coming to my fight! I don't *want* you there!"

Alyssa turns to me, her mouth open wide. "O-oh." She looks down. "Okay. Gosh, I'm sorry. I thought..."her voice trails off.

And just like that, I feel like the biggest piece of shit in the world.

Ricardo looks at me, understanding in his eyes before he turns his gaze on her. "You got attacked the last time, remember? And this time, Tyrone won't be there to help. None of us will; because *he'll* be in the cage and *I'll* be stuck on the sidelines. We can't have you sitting in the crowd all alone. It's not safe."

Well, he's not exactly wrong. It's *not* safe for her. Especially when I put a fucking target on her back because I stopped the fight for her the last time she was there.

I *know* DeLuca saw that shit when he went through the footage. I can only *hope* that he didn't recognize her because it's been so long.

Because thinking that he won't care that she showed up at his club would be a rookie mistake. And if she *keeps* showing up and taunting him like a mouse taunts a cobra...well we're fucked.

I just have to make sure she never goes to the club or the gym...ever.

I gesture toward Ricardo. "Exactly. That's *exactly* why I don't want you there. I'm sorry for being an asshole about it."

She pulls on her lip before saying, "Okay. I wish I could be there for you. But, I guess...I get it. Like you said, there will be other fights."

Great...a temporary solution to a permanent problem. Perfect.

I really need to talk to her about this...in private.

A part of me thinks that maybe I should come clean. Tell her that I work for DeLuca.

But then, she'll expect me to quit...not that I blame her. *God* how I want to be free from his chains that bind me.

Then when I *don't* quit...she'll be upset and I'll have no choice but to tell her *why* I work for DeLuca in the first place.

Then I lose her.

And she realizes that yet *another* person she put her trust in...hurt her and fucked her over.

Then she goes back to doing what she was doing before I met her.

The thought of that *kills* me. I can see the real her now. I can feel her opening herself up to me little by little.

And I *want* every single part of it.

I want to be the person she smiles at.

I want to take this burden she carries on her shoulders away for good.

I want her to see herself the way I see her...see how amazing she is...and realize that the horrible past she has doesn't determine her future.

I want her to start living.

I want her to be mine.

No. I can't tell her. I can't.

I fucking can't.

Chapter 14 (Alyssa)

After Jackson's outburst, the rest of breakfast was a little awkward, to say the least.

"You gonna hurt my boy?" I look up from the sink full of dishes that I'm currently washing.

Ebony eyes that seem to pierce right through me hold my gaze.

I almost drop the damn dish.

"No," I tell her honestly. "That is not my intention at all." I can't help the flush that works its way up my cheeks. "Jackson's incredible. I'd be an idiot to mess up a chance with him." I close my eyes. "My past isn't that great. I've made a lot of mistakes. Some my fault, some not my fault...but I'm working on it. I want to be better," I say.

My eyes pop open with my words.

I never thought it was *possible* for me to want something more out of life again. I never thought I was *worth* anything more after that day in Ford's office.

She makes a face. "Sugar, don't get me wrong. Now, Jackson *is* incredible...that heart of his is incomparable to any others. And while he might *look* like one- he is not some mythical creature or a God. At the end of the day, he's just a man." She holds me by my shoulders. "All I'm saying is that you're a prize, too. You have to cut a diamond in order to make smaller diamonds, darlin'. But you still have to *cut* the original diamond first. So in the end, it's the imperfections that really make us shine so beautifully. It would do you well to remember that."

And with those words she walks away.

After I finish drying the dishes and put them away, I head out to the hallway. It's almost noon and I need to get home and take a shower. I also have the urge to visit my father's grave again.

Which is odd, because visiting it yesterday afternoon was hard enough for me. I hardly ever go because I always feel like an abomination of some sort. Like I don't deserve to even be there because he'd be so ashamed of the person I've become.

I'll never get Ford's words out of my head.

I'm stopped in my tracks when I see Jackson and Momma hugging. It looks like they're having a moment and I don't want to intrude.

I also can't seem to look away. His big arms are wrapped around her and his eyes are closed while she whispers something to him. I almost wish I had a camera to capture the moment because I love how much *love* he has for the woman standing before him.

When he pulls away, she holds his face in her tiny hands. "You're a good man, Jackson," she whispers with tears in her eyes. "You're a *good* person. Lilly would want you to be happy. You *deserve* to be happy." She gives him a kiss on his cheek. "I love you. You're *my* boy and don't you ever forget it."

"Love you too, Momma," he whispers, his voice cracking slightly.

I have to take a few deep breaths to stop myself from falling apart. Momma's tenderness reminds me of my father and the last conversation I ever had with him. I haven't felt what it's like to be truly loved since that day. My mother didn't know how to love me anymore because she was so consumed by her grief.

I know Ford loved me, for a little while at least. In my own twisted head...I think he still does. And I know I cling to it in my darkest hours because it's all I had after I lost my father.

I turn down the hall and head back to the kitchen. I'm still batting my eyes when I hear their footsteps approach.

Jackson gives me a strange look. "You alright?"

"Yeah." I cough. "Just got something in my eye."

He pulls me gently by my elbow and ushers me into the bedroom. "Can we talk for a minute?"

"Sure. I have to leave, though, can we talk while you walk me to my car?"

He rubs his neck. "I'm not kicking you out or anything. I have to head to the gym for a few hours, but you're more than welcome to stay here and relax. You can even spend the night again if you want."

I grab my jacket. "Thanks. But I have to take care of a few things today."

His jaw tightens and he pulls a sweatshirt over his head. "Okay. I guess I'll walk you out then."

I say a quick goodbye to Momma and the guys, purposely ignoring Lou-Lou on my way out. She's not worth my time anymore. Besides, Jackson more than took care of her anyway.

I realize that we've already made it out the front doors of the apartment complex and he still hasn't said a word to me. For someone who wanted to talk to me, he's being awfully quiet. "Penny for your thoughts?" I ask.

He shuffles his feet and plays with the strings on his sweatshirt. "Look, if I asked you to do something...or rather *not* to do something would you?"

I tip my head back. "It would depend on what it was, I guess. But for the most part, I don't see why not. What's up?"

He winds the string around his finger and it's funny because that's exactly how I'm feeling at the moment. Like I'm about to be wrapped right around his finger.

"I don't want you to—" He rubs his face. "Look, I really *need* you to promise me you won't ever show up at the fight club or the gym...ever. It's not safe for you at either of those places. Even if you go with Tyrone. There's no guarantee that something won't happen and he could prevent it."

I don't know how to feel about his request. On one hand, I'm flattered that he's looking out for my safety. On the other, something is a little off. "I guess I can get behind not going to the fight club....but why not the gym? What's so dangerous there?"

His eyes dart to the floor and he shuffles his feet again. "I don't need the distraction when I'm training," he says gruffly.

I don't know whether to be insulted or flattered again.

He lifts his hood. "I can't keep my eyes off of you when you're in the room. I'm liable to get knocked out or something."

"So I'll go to a different room."

He grabs my jacket and tugs me to him. "I'll still feel your presence. I feel you *everywhere*, Alyssa."

Butterflies attack poor Momma's breakfast with a vengeance when he utters those words.

I stare at him wide-eyed as he skims the left side of my cheek with his finger. "Promise me, please. It's a hard limit for me. I can't have you at either of those places."

"Okay, fine. But you should know that I'm holding this as leverage. Just in case, I want to drag you to a chick flick or something in the future."

He pulls me even closer to him. "I'll do anything you want. *Anything*. As long as you promise me this."

He's being so serious, it's almost scary. "I promise."

The next words out of his mouth, confuse me. "If you could do anything for your birthday, besides go to my fight, what would it be?"

I have to think about this for a moment because, in all honesty, I have no idea. Between witnessing my father dying and spending the entire weekend in the interrogation room. The night Ford and I had when I was 17. Heck, even the night of the sex tape fell on my birthday.

My birthday has always been bad. I'm convinced it's officially jinxed.

I close my eyes and feel the crisp, cool October air around me.

And for a second, I pretend that I'm someone else. Someone different. Someone, "Normal," I whisper. "I want to be normal and do something a normal 24-year-old would do for her birthday."

"Like what? Go out to a club or something?"

I open my eyes. "Yes! That's *exactly* what I want. I've never been out to a club because I was 21 when the sex tape happened and feared being recognized." My face falls. "I still fear being recognized. I can't go to a club, Jackson."

He tilts my chin up. "I think you're forgetting something, Damsel."

Normally I hate when he calls me that, but he says it so softly and sweetly, I fight back a shiver. "What's that?"

The corners of his mouth tilt up. "Your birthday falls on Halloween. You can be anyone you want to be." He brushes my lower lip with his thumb. "*We* can be anyone we want to be."

I hug him. I hug him so tight because he's right. And I haven't seen the upside to my birthday in such a long, long time. This is a gift in and of itself.

"But what about your fight tomorrow?" I ask, disappointment floating in the air.

He thinks about this for a moment before saying, "Fuck, I'm the last one on because I'm the main event. I won't be done until a little after 10."

For some reason, I refuse to let this get in our way. "Most clubs don't really pick up until after that."

"True. I'll take a quick shower and meet you at the apartment after...if that's okay? I would pick you up but that would cut more time out."

"Don't be silly. It would make sense for me to meet you at your place. In fact, there's a really good club not too far away from here that has some kind of masquerade theme that night. I saw the fliers for it in your apartment complex."

He smiles and pulls me even closer, crushing me to him. "It's a date," he whispers.

Then he touches my ass.

For a moment I'm convinced this whole thing is a dream...but no, he's really sliding his hand into the back pocket of my jeans.

Then he pulls out my phone. "What are you doing?"

"Rectifying a situation," he responds with a wink, before handing it back to me.

I want to tell him to put it back the exact way he got it, but his voice stops me. "I just texted myself from your phone so I have your number. I'll see you tomorrow, but I want you to text me when you make it home safe. And if you need anything between then and tomorrow night, you can always call me."

"I need a back rub and a pedicure. How are you with those?"

He laughs and releases me. "Trust me I'd have no problem giving you a good rub down, but you definitely wouldn't want me polishing your little toes."

"How do *you* know I have little toes? I could have full on Flintstone feet for all you know."

He wiggles his eyebrows. "I have my ways."

"I'll see you tomorrow night, Jackson."

"See you tomorrow night, Alyssa."

I turn around and face my car. "By the way," he whispers in my ear before he backs away. "I *really* like the fact that you're still wearing my t-shirt. Looks good on you."

I blush the whole ride home.

Chapter 15 (Jackson)

I jog up the stairs to my apartment, happier than I've been in awhile.

She agreed.

She agreed to stay away from the club and she didn't question me about it.

I still have a shot at not royally fucking this up.

I open the door and head for the living room where everyone else is still congregating.

I jerk back when I hear what sounds like Alyssa's voice coming through the surround sound speakers.

My smile plummets when I walk in the room and realize that Alyssa's sex tape is being broadcast on the big screen television while Lou-Lou's standing there with a smirk on her face, holding the remote control.

"Jackson, so glad you came back. We were just getting to the good part."

I fucking lunge at her.

Tyrone and Ricardo try pulling me back, but I'm out for her blood. I have to dig deep and talk myself down from the ledge so I don't actually attack her.

"I swear, man, we had no idea she was gonna play that shit. We didn't see much. I didn't even realize what the hell it was at first," Tyrone yells, holding me back.

"Yeah. What the *fuck* is your deal, Lou-Lou?" Ricardo barks.

Alyssa's voice zaps me. "*What do you want?*"

Then I hear a guy's voice. "*Strip for me. Show me those nice titties of yours.*"

Tyrone and Ricardo lose their grip on me and I lunge forward and get in her face. "Shut it the fuck off *now*, or so help me God. I will tear your head right off your skank infested body," I shout so loud the windows shake.

Lou-Lou's trembling at this point but I literally don't give a fuck. With shaky hands, she presses the pause button.

I want to remind the stupid bitch I said to turn it *off*, but I'm just happy the sounds are gone and it's no longer playing.

Besides, Momma herself decides to get a piece of the action. She reaches for Lou-Lou's arm and begins dragging her toward the front door. "Don't mind me, boys. I'm just taking out the trash." She throws Lou-Lou out the door. "Next time I won't be so kind—" She pauses. "What's that word you like to use again? Oh yeah...*Puttana*," she snarls before slamming the door shut.

She rubs her hands together and looks at Ricardo. "I think it's time for you to find a new distraction."

Ricardo nods. "I still can't believe she pulled that. I always knew she was territorial, but *this*...is going too far."

Tyrone hikes his duffle bag on his shoulder and looks at me. "Maybe I can catch a later flight," he offers.

"No, it's fine." I give him a pound. "Go and get your girl, man. I can't wait to meet her."

He gives me a grin. "Break bad on em' J-man. Call me after you win the fight tomorrow night."

"Will do."

Momma barrels into me and puts her arms around me. "I look forward to seeing more of Alyssa. That girl is something special, I have a sixth sense about these things you know. And my opinion on her hasn't changed one bit. Love you, sugar. There are some left-overs in the fridge for you."

"Thanks. Love you too, Momma. Have a safe flight."

After they leave, I sit down on the couch. I'm *still* reeling from what happened. I force myself to sit on my hands in order to stop myself from putting them through the wall.

"Hey," Ricardo starts. I sit up and glare at him. He blows out a breath. "You want to talk about it?"

"Not really," I bite out.

He holds up his hands. "Okay. I get it, man. I do. That couldn't have been easy to walk in on. Talk about being fucking blindsided. We all were. None of us even knew about that tape or what the hell Lou-Lou was making us sit down and watch. It makes even more sense now why you're so protective when it comes to her. I don't blame you."

I grunt and look away while he continues, "Normally, I'd say this anger would be good for training." He pauses. "But tomorrow is a big fight and I need you to be clear and focused enough to go over strategies." He heads for the door. "So, I'll give you a few hours to cool down before we head to the gym. And I meant what I said, Lou-Lou won't be coming around here anymore."

He stops and taps the wall beside the door. "As your coach, I can't say that I like the idea of you and Alyssa together. You've got one hell of a hero complex and this visceral rage inside you is like *nothing* I've ever seen before. It makes you great in the cage...but it's a liability on the outside. And I'm afraid that she might be the thing to tip the scales in the wrong direction for you." He opens the door. "But as your friend...I think there's something special between you two. I think, in some way that's beyond my understanding; you guys need one another. I think you two get each other in a way that no one else ever will. Anyway, if you change your mind and want to talk about it, I'm here."

"Thanks," I whisper.

I lean back and look at the television. The image on the screen is still paused.

The freeze frame of Alyssa permeates my vision.

I didn't actively go searching for this shit. But right now, this is my very own Pandora's box and I don't know if I can resist the urge to open it.

I know it *won't* change how I feel about her...but maybe it will help me understand her more. At least, that's what I tell myself when I hit the 'play' button on the remote.

The first thing I register is that she looks a little different. Not a whole lot, but there are some subtle distinctions.

For one, her blonde hair is shorter, resting slightly above her shoulders instead of halfway down her back like it is now. She's also wearing less makeup in the video, it makes her appear younger. And the way she's dressed...she's wearing a full sleeved cardigan and her long flowing skirt is almost touching the floor.

It's not a bad look, she's still beautiful...it's just different...innocent.

I can't help but notice that the camera is angled directly behind the guy's head. There's some ridiculously generic tribal tattoo on his lower neck. There's literally *nothing* else giving his own identity away. You wouldn't even know it was the mayor's son filming this.

The camera is *solely* focused and zoomed in on Alyssa. That alone makes my blood boil...because I know this was all a setup.

"*Strip for me. Show me those nice titties of yours.*"

For a moment, I see the hesitation in her eyes before she answers, "*Um. Okay. I can do that.*"

My first instinct is to look down when I see her standing there in her white cotton bra. I'm part enraptured and part disgusted because I can only imagine how many men have ogled what I'm seeing now. How many men just chalked it up to her being some 'whore' and thought they were entitled to watch her like this. Not even caring about the life changing repercussions she suffered from it.

None of those men deserved to be seeing her like this. Hell, I'm not even sure if I do.

"Have you ever sucked a dick before, hot stuff?"

I think I'm going to be sick.

"Yeah. My high school boyfriend," she answers.

"Did you like it?"

She blushes and nods. *"I did."*

I can see even more now why the video went viral, not only is she beautiful in a natural way—which alone is appealing. But these personal questions she's answering? It makes it so genuine and real. Like you're right there in the room with her.

"What did you like about it?"

She appears to think about this for a second before replying, *"Being able to please him with my mouth. Knowing that I was the one responsible for his pleasure. It's empowering."*

And now my dick has officially joined the party in the third circle of hell.

"Yeah? Why don't you finish getting naked and show me how much you like it?"

I hear the sound of a zipper in the background while Alyssa pulls down her skirt. Then she pauses.

"No, sweetie. I want you naked, now. Take everything off," he commands.

The shame hits me hard when she starts stripping. Not just because my dick's reacting to it...but because I could see myself uttering that very same command to her. The turbulent wave of jealousy that washes over me when she drops to her knees before *him* naked steamrolls over any shame that I felt.

Even my dick decides it's too much of a hassle to compete with my mind and gives up.

My mind wants to conjure up its own alternate version that has her putting her clothes right back on and turning the camera around on *him* before taking a fucking bat to his head.

I can't watch any more. I already know what happens next. I don't need or *want* to see another second of it. I'd rather gouge my own eyes out with a rusty spoon. Disgusted with myself, I rip out the wire connecting my laptop to the television.

It was exactly like Pandora's box. I found no answers by watching it...all it showed me was a different brand of evil in the world.

I wish I never watched it at all.

It *still* doesn't change how I feel about her, though.

Chapter 16 (Alyssa)

I'm leaving the cemetery when my phone buzzes with a message.

Jackson: *I know this is random, but I just wanted to tell you how amazing you are.*

I stare down at my phone and hit the 'reply' button as I continue walking.

I stumble back slightly when I bump into someone.

I look up with an apology ready to leave my lips due to my clumsiness.

Deep blue eyes meet mine and I stifle a gasp.

Ford.

Before I can say anything, he grabs my arm and spins me around until my back hits a large marble statue.

"You haven't been answering my phone calls," he growls.

I swallow down the fear rising in my chest. I'm perfectly aware he's called me a dozen times in the last few weeks...I just haven't really been up to talking to him.

"Sorry. I've been busy," I say.

And then I brace myself. I brace myself for his comment telling me that I'm a whore or something else along those lines, but it never comes.

His gaze locks on Jackson's t-shirt that I never changed out of. "These aren't your clothes. Where have you been?"

"I already told you. *Busy*," I repeat.

He leans in close to my ear. "You're getting a little too big for your britches there, sweetheart. Remember who it is that you're speaking to."

I push my shoulders back and look at him, feeling annoyed now. "You know, lurking around graveyards is a little creepy...even for you."

His eyebrows draw up in surprise. I haven't given him attitude like this in a very long time. Since I was a teenager.

He positions one of his hands on the statue behind my head. "You know why I'm here. I still mourn your father, unlike *you* who tarnishes his memory with your internet antics and whore-like ways."

And there it is.

Ever since that day in his office, I've felt like I was made of glass around him.

But not today.

Today...I feel a little bit stronger. Not a lot, but enough to give him a taste of his own medicine. "Didn't stop you from indulging in my *whore-like* ways in your office that day, now did it? Or when I was 17 for that matter."

To say he looks shocked would be an understatement. He opens his mouth to say something but stops himself and looks down at his feet.

"I'm sorry," he breathes.

I'm certain that I must be hearing things. Ford actually apologizing to me is *not* something I ever expected to hear in this lifetime.

"What?"

This time, when he looks at me, I see a glimpse of the old Ford. The one who was always there for me. The one who actually loved me. The one who saved me.

"I should have been there for you that day. I turned you away and I treated you like garbage." He tilts my face up. "I couldn't stand the thought of you giving that part of yourself to someone else. I wanted it to be me that you shared your innocence with." He closes his eyes. "I thought you wanted it to be me."

He cups my cheek and looks at me. "I'm fucked up, Alyssa. You make me that way. I have tunnel vision when it comes to you. But I *know* deep down inside *you* know that no one else will *ever* love you the way I do. They'll only hurt you, sweetheart. And when they do...I'll still be standing here. *I'll* still be loving you when no one else in the world ever will."

I'm at a loss for words. Actually, no. I'm not.

"You hurt me, Ford. That day, you broke something inside of me. I never knew you could hurt me like that."

He pulls me into his arms. "I know, sweetheart. I know. Why do you think I couldn't bring myself to touch you again after that day? I hate myself for doing that to you."

I rub my cheek along the fabric of his suit and fight back tears because it's so familiar and strangely comforting to be held by him again.

"Let me make it up to you, Alyssa."

"How?"

"You know how."

I begin walking away from him, knowing perfectly well why he came here now.

"I told you. I still have to think about it."

Irritation crosses over his handsome features. "It's been almost a *month*. How much time could you possibly need? I already gave you the location and even went as far as to set you up with an interview."

He spins me around. "Don't you want to get vengeance for your father? All I need you to do is go undercover and tell me if DeLuca owns that fight club. We start there and find something we can use. Then we take him and all his other establishments out little by little. I know it's not ideal and it will take awhile. But we need to move stealth-like so he'll never see it coming."

I bite my thumbnail, hating that what I'm about to say will

disappoint him. It's the real reason I've been avoiding him. "I went to the club, Ford."

His grip on my arm is so tight I'm sure he's going to leave a bruise. "And? What the fuck happened? Why didn't you tell me?"

I wince in part due to his tight hold and because I know I failed him and my father...once again. "And it turns out that it's *not* his club. I'm sorry. I wanted it to be...but it's not."

He shakes his head. "No. It *is* his club. Stop *lying* to me. Christ, Alyssa...all I needed you to do was go undercover for a week or two — not really all that difficult."

Easy for him to say, he doesn't have the scars that I do. The scars caused by being a 10-year-old who watched their father get brutally murdered in front of them. All while the killer looked right into her eyes and smirked.

But I *still* walked into that club knowing it might be his. I still took the risk.

"I'm telling you, it's *not* his club. Jesus, you think I don't *want* to help you nail DeLuca? You think I would lie to you about something so important?"

He releases my arm. "How good was the source of your intel?"

Guilt hits me when Jackson's face crosses my mind. Luke, the guy who hired me, was actually my original target. And Lou-Lou quickly became my backup. Well, before I found out what a bitch she was.

I *never* intended to make Jackson my source, but in the end, he provided me with the answers I needed. And I have no reason not to believe him. He's never lied to me before.

"Trust me," I say, while digging in my purse for my keys. "I couldn't have found a better source unless it was DeLuca himself."

Ford's eyes narrow while he holds my car door open for me. "What makes you think this source didn't lie to *you*?"

I think about this for a second before replying, "Because I trust this person."

He looks down at my t-shirt and scowls. "Well, I think *he's* wrong. I'll find another way to get you undercover at a different establishment of DeLuca's." I open my mouth to protest but he grabs the back of my neck. "And when I do...don't *fuck* it up again by spreading your goddamn legs for your source this time."

He releases me and slams the door.

It's only when I'm pulling in the driveway that it dawns on me. How does Ford know my source was a *he* in the first place?

My phone rings and Ford's name lights up the screen. I debate not answering it, but decide to just get it over with.

"Yeah?" I answer.

"Listen, I'm sorry. I was a little too hard on you back there. I wasn't very nice to you and you didn't deserve that." He takes a breath. "I'm under a lot of pressure at work, especially with this new promotion."

Two apologies from Ford in one day? It must be a full moon.

"How did you know my source was a he?"

I hear paper rustling in the background. "What?"

"You heard me, Ford. How did you know it was a guy?"

"What exactly is it that you're accusing me of, Alyssa? You act like you don't trust me anymore."

He sighs when I stay silent. "I assumed it was a guy because you're a beautiful young woman walking into a goddamned underground fight club. For crying out loud, you went undercover as a *ring girl*. Not only would it make sense, but it would be smart for your target to have been male. Why do you think I asked *you* to do it in the first place? Trust me, none of my female agents look like you."

I hear the call waiting signal on the other line. I smile when I see Jackson's name.

"Okay fine. I gotta go. Bye, Ford." I go to press the button to hang up but his voice stops me. "Wait a minute, sweetheart."

"What?"

"Are we okay? Because I really don't like that you felt the need to question me. You know I would never do anything to hurt you, right? I love you."

I roll my eyes because he's already hurt me too many times to count in my short 24 years, despite his love for me. "Yeah, I know. We're fine. Look, I have to go. I have another call. It's important."

I hang up without waiting for a response.

"Hey, you," Jackson's voice greets me on the other line.

Wow, do I love the sound of his voice.

I get so lost in that thought, my keys slip out of my hands when I go to open the front door.

"Hey," I respond. "What's up?"

"Just wanted to make sure you made it home okay." He pauses. "I got a little worried when you didn't respond to my text. I hope I didn't freak you out."

I mentally curse myself for never responding to him earlier. "You didn't. I was at the cemetery visiting my dad when I got it, though. I'm actually just walking in the door now."

I don't tell him about Ford...for obvious reasons. There's no way he'll understand our fucked up dynamic. Hell, I've never understood it. Not to mention, he'll probably be upset that I lied to him in the first place.

"Oh." I hear him draw in a breath. "I'm sorry."

Neither of us say a word for what feels like forever.

I plop down on the couch. "Cue the awkward silence that death always ensues."

"You'd think we'd be experts at getting around it, huh?" He clears his throat. "Okay, change of subject. How was the rest of your day? Did you do anything else?"

"Nope, just that."

"That's good." He sounds relieved...which is *interesting*.

"What exactly did you think I'd be doing, Jackson?"

"Nothing," he quickly says. "I'm just happy to hear that you weren't doing anything."

He curses under his breath. "That did *not* come out right."

I decide to cut to the chase. "Is that your weird way of saying you're happy to hear that I wasn't hanging out with another guy today?"

"Yeah," he admits. 'Yeah, I guess it is."

"I haven't." I sit up and cradle the phone in my ear. "I haven't been with anyone since before we met."

Since the night he saved me from that guy in the parking lot, I think before his voice interrupts my thoughts. "Is it wrong that it makes me really happy to hear that?"

"That all depends. Have there been any other girls in your bed beside me lately?"

"What?" he says. "No. Not at all."

"Then it's not wrong. Because that makes me really happy as well."

"Good. I guess I'll see you tomorrow."

"See you tomorrow, Jackson. Good luck with your fight."

"Thanks. By the way," he says before we hang up. "My sheets still smell like you. And I fucking love it."

Chapter 17 (Jackson)

R icardo was right, tonight ended up being a big fight for me. I won, but my opponent was a good 3 inches and 45lbs heavier than me.

He also managed to land not one, but *two*, solid punches straight into my rib cage. Making it the second time I've been hit now during a match. He knocked the wind out of me for a moment.

But then I thought about Alyssa...and how I *needed* to make it out of there in one piece so I could take her out for her birthday tonight.

It was strange because it was the *first* and only time I didn't think about the night Lilly was murdered while in the cage.

I'm not sure how I feel about it. I *need* that pain as my fuel. I need it as a reminder to never forget. A reminder to never *forgive* myself for what happened to Lilly.

I'm standing in the mirror putting tape across my ribs when I hear a knock on the dressing room door. "Yeah," I say.

The door opens and it's the last person I want to see standing there. She's out of her fucking mind if she thinks I want to talk to her. "Get the fuck out," I bark.

"I'm sorry, Jackson," Lou-Lou says.

"Doesn't matter. You crossed a line that never should have been crossed."

"I was hurting."

I spin around and face her. "Hurting? Really? That's the best you got?" I scream. "Hurting," I grit. "*Hurting* is having someone set you up with a sex tape. Hurting is finding out that the night you lost your virginity was posted online without your consent for all the world to see!"

To her credit, she blanches. "I didn't..."

"Yeah, that's just it, Lou-Lou ...you didn't. You didn't stop and think about how fucked up it was to play that tape in front of everyone. You didn't stop and think about how it would make *me* feel. Hell, you didn't even stop and think about how Ricardo would react to you pulling some shit like that."

She steps back and looks at me. "Wow, you're really falling for her."

I stop and think about this for a second.

No, I'm not in love with her. Not that I would know because I've never let myself fall in love before. But logically, I know I'm not in love because we've *only* known one another for a month. However, if there's a phase that comes right *before* love. Well, I might just be *there*. And something tells me that I *am* going to end up falling in love with her, whether I want to or not.

"This isn't about me," I argue. "What you did was wrong."

"I know and that's why I'm apologizing to you. I was jealous."

Before I can cut her off and tell her that I've never given her a reason to be jealous because I've turned down every advance she threw my way, she continues, "I've *never* had a guy look at me the way you look at her. I've *never* had someone defend me the way that you defend her. Or protect me, or care about me. I've *never* had someone in my corner...not once. I mean, why the hell do you think I'm *like* this in the first place?"

I push past her. "I'm sorry about that, Lou-Lou. I really am. But, it still doesn't make it right."

"I know, Jackson. Trust me, I know. That's why I came to apologize."

"I can't forgive you," I say and her lower lip trembles. "I'm not saying that I'll never forgive you...just not this second."

She lifts her chin. "Okay. I can understand that." She looks down and shrugs. "It's more than Ricardo's willing to give me."

For a second, I feel bad. But then I remember what she did. I put on my shirt and head for the door. "Jackson," she calls out.

I close my eyes and let out a deep sigh. "Yeah?"

"Word of advice? Since Alyssa and I *are* a lot alike."

I turn around and face her again. "You're nothing alike. *She's* not—"

"Damaged?" Lou-Lou laughs. "Trust me, that girl is as broken as they come. It takes a damaged soul to know one. And just because she's trusting you enough to open up to you...it doesn't mean she's cured. It doesn't mean that her demons are gone. They're only temporarily camouflaged until something causes them to flare up again." She points a finger at me. "Because let me tell you something about the broken people, Jackson. If you hurt us...we hurt deeper than others. If you hurt us...you drudge up every past hurt that we've ever experienced and send us into a tailspin right back down the rabbit hole."

I open my mouth to say something but she cuts me off. "Whether you *mean* to hurt us or not. It doesn't matter, because once we're in that tailspin...how do you think we cope? What do you think our go-to is? It's a vicious cycle and we end up taking down a lot of good people with us. People like you, Jackson. So be careful."

I slam the door behind me.

Lou-Lou's wrong. Alyssa's *not* like her. She's stronger than her fucked up past. And she's got me now to help her get through it.

I stop and pick up a bouquet of roses along the way to my apartment. It's not much, especially considering I'm still on the fence about giving her the other gift I have.

I've never really done the whole dating thing before. Between taking care of Lilly, and training at the gym...there never was much time for girls...just sex. I figured I'd settle down after I spent a few years as a professional MMA fighter, but well, clearly my life didn't go down that road.

I have no idea what to wear to this club. I looked at the flier she was talking about and it said costume optional but mask not.

Mask. Maybe this wasn't such a good idea after all. The only time I wear a mask is at the bdsm club. The club where every sexual fantasy and carnal urge I have come to life. The place where I don't ask for control of my life, *I* take it.

Christ...there's *no* way I'll be able to keep my hands off her tonight. Especially since she's now become the object of every sexual fantasy I have lately.

I decide to go with a black button down and dark jeans. On the bright side, at least my opponent didn't hit my face.

There's a knock on the door and I look at my watch. Alyssa's right on time.

My brain short circuits when I open the door.

She's wearing a cropped black jacket and a short red dress that must be made out of silk because it looks as soft as her skin does. And don't even get me started on her legs. I don't know how a girl who's only 5'3 tops, has legs so shapely and long, but I'm not about to question God's beautiful creation. I'd rather just enjoy it and be thankful.

I force myself to stop staring at those legs, which are showcased by a pair of black heels that I'm secretly wishing were digging into my back as she screams my name.

"Are you okay, Jackson?" she asks, her expression puzzled.

No, I'm not okay. I'm not okay because I told her we could only be friends not even 48 hours ago and every second after that has only made me regret ever saying those words. But then I remind myself of my reasons.

I inwardly groan as I reach over and pick up the flowers and hand them to her.

Her eyes are bright and I see that dimple. "They're beautiful. Thank you so much." She bites her lip. "But I can't take them to the club." She pushes me aside and heads for the kitchen. "We have to put them in water or they'll die." She looks around the kitchen, her expression concerned. "You don't have a vase."

Shit, I didn't really think of that. This is a guy's apartment. Of course, we don't have a vase lying around. I'm about to suggest she stick them in a bowl or something, but I hear another knock on the door.

"Here, take this," Ricardo says, handing me a vase.

I raise an eyebrow. "You could probably give Ms. Cleo a run for her money. How did you know I'd need this?"

"Saw you walking up the stairs with flowers. Figured it would come in handy." He grins. "Although I *am* surprised that you and Tyrone's bromance hasn't reached the level of flowers."

"I wouldn't be one to talk, Ricardo," I tease. "*You're* the one who just happened to have a vase." I point across the hall. "Last time I checked, that was a one bedroom apartment. Tell me, what color flowers do you like to get yourself?"

He looks down. "It's not mine. I had it for...someone."

Hmm, maybe him and Lou-Lou's relationship was more serious than I thought?

"Oh hey, Ricardo. Thanks," Alyssa says while taking the vase.

Ricardo looks at her for a second too long before replying, "No problem. Wow, you look gorgeous."

I fight the urge to slam the door in his face. But then I remind myself that he's my friend and it's not his fault he's got a pair of eyeballs.

She beams. "Thanks. It's my birthday. Jackson's taking me out to a club."

Something flashes across his face. But before I can question it he says, "Well, I hope you have a good night. You really deserve to have a good birthday, Alyssa."

She glances up at him and gives him a weird look, but then shakes her head. "Thanks, Ricardo. I'm um—" She pauses. "I'm gonna go put my flowers in water."

"Have a good night," Ricardo says in my direction before he walks across the hall to his own apartment.

What the heck just happened?

I follow Alyssa into the kitchen where I find her filling the vase with water as she mumbles something under her breath. I put my hands on either side of the sink, caging her in. "Everything okay, Damsel?"

She spins around and looks up at me. I didn't mean to end up so close to her, but like a moth to a fucking flame...here I am.

She waves a hand. "Yeah. I'm fine. The flowers really are beautiful by the way. I love them."

"Good. Makes me feel better about the other thing I got you."

"What thing?"

I back away, feeling like an idiot now for even bringing it up. "It's nothing, Alyssa. Really. I shouldn't have mentioned it."

She makes a face. "It's not nothing." She puts out her hand and pouts. "Now give it to me."

I pull the jewelry box out and place it in her hand. Hoping like hell it won't ruin the night. I didn't intend on getting her jewelry— but it occurred to me that I've *never* seen her wear the necklace she told me about. I can only assume that she must have lost it.

"I know it's not an exact replica or anything. But I tried to match up the goblin the way you described."

She looks down and her mouth opens wide. Her expression is unlike any I've ever seen before and she doesn't say a word.

Shit. I made a mistake.

I'm ready to apologize, but then she literally jumps into my arms, wraps her legs around my waist and hugs me so tight I almost send us both flying backward. "I take it you like it?" I ask. I don't even feel the pain in my ribs because her coconut scent surrounds me. And for the record, I was right. Her dress *is* made out of silk.

I hear a small sniffle. "You have no idea how much," she whispers. I stand there holding her for what feels like hours, not that I'm complaining. I would be more than content to hold her all night without ever venturing to the club. But I know how much she's looking forward to it.

"Are you ready?" I ask after I hear her breathing return back to normal.

She slides down my body and I swallow hard. She turns around, hands me the box, and holds up her hair. "Would you mind?"

My fingertips brush over her collarbone as I fasten the necklace around her neck. My lips hover over her ear. "You look breathtaking," I whisper.

Goosebumps erupt along her soft flesh and she fights a shiver. I meant to aim for her cheek, but before I know what I'm doing, my lips are grazing her neck.

Then she moans and my self-control plummets.

I force myself to back away. "Let's go."

"Okay," she whispers.

Before we leave, she reaches into her purse and pulls out a red and black masquerade mask for herself and hands me a black one.

A black mask that is so fucking similar to the one I already have. My expression must give me away because she asks, "Are you okay, Jackson?" For the second time that night.

No...I'm not okay.

I'm the exact opposite of okay.

Chapter 18 (Alyssa)

After Jackson paid the admission and we walked into the club, things got weird.

For the first half hour, he refused to make eye contact with me and practically ignored me.

And since neither of us are big drinkers we didn't spend much time at the bar. Not a whole lot of liquid courage for either of us to rely on.

That only left one thing to do. Dance.

Which Jackson, of course, said he doesn't do.

With only an hour left of my actual birthday, a night that started out so good, was turning out to be a bust.

Which is why I'm currently on the dance floor with some guy wearing a green mask while smoky air and dark sultry music surround us.

I have no interest in my dancing partner other than dancing but even in the almost pitch black room, I can feel Jackson's eyes on me the whole time.

Which is odd, because I swear, it seems like every female's eyes are on him.

And I can't say that I blame them one bit. If only they got a load of how sexy his face is without the mask...I'm pretty sure they'd faint.

My dancing partner grabs my hips and leans in much closer. Through his mask, Jackson's eyes narrow.

The D.J changes the beat up a little and cues up *Meg Myers, Desire.*

The guy presses flush against me and starts getting really into it...until he's suddenly gone and I'm being pressed against a wall instead.

I look up and Jackson's staring down at me, my former dancing partner long gone.

I've never seen Jackson look at me like this before. I don't know if I should be scared or turned on. I choose the latter.

He leans down, his breath tickling my ear. "I've had about as much as I can take, Alyssa. I don't like watching while some other guy puts his hands all over you."

Wow, this sounds a lot like jealousy. Against my better judgment, I decide to provoke him. "Why's that?"

I know exactly what I want. And that's *him*. Now, he needs to decide if he wants me once and for all. This hot and cold business is becoming exhausting.

He closes his eyes. I don't even think he realizes that he's started swaying to the music. And for someone who claims they don't dance, he's awfully good at it.

He raises my hands above my head and slowly grinds himself against me. "I think you know why," he rasps.

I shake my head and bite my lip. "No. Why don't you tell me? Or better yet, show me."

You can cut the sexual tension between us with a knife at this point, but I'm putting the ball in his court. He turned me down when it was in mine.

He leans his forehead against mine, links our fingers together and thrusts against me. "I want to be the *only* one who's allowed to touch your body like this. I want it to be *me* you think about at night when you touch yourself. I want it to be *my* name you're screaming when I'm making you come. I want you to be *mine*, because as far as I'm concerned...I'm already *yours.*"

I'm dizzy with those words. Our lips are so close, we're almost kissing. And my God, do I *need* him to kiss me right now.

"I'm yours. Now kiss me, Jackson."

His thumb brushes over my bottom lip. "Everything will change," he warns.

And he's right. Everything *will* change. But I want it to. I want things with him that I've never wanted with another person before.

I want to give him every single part of me...even the broken parts.

I take off my mask and toss it, not caring where it lands. "Good."

It's *not* a soft and gentle kiss.

It's a kiss that ravages me, consumes me. It's a kiss that claims me...effectively ruining me for anyone else, threatening to haunt me if my lips dare to ever touch another's.

He's putting his mark on me with those lips, branding me with the stroke of his tongue and worshiping me with his every breath.

I've kissed a lot of guys in my lifetime. But I've *never* been kissed like this before.

He nips my lower lip and I let out a groan. His hands are every-where- in my hair, moving up my spine, lifting and pulling me closer to him.

I feel his hardness against my stomach and taste the hint of whiskey on his tongue, his heart beating faster than the speed of light.

We stay kissing for what feels like forever, neither of us daring to ruin the connection we've forged by coming up for air...until someone clears their throat around us.

I open my eyes and realize that Jackson has me pinned up against the wall, my dress is bunched around my thighs and his own mask has slipped off.

"This is a masquerade themed Halloween party. You both *have* to wear your masks. And stay off the goddamned wall," some big guy in a security t-shirt says gruffly before he walks away.

I unravel my legs from around Jackson's waist and I know my face is probably the color of a tomato. I've never been so happy to be in a dark room.

He cradles my face in his hands. "Do you want to stay? We can if you want to."

I shake my head and Jackson takes my hand and heads toward the exit. "Wait," I say. We stop walking and he looks at me. "I have to go to the bathroom."

He laughs as we walk over to where the bathrooms are, making sure to dodge any security personnel along the way.

"I'll be right outside the door if you need me," he says. He bends down and I think he's going to kiss me again, but he kisses my forehead instead.

I turn around but he reaches for my arm. "Hurry up because I'm not sure how much longer I can keep my lips off of you," he murmurs before he releases me and I enter the bathroom.

For a second, I think I must have walked into the wrong bathroom because I see the back of some guy's head as he leans over the sink, obviously snorting some coke. I look at the bathroom door and sure enough, it *is* a women's bathroom. My bladder doesn't discriminate, though so I slip past him into one of the stalls and take care of business.

The guy's still hovering over the sink when I'm done, but I know Jackson's right outside so I walk to the furthest sink away from him and wash my hands.

It's only when I see his reflection behind me that I jump.

It's the last person I ever expected to see here.

Looks like the mayor's son is the next celebrity rehab star in the making.

The last time I saw him, he and his father were threatening me about going to the authorities after he leaked the sex tape.

"Dean," I whisper.

He wipes off some powder under his nose and sniffs. "Alyssa."

In the mirror, I see his reflection eye my body up and down. "You look incredible," he slurs.

"You look like shit," I counter.

"Yeah. I guess I deserve that," he whispers.

I turn on my heels and face him. "No, what you deserve is to have your testicles ripped off by a piranha while being dragged through hot coals." I shrug. "But hey, not all wishes come true now do they?"

He staggers forward until I'm pressed against the sink. "Look, you have every right to hate me," he whispers. "I'm sorry for what I did to you. I know how fucked up it was." His eyes open wide and he sways. "But there are things that you don't know about. Sometimes there are things that are far beyond our control."

He must be high right now because he's definitely not making *any* sense. I stay silent for a moment because I'm just not sure how to process the words coming from this poor excuse for a pathetic mess standing in front of me.

Finally, he slowly backs away from me.

The door to the bathroom swings open and Jackson walks in.

"You," he sneers.

At first, I think he means *me*. But he's looking right at Dean. Or rather, looking at Dean's back because he's still facing me.

Before I know it, Jackson's yanking Dean by his shirt and bashing his head into a wall.

Dean doesn't fight back for the first minute or so. But then the coke must kick in because he starts struggling against him and attempting to defend himself. Both of them are evenly matched in height, but Jackson's got a solid 30lbs of muscle on Dean. Not to mention, a temper like a raging bull right now.

I'm torn because a big part of me wants to see Dean get what he deserves...but then Jackson bashes Dean's head into the door of the bathroom and I see blood trickle down.

Shit. He's really, *really* hurting him.

Then it hits me...why the *hell* is Jackson fighting Dean anyway? It's not like *he* knows who he is. There's no way he heard our conversation because the door to the bathroom was closed and our voices were barely above a whisper.

The only thing I can come up with is that Jackson's jealousy got the best of him when he walked into the bathroom and saw a guy near me. If that's the case, and it must be; then his reaction is excessive and is quickly crossing over the line to insanity.

"Jackson, stop!" I scream.

It's like he doesn't even hear me. He just continues beating the ever living shit out of Dean.

For a second, I think Dean's down for the count, but he moves and Jackson's next punch misses him.

And that only makes Jackson's temper flare up more. I've never, *ever* seen him like this. He's like a wild animal unhinged.

I scream and chase after them when they both go flying through the bathroom's swinging door. Not before long, Jackson's on top of Dean and a crowd of people have gathered around us. Some even stopping to record the whole encounter on their phones.

Jackson's not missing a beat with his punches and Dean's face is starting to resemble ground beef. His body's starting to resemble a rag doll.

If Jackson keeps this up, he's going to end up killing him.

"Jackson, please stop!" I scream.

"You ruined her life and now I'm gonna ruin yours," Jackson growls between punches.

What?

I don't have time to think about that statement, because some girl starts shrieking, "Someone call the police! I think that's the mayor's son."

My stomach drops to the floor. I try getting between them, but a large arm wraps around my waist and pulls me out of the way.

I look up. *What the hell is Ricardo doing here?*

Ricardo's smart enough to know he can't stop Jackson in this state. Instead, he waits for the split second in between Jackson's next punch and slides Dean's now unconscious body out of the way and hands him over to two big men wearing suits.

That seems to break Jackson out of his haze.

The girl is still shrieking and going on and on about calling the police but Ricardo takes her phone and snaps it in half. "*No* one is calling the police," he booms.

He quickly turns to the three people who have their phones out recording what happened.

He then proceeds to stomp on each and every one of their phones.

I watch as everyone looks at him with fear in their eyes, including me.

The look in *his* eyes tells me that he'll accept nothing less. He commands power.

My stomach drops for a different reason entirely then...because I've seen that look in someone's eyes before.

I shake my head. *No.* I'm crazy. I'm fucking delusional.

"Alyssa," Jackson says.

I turn my head to look at him, but all I hear are those words that he said to Dean. "*You ruined her life and now I'm gonna ruin yours.*"

It's then that I realize.

Jackson watched the video.

Chapter 19 (Alyssa)

W e head back to his apartment.

All that's going through my head is—he told me he would never watch the sex tape.

I tell myself to calm down...that maybe, just *maybe* I'm overreacting and Jackson didn't watch my sex tape after all.

I tell myself that *maybe* he just blacked out in the middle of the fight and had a flashback of some kind that caused him to say what he did. He *did* look out of it, like off in another zone completely.

I don't know what to think right now. I feel like I'm grasping at straws because it's better than the alternative I'm faced with.

I mean, *why* would Jackson do that to me? He *knows* how much pain that video caused me.

"I'm gonna go clean up," he whispers before heading for the bathroom.

Those are the first words that either of us have said since we left the club.

I want to ask him...but I don't want him to lie to me.

There's only one way to know for sure if he watched the video.

I have to look at the history on his laptop.

I'm not proud of myself. Jackson's been my boyfriend for all of an hour at this point...but I *need* to know. I have to. Desperate times call for desperate measures.

As luck may have it, I notice his laptop on the couch in the living room.

I flip it open and say a silent prayer.

A silent prayer that turns right around and bites me in the ass when I see that I don't have to go through Jackson's history after all.

Because it's right here in front of me. Still on the fucking screen.

He watched it recently. *Very* recently.

And that makes it even worse. I could forgive him for watching it when he didn't really know me. I could even understand it...he *is* a guy.

But the fact that he watched it *after* I already started opening up to him.

After I told him things I've never told anyone. After I had convinced myself that Jackson was different. That *he* wouldn't hurt me.

That kills me. Wrecks me.

Another thought hits me and I want to fucking cry. No wonder Jackson got physical with me tonight.

Two days ago he was telling me that I wasn't a whore and that it was best to just be friends until I discovered my self-worth.

Then tonight...*after* he watches the video, he's talking about wanting me to scream his name and pushing me up against walls while he kisses me in a club.

I'm so stupid.

I know exactly how Jackson feels about me deep down inside. I *know* how he sees me now.

Just like everyone else in the world does.

And just like that...the scab comes off my wound and I feel it.

I feel all of it in a single rush.

The pain, the heartache, the despair.

There's only one way to cope when I shatter. I go to that place inside myself. The place that screams for me to acknowledge what I truly am and punish myself for it.

I also want to punish Jackson for what he's done. And there's only *one* way I can think of to accomplish both. The only weapon I have in my arsenal.

I slam the laptop and put it back where I found it, feeling myself morph into the person I've come to know so well.

"You only did it to yourself, Alyssa," I whisper to myself.

"I think we should talk," Jackson says.

I stand up and face him, putting on my game face. I throw my purse, not even caring where it lands and take off my jacket. "I don't want to talk."

"But—"

Jackson doesn't get a chance to finish that sentence because I jump on him and start kissing him.

I kiss him so hard I back *him* up against a wall.

It's nothing like our first and last kiss. I don't let myself feel anything. I shut everything off. I only focus on what needs to be done.

"Whoa," Jackson says pulling away from me.

"What?" I question. "Didn't you say something back at the club about not being able to keep your lips off me?"

"Well yeah," he says. "But that was before the fight and—"

I put my finger to his lips silencing him. "I don't want to talk about that, Jackson."

I kiss his neck. "I just want you—" I run my tongue along the shell of his ear. "To get naked for me," I whisper while my hand ventures lower and I grab his package. I smile when I feel him start to thicken in my hand through his jeans.

"Jesus Christ, Alyssa," he groans. "I think we should slow down. Especially since you don't want to talk about what happened. We *need* to talk about what happened."

"Take off your shirt."

He raises an eyebrow. "What?"

I lift my chin. "You heard me. Take off your fucking shirt. I want to see you naked, now."

He gives me a look that I hate. "No. Stop and *talk* to me, Alyssa."

I shake my head. "I don't want to talk. I'd much rather suck your dick instead."

His eyes open wide. "Not like this...not when you're *acting* like—"

I smile because it would be so much better for me if he said it. Like throwing another log into the fire. "Like what, Jackson? Tell me."

"Not like *you*. Not like *Alyssa*. *My* Alyssa."

I'm going to actually have to work for this. "You're right. I'm sorry." I walk over to him and kiss him sweetly, tenderly.

Then the worst thing of all happens. I start responding to his touch. I start losing myself because it's no longer my kiss...it becomes his kiss.

He cups my face as his tongue parts my mouth and I fall into him. His hands run along my hips before resting on my behind and I can't help but moan.

And just when I think I'm going to float to another dimension...he pulls away and kisses my forehead. "Now let's talk."

I don't want to hear anything he has to say. Nothing will change what I know to be true.

I kiss his neck again before whispering, "I don't want to talk. I just want to be close to you. I need to be close to you right now, please."

He looks contemplative for a moment and I think he's going to reject me. But instead, his thumbs brush over my cheeks and his lips find mine.

I reach for the button on his jeans but his hand lands on top of mine. "Stop, baby. Why are you rushing things?"

The term of endearment sounds so sweet and loving coming from him I have to fight off a shiver. And I have to remind myself why I'm doing this.

My other hand reaches down and starts rubbing along his length. "Let me do it, Jackson."

He bites his lip and closes his eyes. I've seen that expression before. He's fighting a war with himself right now. "Not tonight," he says.

Too bad he chose the wrong side.

"Fine," I say backing away from him.

I know I'm about to go in for the kill. "I'll just find someone else who wants me."

His hands clench at his sides. "Why are you acting like this? You don't have to be this way." He slams the wall beside him. "Tell me what the *fuck* is going through that head of yours, now," he barks.

I lower the straps to my dress. His expression is a combination of both anger and lust. Which I can definitely work with. "Because you keep telling me no and I want you." I slide the top of my dress down revealing my lacy bra. "I want to take you in my mouth so bad. I can't even see straight."

His jaw tightens and he swallows hard. "Prove it."

I begin sinking to my knees but his voice halts me. "No. Not like that."

For a minute...I panic. It feels like he's taking all the control from me. I stand back up. "Then how?"

He looks me in the eye, his expression giving nothing away. "Take off your panties."

It's amusing that he's trying to call me on my bullshit. Lucky for me, I have no problem stripping for him. Besides, he already saw everything when he watched the video.

I give him a sly smile, lift my dress and slip out of my thong. His eyes darken when he looks between my legs before traveling up to meet my eyes.

I twirl my panties around my finger and give him a smirk. "Good enough?"

"No. Come and bring them to me."

"Why?"

His gaze is penetrating. "I want to see how wet they are."

I know I'm blushing.

He knows he's got me.

And it's *not* because my panties are dry. Quite the opposite.

He's playing me at my own game. Twisting it around and turning me on against all odds. Making it so that it doesn't feel like a punishment, but a reward.

I also know that a part of him is hoping I don't take the bait. Hoping I'll back down and reconsider doing whatever it is that I'm doing. Hoping that I'll cool off and hear him out.

Too bad for him that's no longer an option. I'm bringing Jackson into the dark with me and I won't stop until I make him pay. I'll show him my fucked up underworld. He can find his own way out when I'm through with him...unlike me who never will.

Steeling myself, I take the few steps forward until I'm standing directly in front of him.

He takes my panties out of my hand and his eyes blaze when he runs his thumb along the crotch of them. His head rests against the wall and he closes his eyes. I watch his adam's apple bob, straining against his throat as he begins to unbutton his shirt.

For a second, I wince when I see the tape across his ribs, hating the sight of him hurt. I force myself to put it out of my head and focus on the task at hand when he shrugs out of his shirt.

He opens his eyes and his hand reaches out for my cheek. His gray orbs are obscured with both lust and turmoil as his pupil's drill into me. We both know this is the final step before takeoff, the last chance to stop myself.

I slowly drop to my knees. And because I'm more fucked up than I ever realized, I decide to prolong his torture by saying, "Tell me exactly what you want me to do, Jackson."

He groans, his hands tightening at his sides. "Undo my pants and pull me out," he says, low and deep.

I undo his belt buckle and unzip his jeans before sliding them down his hips.

I expect him to be wearing boxers, but he's going commando. My breath catches because his erection is both long and thick. My eyes focus on the glint of metal from the barbell going through the engorged head of his cock. I also can't help but take in the veins and ridges encompassing his shaft and the pure masculine scent radiating off him.

I'm so turned on, I can't find my way into the darkness. I'm completely out of my element now. All I can do is succumb to my own arousal.

I dip my head forward, look up at him and plant a kiss on the small drop of fluid leaking from his tip.

His eyes glaze over and the tight cords of his muscles flex in restraint. I'm struck with the overwhelming feeling of wanting to see him lose control.

I take him in my hand and pump him while I run my tongue along the seam of his balls. My tongue travels back up to his length and I lick the throbbing vein running across his shaft.

"Fuck, Alyssa," he rasps.

I open wide and proceed to fill my mouth with as much of him as I can. I start sucking him with earnest then. His hand wraps around my hair and he thrusts his hips forward. "That's it, baby. Just like that. God, that feels so *fucking* good," he groans, his voice husky.

I don't let up, my mouth bobs up and down, barely stopping for air. I continue even when I begin gagging and his piercing hits the back of my throat. I look up and notice that his eyes are closed, his mouth is parted, and his breathing has become erratic. He's so far gone in the throes of ecstasy, chanting my name like a prayer.

I'd be lying if I said it wasn't the sexiest sight I've ever seen in my life.

"I'm close, baby," he warns. I feel his cock pulse in my mouth and I swallow every last drop of his release while gently tugging on his balls.

"Holy...shit," he grunts.

Before I know what's happening, he's hauling me up to him and crushing his mouth against mine. "That was incredible," he whispers.

I'm brought back down to reality and I give him a menacing smile.

He looks confused for a moment...until I utter my next statement and his face falls.

"Was it better than the blow job you saw me give when you watched the video, Jackson?"

Before he can answer or stop me, I adjust my dress, find my jacket and keys and head straight for the front door.

His hand reaches for my wrist when I touch the doorknob. "Alyssa. It's not what you think."

Anger rips through me. "Oh, so you're going to try and deny it?"

He shakes his head, his expression hurt. "No. I won't lie to you. I...I watched it." He sighs. "Well, part of it before I had to turn it off—"

I didn't think I could feel any worse about the situation. I didn't think there was any more hurt left to experience in my lifetime.

I was wrong.

He's disgusted by me. And why wouldn't he be? He just witnessed who and what I am first hand.

Ford's words from that day echo in my head, shredding my insides. I have no value...no one could or ever will love me.

My hands reach for my necklace and I tug on it until it falls. "Goodbye, Jackson."

Chapter 20 (Jackson)

"Goodbye, Jackson."

With those words, she slams the door and takes off. Her necklace tossed on the ground.

I know I fucked up. I know I shouldn't have let her do what she did. Even if it was the best blowjob I'd ever received.

I wanted to wait awhile before we did anything sexual, I didn't want to rush things and screw it all up. But when she uttered those words...about being with another guy...I saw red.

And in all honesty, I *thought* she was into it after I called her on her bullshit. That look in her eye was gone, and her manipulation was replaced by lust. In some fucked up way, I thought it was a good thing.

Clearly, I was wrong.

But I *still don't* regret going after that piece of shit tonight.

She was taking too long in the bathroom and I thought something happened.

Something happened all right...that shit stain was standing right in front of her. How he ended up there in the first place is anyone's guess.

I recognized his tattoo immediately. I was hoping I was

mistaken, but deep down I knew it was him. I went into that place inside my head and I blacked out. I barely even remember any of it.

I thought I was in the cage...defending Lilly.

It wasn't until my fist hit the floor and I heard Ricardo's voice that I was brought back to reality.

Then I saw the look on Alyssa's face. She was petrified.

And why wouldn't she be? She just saw her boyfriend for all of two seconds on the verge of killing another person.

And trust me, if Ricardo wasn't there...I would have killed him.

For all I know, I might have.

She didn't utter a word the whole walk home. She just kept her head down and her arms crossed over her chest, shielding herself. I knew we had to talk about it. I knew I had to come clean about watching the video. I knew she would put two and two together and she deserved answers.

I wanted to give her those answers. But when I came out of the bathroom...something happened.

I didn't understand it...but she became someone else. All I knew was that it was because of me.

I tried to talk to her, but she kept telling me she didn't want to talk. Then, she kept throwing herself at me...and kept taking the control away from me. I knew I had to let her have it, within reason...but when I saw it going down a bad road my suspicions were confirmed.

I knew exactly what she was doing.

And the fact that she was doing it with *me*? Even though I made it clear to her time and time again that I didn't want to be used by her....well, I couldn't let it go down like that.

And I sure as hell *wasn't* going to let her go running off to fuck some other dude. That would only make things worse...not to mention, it would kill me.

So, I did the next best thing...I let her have what she was asking for.

Only, I was going to see to it that she wouldn't be punishing herself. That this would be different. It felt like I was fighting against something that was even stronger than me...but I saw the moment the real Alyssa peeked through.

I let her take the control from me...let myself get lost in her, which is something I never, *ever* do. Not that I really had much of a choice in the matter because the things she did to me?

Well, *fuck*.

Porn stars could learn a thing or *several* from her.

Then she looked up at me and gave me a smile that chilled me to the bone. My favorite dimple was nowhere in sight.

I told her the truth about watching the video...I didn't lie. But she never let me explain myself because she took off.

Worst of all? She didn't let me tell her how brave and strong I thought she was for making it through something like that. She didn't let me tell her that I was falling for her. I knew I was a goner the second my lips touched hers in that club.

I want to chase after her, but I know she needs time to cool off. I know that when I push her too far, she doesn't come bouncing back harder and stronger like I wish she would.

We might be similar in some ways, but *unlike* me, my girl's not a fighter...she's a runner. And even though I hate that...I'll accept it because it's who she is and I want all of her.

I hear a knock on the door and I can't get there fast enough.

I'm disappointed when it's Ricardo staring back at me. Not that I'm not thankful for his help.

Although, I still don't know *why* he was there in the first place.

I open the door, gesture for him to come inside and cut to the chase. "Why were you there?"

He looks at me hard and I know I'm not going to like what he's going to say. "No offense, but your girl was dressed to kill tonight. Even I couldn't ignore how hot she looked. That being said, I already told you I was concerned about what would happen on the outside. I was going to tell you not to go. I didn't have a good feeling about it." He shrugs. "But then she mentioned that it was her birthday and I saw how excited she was. It doesn't take a genius to figure out that she must not get out much because of the video. My bad feelings were confirmed, though after you beat the mayor's son to a bloody pulp. "

Fuck, DeLuca was not going to be happy about this. Not one bit.

Ricardo must notice my expression because he says, "Don't worry, I took care of everything."

"How?"

"I had a few of DeLuca's men waiting on deck, just in case something happened. Plus, I was in the wings myself. I wish I got to you sooner, but I didn't see you go into the bathroom. I thought you left because I saw you both head out for the exit. I stayed back chatting it up with some hot redhead. Then I heard the commotion."

He runs a hand through his hair. "You fucked him up bad, Jackson. He's got some serious damage. On the bright side, he was so zonked out of his mind he doesn't remember shit before or after. He had no idea he was talking to Alyssa in the bathroom or that he got into a fight."

He smirks. "I had Freddie wreck his car and stage it like he got into an accident because he was too stoned. I also issued him a warning. Not only did I tell him that you were in DeLuca's circle and ran with him. I mentioned that if his memory about tonight were to ever come back, he and his car would be found at the bottom of the Atlantic."

Part of me wishes that the bastard does end up remembering now. It's what he deserves.

"Thanks. I owe you." I pause. "But what about DeLuca's men? What if they say something to him?"

I want to tell him that what I'm *really* worried about is someone mentioning Alyssa being there with me. But, as much as we're friends—I can't.

I'm in a bind because I don't want to reveal Alyssa's past. Partly because it's not my place and partly because I really don't know how strong Ricardo's loyalty is to DeLuca. For all I know, *he* could spill the beans to DeLuca himself.

He jerks a shoulder up. "They won't. They owe me a few favors.

But, if DeLuca finds out, I'll handle it. I don't really see him flipping out over some stupid bar fight, anyway. He's got much bigger shit to worry about. It's not like you ended up in jail or on the news."

His words should comfort me but they do the exact opposite. My memory kicks in and I remember that people had their phones out recording the fight.

"Shit. What about the cell phones? It was the mayor's son. You know someone will be more than willing to sell the footage to tmz or post it online."

"Took care of that too," he says.

I vaguely remember him breaking a few cell phones. "What if you missed one? Then what?"

He considers this for a moment. "Then we take care of it."

He looks around. "So where is Alyssa?"

I briefly tell him how I fucked up. I leave *out* the part about her giving me a blowjob...but not about me watching the video.

"Fucking Lou-Lou," he growls. "She doesn't know when enough is enough. Always causing problems."

I don't miss the intensity in his eyes when he says that.

"Yeah, but it was still *me* who watched it. I have no idea how the hell to fix this."

"Maybe it's best to just leave it alone and let it perish. Some things are better that way."

Something tells me that it's not me and Alyssa he's talking about when he utters that statement.

I shake my head. "No. She's special. I can't let it end like this."

He stands up. "Then do what you do best." When I give him a weird look he says, "Fight for her, dummy."

He's right.

I've already tried texting her multiple times, though. I told her how sorry I was and explained what really happened with the sex tape.

I also told her that my feelings for her never changed after watching it. Nor have they changed after tonight...after I saw the other side of her. I told her that if she was willing, we would get through it together because I wasn't giving up on her or us.

Then I told her that I was falling for her.

She still hasn't responded.

I scan the living room and notice that in her rush to leave, she left her purse here.

Maybe *that's* why she never responded to any of my texts.

I pick it up and can feel her phone vibrating through the material.

That's when I realize what an idiot I am. I shouldn't be telling Alyssa those things via text. I should be saying them to her in person. Fighting for her like Ricardo said.

I turn around and face him. "I need another favor."

"What's up?"

"Can I borrow your car?"

A fter promising Ricardo over and over again that I wouldn't crash his prized Mustang. He handed over the keys.

I got Alyssa's address off her license and plugged it into the gps on my phone. The drive wasn't as bad as I thought it would be.

Her neighborhood is quiet and the houses that line the streets are all large and upscale.

The lawns are green and the streetlights are all in working order. There's no sign of drug dealers or garbage littering the sidewalks.

It's the perfect suburb life. So different from the environment I grew up in.

I decide to park right behind her car in the driveway. I notice another car parked there as well...but from the looks of things, her house is so big, maybe she has a tenant or two living there.

Her driveway is long and her house sits on top of a large hill, meaning I've got a little bit of a walk ahead of me. Dozens of large oak trees line the property. After a solid three minutes of walking, I see a glimmer of light up ahead and I know I must be close.

The light from the porch becomes brighter and after another minute, I'm standing right in front of her house.

Then I see her.

But she's not alone.

I see the back of some other guy, one who's wearing a gray suit.

I can't hear what he's saying, but I watch as he gets down on his knees in front of her and grabs her hips.

His hands are all over her, touching her everywhere...then he leans in and lifts up her dress.

Since her panties are still on the floor in the living room of *my* apartment, she's fully exposed.

I'm less than a second away from charging full speed ahead and pummeling the asshole.

Then I hear her shout something that takes the breath from my lungs. "I love you, Ford."

I quickly turn away and run back down the hill.

I'm running down the hill as fast as I can, so I don't go back and do something stupid...like beat the ever living shit out of an FBI agent.

An FBI agent she specifically told me wasn't in her life anymore.

He sure as *fuck* looked to be *very* much in her life...especially while he was positioning himself to go down on her.

I don't even know what to think at this point. The only thing I feel is betrayed, hurt, and lied to.

And I know...I lied to her, too.

But unlike *her* lie, my lie was to *protect* her from harm.

I've done *nothing* but try and be there for this girl...I didn't use her, intentionally hurt her, or betray her.

The question is...why the fuck did Alyssa feel the need to do *all* of those things to me?

I know she's got her demons...I saw them up close and personal tonight. I also know that she thought the world of her dad's old partner. I guess I know why now.

My chest tightens when I think about what she said. She *loves* him.

I made the mistake of falling for a girl who could never be mine because she already belongs to someone else.

My blood boils at the thought.

But if she loves *him*...why did she lead *me* on?

No. *Fuck*, no.

She wouldn't do that. It would be stupid and *dangerous* to do that.

I force myself to breathe. I have to remind myself that *if* Alyssa was in fact, attempting some undercover shit...then she wouldn't have told me about what DeLuca did to her dad.

Unless she made it up?

No. I saw the agony in her eyes that night when she confided in me. I felt it. There's no way that was false.

At least, that makes one thing she told me true.

Tyrone tried to warn me about her in the beginning. Hell, even *Lou-Lou* warned me about her. I just refused to listen. I didn't want to believe it.

I thought I saw something inside of her that called to me...connected us. Something I wanted to take care of. Something I would have cherished until my dying breath.

I pull the car door open and grab her purse from the passenger seat of the Mustang.

I'm sure as shit not going back up that hill, but I also don't want to have any of her stuff near me. I don't need to be reminded of what a deceitful bitch she is because I'm certain I'll never forget.

And because I'm feeling extra spiteful at the moment, I snatch the necklace I got her. I put them both on the hood of her car. Now, I have absolutely no reason to ever see her again.

Although, if she ever showed up at my place; I'm sure I could have Lou-Lou play along and answer the door for me. I *could* make Alyssa think I was fucking her. I could hurt her the way I'm hurting now, but I'd rather just be done with her for good.

I briefly consider keying her precious BMW, but quite frankly, I don't have the energy to go all Carrie Underwood on her ass. I still have over an hour drive ahead of me.

Besides, I'm sure Mr. Special Agent, *Daddy Warbucks* would just offer to buy her a brand new car. Hell, maybe he's the one who bought her the one she has now.

I *almost* let myself love her. I was right there...on the fucking cliff...already falling...about to land.

I just never knew I was headed for a crash landing.

Chapter 21 (Alyssa)

F uck, I forgot my purse.

I briefly consider turning around. But for what? How the hell can I even begin to explain what goes on inside my mind to Jackson? He'll think I'm a psycho. Hell, I probably am.

A part of me wants to turn the car around, but Jackson will just want to talk about everything. How can I tell him about this place I go to inside myself that causes me to do these things? How can I tell him that when he hurt me...all I thought about was Ford.

How can I tell him about Ford?

I know, deep down inside that Ford is the gatekeeper to this hell-hole I'm trapped in. But I *can't* live without him...because he's the *only* one who ever showed me love after that horrible day. He's the one who cared when I had no one else. He's the only tie to my father I have left. And if I severe our relationship...I'll have nothing.

I know our relationship isn't healthy. It hasn't been since that day in his office, maybe even before that if I'm being honest with myself.

But I know *he* loves me. I know he cares...and I know he will always be there for me.

Like now, I think, as I pull into my driveway and see him waiting for me in his car.

As soon as I get out of my own car, his arms are around me.

"What happened, sweetheart? You don't look happy." His blue eyes are piercing tonight and his expression is particularly kind.

I'm immediately uneasy. Ford hasn't treated me like this in a *very* long time. Usually, he's upset with me about something or telling me all that I do wrong. I almost want to ask him when the last time he saw me genuinely happy was...because I'm always miserable when he's around.

I shrug as we begin walking toward the house. I don't really want to tell him about Jackson. Besides, anytime he suspects that I've been out with a guy...wow he gets mad.

I decide to stay silent. Because I know that when it comes to Ford, anything and everything I say will eventually be used against me.

We walk up to the house, but I don't invite him in. I'm too exhausted to deal with whatever it is he came here for tonight. "I'm tired, Ford. I think I'm just going to go to bed. Have a good night."

His hand wraps around my arm and he spins me around. Then I see it. The moment he looks down at my dress and his expression fills with disgust. "I wonder why that is, Alyssa."

When I don't respond, he pushes me further. "I know you've been *seeing* someone."

He says this like the concept of me actually having a relationship with anyone is utterly barbaric.

I let him continue because I'm not sure what I'm supposed to say to that. I don't want to correct him and tell him that we got into a fight and might be over; because I don't want him telling me that he told me so and that no one will ever love me.

"I know you stayed at his apartment in the city the last time I saw you. *He* was also who you hung up on *me* for during our last conversation."

I don't know how he has this information or *why* it matters so much to him. "Yeah...and? What's your point?"

He steps closer to me and I swear his features change right before my eyes. His eyes narrow, his jaw goes rigid and his lips form a tight line. The hand around my arm squeezes so hard I wince. "You said *he* was important, Alyssa."

I laugh, I laugh so hard I must sound like a crazy person. "So? He *is* important. What the hell is your deal?"

"My deal," he grits through his teeth. "Is that there should be *no one* in your life more important than me, do you understand me? You are mine. *My* goddamn whore, you hear me? Not his!"

And then he slaps me. Hard. Right across my left cheek.

And then I'm crying. Because the truth fucking hurts.

All of it hurts.

I want to go numb.

"Goddammit," he screams. "See what you made me do?"

"I'm s-sorry."

"Stop stuttering, Alyssa. I forgive you."

I only stutter like this when I'm terrified or upset.

I'm about to apologize again, but I realize what he said. He forgives *me*? For what? I've done nothing wrong. "I don't forgive *you*, Ford."

He appears confused so I continue, "I don't forgive you for that day in the office. I don't forgive you for the way you treat me. And I definitely don't forgive you for slapping me."

He looks astonished but I'm not done yet. I jab a finger in his chest. "So what? I have a boyfriend. And you know what the best part about Jackson is? He doesn't treat me like *you* do, Ford. He's *nice* to me. He respects me. He doesn't treat me like I'm his property and he certainly doesn't treat me like I'm a whore."

Ford looks at me with so much pain in his eyes...I almost crumble.

He grabs my face. "I'm so sorry, sweetheart." He leans down so we are eye level. "I love you, Alyssa." He kisses my cheek. "Can you forgive the beast?" He kisses my other cheek. "For only trying to save her," he whispers.

I close my eyes because *this* Ford is so familiar. This is the Ford I know in my heart. This is the Ford I love.

His hands find my waist and his thumbs skim over my rib cage. "Please," he pleads.

I open my eyes and look down as he drops to his knees. I've never seen Ford look so sad or desperate before.

He looks up at me. "I know you love me. Don't punish me for loving you back. Please don't punish me for being the only one who could ever love you."

Something about that statement tears at my soul. I can't respond to him, because if I open my mouth...something inside me will crack further. And I won't know how to fix it all by myself.

His hands grip my hips forcefully. "You love *me*, Alyssa. You fucking love me. Let me hear you say it. I *need* to hear you say it."

But I can't. I can't say it. He looks so wounded in this moment, it physically causes me to ache.

But I *still* can't say it.

He fists my dress. "I'll *make* you say it then," he sneers.

What? No. Fear renders me captive and I attempt to shake my head, but I can't move.

He cups my mound through the silk fabric of my dress. "Tell me, does he touch you like this?"

I stay frozen, refusing to answer him. He lifts my dress and the cool breeze hits me, leaving me vulnerable and exposed. "He's never made you come before has he?" He clicks his tongue. "But then again, no one has...have they, sweetheart?"

I don't answer him and he laughs. "You want to know why that is?"

I don't. I really, really don't. Because I think I already know the answer.

I just never wanted to believe it.

His head dips forward and I know there's only one way to make this stop. "I love you, Ford," I shout at the top of my lungs.

But he doesn't stop.

204

"I own your mind," he whispers, his breath tickling my core. "Because I was the first one to fuck *that* and make it mine."

I crack. My body feels both lighter and heavier at the same time.

He smiles. He's giving me that movie star smile that now makes me feel sick. "I love you, Alyssa."

The tears hit me fast and hard.

What *kind* of man loves like *this*?

That's easy. No man.

Because what Ford feels for me isn't love. "No, you don't."

Something deep inside me snaps with that final realization. I push him off me and open the front door. He chases after me, following me into the kitchen. "Get out, Ford! Get out!" I shove him. I shove him as far as I possibly can and he stumbles back. I need him to *leave*. I never want to see him again.

I scream and pull my hair. Ford looks at me like I'm insane.

Good. Let him see what he's created.

Before I know it, I'm reaching for a knife and aiming it at him. "Get the fuck out!"

His eyes open wide and for a moment, I think he's going to reach for his gun. But he holds his hands up instead. "Put the knife down, sweetheart. Look, I'm sorry for what I said. I didn't mean it. I only wanted to hear you say that you loved me."

"It's your fault!" I scream. His mouth drops open and for a second, I swear, panic flashes across his face.

I'm crying so hard I can barely form words. "It's your fault I'm like *this*. You broke me." I begin shaking. "And the worst part is...in my darkest moments...when I go to that place inside myself. I'm just like *you*."

And it's true. It's so fucking true. I treat others like they're disposable. I treat myself like I'm worth nothing. I manipulate people to get my own way. And I can honestly say, that I don't love myself.

The cold, hard reality is like being thrown outside naked in the middle of a blizzard.

I wipe my nose with my sleeve and fall down to the floor. "You don't love me, Ford."

He begins pacing, looking at me like I'm a mental case. "Of course, I love you!" he screams.

I look him in his eyes for the last time. "No. Because *if* you loved me...you would *never* keep insisting that I go undercover for my father's killer...knowing that he might end up killing *me* if he ever found out."

He opens his mouth to speak but I hold up my hand. "You would want to *protect* me. You would want me to be safe. You wouldn't send me into the eye of the storm. You wouldn't set me up."

A tear falls from Ford's eye. "Alyssa. I—"

"Just leave, Ford. Please, just leave me. That's the only way you can ever make any of this okay."

I hear the sound of the door closing and breathe...actually breathe for the first time in years.

I drop the knife and curl my arms around myself...because I'm all I have left now.

And I have to be okay with that.

Three months later...

Chapter 22 (Alyssa)

"I need a glass of coke and a splash of jack."

I wink at my customer. "Ah. You take your whiskey like I take my coffee. Cup of cream and sugar and a splash of coffee."

He looks embarrassed. "I guess that makes me sound like less of a man, huh?"

I wave a hand at him and continue fixing his drink. "Nah. You gotta do what's right for you. Don't ever let anyone tell you different."

He leans in. "And what if I told you that getting your number would be what's right for me?"

Somewhere in back of me, someone clears their throat. "I would say that what's right for *me*...is punching you in the face for hitting on my girl."

My customer quickly leaves after that.

I roll my eyes and look up at my friend. "What the hell, Shane?" I nod my head in the direction of the cute musician who hasn't stopped looking at Shane since his shift started. "Your *boyfriend* is sitting right over there watching you."

He flips a bottle in the air. "I know. I'm wearing the jeans that make my ass look great." He begins filling the glass in front of him.

"I thought I'd run interference. Besides, I said my *girl*. Not *girlfriend*. If he was really interested in you for more than one night, he would have clarified." He shrugs. "Guy looked like a douche anyway. "

I shake my head. "You're crazy."

He purses his lips. "Yeah, but you love me."

I smile because I can honestly say that I do. Shane gave me a job when no one else would. Not only did he hire me, but he also lets me rent the apartment upstairs from the bar.

And when I had a full blown panic attack over possibly being recognized that first night...he wiped my tears away and suggested we dye my hair. He didn't judge me when I told him about the video and he never uses my real name around customers.

I toss my long dark hair over my shoulder and kiss his cheek. "Call me if it gets packed. You know where I'll be."

He laughs. "It won't now that you're off the clock. But I'll call you anyway."

I walk around the bar and head upstairs to my studio apartment.

A lot has changed over the last three months.

For starters...I no longer visit the city. I live here now. I moved out of my father's house two weeks after the last night I saw Ford.

I used the money I got from selling Ford's BMW which was apparently equipped with a hidden gps tracking device to help me move.

That's how he knew I spent the night at Jackson's.

Jackson.

I have to close my eyes at the thought of him.

I went out to my car the next day and found my purse along with the necklace he got for me. I also dug my phone out and wept while I read all of his text messages.

I didn't even think about it, I hopped in my car and went straight to his apartment.

Where he proceeded to ignore me for hours upon hours.

So, I left and came back the next day.

Only to face an angry Tyrone.

He didn't want to speak to me...but after he saw the state I was in...he relented a little. He said that Jackson wouldn't go into much detail about it, but that he saw me with some other guy at my house.

Apparently, he came to my house to talk to me that night and showed up just as Ford got down on his knees and I was screaming that I loved him. He left shortly after that and never looked back.

I never thought it was possible to hate Ford more. But, I really only had myself to blame. I *should* have been honest with Jackson and I *should* have kicked Ford out of my life a long time ago.

I told Tyrone...well, it was more like *begged* Tyrone to talk to Jackson for me and set him straight.

I told Tyrone to tell him that what he saw between Ford and I *wasn't* what he thought it was.

The verdict?

It didn't matter. Jackson was done with me.

I still wasn't done with him yet, so I made one final attempt.

This time, it was Jackson himself who answered the door. He never let *me* get a word in, but I'll never forget what he said- *"I'm all out of fucks to give. Maybe Ford can give you a few."*

Then he slammed the door in my face and locked it.

Yup...I hurt him that much.

And I never, ever got a chance to apologize to him or explain what happened.

I tried for two weeks straight to make things right. But the same thing happened every time. Tyrone would come out and tell me to go home. Nothing was going to change.

It got to the point where even freakin' Lou-Lou was looking at me with pity whenever she saw me in the apartment lobby.

I didn't want to, but I had to let him go.

I can only hope, that our paths will cross again one day.

Chapter 23 (Jackson)

"I love you, sugarplum."

Ricardo and I exchange a glance.

"I promise I'll call you later, sugarplum," Tyrone continues. "I've missed you so much. I can't wait to see you, sugarplum."

"So help me god, if he says *sugarplum* one more time," Ricardo says under his breath.

I pinch the bridge of my nose and lean forward. I don't know how much more of this *sugarplum* shit I can take.

I'm about ready to hand over *my* balls just so he can feel what it's like to have a pair again.

Is this what I would have turned into if things hadn't gone sour with Alyssa?

Nope. Not going there.

Five more sugarplum's and three 'I love you's' later, Tyrone finally gets off the phone.

He turns around and makes a face at Ricardo and I. He's been doing that a lot lately.

Ricardo and I exchange another glance because we both know what's coming, and neither of us are up for it.

"Guys," he starts. "Y'all could be just as happy as I am if you would both stop being so stubborn."

I grunt and Ricardo reaches for his beer.

He points to Ricardo first. "You going out and screwing anything in a skirt night after night isn't helping you. You need to walk down the hall and talk to Lou-Lou. I don't care what you say, man...she meant more to you than you're letting on."

His eyes swivel to me. "And *you*. You haven't been the same since that night you went to Alyssa's house."

My entire body stiffens at the sound of her name.

"You've *changed*, Jackson. You're always in a bad mood these days. All you do is work out and go to the fight club."

I shrug. "That's always what I've done, Tyrone."

He tsks at me. "No. You're different. Even angrier. Like the entire world is your own personal fighting cage now."

He rubs the back of his neck. "I don't think you gave her the benefit of the doubt. I don't understand why you don't just call her up and let——"

"Enough," I warn.

There's absolutely no reason to call her. Why? So she can just lie to me about Ford again. Make me start falling for her and turn myself inside out.

Been there done that.

I rub my temples...trying to push my other thoughts away.

Thoughts like—What if there *is* more to the story? What if she's truly sorry for what she did?

Or worst of all? What if I let myself forgive her?

Then I'll be right back where I started.

Having no choice but to lie to her about working at DeLuca's club and my reason for working there in the first place.

And when she finds out, she'll leave me anyway and it will hurt worse.

No, I'd much rather let my anger and venom for her stew. Let it turn me into a cold, heartless bastard.

He blows out a breath and looks at the both of us. "I'm tired of this, y'all. So, here's what we're gonna do. We're going to *talk* about it."

I rub my hands over my face. I've had enough of this shit. "Oh for fucks sake!" I roar.

Tyrone stops talking and Ricardo laughs.

Tyrone claps his hands. "Okay, this is progress. Let it out. Jackson, why don't you start first. How did it make you *feel* when Alyssa hurt you?"

I look at Ricardo and he smirks. "You gonna answer that?"

I get up from the couch. "Fuck no. Let's grab a drink." I look at Tyrone. "Feel free to stay back and watch some more Doctor Phil."

"And bake some cookies while you're at it, *sugarplum*," Ricardo adds.

Tyrone gives us the finger. "Fuck you both. I was only trying to help."

I toss him his jacket. "If you wanna help you can buy us a round at the bar."

Ricardo looks at his phone. "You guys down to try a new spot? It's kind of a hole in the wall, but rumor has it the bartender is easy on the eyes."

I open the front door. "Fine, but I'm not looking for pussy. I'm just looking to drink."

"I s there something you'd like to tell us, Ricardo?"

Beside me, Tyrone laughs.

Ricardo rolls his eyes. "I guess I just *assumed* the hot bartender was a girl."

The giant bartender with frosted blond tips looks up and gives Ricardo a wink.

That only makes Tyrone laugh harder. "Ah. So you *do* think he's hot?"

The bartender saunters over to us. "What can I get you, boys?"

Ricardo takes a seat at the bar. "Are you the only one who's working tonight? Because there's supposed to be a *hot* bartender who works here."

Frosted blond tips and eyeliner aside, the dude's built like a linebacker who could probably give Ricardo a run for his money.

The guy looks offended, so I clear my throat and cut in. "I think what my rude buddy means is—is there a *female* bartender working here?"

"A hot one," Ricardo interjects.

The guy gives Ricardo a dirty look before focusing his attention back to me and holding out his hand. "I'm Shane."

I shake his hand. "I'm Jackson." I quickly introduce Tyrone and Ricardo.

Shane flips a bottle in the air. "I like you, Jackson."

Well, now this is awkward.

He flips another bottle in the air and winks at me. "So, you know what I'm gonna do for you, sexy?"

Next to me, Tyrone pats me on the back and whispers, "I'm so glad I came here tonight. This is *awesome*."

I'm going to *kill* Ricardo for bringing us here.

Shane slams his hand down on the bar. "I'm going to introduce you to my employee."

I raise an eyebrow. "Come again?"

"The hot female bartender...you're interested right?"

I shake my head. "No." I gesture to Ricardo. "*He* is. The only thing I want is some whiskey if you have it."

He fills up a glass and hands it to me.

Ricardo leans in. "When will she be here?" he asks Shane.

He looks at the clock. "In about 20 minutes. But if you're looking for a quick screw, trust me...she's *not* it," he says before turning to a different set of customers.

"If she's hot, I'll have no problem giving her a long and slow screw," Ricardo says under his breath.

Tyrone looks at him and shakes his head. "I already told you, man. You can screw as many women as you want. It's not going to keep your mind off of Lou-Lou. Just *talk* to her."

"Drop it," Ricardo barks.

I finish my drink and put money on the bar. "Ready to go?"

Ricardo shrugs. "Nah. We're here now. We might as well stay awhile." He swirls the amber liquid around his glass before downing it. "We came here to drink our troubles away anyway."

I click my empty glass against his. "I'll drink to that."

Three games of darts and five rounds later we walk back to the bar for another round.

Or in my case, stumble because I slammed three shots of 151 during the last round that we had and I'm pretty sure I've reached my limit.

It's semi-crowded now, so we're forced to take the last three seats at the end of the bar.

I'm drunk as fuck, but I notice there's a subtle shift in the atmosphere and it seems like everyone's eyes are glued to the same thing.

When I look up, I find out why.

There's some girl bent over a large cooler located at the back of the bar. Her shiny dark hair cascades down her back, but I'm too focused on the way her perfect little ass looks in the skirt she's wearing to notice much else. She leans down even further and I feel myself lean with her as I notice her skirt rising higher...hoping to be rewarded with a glimpse of her cheeks.

I look over and Ricardo bites his knuckle. "Fuck me that's hot."

Tyrone shakes his head and looks down. "My dick belongs to Shelby. This is *Shelby's* dick," he chants to himself.

Ricardo and I burst out laughing.

It feels good to laugh again. Even if it's only because I'm feeling the effects of the alcohol.

I turn to him. "Goddamn, man. How can you ignore *that*? Even *I'm* looking at her," I say. I point in the direction of where she last was and ignore Ricardo's tap on my shoulder. "I mean, she sure as *fuck* is putting it all out there. She's obviously looking for attention and a good time."

I turn to Ricardo, but he's shaking his head at me. I proceed to ignore him. "Looks like you found your quick fuck after all. I bet you won't even have to take her home to get it."

I swipe my hand in the air. "Hey, hot stuff," I call out. "Thanks for the free show. But can I get another glass of whiskey?"

When I turn my head back to the bar, I'm greeted by a pair of gorgeous, but furious hazel eyes.

I must be drunker than I realized, because I swear, I see an exact replica of Alyssa standing before me, only with dark hair.

I turn to Tyrone. "Are you seeing what I'm seeing?"

He puts a hand on my shoulder. "Yeah, brother. And I think it's time to get you home." He casts a sympathetic glance at Alyssa. "Look, he's really drunk right now. He doesn't know what he's saying."

Ricardo nods. "It's true, Alyssa. He's not exactly himself at the moment."

She crosses her arms over those perfect tits of hers and I groan.

But even in my drunken state, I know this woman is poison. I have to get the fuck out of here.

I put one arm around Ricardo and another around Tyrone. "You guys better get me home before her FBI—sugar daddy... and I do mean *daddy* because he's *old* enough to be her daddy...arrests me."

"Fuck," Ricardo mutters.

"Bro...*shut* up," Tyrone yells.

Before I know it, the glass of whiskey I asked for is being thrown in my face and Alyssa's storming off.

Chapter 24 (Jackson)

From what I'm told, everyone has at least *one* night in their life where they get too drunk and end up regretting it.

I never had that night.

Until *last* night.

When I was a teenager, I was too busy taking care of Lilly...and when I was 21, I was too focused on MMA training.

For most of my adult life, I avoided getting drunk altogether. Between having an addict for a mother, along with hating the feeling of losing control, I saw no reason to drink to the point of being obliterated.

And this afternoon...I'm adding one more reason to that list.

It makes you act like a dumbass and say stupid fucking things.

Whoever said that a drunk mind speaks sober thoughts...was clearly still drunk off *their* ass.

Tyrone told me everything I said last night...not even bothering to mince words.

I never had any intention of seeing or talking to Alyssa again.

But...I do owe her an apology for how I behaved last night.

Which is why I'm currently making my way *back* to the bar that Alyssa now works at.

If I'm being honest, a small part of me was hoping she wasn't working now so I wouldn't have to go through with this.

But here she is, wiping down the surfaces of the almost empty bar. She's wearing a black t-shirt with the name '*Finnley's*' written across it in white lettering and every time she moves I see a tiny sliver of her toned abdomen.

She's also wearing pants now.

Because I'm a dick.

Shane nudges her and she looks up at me. Her expression tells me that I'm the last person she ever expected to see walk through that door. Shane leans down and whispers something in her ear. She shakes her head and he begrudgingly walks away...but not before giving me a dirty look.

Guess he doesn't like me all that much anymore.

I take a cautious seat at the bar and look around a little. It's not a big place, pretty small actually...but it does have a very laid back vibe going for it. It's definitely not one of those flashy bars that you hear about celebrities going to.

That's when I take another look at her hair.

It's a bit longer now and very dark, almost jet black.

I'm not going to tell her...because then I'd have to acknowledge the fact that I still, somewhere deep inside of me; have feelings for her...but I like it. *Really* like it.

I mean, she looked great as a blonde. But the dark hair?

It makes her hazel eyes pop even more and it complements her ivory skin.

She makes her way over to me after finishing up with the only other customer in the place.

I don't miss the way her smile falls and her full lips form a tight line. Or the way she lifts her chin right before she walks over to me like she's preparing herself, putting on a brave face.

And I definitely don't miss the look of sadness in her eyes before they turn intense. "Whiskey?" she asks.

I detect a hint of snarkiness in her tone and I'm surprised to find that I actually miss her sassy side. Now that she's standing right in front of me, there's a lot of things I find I miss about her.

But I have to force myself not to focus on that because if I do...I'll be reminded of the things I hate about her as well.

Like what she did to me...how she hurt me.

I fucking hate that she hurt me.

Almost as much as I hate that I'm never going to kiss those lips or see that dimple again.

I meet her gaze. "No...I think I had enough to drink for a lifetime last night." I give her a smile. "And if I want more, I can always wring out the clothes I wore last night, right?"

A ghost of a smile touches her lips. I can't tell if it's because she's recalling the memory, or smiling at my lame-ass attempt to break the ice.

A part of me is hoping for the former because a part of me is proud of her for standing up for herself and throwing the whiskey right in my face.

Alyssa's always been finicky when it comes to that sort of thing. Sometimes she defends herself...sometimes she runs.

But she's not running now, which is good. Because I really do owe her that apology. "I'm sorry, Alyssa. There's no excuse for the way I acted or the things I said last night, so I'm not going to waste your time giving you any. I was wrong. Plain and simple."

There, I said it. Now my guard can go back up and I can walk away from her.

She inhales deeply and bites her bottom lip. "I accept your apology. I know it wasn't easy to have to see me again."

She pauses, appearing to be debating the next words out of her mouth. "I wanted to look pretty," she whispers, looking down at the floor.

I have no idea what she's talking about. "Pardon?"

"The reason I was wearing a skirt," she says. "I, um. I wasn't looking for attention or anything. I wasn't trying to put it all out there like you said."

I open my mouth to apologize again, but she continues, "I haven't worn a skirt or a dress in over three months. I didn't want any reminders of the person I used to be...or the things I used to do. But last night, for whatever reason, I wanted to look pretty." She pauses and draws in a shaky breath. "I realized it was a bad idea when a group of guys kept asking me for the bottles of beer that we keep in the cooler instead of what was on tap. Shane had an emergency and it was too late to change since I was by myself and it was getting packed."

Her brow wrinkles. "I heard your voice and it made me happy. But, then I heard the things you were saying about me. And whether I liked it or not, I had to accept that there were people in that bar who might have shared your thoughts. Maybe even some who thought I was a whore."

She looks me in the eyes. "But I'm not a whore, Jackson." She gives me a small shrug. "I just wanted to tell you that."

There are moments in your life that you'll never forget. Some good, some bad, some life-changing.

However, I never thought it was possible to fall in love with a single moment.

Especially a moment with a person who's caused you so much pain.

Especially when the moment puts you in your place for being a monumental asshole.

But this moment right here?

I *love* this moment.

Despite what happened between us in the past, I *still* love this moment.

There's so much strength, growth and beauty in this single moment pouring out from her.... I almost don't want to ruin it by talking.

But I have to, if for nothing else then to say, "You're right, Alyssa. You're not a whore. You never were." I wipe the tear from her cheek with my thumb and stand up. "I was wrong for the things I said last night. And I'm sorry."

I give her one last smile before I walk away.

Then I put my armor up because I *have* to.

I'm stepping out the door when I hear Alyssa's footsteps behind me. "Jackson, wait. Please." I turn around and she grabs my hand and leads me to a small corner of the bar, giving us more privacy.

"I'm sorry," she says.

I open my mouth to stop her, because although the moment we just shared was incredible, it doesn't erase what happened.

And it doesn't change the fact that I'm still irate with her about it.

"Please, I'm begging you to just hear me out," she pleads. I go to turn away, but she tugs on my hand. "Ford was never my boyfriend. I was never with him!" she blurts.

"Although, there was a point in my life when I thought I wanted that," she amends.

I pull my hand away and begin walking again. "I shouldn't have lied to you about him being in my life," she calls out. "But if you knew about the things between us. The things that went on."

I stop mid-stride and turn around. "I don't *want* to know about those things, Alyssa. Keep them to yourself. Trust me, I really *don't* need to hear all about how you loved him and fucked him."

I didn't mean to raise my voice, but I didn't come here for this shit. I came here to apologize and go on with my life. Why can't she just let me?

"But...Jackson. You don't understand."

No, *she's* the one who doesn't understand. "Did you have sex with him?"

She steps back with a guilty expression her face. "Yes. But it was—"

"Did you love him?" I interrupt.

She worries her bottom lip between her teeth before answering, "Yes. But it wasn't—"

I cut her off. "Did you lie to me about the nature of your relationship with him?"

She looks down. "Yes."

I lean in close to her ear. "You see, Alyssa. It really doesn't matter what you think it *was* or what it *wasn't* between you and him. That's none of my business and quite frankly, I don't give a shit. The only thing that matters to me is that you loved him, you fucked him, you *lied* to me about him and all three of those things ended up hurting me."

I walk away from her this time with no hesitation.

The only thing that causes me to pause is when I hear her whisper, "I didn't have sex with him that night. I wouldn't do that to you." But I still force myself to walk right out that door.

Because I don't want to forgive her...I don't want to fall for her. But most of all?

I don't want to have to lie to her about who I really am...again.

Chapter 25 (Alyssa)

S hane nudges my hip as he leans in and whispers, "I thought you said he didn't want to talk to you?"

My eyes scan the bar before landing on Jackson. He's standing in the back playing a game of darts, by himself. Probably wishing it was my face that made up the board. I exhale sharply as I take in the way his gray henley shirt stretches across his broad chest and outlines the muscles of his arms. I force myself not to let my gaze drop to his faded blue jeans, which I have no doubt fit his ass and strong thighs perfectly.

My eyes betray me anyway...and dammit, I was right. They totally do.

"He doesn't." I shrug. "He still hasn't said a word to me."

And it's not like it's because the bar is so crowded or anything. We have a few customers, but there are plenty of seats at the bar.

Which he has yet to walk up to...because he still has yet to order a drink.

Which can only mean one thing. He's here to see me.

And he's been doing plenty of that because, over the last two hours, I've caught him stealing glances at me 32 different times now.

Make that 33.

Those gray eyes of his are burning into me yet again, heating my entire body with a single look.

The corners of his lips twitch. And that's when I know. He totally caught me checking him out just a second ago.

My mouth goes dry when his own eyes drop down, then slowly drag back up my body seductively, finally landing on my face. My brain fizzles. The 'this is your brain on drugs' warning, should also issue a 'this is your brain when Jackson Reid looks at you like *that*,' warning.

"He's been here four nights in a row," Shane says. "I don't understand why he won't speak to you. Want me to kick him out?"

"Absolutely not," I reply.

Jackson might not be talking to me, but the fact that he's been here night after night watching me tells me something.

He still has feelings for me. Feelings that some part of him can't ignore.

Either that, or he wants to see if Ford will show up here. Maybe, see if I was telling him the truth the other day.

I knew I hurt him...but even I wasn't aware of just *how* much I hurt him until his drunken outburst happened and our last conversation took place.

I wish he would just let me explain everything...I know it won't be easy for him to hear, but for some reason, he won't let that happen.

"You gonna be okay to close up by yourself?" Shane asks while casting a look in Jackson's direction.

I glance at the clock, I didn't realize that it was time for last call already. "I'll be fine."

We announce last call and Shane and the last few stragglers leave.

With the exception of Jackson...because I'm certainly not kicking him out. Plus, he'll have no choice but to speak to me if we're the only two people here.

I walk to the door and proceed to lock up and put the alarm on.

I'm wondering why Jackson doesn't leave when he sees me doing this, but he doesn't seem to care that I'm closing the bar. I turn off the lights above the bar but make sure to keep the one on in the back where he is.

I walk over to him, my heart beating like a jackhammer the whole time.

"I like your hair," he murmurs in my direction.

It's such a random statement, but I'll take it. I open my mouth to say thanks, but he gives me a hard look effectively silencing me.

His jaw ticks and he goes back to playing his game of darts. "I hate that you used me that night," he says before throwing a dart at the board.

He hits a bullseye.

"I'm sorry."

He pulls the dart out and takes a step back. "I hate that I watched the video."

He throws another dart, bullseye.

"I know what Lou-Lou did, Jackson. I read your text messages after I found my purse that night. I know you were disgusted with yourself for watching it and I *know* you're sorry."

I tuck a piece of hair behind my ear. "I've had a lot of time to think about it...and I never once asked or told you to not watch the video. You didn't do anything wrong."

He shakes his head. "No. I *was* wrong. *I* told you I wouldn't watch it and I did."

"I forgive you."

"You shouldn't," he says gruffly.

We stay silent after that. I decide to sit on top of the pool table and watch him throw more darts, hoping he'll continue talking to me.

"I hate that his hands were on you, touching your body. Touching what I thought was mine," he finally says.

He throws the dart so hard I think the board's going to come off the wall.

"I didn't want his hands on me."

He snorts. "It didn't look like it from where I was standing. And it certainly didn't sound like you didn't want his hands on you when you told him you loved him." I open my mouth to argue, but he cuts me off. "Don't," he warns. "Because I swear to god, if I hear you say his name again...I'll fucking lose it, Alyssa."

I stay silent. I want to shout everything about my relationship with Ford at the top of my lungs, but I don't want him to walk away from me. Especially now that he's *finally* talking to me.

I desperately want him to give me another chance...because this time around, it won't be tarnished by my past or lies. I feel like I can actually let myself fall in love with Jackson. I can love him the way he deserves to be loved.

He throws another dart, and another, and another. Until he's firing them all at the board like a round of bullets. "I hate that I still want you. Especially when I should know better."

My heart drops with those words.

Then he turns around and the look he gives me, makes the entire world stop. I hold my breath but he steals it from me when his lips land on mine.

The kiss is saturated with need, longing and desire. His tongue probes every inch of my mouth, his teeth crash against mine, and his hands touch my body like it's his possession.

My back hits the surface of the pool table and I moan when I feel Jackson move on top of me. I wrap my legs around his waist and grab onto his shoulders. "My apartment's upstairs," I pant.

Jackson doesn't waste another second, he picks me up and we make our way up the staircase.

He slams me against the door to my apartment and his teeth nip at my neck while his hands dig into my ass. "Hope you have another t-shirt," he growls.

I'm about to ask why, but I soon find out when he shreds the material right down the middle and buries himself between my breasts.

"I need these perfect fucking tits in my mouth," he rasps as he yanks down the cups of my bra and pulls my nipple into his mouth.

He lavishes it with his tongue, sucking on it like it's his favorite thing in the entire world.

I whimper when he pauses. But then he moves on to my other breast and pays it the same attention. Bolts of pleasure jolt me when he reaches down and pops open the button on my pants.

He's sliding them down when he stops abruptly and bangs on the wall beside my head. "I can't."

"Can't what?" I ask, still in my delirious fog. He puts me down. "I can't do this to you."

I don't understand how one second he's tearing my clothes off and the next he's walking away. He quickly backs up. "I need to leave."

"Why? I thought...I thought that we were—" I pause because I realize that maybe I misconstrued the situation entirely and this wasn't what I hoped it was after all.

"I thought we were trying again," I say.

He gives me the coldest look I've ever seen. "Well, you thought wrong. I'll stay out of your life for good from now on. I promise."

What the hell is going on with him? None of this makes any sense.

He heads for the exit stairs but I stop him. "No. I don't want you out of my life. I want *you*, Jackson. Talk to me, don't run away."

"Yeah, because you know all about that. Don't you?" he scoffs.

I want to punch him for being so callous right now. With the exception of his drunken episode. He's never been this cruel to me without reason. "Yeah I do. So, take it from me when I tell you that it will only make things worse."

He begins walking down the stairs and I'm right behind him. "I know you. Something is—" I start to say before he cuts me off.

"You don't know me, Alyssa. Trust me."

And with those words he walks away.

Chapter 26 (Jackson)

"You straight?" Ricardo asks.

I look at myself in the mirror. "As a motherfucking arrow."

"Big fight tonight."

"It's always a big fight."

I know he's on edge because we just got word there was a last-minute change regarding my opponent...but unlike Ricardo, I'm not worried.

Ricardo meets my stare. "The guy fights dirty and he's almost three times your size. He's not a boxer or an MMA fighter. He's a pure street fighter, which means he's a wild card. I don't know how much fucked up shit you have stored in that reserve of yours, but as your coach...I need you to tap in and empty it."

His gaze shifts from one of concern to nervousness. "And as your friend, I'm telling you...I need you to give it everything you got. DeLuca's got a lot of money riding on this tonight."

"He always does."

"Not like this, Jackson," he says before he walks away.

I close my eyes and force myself not to think about Alyssa.

I almost faltered, but I wasn't going to make the same mistake twice.

It's been a week since I pushed her away on purpose.

I was harsh, but I don't regret it one bit.

I knew the best way to get her to stay away for good, was to make her believe that for a fraction of a second we had a chance...then dash all her hopes.

My blood burns for her and I want her every second, of every day. But, you have to be cruel to be kind...and there's nothing kinder than saving her from who I really am.

And of course, the devil himself, DeLuca.

On second thought, maybe it's best that I use the fact that I can't have her as my fuel tonight...because there sure as hell is nothing and no one that I want more than *her*.

I open my eyes, suck in a breath and give myself one last look in the mirror.

Then I punch it, watch it shatter and walk out to the cage.

I turn into the machine.

Chapter 27 (Alyssa)

"Y ou putting money on any of the fighters tonight, little lady?"
I look up at the big man and hand him my wages for the
past week. "Five-hundred on Jackson Reid."

"You mean Jack the Ripper?"

"Yeah."

"Good pick, he doesn't lose. Go on in."

I smirk. "I know."

I gave Jackson a week. A week to come and find me, a week to
make it right. A week to talk to me about whatever it is that's going
on with him.

His time is up.

I didn't want to go back on my promise to him, but there was no
other way I could track him down. He pulled a complete Houdini
act, so I'm pulling one of my own. I know he won't be happy when
he finds out I came here, but if I have to provoke him just so I can
get some type of response from him, well, then so be it.

I'm not giving up on him and I'm not letting him run away
from me.

He's seen all my demons...now it's time to see his.

The large room is full and the crowd is already going crazy by the time I make my way in.

I look up at the steel cage and fight back a shiver. It's monstrous, barbaric and to be honest, it intimidates me a little bit. There's something so unsettling about it. I can understand why Momma doesn't like watching the fights.

Out of the corner of my eye, I spot Tyrone in the crowd. I turn away and flip the hood on my jacket up.

I have every intention of Jackson finding out I'm here, but not until *after* the fight. I already know that he looks to Tyrone before he starts and he'll spot me right away if I walk up to him.

Besides, there's always the chance that Tyrone would kick me out because Jackson told him to.

I study Tyrone's profile for a bit and I can immediately tell that something is wrong. He looks unsettled and he's biting his finger-nails while looking up to the sky.

I'm a little worried myself after seeing that now. I mean, what could be so different about *this* particular fight than any other fight?

The crowd's cheering picks up and I focus my attention back on the cage. This time, I see Jackson walking out in his green trunks. I take a moment to admire his 8 pack abs, muscular arms, and the rest of his beautifully toned physique.

I also notice his demeanor. He looks *completely* in the zone. His expression is controlled, his posture resembles that of a brick wall, and well, he looks a little frightening.

Actually, make that a lot frightening. It reminds me of the time he fought Dean in the bathroom.

I can barely even hear the announcer right now because all I hear is the crowd chanting, "Ripper! Ripper!" I'd say the crowd is about 90% male...so the female voices are much easier to pick up on.

I grit my teeth when some woman yells, "You're so hot. I want to have your babies." Followed by another woman screaming, "I'll let you do anything you want to me. You can stick it anywhere!"

On second thought, maybe it's best that I take a page out of Jackson's book and tune out the crowd.

They finally announce Jackson's name and I can't help but let out a few cheers of my own. I know he won't be able to hear me over the frantic cheering that's going on right now.

Like the flip of a switch, the general mood around the room shifts just then and I don't know what to make of it.

But then I see someone else walk out on stage.

My jaw drops and my stomach knots up.

There's no way Jackson's about to fight *this* massive beast.

He looks like some kind of a science experiment gone horrifically wrong. His muscles are way too big to be natural, his veins are bulging and his head looks too small for his massive body. This guy is a tank...he probably eats people *my* size for freaking breakfast.

They announce his opponents stats and I'm sure I must be hearing things, but when I take another look...I know I'm not.

How the hell is Jackson going to fight and *win* against a guy who's 6'7 and 388lbs?

Jackson's 6'3 and 235lbs. This is a completely uneven match.

I know this is an underground fight club and all...but this guy could fucking kill him.

No wonder Tyrone looks so nervous.

Ricardo taps Jackson on the shoulder and says something in his ear.

Jackson then looks out to the crowd to find Tyrone. Tyrone doesn't give him his usual happy musings, instead, he taps the spot over his heart.

Jackson's eyes flash as he pats the tattoo over his own heart where Lilly's name resides and I realize that Tyrone's gesture was much more significant than I thought.

I watch as Lou-Lou walks up with her cue cards, wearing the green flashy costume that I myself once wore, and even *she* looks uncomfortable about what's about to go down.

I don't even have the heart to mentally curse her out when she gives Jackson a small smile and a thumbs up sign before stepping down.

The bell dings and Jackson's off to a good start.

I figured he'd start swinging like a bat out of hell, just like in the bathroom...but he's sidestepping and dodging the beasts punches like a pro.

No wonder he almost never gets hit. Despite his muscular build and the fact that he's in the middle of an underground cage fight, he looks so graceful and poised. He's a natural up there, like his body was made to do this.

He looks so comfortable in his habitat it's amazing to be able to watch him.

Then the big brute he's up against grunts and lunges at Jackson out of nowhere. I'm not sure if Jackson even saw it because it happened so fast.

I hold my breath when the guy punches him straight in the kidney.

The crowd lets out a collective big gasp and even some 'Oh, shit's.'

Jackson stands tall and I feel my entire body relax.

Until the big ogre lunges at him again and his fist connects with Jackson's jaw.

Jackson rebounds, though and gets him with a few quick jabs and a sharp kick. The guy stumbles and teeters, appearing seconds away from keeling over.

I channel my inner *Adrian* and before I can stop myself, I shout, "That's right, baby. The bigger they are the harder they fall."

Some guy next to me apparently agrees with my statement and lets out an,"Oh, yeah! Let him have it, Ripper!"

I'm smiling and laughing...until the beast lunges again and takes another swing at him. He connects with Jackson's face again and blood sprays.

Jackson staggers back and the beast uses the opportunity to send a kick to his ribs.

There are murmurings in the crowd then...things like, "He's

never been hit more than twice in the cage, this makes four times in a row now." And, "This is the longest a fight has ever lasted while he's in the cage."

I can't help but look at Tyrone. His palms are drawn together and he's silently whispering something to himself.

Then I realize what he's doing. He's praying for him.

My eyes become glassy and I issue a silent prayer of my own. I'm so worked up I have to take off my jacket and bounce on the balls of my feet to get rid of some of this anxiety.

The guy's about to strike again...but Jackson dodges it and this time, he gives him a menacing smile.

I start screaming along with the crowd when Jackson loses his damn mind and starts unleashing punches and kicks so quick, that if I blink I'm sure I'll miss a few.

Everything is perfect...until the big beast rears his ugly head and deals a hard karate chop to Jackson's neck and headbutts him at the same time. The move is so savage and so ruthless the crowd becomes angry and starts calling for the match to be paused.

Especially now that Jackson's body has gone limp.

My. Heart. Stops.

I realize two things at that moment. One—I swear, I'll go toe to toe with this beast myself if he ever lays another hand on him. And two—that I'm completely in love with Jackson.

I'm soon pushing people out of the way and running toward the cage screaming Jackson's name so loud I think my vocal cords have ruptured.

Tears and screams are ripping right out of me...it feels so similar to the moment I lost my father that it only causes me to scream even harder. "Please, No!"

I feel a pair of strong arms haul me back at the same time Jackson gets back up.

His eyes connect with mine and I'm so relieved I'm about ready to declare my eternal love for him in some massive poetic moment.

Then his eyes narrow and he gives me a look that's so deadly, I immediately know I've made a huge mistake by coming here.

Jackson's not just ticked off or pissed that I'm here. He looks like he wants to annihilate *me* and rip me to actual shreds.

I knew he wouldn't like it. I took that gamble...but I never knew he would get *this* mad about it.

"Jackson's fine, Alyssa. He was just pretending to be down since his opponent was playing dirty," Tyrone whispers in my ear.

I look up and watch Jackson proceed to pummel the giant beast into a bloody pulp, that same look he gave me, now turned on him.

Jackson wins the fight in no time and is declared the victor.

When he scans back over the crowd, his eyes fall on me and he gives me the same death stare as before. Only this time he mouths a word that literally causes me to shake. "Run."

Chills creep up my spine and I hightail it the fuck out of there.

I run back to the bar and try to calm myself down. I'm almost positive that Jackson wouldn't actually hurt me...or at least, I *was* before tonight.

Because I need something to distract myself, I offer to close the bar for Shane who happily takes me up on it.

That's when it hits me...I never collected my winnings. *Dammit.*

I'm just going to have to cut my losses, though because I don't even want to know what Jackson would do to me if I went back there right now...or ever for that matter.

After a few hours, I'm calmer than I was and I proceed to close up the bar.

I'm shutting the door when a large black boot lodges itself in the door frame, preventing me from shutting it all the way.

I look up and stifle a scream when I see a large figure standing before me dressed in a black hoodie and jeans. Their hood is pulled up and since it's dark out, I can't make out their face.

They tilt their face slightly and the light from the streetlight catches illuminating their features.

Jackson's normally gray eyes are the darkest I've ever seen them.

He pushes the door open and I immediately start to back away because I can honestly say, he's scaring the shit out of me.

He doesn't say a word to me, he just slams the door shut behind him and starts dead bolting it. Then he grabs my arm and nudges me toward the alarm.

With shaky fingers, I reach up and set it. I briefly contemplate pressing the panic button and informing the alarm company about a break in because I just don't know what he's playing at or what his deal is right now.

He seems to sense my thoughts because he leans down and whispers, "Go ahead. I dare you," in my ear.

I take a few steps back wishing that I hadn't already turned all the lights in the bar off.

I steel myself and lift my chin. His little game has gone on long enough as far as I'm concerned. "Why are you here, Jackson?"

He takes a step forward and I take a step back. His large frame is looming over me and I've never felt smaller in my whole entire life.

He gives me a smile that reminds me of a crazed killer, albeit a very hot one. "Why am *I* here?" he repeats. "Are you saying that I'm not allowed to be here?"

I fold my arms across my chest and glare at him. "I..um. Y-yeah."

Good job Alyssa, your intimidation level is equivalent to that of a puppy.

Jackson rubs his jaw. "Good thing I don't give a fuck then, huh?"

I open my mouth to say something, but he cuts me off by shouting, "Just like *you* didn't give a fuck when you went down to the fight club tonight, and I specifically told you not to *ever* go there."

He takes another step forward. "You promised me that you wouldn't."

"I'm s-sorry," I stutter. "Look, you're really starting to scare me, Jackson."

He smirks, takes another step forward and removes his belt,

which both terrifies and excites me. "I thought you liked danger, Alyssa? You sure put yourself in harms way tonight."

I shake my head. "No one attacked me this time."

"This time," he mocks before his expression turns serious. "Do you remember what I told you to do tonight?"

"Well, yeah but you can't actually be serious—" I start to say until the crack of his belt against the wooden table causes me to jump.

"Oh, I'm *very* serious. As serious as *you* were when you walked into that club tonight. You have 30 seconds," he sneers.

I don't know whether to laugh or cry at this point. Where exactly does he expect me to run to? Especially when he dead bolted the doors?

When I still haven't moved, his eyes narrow. "15 seconds. I suggest you do what I told you to now, Alyssa. You're only making it harder on yourself."

Since it would take me twice as long to run up the stairs to my apartment, I take off in the direction of the bathrooms.

I fly through the swinging doors and fight to catch my breath. I debate hiding in one of the stalls, but mere seconds later Jackson enters the bathroom.

I shouldn't feel so turned on over this little cat and mouse game he started but I am.

I'm nervous too because he's never acted like *this* with me before.

He begins walking toward me and I notice that he's stripped off his hoodie. I also see the few bruises on his face from the fight. I instinctively reach up to touch his face, but he bats away my hand and grips my ponytail while backing me into the stall door.

"What are you doing, Jackson?"

He pulls my hair tighter. "Trying to figure out the proper way to punish you so you don't pull this shit again."

"Look, I'm sorry, okay? I've learned my lesson."

He presses me against the stall. "Not okay. You make me a promise you fucking keep it, understand me?"

"I won't show up at the club again. I promise," I say. My vision gets blurry and I want to kick myself for giving into my emotions right now. But I know there's no point in fighting them.

I draw in a shaky breath. "Believe me, there's nothing you could do to me that would ever be worse than thinking you were seriously hurt in that cage. It was the second worst experience of my entire life." I close my eyes. "So go ahead, Jackson. Do *your* worst. I can take it."

His mouth smashes against mine with so much force I'm certain my lips will be bruised, but I don't care. It's the most violent kiss I've ever had and the passion flowing through us both right now is enough to bring me to my knees. I feel myself drop, but one of Jackson's hands latches onto my hip while the other tugs on my ponytail so hard I yelp.

And when I do, he nips my lower lip hard enough that I taste a hint of copper. He groans and sucks my bottom lip into his mouth until I'm lightheaded and fighting for air. Before I know it, he's dragging me until we're stopped in front of the mirrors and he's directly in back of me.

He lifts my shirt up and his fingers trail down my abdomen before he flicks open the button on my jeans.

I'm about to close my eyes, but he shakes his head and whispers, "Watch," deep and low in my ear. His hand moves inside my jeans, brushing over the damp fabric of my panties.

The sight of his large hand inside my pants as he's stroking me is enough to make me blush. It's such an erotic sight and I'm so wound up I feel like a slingshot that's about to launch into outer space. That feeling only grows when he pushes my jeans down lower, along with my panties, leaving me completely exposed to him.

He positions one of his legs between both of mine until I'm pressed flush against his chest and I can feel the strong effect I'm having on him through his jeans.

Embarrassment courses through me when he slips one of his

fingers inside me and we both hear just how wet I am. He curses under his breath as he begins slowly moving deep inside me.

I've never been more turned on in my entire life, but I really need him to know something before we take this any further.

"I didn't sleep with Ford that night. I kicked him out of my life and I haven't seen him since. I only want you."

The sting from his other hand slapping my ass causes me to jump.

"Don't ever and I mean, *ever* utter another man's name while my fingers are inside you."

"I'm sorry," I say frantically. "I just wanted you to know that Ford—" I'm cut off by another sharp *whack* across my ass. This time, it sends a jolt of pleasure up my spine.

"What did I say?" Jackson warns, his voice harsh and rough.

He removes his finger before entering me again, this time adding another finger and stroking me even deeper.

"You want me?" he says, his breath tickling my ear. "Well, you fucking have me. But it comes with contingencies, now."

I open my mouth to find out what he means but he leans down and bites my neck. "I've tried going easy on you. I treated you like you were fragile before. I thought that's what you needed. But not this time, Alyssa. I'm not gonna treat you like you're some sad, broken, and damaged damsel...because you're not, are you?"

"No—" I start to say but it's cut off by my moan when he flicks my clit. "Glad we reached an understanding. Now start riding my fingers until you come like a good girl."

His words light me on fire and I reach up and snake my arm around his neck as I begin doing what he told me to.

But then my pleasure crumbles because although I've been working on myself and changing for the better, there's still some things that haven't completely gone away.

That dark and destructive place inside me taunts me and I feel shame wash over me because I know I won't be able to do what Jackson wants. No matter how much I want to, that place inside me associates my own sexual pleasure as something bad.

I stop responding to his touch. "I won't be able to come, Jackson. I'm sorry." Before he can interrupt me, I continue, "I've never been able to before. It's not a line and I'm not saying it to issue you a challenge. I'm just trying to be honest. So, you can stop and I'll take care of you. I *want* to take care of you. I like being able to turn you on, it makes me feel good. I just don't want you to be disappointed with me for not being able to come and I don't want to fake it with you."

To my surprise, Jackson doesn't stop. He continues fingering me, alternating between shallow and deep strokes. He places a gentle kiss on my temple. "You let *me* worry about your pleasure, Alyssa."

I'm about to protest, but his thumb swirls around my clit and I swear, I see stars. "Give it to me," he demands as his finger plunges into my slickness. "Give me every single ounce of pain you have when you go to that place of yours and trust me enough to take it all away and make it better."

"Okay, I'll try," I whisper.

"Do you like the way my fingers feel inside you? The way I'm stroking your pretty pussy?" he asks.

I blush and shiver at his dirty words. "I do," I respond honestly.

He pinches my clit and I moan. "I know you do, baby. You know how I know?" He pushes his erection into my behind. "Because your juices are dripping down my hand, making me harder than a fucking rock right now."

I mewl and begin moving my hips in time with his touch. He circles my clit again before he submerges his fingers inside me. "Let your pussy grip my fingers, baby. Don't fight it. Just breathe and focus on the way I'm touching you and exploring this tight pussy of yours."

"Oh god, Jackson. Your mouth. It's so dirty."

He licks the shell of my ear. "Trust me, you have no idea how dirty my mouth can get. Just you fucking wait. I'll be tasting every part of you."

I gasp and my hips buck against his erection when the first ripple hits me. I almost want to tell him to stop, because it's too much, but then the second wave happens. It causes such an intense rush of absolute pleasure, I'm screaming my own dirty words and jerking against him.

Jackson holds me while I fall apart in his arms, my movements finally coming to a slow stop as I fall into his chest.

I look up as he brings his fingers to his mouth before sucking on them and closing his eyes.

I'm still catching my breath, trying to gather my bearings when Jackson nudges me forward until I'm bent over the sink. "Spread your legs and hold onto the edges of the sink," he tells me.

I do as he says without protest. I'm expecting him to start fucking me, but he doesn't. He gets down on his knees instead.

Seeing as I just came not even moments ago, I'm confused. "What are you doing?"

He pulls my jeans down all the way and lifts my leg. "That first orgasm was for you. This one's for me," he informs me.

Then faster than I can form my next thought, his mouth is covering my pussy. There are no dainty or teasing little licks, he's eating me like I'm a delicacy that he intends to savor every drop of.

"I was wrong," he rasps while lapping at me. I'm about to ask what he means, but then he says, "You taste even better than you smell."

White blinding light hits me when he sucks my clit into his mouth and I can't help but scream out his name. That only makes him ravish me more with his skillful tongue until I know I'm about to start convulsing again.

If I thought my first orgasm was intense, it has nothing on this one. I'm in a whole other world, so far off the beaten path that all I feel is Jackson. He's permeating every sense of mine. I twitch so hard Jackson has to hold my hips so I don't fall and I scream his name like it's the last word I'll ever say in this lifetime.

All my feelings for him flood through me at that moment, I think about how I felt just hours ago when I saw him in that cage. When I thought I might lose him forever. I need him to know how I feel, I need him to know how much he means to me. "I love you, Jackson," I whisper.

He lifts his head, wipes his chin and stands up. The look on his face is like nothing I've ever seen before and I'm not sure what it means.

My heart is beating so hard, I feel like I'm about to faint, but I know I need to do this.

One of the things I will always remember the most about my father was how much he loved me. He gave me the gift of unconditional love for 10 years, and although I lost my way after he died and it got buried with my shame over the sex tape, and my toxic relationship with Ford, I remember now how special it was to know and feel that.

I look him in the eyes this time. "I love you, Jackson," I repeat.

He just stares at me, not saying a word. I didn't expect him to say it back, but some kind of response would be nice.

I put myself in his place and realize that maybe I've just blindsided him with this weighty statement since it did come out of nowhere. I also probably need to be a little bit more specific with how I feel and what I want.

I move toward him. "I want you, Jackson. I want to try again. I know we've both made some mistakes. I know we crashed and burned right after take off the last time around. But, I also know...there's no one in the world that I want more than you. I honestly don't think there ever will be. No one has made me feel the way you make me feel."

His closes his eyes and his thumb brushes over my bottom lip. "Alyssa," he whispers.

I give his thumb a small kiss. "I'll go all in and give you every single part of me. I'll never, ever lie to you again or break a promise...and I swear, I will do my damnedest not to hurt you." My voice begins cracking, but I continue, "I'll fight for you with every single breath I take, Jackson. And if you're too scared to take the risk and roll the dice with me...don't be...because I'll hold your hand for the rest of my life."

His face contorts in pain so I reach for his hand, hoping to prove it to him, but he rips it away. "No," he says, his voice gravelly. "Get over me and find someone else. Someone that's not me. Someone who can give all of that back to you because I can't."

The impact of his words is like pouring battery acid on a wound. It's tearing me apart, burning me and leaving me scarred. I don't know why he's hurting me like this or saying these things, but my heart pulls when I see the emotion on his face.

He heads for the door and I follow him. "Don't chase me, Alyssa," he shouts. "Let me leave...because if I don't leave right now —I'll *never* be able to stop myself from doing the right thing when it comes to you. And I *have* to do that. Please, just let me give you up."

I try to open my mouth, but the tears are lodged in my throat, clogging my voice. I don't understand any of this.

He pauses right before he leaves. "I'm not who you think I am. But for the very *first* time...I *wish* I was." His voice cracks with his last statement and he slams the door.

Chapter 28 (Jackson)

I'm running through the city streets like a madman and screaming Lilly's name...wishing everything was different.

I never once regretted killing him.

I never once regretted taking his life...never had a single ounce of remorse for being a murderer.

I never thought I would.

I never had a reason to.

My soul feels like it's split right down the middle.

Half of it belongs to Lilly- I know that even in the after-life...we're tied together and our bond will never be broken.

The other half of my soul belongs to Alyssa.

The rest of me is stuck in turmoil because I don't know how to process this new feeling and I don't think I can handle what it must mean. Because if it means, what I think it means...I don't think I can live with myself.

I reach my apartment...at least, I think I do. I'm a complete mess. I don't know how I'm functioning or taking in air.

I must be worse off than I thought because when Lou-Lou finds me on the floor in the lobby. She freaks the fuck out, picks up her phone and dials Tyrone. "I don't know, Tyrone. He just keeps screaming for Lilly. Get your ass down here!" she yells into the phone.

Less than a minute later Tyrone's helping me up the steps. He tells me that it's going to be okay. He also mumbles something about him calling Momma and her taking the next flight out here.

I'm too far gone to be embarrassed by being such a wuss at this point.

He sits me down on the couch and pats my back. "Jackson, please talk to me. I know you hate talking. But right now you're really scaring the fucking shit out of me."

I feel some wet shit on my face and I can't stop myself from screaming Lilly's name again.

I keep imagining what it would be like if she was still here now....*living*. She would be gearing up for graduation, probably valedictorian because she was so fucking smart...and I would be so proud of her. I would tell her how proud of her I was.

I'd sneak into her first courtroom case and cheer for her in the background. I'd probably be fighting the urge to punch the judge if he ever dared to rule against her. But, I'd make her hot chocolate with cinnamon and whipped cream if she lost the case.

I close my eyes...the wet stuff on my face is getting worse, and my thoughts are firing off like a cannon.

Maybe, she'd be an aunt now. I always wanted to have a family. My kids would adore her...I know they would. She would be the best aunt in the entire world.

Lilly would have liked Alyssa. She would have been concerned at first, like the good sister she was; but I know she ultimately would have ended up loving her, just like I do.

The reality slams into me like a blazing wildfire.

I'll never have any of that now. And neither will she.

There's no graduation, no first courtroom case, no hot chocolate, no family, and no Alyssa.

Because Lilly's tiny body is dead on the floor beside the couch. Her pink nails have blood caked under them...because she fought like hell. Just like her big brother would have wanted her to.

But she lost her fight. Because I didn't protect her like a big brother should.

But I got vengeance for her.

I murdered that son-of-a-bitch for killing my baby sister.

So, how could I have a moment of regret?

I wipe the tears off my face and look at Tyrone. "If I love Alyssa...it will mean that I love Lilly less. It will mean that I accept Lilly's death and that in the end, I'm okay with what happened to her because I had a moment of regret for murdering Mike when Alyssa told me she loved me."

He looks confused but I continue, "So you see, I can't love Alyssa because I can't *not* love Lilly. If I love Alyssa, then I have to regret both loving Lilly in the first place because I have to be fine with her death and regret killing him."

Tyrone shakes his head. "I'm not following you. Did you tell Alyssa the truth about everything?"

I lean forward and put my head in my hands. "No. But let's just say that I'm certain she'll want nothing to do with me if she ever finds out."

He scowls. "You don't know that, Jackson. There are extenuating circumstances and you know it. Again, I think you're not giving her the benefit of the doubt here and just assuming——"

"Her father was murdered. I can't go into any more detail about it because it's not my place, but her father was murdered when she was a kid. Let's just say that she has a very set in stone outlook when it comes to murder in general. Trust me."

He stands up and runs a hand along his jaw. "It's not always black and white or cut and dry." I open my mouth to tell him that for *her* it is, but he cuts me off. "And I think that if you told her, not only would she see that...but you would as well." He holds up a finger. "However, we have a few more things to work out before we come back to that. Starting with you and your feelings. First, I do think you need to accept Lilly's death. It doesn't mean that you loved her any less and it sure as heck doesn't make you a bad brother for accepting it. It simply means that you are aware that her death happened, that you processed it." He sighs. "And you need to process it, Jackson...because she's *not* coming back. No matter how many people you beat up in that cage or how much you blame yourself—it will never bring her back. Her life is over...but yours doesn't have to be. She wouldn't want that...she would want you to go on living. You know I'm right, brother."

I nod my head softly and he continues, "Which brings me to Alyssa. Now, you said before that you can't love her because you felt this moment of regret about killing him."

"Yeah. I've never had that feeling before. I don't know how to explain it. But, I know I don't regret getting vengeance for Lilly. So I don't understand how I had this moment of regret because—" I pause because my heads going around in circles right now and I don't know how to sort out my thoughts.

Tyrone looks at me. "It's because Alyssa loves you...*but* you don't think that she can because, in *your* eyes, she doesn't know who you really are. And because you love *her* and you hate the thought of losing her you wish that you were different. You wish that you were who she thinks you are...correct?"

I think about this for a moment before replying, "Yeah, sounds about right."

He smiles. "Well, you're wrong."

Now I'm completely confused. "But you just said—"

He cuts me off. "I said that in *your* eyes she doesn't know who you really are."

"I don't know where you're going with this, Tyrone."

"You don't have regret about killing Mike and getting vengeance. You regret who you *think* you are. Your own self-identity is tied to being a murderer and all that it entails."

He looks me in the eyes. "You're a good person, Jackson. You're the most loyal person I've ever met. You will fight to the end of this earth and back again for those you love. There's not a thing you won't do for us. Momma's right when she says that you have an incredible heart that's incomparable to others because you lead with it. Your heart is who you are and it's one hell of a good heart. And you know what that means? It means that Alyssa already knows who you are on the inside. You shouldn't wish to be anyone else because it's your heart and you who she loves."

"But I'm a murderer."

"And that brings me to the next point we need to sort out in that head of yours. Remember what I said about it not always being so black and white or cut and dry?"

I nod my head again.

He takes a deep breath. "Would you call a soldier a bad person? Would you think of them as a murderer or a killer?"

"Absolutely not. They're heroes who are defending and protecting others."

He nods. "You're right. They are and they do."

"You've lost me again, Tyrone. Because if you're insinuating that I'm some sort of hero...you're wrong. Heroes *save* people. So, what is it that you're saying?"

"What I'm saying is that it's not always mutually exclusive. There are exceptions to every good thing and every bad thing. Think about it...if a person donates a shit-load of money to a charity, we automatically assume that it makes them a good person." He pauses. "But, if you find out that they only donated to the charity to claim it on their taxes and not from the goodness of their heart. That changes your perception about them a little, huh?"

"Yeah."

"Now, what if a person murders someone? We automatically assume that it makes them a bad person. But, what if you found out that this killer had walked in to find their little sister whom he loved more than life itself brutally murdered?" He draws in a breath. "And in the *very* same moment, his best friend whom he *trusted*, walked out and admitted to killing his baby sister. Which in turn, caused him to black out in a rage that ended in murder. Wouldn't that change your perception about this killer?"

"Yeah."

He gives me a hug. "Let Alyssa decide for herself what her

perception of you is. Let her show you that she knows exactly who it is she's giving her heart to. Have some faith and trust in the girl."

I hug him back. "Thanks, Tyrone. I really don't know how I would have figured that all out by myself. I owe you."

"So, you're going to tell her?"

"No. I'm gonna do more than that."

He raises an eyebrow. "How?"

"You still have that camcorder?"

His stares at me wide-eyed. "You sure about this, man? I mean, there's putting your trust in someone and then there's putting your *trust* in someone. She could do anything with that confession, Jackson. In the wrong hands, you could end up right back in jail. And if that happens, dropping the soap will be the least of your worries, brother. DeLuca will have you killed in jail for outing him about staging the cover up."

"You said to have some faith and trust in her, right?"

An hour later I find myself making my way to Alyssa's apartment.

I'm choosing to tell her about what happened on video because, in some way, I'm trying to show her just how much I love her.

I know that the sex tape ruined her life. It left her vulnerable, naked, exposed and judged for the whole entire world to see.

Although this is a different circumstance entirely, this video very much leaves me vulnerable, naked, exposed and open to her judgment.

There's no way to match her love and give her every part of me if she doesn't know my past and what I've done.

Alyssa's video never changed my opinion about her. It only made me fall for her more.

I guess in some way, I'm hoping that she feels the same about me after she watches mine.

I knock on her door with an eerie feeling in the pit of my stomach. On one hand, I'm more nervous than I've ever been in my life. On the other hand, it feels like a giant weight is being lifted off my shoulders.

She opens the door after the second knock and looks up at me.

I shove the disk in her hand. "I need you to watch this. It's everything important you need to know about me."

She opens her mouth to say something, but I guess the look I give her stops her. Instead, she gives me a small nod before closing the door.

I hear her rummaging around briefly on the other side of the door.

Then I hear the words that will change everything.

"My name is Jackson Reid. There are two things you need to know about me. The first—is that I'm in love with Alyssa Tanner. The second—is that I'm a murderer."

With my heart completely in her hands, I walk away.

Chapter 29 (Alyssa)

"Now you know, Alyssa. That's my story. He killed Lilly and I don't regret avenging her death. But I do regret not telling you sooner."

I watch as Jackson moves closer to the screen before pausing. "And just in case I never get the chance to say it again. I love you," he says before the camera shuts off.

I wipe my eyes and stand up.

Then I run.

Only this time...I'm not running from anything.

I running toward something.

I'm running as fast as I can to the man I love.

The man that I *still* love. Maybe even more now.

It's almost 4 in the morning and the rain is falling hard outside, It's coming down in buckets, causing me to almost slip on the concrete a few times, but I don't care.

By the time I reach Jackson's apartment, I'm a shivering wet mess. I'm also pretty sure my lips are blue and I'm going to catch pneumonia, but I still don't care.

Tyrone opens the door and I expect him to be surprised that I'm here but he's not. He just gives me a knowing smile and tells me that Jackson is in his room.

He then offers me a blanket but I decline. Instead, I ask him if he would mind if I rummaged around the kitchen for a bit.

He smiles even wider...until I inform him I'm not cooking him anything.

I don't even knock on Jackson's door, I just walk right in.

He's sitting up against the headboard of his bed, he's shirtless, his eyes are closed and the acoustic version of *Shinedown's, Simple Man* is playing on repeat in the background.

I clear my throat and he startles. When he sees me his eyes flicker and his breathing picks up.

He takes in my appearance and opens his mouth to say something, but I put my finger to my lips and hand him what's in my hand.

He looks down at the cup of hot chocolate containing both cinnamon and whipped cream and his breathing becomes shaky.

His eyes are glassy when he looks back up at me and his hand reaches out for mine.

I take his hand and position myself on top him with both my legs on either side of his. I wrap my arms around him tighter than I ever have and my head falls against his chest. Then I plant a kiss over Lilly's name.

We stay like that for a while, neither of us saying a word, which is fine because this moment is too profound to ruin it with words.

He's rubbing slow circles over my back and it feels amazing, but I have to fight off another chill due to my drenched clothes.

Jackson notices this and hauls me upright so that I'm facing him. He motions for me to raise my arms and I do. He starts lifting my shirt, and since I ran out of my apartment wearing nothing but pajamas I'm not wearing a bra. He quickly balls my wet shirt in his hand and throws it across the room causing it to land with a wet thud.

I feel the flush in my cheeks due to being topless in front of him, but it quickly turns to arousal when Jackson leans down and flicks his tongue over my nipple. He does the same to my other nipple and I feel the warmth that he's providing me spread throughout my body.

He lets out a low groan as he begins massaging and kneading my breasts and I can't help myself from sighing his name.

Not before long, my pants are joining my t-shirt on the floor and I'm completely naked before him.

His eyes blaze as he scans over my body and pulls me back to him.

I straddle him and his hands dig into my lower back as he plants gentle kisses along my chest leading up to my neck and finally my lips.

I feel his erection through the flannel of his pants and I grind against it shamelessly, wanting more than anything to feel him inside me.

He runs his fingertips along my hips and blows his breath across my nipples, the sensations causing goosebumps to break out over my skin.

His mouth finds the pulse point on my neck and he drags his tongue along it as his finger dips inside me. The sound of his fingers plunging into my wetness fill the room, but I'm too turned on to feel self-conscious at this point.

I'm on the verge of having an orgasm when Jackson pauses and pulls his pants down. He holds the base of his erection and slips his length between my folds, but doesn't enter me. I look down and lick my lips when I see that my slickness is coating his cock, making it glisten.

He gives me a smirk before he circles the barbell of his piercing directly over my clit causing me to come harder and faster than I ever knew was possible.

He peppers my neck with kisses as the last of my climax trickles out of me and onto him. I'm desperate to have him inside me at this point and I know he feels the same because he reaches into the nightstand drawer and gets out a condom.

He looks at the condom then back to me and I nod my head, letting him know that I want this.

I'm waiting for him to put it on, but instead, he cradles my face in his hands and gives me a look that steals my breath. His eyes penetrate me and I can feel how much he loves me with a single glance.

He puts the condom on and pulls me in for another long and sultry kiss. I think he's going to enter me and start fucking me, but he doesn't.

Instead, he grips my hips and gently lifts me before slowly setting me down on top of his erection. I feel him enter me inch by inch gradually—purposely taking his time to make sure I'm not in any discomfort.

Once he's filled me up to the hilt, I begin bouncing on top of him rapidly, wanting to make it good for him. He groans my name and curses under his breath. Then his hands press down on my thighs causing me to pause my movements while he pulls me in for another slow kiss.

In a single movement, he flips us so that he's the one on top before he begins thrusting inside me. His thrusts are both deep and gentle rendering me breathless. He looks at me as he reaches down and links our fingers together before bringing them above my head.

This concept of going slow and sweet is so new and foreign to me. I'm far from a virgin, but I've never had sex like *this* before. I've never had anyone take their time and worship me or my body. It makes me feel loved and cherished in a way I never knew was possible.

Jackson brushes the tear from my cheek and leans his forehead against mine. "I love you," he whispers. I tell him that I love him too and it's such a tender moment between us, I know I'll never forget it.

I always thought that when Jackson and I had sex it would be a frantic frenzy filled with lust, with him racing to the finish line. I never knew that it would be this passionate and powerful or that it would somehow intensify the connection between us.

Our guards are down and our insides have been stripped, leaving us bare in so many ways. There's something so beautiful and raw about what's happening right now.

My legs start to shake and an all-consuming climax begins to take over my body, heightened by the emotions flowing through me. Jackson stares down at me, watching me with hooded eyes.

His face is strained and I know he's trying to hold off, but I want him to let go at the same time I do. I untangle my hands from his, skim over his broad back and grab hold of his ass while my walls clench around him and I sigh his name. I watch as the muscles in his forearms flex and his mouth parts open before he whispers my name and his release swiftly follows mine.

Chapter 30 (Jackson)

I prop myself up on one elbow and watch as she yawns and stretches while sprawled out on my bed.

Her eyes are still closed and she mewls my name in her sleep, which only encourages the morning wood I'm sporting.

Her hair is a perfect combination of bed head and just been fucked hair. I lean in and get a whiff of that coconut scent that I love so much.

She stretches again, only this time the sheet falls and her breasts are fully exposed to me. Her pretty pink nipples are just begging to be sucked on.

A man can only be strong for so long. I don't know where to start first because I want to taste every part of her body. Since her breasts are mere centimeters from my face, I decide I'm gonna start there and work my way down.

I move forward and give her right nipple a little lick and wait for her response. And what a response it is, she moans and arches her back, shoving her breasts into my face.

I suck one nipple into my mouth while kneading the other one with my hand. Her eyes are still closed, but I notice the coy smile on

ASHLEY JADE

her face. This little minx has been awake the entire time, purposely teasing me with these pretty titties of hers.

In one fell swoop, I dive under the sheet and spread her thighs apart. I loved making love to her last night and baring my entire soul to her...it was the single best moment of my entire life.

But right now? Right now her sex is wet for me and I need to issue my own brand of teasing.

When I look up, I notice her eyes are still closed and she's *still* trying to feign sleep and innocence, even though the little coy smile hasn't left her perfect face. Part of me thinks it's adorable, but the other part of me wants to spank that luscious ass of hers for putting on an act in front of me.

I lift the sheet off her body and throw it on the floor. I position myself between her thighs again and kiss her navel before lavishing it with my tongue. Her hips push up but I grab onto those hipbones of hers that make me lose my mind. "You move and I'll stop," I inform her. "You wanted to be cute and pretend to be sleeping while you teased me with this gorgeous body of yours...didn't you?"

She nods and I bite the inside of her thigh. "I said don't move."

She immediately goes still and I hear a whimper escape. The sound goes right to my cock and I have to suck in a breath.

I inhale the scent of her arousal combined with coconut and I barely suppress my growl. I work my way down her body all while whispering how beautiful she is.

I might be taking the control and teaching her a lesson, but I don't want her to get the wrong idea and think that I'm any less appreciative of her beauty and the gift of her body that she's trusting me with.

I'm very appreciative. I know I'm a lucky man. I've got what most men can only hope and wish to find in their lifetime. I've got a beautiful woman who loves me unconditionally, despite my past. And I'll spend the rest of my life matching that 10 fold.

I draw little circles on the inside of her thighs with my tongue that has her gasping. I see her hands clench at her sides and I bite the inside of her thigh again in warning.

She blows out a breath and I know she's becoming frustrated

I move my head down until I'm directly in front of her pussy. It's pink and smooth, except for the thinnest and tiniest of landing strips, giving away that she is in fact, a natural blonde. I rub my nose against it, inhale sharply, and savor it for a moment. Then I slide up her slit, finishing my slow graze with a flick of my tongue against her clit.

She whimpers again but doesn't move. *Good girl.*

I decide to reward her for being so compliant. If I'm being honest, I'm really rewarding myself because there's nothing like diving face first into her heat.

I eat her and suck her folds into my mouth like they're made out of goddamn candy and I'm the gingerbread man.

That's when she ruins her streak, pivots her pussy into my face and grabs hold of my hair. I let myself enjoy it for a moment because, well—it's fucking awesome.

Then before she knows what hits her, I wrap my arm around her waist, flip her over and prop her up on her knees. Her ass is sticking straight up in the air and I can't help but admire it. More than admire it, I want to build a shrine for that ass of hers and pray to it every day.

I run my finger down the seam of her ass and she jerks up in surprise. I couldn't give a fuck less about her not moving at this point, my desires are now focused elsewhere.

I repeat the gesture and her body tightens. "You've never had anyone play with your ass before...have you, baby?"

She shakes her head and I can't help but thank my lucky stars for being the lucky bastard that's going to bring her pleasure to new heights.

But, I'm not an idiot. I know that this is something that she needs to work up to slowly. Anyone who tells you that first-time anal sex is a 'wham bam thank you ma'am' with no prep—is a fucking moron who has no business participating in the act.

I kiss one of her ass cheeks and slip a finger inside her pussy.

Her back bows and she sighs my name. "At some point," I whisper. "You're going to let me have your ass."

Her entire body goes rigid, so I rub one hand down her back in a calming motion. "But not until you're ready to give it to me."

She visibly relaxes and I plant a kiss on her other cheek. "Do you trust me?"

"You know I do, Jackson," she whispers. My heart swells at the statement.

I slowly slip the finger that's wet with her arousal into her ass. She blows out a shaky breath and goes stiff. "I'm not going to hurt you, baby," I reassure her.

Making sure not to push my way in, I make small circles around the tight bud. With my other hand, I sink a finger back into her pussy and begin playing with her clit.

After a moment, she's calm again and moaning my name. Then she starts bearing down on my finger. I'm not sure if she realizes what she's doing, but it sends my own arousal into overdrive.

"You want me to stick it further in your ass, baby?"

"Yeah. It feels—" She pauses, and I wish I could see her face right now because I know she's blushing.

"It feels what, Alyssa? Tell me, I want to hear you say it."

She pushes down on my finger until it's fully inside her. "It feels good when you play with my ass and my pussy at the same time."

My dick twitches at those words, and I have to remind myself not to pounce because as much as I want to, I'm not taking her ass right now.

She straightens her spine and sits upright. Then she does something that almost makes me come right on the spot.

She partially sits on my lap and begins riding the finger I have in her ass. I move my other hand around to her front so I can trace her clit at the same time. "I need you inside me," she pants. "I want you to fuck me at the same time you're doing this to me."

I'm so turned on with her statement and the fact that she's embracing her own sexual pleasure like this. I eagerly comply and begin to enter her, letting out a groan when I'm all the way in.

"Oh my god," she screams. "It feels even better than I thought it would."

Hell yeah, it does. There's no way I'm going to be able to hold off if she keeps riding my cock like this. I'm going to have to speed things along in order to make sure she gets off before I do. I look down at where our bodies are joined and I quickly realize why it feels exceptionally good.

I'm not wearing a fucking condom. I bring both her and my movements to a rapid halt and slip out. "I have to put a condom on. I'm sorry, I should have been more careful."

She doesn't freak like I assumed she would. Instead, she says the words that every straight man loves to hear when he finds himself in this predicament. "I'm on birth control. I've also been tested and I'm clean—"

She doesn't even get to finish that sentence because I thrust into her. Since one of the membership requirements of the bdsm club that I won't ever be going back to, was getting tested semi-annually, I know I'm clean as well.

I hold onto to both her breasts while she bounces up and down on my dick. The friction between us is better than any I've ever felt before. "Oh my fucking god, Jackson," she screams so loud I know Tyrone's going to hear, but so be it. Lord knows, I've heard him in the act more times than I can count.

I switch positions then so that I'm thrusting into her doggie style, circling her other hole with my finger, and watching her ass jiggle with my every move. Alyssa's loud moans along with the sound of my balls slapping against her fill the room and it only enhances the act.

A moment later, I get ready for my favorite part. Alyssa's orgasm.

I've never witnessed someone orgasm the way she does. It's truly an experience to watch and if I'm being honest, I really revel in the fact that *I'm* the only one who gets to see her come apart like this. She orgasms with her entire body. She jerks, she pants, her breasts push up into the air, she curses like a sailor, her legs shake, her little toes curl, and her pussy grabs me tighter than a damn vise.

She's on the first wave of her climax, sputtering curses into the air, when she hits her second wave and starts milking my cock, sucking every ounce of come from my balls. It feels so fucking good I begin roaring obscenities over her loud screams until I fall on top of her in a sweaty heap.

I feel her twitch underneath me slightly but I'm too distracted by the sight of my come leaking out of her.

"Momma," she screeches.

"Momma?" I question with a smirk. "You mean like, Whoa, Momma that sure was some amazing sex we just had?"

She leaps up from the bed and her cheeks flush. "I meant *Momma*, Jackson! As in Momma just walked in, did the sign of the cross while saying the Lord's name, covered her eyes, and walked right back out!" she screams.

Oh, *that* Momma. Well, shit.

I forgot that Tyrone had mentioned something about Momma flying out here. If I thought Momma had bad timing the *last* time Alyssa spent the night, it has nothing on *this* time.

I try hard not to laugh at the way Alyssa's freaking out right now. Momma's caught her *own* son in the act quite a few times, I doubt she'll even make a big deal about it. "It's okay," I assure her.

"Easy for *you* to say. Despite who gave birth to you, that woman *is* your mother. And the last memory that woman has of me is watching me strip down for a sex tape. Not to mention, whatever you told her about me when we broke up. This is *so* not okay. This is mortifying."

Guess I didn't think of it like that.

I walk over to where she is and hold her in my arms. "I love you, Alyssa. I will never let anyone talk bad about you. Please, don't feel ashamed or embarrassed. Everything will be fine."

I walk to my closet and throw on a pair of shorts. I hand her a t-shirt and a pair of my sweatpants. "You'll have to roll them up until they fit, but it's the best I can do right now."

She still looks nervous so I pull her into another hug. "It's okay, baby."

She gives me a small smile and I tilt her chin up. "That's my girl."

The corners of her lips twitch. "It was some amazing sex by the way."

I give her a wink. "Oh, I know ."

She begins changing and I head for the door. "I'm gonna go out there first," I say. "But seriously, don't worry. Momma's not judging you. She's the sweetest, least judgmental person I know."

T he swipe of the newspaper against my arm almost causes me to laugh. "Jackson Mathew Reid," Momma screams. "You think this is funny, boy?"

This is the first time Momma's ever middle-named me. Heck, I didn't even think she knew what my middle name was.

I ignore the howling of laughter coming from both Tyrone and Ricardo seated at the kitchen counter.

She swipes me again with the paper. "I'm fixin' to lay a real hurtin' on you. I trucked all the way to New York because I thought you were going through a hard time and needed your Momma. Then I come to find you screwing some hussy. *You're* supposed to be the good one!"

"Alyssa's not a hussy," I growl.

She stops mid swipe. "Alyssa? Well, of course, Alyssa ain't no hussy. I'm talkin' bout that two- bit—"

I almost laugh again when I realize. "Momma, that *was* Alyssa. She just has dark hair now."

She puts the newspaper down. "Well, I see. Glad to hear you worked things out with that girl. Bout' time. Now give me a hug."

I pull Momma in for a big hug and Tyrone wiggles his eyebrows at me. "From the sounds that were coming through that bedroom of yours all night *and* this morning. I'd say you two *definitely* worked things out with each other."

I open my mouth to tell him to knock it off, but Alyssa walks out, takes Momma's newspaper and swipes him across the head with it.

Momma claps her hands. "I knew I liked this girl." She lets go of me and pulls Alyssa into a hug. "How you doin', sugar? I like the hair."

Alyssa chuckles. "I'm fine, Momma. Need any help making breakfast?"

She waves a hand and motions for us to sit down. She scans the room and her eyes land on Ricardo. "I reckon I'm gonna be one plate short?"

He gives her a soft nod and she wipes her hands on her apron. "Hmm."

"Hmm?" Ricardo says. "What's hmm?"

"Well, I never thought I'd say this because that Lou-Lou girl really dills my pickle, especially after she pulled that stunt. But maybe you ought to suck it up and talk to her. That sparkle in your eyes is dimmer, Ricardo. That girl had some kinda effect on you whether you're willing to admit it or not."

Tyrone grins. "That's what I've been telling him, Momma."

I take the stack of pancakes from Alyssa. "You know, I have to say. I'm on their side of the fence now. Running into Alyssa again was the best thing that could have happened. Even if I did screw it up by getting drunk at her workplace and saying some really messed up stuff. It led me back to her. Lou-Lou's right across the hall, you guys have been ignoring one another for months now."

To my surprise, Alyssa nods. "It's true. Don't get me wrong, I was pissed at what Jackson did that night. But, I wanted nothing more than to talk to him and work out our issues. I'm sure she feels the same about you. I don't like Lou-Lou...for obvious reasons. But it's obvious that you both have something—" She pauses and makes a face. "Well, you have *something* together. And if she makes you happy that's all that really matters."

Ricardo rolls his eyes, clearly hating that the focus is on his and Lou-Lou's former relationship. Then he looks at me and gives me a wink. Now I know he's going to somehow use me to deflect the attention off of him. "Hey, Jackson. Did you tell Momma how you basically said that Alyssa was nothing but a good time at the bar that night?"

Asshole.

Momma gasps and reaches for the newspaper again.

"He was drunk, Momma. He didn't mean it," Alyssa says, rushing to my defense. I reach for her hand and give it a kiss.

Momma puts the newspaper down and picks up the spatula. Then she turns her gaze on Alyssa. "You work at a bar, young lady?"

Shit, I was hoping Momma wouldn't pick up on that. Fucking Ricardo.

Alyssa crinkles her nose. I squeeze her hand as a signal to deny everything, but she doesn't take the hint. "Well, yeah. I mean, it's nothing crazy or anything. It's low-key and—"

Momma cuts her off. "Do you really think that's safe? You're a pretty young thing...who knows what could happen to you." She points the spatula at me. "I can't believe you're *okay* with this, Jackson."

Alyssa waves a hand. "It's fine, Momma. Trust me, my friend Shane who owns the bar is usually there with me and he would never let anything happen to me. And it's perfectly safe, there is an alarm system and everything. I always make sure to put it on right after I close up and head upstairs to my apartment."

This isn't good.

Momma puts her hand over her heart and takes a step back dramatically. "You *live* at this....this *bar*? What if one of the customers follows you up to this *apartment*? Or even worse hides up there and attacks you? Or attacks you when you're closing one night and this Shane character isn't around?" She shakes her head. "No. This just won't do."

I've never thought about it like that before, but seeing as I pretty

ASHLEY JADE

much did that to her not even 24 hrs ago...Shit, Momma has a point.

Alyssa opens her mouth to answer, but Momma looks at me. "How can you let this happen?"

I open my mouth to defend myself...but I've got nothing. What Momma's saying makes complete sense.

I look over at Ricardo and he's happily eating his breakfast and humming to himself. I fight the urge to throw my biscuit at his head.

I look at Tyrone and he shrugs.

"Momma," Alyssa starts. "I like it there and even more, I can *afford* the rent there. New York is a ridiculously expensive place to live. What Shane charges me for rent is a steal."

She points the spatula at her. "Until someone steals you away in the middle of the night and you end up on the news."

The thought of that happening makes my stomach knot up.

Alyssa stands up. "You should come there tonight and see it for yourself. It's a safe place. Come and have a few drinks on me and enjoy yourself."

Tyrone snorts. "Momma ain't going to no bar, Alyssa. She can't hang like that."

Momma folds her arms across her chest and glares at him. "I can most certainly *hang* like that. And seeing as I'm here for the next two weeks...it wouldn't hurt to appease Alyssa and see this *bar*." Tyrone chokes on his food, but Momma turns her ebony eyes on me again. "I'll see this bar, but I reckon a few changes will be happening by the time I hop back on that plane."

I give her a subtle nod and finish the rest of my breakfast while answering her questions about the fight and the two bruises on my face.

I stand outside and watch Alyssa through the glass window of the bar. Everyone, including Momma, is there waiting for me to arrive, but I'm enjoying just watching her for a few moments.

After Breakfast, I walked Alyssa home and I went to the gym. After our workout, I told the guys to head to the bar first and said I'd catch up in a little while.

I needed the time to think.

I have no idea how to go about the situation regarding Alyssa and her apartment at the bar.

I would ask her to move in, but that would only make it that much easier for her to find out about DeLuca.

And I don't care how much of an asshole it makes me, there's *no* way I'm telling her about him. Her not knowing will keep her safe.

She's got a bit of a wild streak at times and I don't know how she'll take finding out about everything. But one thing is certain, if she does anything to DeLuca...he will have *no* problem retaliating by having her killed or doing it himself.

I just can't take that chance.

The only reason I'm not more freaked out about her showing up at the club last night is because of her new hair color. I'm hoping that DeLuca won't realize it was her...even though I know it was a big fight for him and he's checking out the footage.

Ironically enough, it was seeing Alyssa there that helped me win that fight in the first place.

My opponent was the toughest one I ever faced at the club. There was a couple of times I thought I was going to lose.

Luckily, I looked out in the crowd and saw Tyrone doing the praying possum. As silly as it sounds, I knew that was his way of giving me advice. When he was a kid and got bullied on the playground by some racist pricks, he used to drop and 'play dead' in the middle of a fight, just like possum's do. It threw the bully off for a moment and Tyrone would use the opportunity to sprout back up and defend himself.

I saw the karate chop at the very last second and tucked my

chin. His hand slipped and I swear, he just missed my carotid artery. However, the headbutt that he dealt got me bad. Bad enough where I did go down and I wasn't sure I was going to make it back up again.

I was temporarily knocked out, but I heard Alyssa's guttural cries and I thought someone was hurting her. With strength I didn't even know I possessed, I managed to get back up. I was relieved to see that she was okay, but I was beyond pissed that she was at the fight club. I used that rage as fuel to win the fight. Without her, I don't know if that would have happened.

Just like I don't know what will happen or how to go about her apartment situation.

I could ask her to move in, I'm sure Tyrone would be fine with it...but then I'd have to tell her about DeLuca...and *she* most definitely won't be fine with it.

I could always lease her an apartment. I'm not a millionaire or anything but I do have a decent chunk of change saved up from fighting the past few years. I could put it toward that...but something tells me Alyssa won't go for that.

Not to mention, that somewhere down the road; I figure in the next few years or so...she *will* want to take the next step and move in together. She'll also want to get married and have kids.

I want the same things, but I still have another 6 years and change left in my contract with DeLuca. And that's *only* if I continue to win at least, 99% of my fights, which in and of itself is a whole new set of problems.

The problem isn't that I'll be 33 by the time I'm done. That's still young enough to enjoy the rest my life without feeling like I'll be missing out on anything like having kids and starting a family.

The problem is, and every great fighter and athlete know this...you just can't stay on top forever. You hit your prime and only go down from there. Right now I'm 27...but I'd be an idiot to think there won't be someone younger, tougher and stronger for me to compete against in the next 6 years. Someone who could end up taking me down.

I know that's why DeLuca makes the stipulations that he does and makes the contract for as long as he does. It really *is* making a deal with the devil.

I rub my temples and try to focus my thoughts back on the here and now. I watch through the glass as Alyssa hands Momma a shot and Ricardo and Tyrone start doing a countdown.

I laugh when she tilts her head back and makes a face like it's horrible. Tyrone hugs her and yells, "Roll Tide!" while everyone in the bar cheers.

Alyssa is smiling from ear to ear and I swear, she's absolutely radiant. Her dimple is out and her eyes are gleaming. You wouldn't even know that she barely slept the night before.

"She's beautiful...isn't she?" some deep voice says. I turn around to face the man who's not only interrupting my thoughts but is checking out my girlfriend.

He's about an inch or two shorter than me, he looks about maybe 15 years older than me; and he's wearing a gray suit that looks vaguely familiar.

He looks to be a professional of some sort, so it's kind of odd to see him hanging around some hole in the wall bar.

For once, I decide to remain calm. Of course, I want to punch the guy...but the reality is that he's only admiring how beautiful Alyssa is. As much as I hate it, she's going to catch the eye of other men. I can't go around beating up most of the male population.

"She's gorgeous," I tell him. I silently add '*and all mine*' to the statement. He stands next to me and watches her through the glass. He's got about another 10 seconds to get his fill before I take back my previous thoughts about not punching him.

My hand's ball at my sides when I see that his eyes still haven't moved off of her. Then he says something that makes my insides twist. "You know, I preferred her as a blonde. She looked more innocent that way. But there's something to be said about the darker hair. It really brings out those eyes of hers. I think I like it."

I snarl and shove him against the glass. He gives me a smirk and flips the inside of his suit jacket open, revealing a badge. "Careful,

273

Jackson. You don't want to go to jail for assaulting an officer." The corners of his eyes crinkle. "Not that it would be your first time in a jail cell...now would it?"

I look at the badge and struggle not to lose my shit. *Ford*. Special Agent Ford fucking Baker to be exact...what the fuck kind of name is that, anyway?

I grit my teeth because it's the name belonging to the man who had his hands all over my girl that night. The man who's *fucked* my girl before. The man my girl said she loved.

To hell with it. I'm taking my chances and punching the bastard. One solid punch, that's all I need to feel better.

He seems to sense my thoughts because he holds up his hands and says, "DeLuca wouldn't like it if you ended up in jail. You know that as well as I do, son."

I grab a hold of the hood to my sweatshirt so I have someplace to put my hands for the time being...because being wrapped around his neck...is looking real fucking good right about now. I decide to hit him with a low-blow of my own. "Son," I snort. "*I'm* only 3 years older than her. So tell me, did you call Alyssa your *daughter* when you fucked her, you fucking pervert?"

His nostrils flare before he says, "No, I was too busy calling her a whore instead."

That's. Fucking. It.

I lunge at him and my hands tighten around his throat. I don't give a fuck about DeLuca right now, I'm *never* going to stand by and let some piece of shit call my girl a whore.

He makes a choking sound, and his beady blue eyes begin popping out of his head.

Then it occurs to me. Alyssa might be able to understand and accept the first murder I committed...but I'm not so sure she'll forgive me for this one.

Begrudgingly, I let go of his throat. He collapses on the pavement and gasps for air.

"Fucking asshole," he croaks. "I came here to offer you a deal."

I bend down and laugh hard in his face. "A deal?" I laugh again.

"Fuck your deal and fuck you. There's nothing you could offer me that I would want." I gesture toward the window and give him a cocky smile. "Or that I don't already have."

He stands up straight and makes a face. Looks like I'm not the only one trying to restrain myself now. And boy do I want the fucker to hit me. I want him to hit me so I can wipe the fucking pavement with him.

He fixes his tie and looks through the window again. "What about a life with Alyssa," he whispers.

"Already have that, " I reply.

I fight the urge to tell him certain details about our life together—like how I was the first one to ever make her come, or how great her ass looked when I took her from behind this morning after licking her sweet pussy. And most important of all; the way her face lights up when she tell me that she loves *me*.

He clears his throat and faces me. "I think you know what I mean."

"Nope."

"Then you've taken one too many hits to the fucking head," he growls. "Do you think you can actually provide a life for her? The kind of life that she deserves?"

I'm not going to let him know how much that comment gets to me so instead I reply, "I can give Alyssa anything that she wants. And if I can't—I'll find a way to make it happen."

"Yeah. But in how many years, Jackson?" he gripes. "If you're even still alive by the time your deal with DeLuca is up. If you even *last* that long in the cage."

The fact that he knows about DeLuca's underground fight club unnerves me. It occurs to me that for all I know, he has a wire on him and I'm sure as fuck not giving DeLuca up.

I roll my shoulders back. "I have no idea what you're talking about. I don't know who this DeLuca is that you're referencing and I know absolutely nothing about this cage you're referring to. Now, if you continue to talk to or question me without a lawyer present there's going to be a problem."

He pinches the bridge of his nose. "I'm not wearing a fucking wire. I'm just trying to help you." He gestures toward the window. "But most of all, help *her*."

"She doesn't need your help. She has me now."

"For how long?"

"Long enough to spend a lifetime with her and grow old with her."

He snorts. "Quite some fairytale you're living in."

I look at him out of the corner of my eye. "I'll do whatever I need to, in order to make sure that happens. I'll make sure I'm around for her."

He folds his hands and touches his pointer fingers to his lips. "I'm sure you will. But, I was referring to her."

I grab his collar and shove him against the glass again. "Is that supposed to be some kind of threat? Because if you hurt her it will be the last thing you ever do."

"I was talking about DeLuca, Jackson. You know, the man who killed her father." He looks at me skeptically. "Unless she didn't trust you enough to tell you the truth about her past."

"I know everything."

I release him and he fixes his collar. "Then you know that she witnessed DeLuca do it. Now, I've done my very best to protect her. I brainwashed her and I manipulated the hell out of her...starting with forcing her to deny to everyone who her father's killer really was. I'm not proud of myself, but it needed to be done."

He looks down at the ground. "I even went so far as to turn her into a broken girl in order to get DeLuca to forget all about her because I hoped he'd see that she was already miserable and suffering enough. That's how much I love her."

I can't help but look at him with disgust. "Sounds like you pretty much tried to kill her yourself then. Good thing she's a hell of a lot tougher and stronger than anyone gives her credit for."

"She is...but she's no match for him. And assuming that you know how he operates, you know that he will get his payback. It's not a matter of if...it's only a matter of when. He likes his revenge best when it's served cold. He likes to watch his prey find happiness and flourish...before he swoops in and snaps their necks." He blanches. "Or bashes their skulls in with a crowbar."

He's got DeLuca pegged right, but I still can't help but wonder. "What makes you think that she's even on his radar in the first place? Trust me, if he was waiting for the perfect opportunity he's had a couple," I say, recalling the two times she's shown up at the fight club.

"She's on his radar because of you, Jackson."

I open my mouth to argue, but I can't.

He takes the opportunity to continue, "She showed up at his fight club on her own a few months ago. She got wind that he might be the owner and she was out for his blood, Jackson. Luckily, you saved her by denying he was the owner. I'll never be able to thank you enough for that." He pauses. "However, If you know her well enough, you know that she can be reckless at times. She's not always mentally with it. Just look at how the sex tape came to be...*she* actively chose to sleep with her step-father's opponent's son. I'm not saying that it was her fault that he filmed it...but it was still her own thoughts of revenge that put her in the position in the first place. She puts herself right into the eye of the storm without thinking about the consequences."

He looks at me, but I stay silent. I hate what he's saying but a small part of me knows it's true. She did defy me and show up at the fight club when I told her not to.

DeLuca aside, because she has no idea that he runs it ...she *knew* there was a chance that she could get attacked at the fight club by *any* guy because it happened before. And she still showed up there, all by herself. She was so determined to see me and have it out with me...she didn't care about the consequences and took that chance.

"She showed up at the fight club last night...even after I forbid her from going there. Even after she promised me that she never would."

He points at me. "See? You *know* how she is. You're perfectly aware of how stubborn she can be. Now do you see where I'm going with this, Jackson?"

I nod, my heart crashing to the floor with the realization. "So what you're 'deal' really entails is me breaking up with her. And if I don't, you'll bust me for being apart of an underground fight club. And DeLuca will kill me anyway once he finds out that I led the feds to it."

I punch the wall beside his head, hating the fact that no matter what fucking corner I go down, or how much I try...there's always something waiting in the shadows to break Alyssa and me apart.

I just want to be happy with her. I just want to wake up next to her every day of my life with her safe in my arms. I just want her to be my wife and the mother of my future child. I want to have lazy Sunday's in bed, make love to her at night, see that favorite dimple of mine every day, and spend every second of my life loving her.

He gives me a weird look and I'm not sure what to make of it, until he says, "No. That's not my deal. Alyssa's far too much in love with you for that to even be effective. She'll just chase you...and I know all too well how hard it is to resist her. And seeing as you're tied up with DeLuca, the chase will most likely end with her getting killed."

He sighs. "What I'm offering you is an actual chance at a life." He closes his eyes. "With her."

My ears perk up at that. "You mean like witness protection or something?"

His eyes open and narrow into tiny slits. "No, something much better than that. DeLuca would find you eventually in witness protection, and it would only piss him off that much more knowing that you tried to run and hide. Why do you think I never put Alyssa into it?"

On some level, I guess it makes sense. "So what's this deal then?"

"I want you to kill DeLuca."

I must be hearing things. "Yeah, because it's so easy to kill one of the most powerful mob bosses who ever lived." I snort. "Wow, I assumed that you were still way too young for senility to be setting in."

He gives me an eye roll before his expression turns serious again. "I would set it up. It would take a few weeks, but I'll make it happen. There would be no witnesses...other than me."

I push my shoulders back. "If that's the case why don't you just off him yourself?"

He sucks his teeth. "Because I'm an FBI agent, Jackson. If I'm the only one at the murder scene...it will all point back to me. And if it all points back to *me*, I won't be able to get you cleared—"

"And what about *me?*" I interrupt. "I'm tied to DeLuca. And if *I'm* the only one at the murder scene it will all come down on me. Not to mention the fact that his blood will be on my hands. How the fuck can I ever walk away from that alive or without spending the rest of my life in jail?"

He runs a hand through his hair. "Because you won't be the only one there...I'll be there with you. I will protect you and you won't go down for it. It will be pinned on someone else who I'll set up to be there. Someone who I have a special arrangement with. Someone who has more motive than you could ever imagine."

Chills creep up my spine. "If you mean Aly—"

"Are you fucking crazy? Of course, I don't mean her. I love her. I would never put her in the direct line of fire, ever."

"Then who is this person?"

He clicks his tongue. "No. You're not privy to that information until you make this deal with me. And even then, you won't know until you're standing in that room holding that gun. Trust me, it's better that way and it's the only way all the chips will fall into place."

I lean down and rest my forearms on my thighs. This is a lot to think about and take in. There's one hell of a difference between killing someone in a rage because they killed your sister and taking out one of the world's biggest mob bosses. Not to mention, trusting a man that you pretty much hate. "I don't know. My gut feeling is telling me not to trust you. And I have no guarantee's that this will go off without a hitch. I have no guarantee that I can trust you."

"Jackson, I'm an FBI agent. Who would know how to commit the perfect murder better than me? And you don't need to trust me, you only need to love Alyssa enough to take care of DeLuca. She'll be safe forever then. But you have my word that you won't end up doing time for it."

I shake my head. "No. I'm sorry, but no. There's too much of a chance for this to backfire. I'll take my chances with DeLuca. He hasn't come after her yet. For all I know, maybe the fact that she's with me is working in her favor. I make DeLuca a lot of money. I'm the best fighter he has. Maybe he knows that if he fucked with Alyssa that he would end up losing me and it would impact his business. He is a businessman first and foremost."

I close my eyes and sigh.

Maybe there's a way I can talk to DeLuca.

I'll have Ricardo set it up for me and I'll put it all out on the table and be honest with him. I'll tell him that I'm loyal to him and I'll continue to be his best fighter...the only thing I ask is that he doesn't retaliate against Alyssa.

I'll tell him to increase the terms of my contract as a sign of good faith...make it 20 years or some shit. I don't know.

All I know, is there's gotta be a better way. Hell, maybe I should tell him that an FBI agent was plotting his murder and trying to enlist me to do so he'll really believe that I'm loyal to him.

Irritation crosses over his features. "I know it's a lot to think about." He pulls his card out of his wallet and hands it to me. "This deal won't be on the table for long. A few weeks at most."

He goes to turn around but pauses. "The only thing I ask is that you don't tell Alyssa I was here or that we spoke about this. She doesn't want me in her life anymore and I don't want to upset her more than I already have."

"Okay," I agree. Not because I want to keep this conversation from her, but because I can't tell her about talking to Ford without giving up my involvement with DeLuca. A part of me wants to tell her about Ford lurking outside her bar, but there's no guarantee that she won't find him to confront him about it. And if she does, I'm sure he'll tell her all about my involvement.

After I watch him go to his car and drive off I head inside the bar.

Momma's got a line up of shots in front of her now. It seems that everyone in the bar is enamored by Momma and wants to see her get drunk.

I shake my head and laugh. Alyssa's eyes catch mine and she lets out a little squeal before running and jumping into my arms.

She gives me a kiss and I begin to lose myself in her, not caring about anything else. Only her.

I pull away and look at her. "I love you."

She gives me a smile and I put her down. "I love you, too," she whispers.

Then she collapses and passes out cold.

I barely even have time to catch her before she hits the ground, taking my entire heart with her.

Chapter 31 (Alyssa)

I hear shouting somewhere in the distance but I'm unable to move.

I'm so cold. My head feels like it's submerged underwater and I'm floating. There's pressure on my chest and chills are raking up and down my spine.

"Did she have anything to drink?" I hear Jackson's voice growl.

There's mumbling in the distance.

"No, I'm not talking about alcohol, Momma," Jackson says. "She doesn't drink alcohol. I'm talking about a regular drink. Water? Juice?"

"I think she had some water," Ricardo says. "I'm not sure, though. We were all paying attention to Momma."

"Well did she leave her cup anywhere? Fuck, maybe someone slipped something into her drink," Jackson barks.

I hear some shuffling before I have the feeling of being lifted in the air. Which only does wonders for the feeling of floating that I have. The chills are getting worse and my body is breaking out in a sweat.

My eyes flutter open, but the weight on my chest feels like it's made out of bricks.

"I swear to god. If any of you fuckers slipped anything in my girls drink," Jackson shouts, addressing the entire bar. "I *will* find you and you'll need a good plastic surgeon by the time I'm through with you."

"We need to get her to the hospital, Jackson," Momma shouts. "She's shaking like a leaf. I think she's sick!"

"What do you mean sick? She was fine this morning and five minutes ago. She's not sick. Someone shithead did something to her," Jackson roars.

"Wait a minute, Jackson. Think about it, she did run to our apartment last night in the pouring *ice* cold rain, wearing nothing but a pair of pajamas. It's still winter outside, she must have been freezing," Tyrone says, worry in his tone.

"Shit. That's right. I should've been paying better attention to her and warmed her up sooner."

I soon feel a wet cloth on my head courtesy of Momma. "Yeah, she's burning up. She feels feverish. I don't think no one slipped anything in her drink, Jackson. But we better take her to the hospital just to be sure."

She runs her hand through my hair. "It's alright, Alyssa. Momma's not gonna leave your side. I'm right here, sugar."

I want to speak, tell her how thankful I am for her, but this feeling is only getting worse. The chills are so bad I feel like I'm going to drop right out of Jackson's arms.

Jackson peers down at me. "Rest if you need to. I've got you. Everything will be okay, baby."

———

Two hours later, the doctors eyes appraise me over a pair of glasses. He flips open his tablet and scans the rest of the small hospital room, his eyes fall on the three huge men taking up most of the space.

In other words, Jackson, Tyrone, and Ricardo. In addition to Momma, who hasn't stopped holding my hand the entire time.

He clears his throat. "Are *all* these people members of your immediate family, young lady?" Before I can open my mouth, Momma and Jackson shout, "Yes! Now tell us what's wrong."

The doctor's lips twitch. "I see," he says before focusing back on his tablet. "Well, my dear, it seems that you have a touch of bronchitis, a touch of an ear infection, and the beginning stages of what looks to be walking pneumonia."

"Jesus," Jackson says while sitting up in his chair. "Is she going to be okay?"

The doctor waves his hand. "She'll be fine. She collapsed because the ear infection threw off her equilibrium, her chest hurts because of the bronchitis, and she has chills because of the pneumonia. Luckily, we caught the pneumonia in the beginning stages. A course of antibiotics will clear everything up."

The doctor pauses and fixes his eyes on me again. "Young lady, might I suggest that you don't go for a jog again in the middle of the night wearing nothing but pajamas while there is ice and rain falling from the sky during the first week of March."

"Thanks, Tyrone," I mutter.

He holds up his hands. "Don't 'thanks Tyrone' me. If you don't tell the doctor everything, how is he supposed to be able to diagnose and treat you properly?"

I roll my eyes and turn my attention back to the doctor. "So can I go home?"

He shakes his head. "Yes, but not right now. I want to get some fluids in you first. The nurse should be in soon to start an IV. You can go home in the next couple of hours." He looks at Momma. "But I do want to ensure that she has someone to take care of her for the next few days. I don't want her collapsing again." He looks back at his tablet and makes a face. "I see that your address is the same address as the bar called "Finnley's'."

I wonder how he knows that my apartment is at a bar, but before I can ask he says, "My son's a musician who frequents the bar. He's also dating the owner, Shane. Nice guy."

I give him a smile. "That he is."

Momma stands up. "Don't worry, Doctor. I will see to it that she gets the very best care."

She turns to Jackson. "And she won't be staying at no *bar*. She'll be coming back to the apartment with us."

I open my mouth to protest, but Jackson cuts me off by saying, "Yes, of course. And you won't be the one taking care of her, Momma. I will."

Momma smiles and says, "Well, I'm helping. No one makes soup for the soul like I do."

"It's true," Tyrone says. "Momma makes the best chicken soup in the world."

With that, the doctor nods. " Looks like you'll be in good hands. Here's your prescription. But the nurse will be here in a few moments. She'll give you your first dose of antibiotics and she'll start your IV. After that, you're free to go. Take care."

I take my prescription and thank him.

Ricardo and Tyrone stand up. "We can run that over to the pharmacy for you if you want."

"Thanks, guys," I tell them before they leave.

Momma kisses my forehead. "Well, I have to run to the ladies room. You gonna be okay, sugar?"

"I'll be fine, Momma Thank you."

When she leaves, Jackson envelopes me in his arms. "Don't scare me like that again." He closes his eyes. "I swear, my heart stopped."

I want to kiss him so bad, but I don't want to get him sick. "I'm sorry. I thought I was fine. I hope I don't get you sick."

"Nah, I'm strong like bull."

"Thanks for offering to take care of me. But honestly, I'll be fine. I'm sure Shane will check on me."

"Nope in my bed is where you will be. Where Momma and I can nurse you back to health. Speaking of nurse's...where is she?"

I hear the sound of someone clearing their throat and I look up.

"She's right here," a woman with long blonde hair, who's wearing pink scrubs informs us curtly.

Jackson makes a face and I know what he's thinking because I'm thinking it too. The nurse looks a lot like *me*. She's about 10 years older than me, but she has the same build, similar features, my natural hair color, and even the same eye color; although hers are more of a brown hazel rather than green but still, it's eerily similar to mine.

It's like I jumped into a time machine and pressed 'future.' I'm suddenly struck with the feeling of wanting to apologize for any troubles that she might have endured in her nursing career due to my sex tape.

Then I look at her name tag and see the name staring back at me. I almost pass out again.

"Oh, god," I whisper. Jackson immediately looks concerned.

But I'm too distracted when the nurse gives me a cold smile. "Yup. I'm the woman whose husband you stole. You little adulteress whore."

The brick on my chest practically caves in with that statement.

Jackson stands up and scowls. "First off, don't ever call my girl a whore again. Or I'll be lodging a complaint with the hospital. Secondly, I'm positive that Alyssa isn't responsible for whatever problems you have with your husband."

She puts her hands on her hips and glares at me. "Clearly your new boyfriend knows nothing about who you really are."

My stomach heaves because as much as I don't like it. This woman is right and I do owe her one hell of an apology for my transgressions. I can't put everything on him.

I open my mouth to start, but Jackson takes a step closer to her. "I don't know who you are, lady. But I do know exactly who *she* is. Now I'm only going to tell you this once—leave. Because when the sassy Southern woman, otherwise known as my Momma, comes back in here and hears you speaking to Alyssa this way. Trust me, you're going to wish you had."

I somehow find my voice. "Jackson, stop. She doesn't deserve to be treated like this, she has every right to be furious with me and call me those names. You don't know who she is."

Jackson's eyebrows shoot up. "Who is she?"
"She's Ford's wife."

Chapter 32 (Alyssa)

"Ex-wife," she informs me. "Well, thanks to *you*."

"I'm sorry."

She frowns and begins setting up the supplies to start my IV. "Save it. You can't apologize for ruining someone's marriage, it's unforgivable."

Jackson points a finger at her. "Look, if you think I'm letting you stick a needle in her arm after you've just verbally attacked her, think again. I want another nurse."

"Jackson, give us a minute."

When he begins to protest, I add, "Please."

He kisses my forehead. "I'll be right outside that door." He looks at Penelope. "And so will my Momma."

I sit up in bed and look at Penelope. "You're right. I can't ever apologize for something like that. It *is* unforgivable. But I will tell you that I'm not proud of myself. And I will tell you that woman to woman, I'm the lowest of the low and I'm ashamed of myself for that."

Her cold demeanor shifts a little and she takes a deep breath. "It wasn't all your fault." She closes her eyes. "In fact, I'd say that a lot of it wasn't your fault. Especially when it started."

She wipes a tear from her eye and looks down. "I don't think you were really old enough to make the adult decision to be involved with a married man back then...were you?"

"I- um," I stall, because being an *actual* adult now, I'm not entirely sure.

"I mean, what were you, like 16?"

I fidget with my hands. "It was within hours of 17th birthday. *I* begged him to see me for my birthday, though. Let's just say that I was with him when the clock struck 12. I felt like Cinderella at that moment. But looking back now, it was never a fairytale. It was a nightmare."

I look her in the eyes and hold out my arm. "But that's still no excuse for my part in hurting you, because I didn't stay 17 forever, Penelope. And although I only had actual sex with him once and hated myself right after. I still wanted it beforehand...and I was 21 years old when it happened."

Another tear falls down her cheek as she puts the tourniquet on and inserts the needle.

"And if I'm really being honest, Ford and I always had an inappropriate relationship. I should have kicked him out of my life a lot sooner than I did. I was too codependent on him...and it was toxic. He was toxic."

She sniffles and I wish I could hug her. I hate that he took down another woman. And I hate that I played a part in it.

She reaches for a tissue and wipes her face. "He is. I realize that now. I think I *finally* got it when our divorce was finalized a little over three months ago. After I discovered everything about the two of you. But he has this way about him, you know? And it's more than just his good looks...it's this way he has of just sucking you in. He tells you what you want to hear. Then he fucks up, you call him on it, and he apologizes and treats you like you're the most important thing in the world again. Until you're not anymore. It's a never ending cycle. Sometimes all in the same night."

She worries her bottom lip between her teeth. "And this whole time...you *know* he's just working his magic. You know he's altering your psyche in some way that you can't explain. But every time you reach to turn that light on...and you get that much closer to realizing it. Bam...he's onto you...and he's ready to strike again and lure you into his trap. The worst part is, you don't even realize how much damage he's caused until it's too late."

I nod my head, knowing all too well what she means. "He's a master manipulator. He's the human version of snake oil. Pretty package, and he'll sell you anything you want...but in the end...you realize that the real snake was him."

"Yeah, that sums it up perfectly. Look, I'm sorry for calling you a whore. I'm a 34-year-old woman. No matter how upset I am, it doesn't give me a right to slut-shame another female. And I should have left him a long time ago. Hell, I should have figured it out right when you called that night. I was so excited to get married to him, though. I thought we would have the picture perfect life. The nurse and FBI agent and our 2.5 beautiful children."

I reach for her hand and she lets me. "Hey. It's not too late to have that. You're nice, sweet, accomplished, and 34 is still young. I would call you beautiful but I'm afraid you would think I'm conceited."

She laughs and I feel a weight lift off my chest. "It *is* a little strange, huh? I mean, even with the dark hair you have now, we still look a lot alike. Obviously, you're younger and your tits don't sag quite like mine yet...but being in the same room with you is like being in the twilight zone."

I think back to all those times when I wished that I was the one Ford chose instead of her.

Oddly enough, I feel relieved because this is like a glimpse into the future of what it would have been like. There's no doubt in my mind now that he would have done the same thing to me and I would have ended up heartbroken like Penelope.

I give her a small smile. "Well, Ford might be the world's biggest asshole, but at least he has good taste." I look down. "And your tits don't sag. You're still rocking it. I can only hope to look as good as you do when I'm 34."

Then she does something that I definitely wasn't expecting. She pulls me in for a hug. "I didn't like you when I first walked in here. But now, I'm really glad we had this conversation."

I hug her tighter and I feel the tears start falling. "Me too. And for the record, I really am sorry. I wish I could take it all back and I wish you never got hurt in any of this."

She pulls away and pats my cheek. "Me too...but I also see now that I wasn't the only one who got hurt. Take care of yourself, Alyssa. Despite what I thought earlier, you're a good person. A good woman."

"Uh. Everything okay here?" Jackson questions, his eyes darting back and forth between us cautiously.

Penelope squeezes my hand. "Yeah, everything's okay. You got a good girl, here. Take care of her." She looks at me. "Maybe one day I'll find my own handsome knight in shining armor like you have."

"I hope so. Because you deserve that, Penelope."

She wipes her eyes and heads for the door. "I'll be back to check on you in a little while."

Jackson stuffs his hands in his pockets. "I'm not sure what I'm supposed to say right now."

"That makes two of us. I never thought I'd say this, but I'm glad I met her. I'm happy I got a chance to have that conversation with her."

"It's fucking weird how much you look alike, though, huh?"

"Can you blame the man for having good taste?"

He walks over to me and puts his arms around me. He looks like he's about to say something, but Tyrone, Ricardo, and Momma walk into the room.

Ricardo whistles. "Did you guys see that smokin' hot nurse walking down the hall."

Jackson grunts but I put a hand on his arm. "You should get her number, Ricardo. I happen to know for a fact that she's single." He looks excited, until I add. "However, she's not a 'hit it and quit it'. So if you pursue her you better be serious. She's been through enough."

"Nah. I already learned my lesson when it comes to broken and damaged girls."

Jackson and Tyrone look at him but he averts his gaze and rubs his neck. "I'll meet you guys in the car."

"I knew he had it bad for Lou-Lou but *damn*," Tyrone declares after Ricardo walks out.

"There's definitely a story there," Momma says. "Poor guy is all kinds of hurtin'."

Jackson nods but turns to look at me. "I'm gonna ask Shane to bring some of your clothes to my apartment, okay?"

"Are you sure? I really don't want to impose."

He lifts my chin. "Alyssa, I take care of what's mine and what I love. Don't you ever forget that."

Almost a week later I'm feeling much better, but since I'm just getting my appetite back, Momma says I'm still not allowed to live at my bar. Those were her words, not mine.

Jackson has been nothing but attentive and caring. He's held me through the night, brought me tissues and magazines, rubbed my feet, and brought me a hot bowl of Momma's soup every hour on the hour, even when I could only stomach a few small bites.

He never *once* made me feel like I was imposing on him and his life. In fact, every time I tried to go back home, he'd sic Momma on me. I learned very quickly that Momma's not a person you want to argue with because I'd be sure to lose every time.

I turn over in the bed and watch Jackson as he sleeps. The mid-morning sun is peeking in through the corner of the curtain giving me just enough light to be able to enjoy the visual of his beautifully sculpted body.

Nothing puts a damper on a couple's sex life like being sick. Needless to say, Jackson and I haven't been able to enjoy one another in that capacity.

But seeing as I'm feeling almost good as new now. I'm thinking it might be time to indulge a little.

I brush my lips against the sexy stubble grazing his jaw before making my way down his neck.

When I look up I notice that Jackson's eyes are still closed, but the boyish lopsided grin on his face tells me that he's very much awake.

I kiss his chest and continue down lower. I run my tongue along both sides of the V of his lower abs and I hear him let out a low groan.

That deep groan of his only fuels me on. When I slip my head beneath the sheet, I see just how much he's awake. I lick the small drop of precome that I see on the fabric of his boxers. Deciding to tease him a little, I place my mouth over the material covering his erection and suck. I find the opening of his boxers and flick my tongue against it, needing to taste him.

Jackson lets out a curse and raises his hips. I eagerly repeat the movement and he reaches down and twirls my hair around his hand before looking down at me. "Are you sure, baby? I mean, are you feeling good enough for this?"

I nod and pull his boxers down all the way. I open my mouth, but Jackson hauls me back up and lays me across his chest.

I frown, until he cups my face in his hands and searches my eyes. "You're so beautiful it hurts sometimes, did you know that?"

My heart soars...until I think about how I must look right now. My hair is in the messiest of messy buns, my eyes are puffy, and my nose is raw from all the tissues I went through in the past week.

This is not just some smudged mascara and chapped lips. Oh, no. This is me looking like a cross between a zombie and a corpse.

I bury my head into his chest and cover my face with my hands.

"Wow, you really know how to take a compliment," Jackson says, his voice light with humor.

"I look like I could audition for *The Walking Dead* right now, Jackson."

He laughs. "Some of those zombie chicks are pretty hot."

I take the pillow from my side of the bed and hit him with it.

He wraps me in his arms and I can feel his heart pounding rapidly against my back causing me to lean into him.

He gives my shoulder a kiss. "Remind me never to tell you how beautiful you are right when you're about to wake me up with a blowjob again."

I turn slightly and raise a brow. "Please, you were definitely awake."

His gaze turns sultry as his fingers begin grazing my upper thigh underneath my shorts. "Maybe," he whispers.

I moan as the pad of his thumb skims the edges of my panties. "I can still give you one, Jackson."

He moves my panties to the side and his pointer finger trails along my outer lips. It takes everything in me not to fall apart and start writhing like a cat in heat. "Rain check," he whispers. "Because right now, I'm too busy loving how wet you get for me when I'm barely even touching you."

He traces my slit with his middle finger. "I love that you're soaking my finger and I'm not even inside you yet." He repeats the teasing motion. "Tell me, baby, how wet are you gonna be for me when I stick my finger in this pretty pussy of yours?"

I'm so worked up I don't care anymore, I grind my ass against his cock and let out a small gasp when he presses his thumb against my clit. "Answer me, Alyssa."

"Why don't you find out?" I tell him. He doesn't waste another second, he pulls my shorts down and two of his fingers dip inside me. "Fuck, baby. You're drenched."

I suck in a breath and swerve my backside against his erection again. He nibbles my earlobe. "You trying to tell me that you want something?"

I nod eagerly and he thrusts into me. "Well, if you want me," he rasps. "Put me inside you."

Desire strong enough to make me dizzy infuses me as I reach behind me, take him in my hand and slowly proceed to slide him inside me.

He lifts one of my legs and rests it on the outside of his before he begins thrusting inside me. This is the sexiest spooning I've ever been apart of—this position is so intimate.

He reaches around and swirls my clit with his fingers. "Oh fuck, don't stop," I scream. His pace picks up and a minute later I'm a cursing, twitching mess around him as my orgasm takes hold of me.

"Fuck, I love the way you come all over my dick, baby," he says. His body tightens, his own breathing is labored and he thrusts into me one last time before I feel the spurt of his release.

He rolls me over until I'm underneath him and kisses my nose. "You're still so beautiful it hurts. Zombie or no zombie."

I fling my arms around his neck and breathe him in. "I'm in love with you, Jackson Reid. You've ruined me for anyone else."

He rubs his nose along my jaw. "I'm in love with you. You're my first, my last and my only love, Alyssa Tanner." He looks up at me and my heart flutters. "I want to grow old with you," he whispers. "I want to let you win at bingo, I want you to help me find my dentures, and I want to spend the evening watching the sunset with you every night from our two rocking chairs." He rests his head on my heart and my eyes fill with tears. "And when I die, you'll be my last thought. When my life flashes before my eyes, I'll see nothing but you. Because you already are the very best part of my life."

"You're mine," I whisper. "Finding you made all the pain I've ever endured worth living through."

I run my fingers through his hair. "We'll have those rocking chairs, Jackson. I know we will."

He wipes the tears from my eyes. "Yeah, baby. We will. I'll find a way to make it happen."

The end of his statement throws me off a little, but I'm soon distracted by the sound of my phone ringing.

"Hey, Shane. What's up?"

"Look, I know you're still probably sick and I know you're moving soon, but do you think you can work at the bar for a few hours tonight?"

"Of, course. It's the least I can do since you've been so cool with me being out this week. Wait a minute—" I pause, unsure if I understood him right. "What do you mean I'm moving soon? Are you kicking me out?"

Beside me, Jackson sits up in bed and puts his boxers back on.

"Kicking you out?" Shane sputters. "No. I'm talking about you moving in with Jackson, silly."

I stare at Jackson then, the way he's avoiding my gaze and the guilty expression on his face tells me everything I need to know. "Yeah," I respond my tone harsher than I intended. "I'll be there at seven."

"Oh, um. Okay, great. See you then," Shane responds before he hangs up.

I crinkle my nose and narrow my eyes. "Something you want to tell me?"

Jackson stands up and opens his arms wide. "Surprise, baby."

I wrap the sheet around me and stand in front of him. "Yeah, *I'll* say. You know, couples usually discuss moving in with one another. Because both parties have to be in agreement. That's the way a relationship works."

I open my arms wide, mocking him. "It's not supposed to be '*surprise, baby*' I've told your landlord / boss that you're moving. Especially when you haven't even discussed it with your actual girlfriend first!" I shout.

He opens his mouth but I cut him off. "I mean, did you even ask *Tyrone* about it? Or is he just as in the dark about all this as I am?"

Jackson holds a finger up and opens the door. "Yoo, Tyrone," he calls out.

I stand there with my mouth open in disbelief.

"Yeah?" Tyrone shouts.

"Is it cool if Alyssa moves in with us?"

"It's cool," Tyrone answers, before adding. "As long as she cooks every once in awhile."

Jackson shuts the door and shrugs. "See? Everything's cool."

I'm so frustrated I begin stomping my feet on the floor like a 2 - year-old. "And what about me? Did you ever think to ask *me*?"

Jackson scratches the back of his head and pouts. "Are you saying that you don't want to live with me?"

I open my mouth to answer but he walks over to me and scoops me in his arms. "I thought we just told one another exactly how we felt about each other?" He kisses my cheek. "Remember? Rocking chairs? Sunsets?" He kisses my chin. "Best part of my life?" He kisses my neck. "Great morning sex?" He moves lower to my breasts and the sheet falls. "Hot zombies?"

I roll my eyes and let out a giggle. "It's a big step, Jackson. We haven't been together long at all."

His expression is sad and it pulls on my heartstrings. "Are you saying no?"

I think about this for a moment. I weigh the pros and cons. Pro's being- waking up next to Jackson, his apartment being in a safer area, kissing Jackson, making love to Jackson, falling asleep next to Jackson. The only con I can come up with is that it's a 20-minute walk away from my job. Unless he expects me to stop working there?

"I'm still working at Finnley's," I tell him.

He looks hopeful. "Of course. I know you like it there. I wouldn't ever expect you to stop. Only now, I'll be walking you home every night. Well, *if* you want me to that is."

"Okay," I say.

"Okay?" he repeats. "Okay, like you'll be moving your stuff in soon? Or, okay you're an asshole and I still can't believe you sprung this on me?"

"Yes. I still hate that you sprung this on me, and I hate that it wasn't discussed and there was no romantic gesture or anything, but okay I'll move in with you."

"Thank you."

Before I can respond he gets down on one knee. I stare at him wide-eyed. "Whoa, too soon. *Way* too soon!" I start. "Don't get me wrong, my gut instinct is telling me to say yes, but we can't get married right now. I need time, Jackson! Like a year or two, at *least*," I begin babbling a mile a minute.

He stares at me like I'm crazy until he looks down and adjusts his position so he's kneeling down on both knees. "Relax. I wasn't asking you to marry me," he says. "Not that I won't be asking you to do that at some point in the future," he quickly says."But trust me when I do, it will be way more romantic." He grins. "And it's good to know that you'll say yes."

"So, what are you doing then?" I ask, half relieved, half nervous.

"Alyssa," he pauses. "Shit, you never told me your middle name," he whispers.

"Trust me. You don't want to know my middle name," I tell him.

"Of course, I want to know your middle name. I would tell you mine but I'm sure you heard Momma shout it last week."

I bite my bottom lip, wishing I didn't have to tell him.

Jackson stands back up. "What? It can't be *that* bad. Let me guess, Marie? That's a nice name, baby."

I shake my head, not wanting to play this game.

He raises an eyebrow playfully. "Is it Gertrude? Can I call you Gerddy for short?"

"It's Ford," I whisper.

"Huh? What the hell does *he* have—"

"That's my middle name," I say, cutting him off. "He was my dad's best friend. When they were kids they made a pact that the first one to have a son would be named after the other one. Ford doesn't have children and since I ended up being a girl, my mom chose the name Alyssa. But my dad still wanted Ford to be my middle name. I'm sorry, Jackson."

He kisses my hand. "Don't be sorry, Alyssa. I love every part of you. Even the parts I don't always like." He clears his throat and looks at me. "Alyssa Ford Tanner, would you do me the honor of moving in with me?"

"And Tyrone!" Tyrone shouts from the other side of the door.

"And Tyrone," he amends.

My face hurts from smiling so hard. "Yes. I would love to," I say.

I hear Momma and Tyrone cheer from the other side of the door and I can't help but laugh with them. Jackson pulls me into another hug, but I don't miss the strange expression on his face.

"What?" I ask.

He appears to be lost in deep thought before saying, "Your dad really trusted Ford, didn't he?"

"Yeah," I whisper. "Ford's an asshole when it comes to the way he treats women. But that aside, my dad trusted him with his life."

Jackson nods before kissing my forehead. "I'm gonna take a shower."

"Want some company?"

He doesn't respond but he pulls me in for a kiss that answers my question.

Chapter 33 (Jackson)

Alyssa's father trusted Ford. He was his best friend.

That thought keeps echoing throughout my head.

Not that I'm actually considering taking that deal with him...but it's good to know that *if* I did...he would uphold his end.

I'm not taking *that* deal, but I do have to figure out a way to deal with this whole Alyssa situation. I'm ecstatic to know I'll be waking up beside her every morning, but I still have to work out how I'm going to keep her from finding out about DeLuca.

I figure, the best way to go about it will be to tell Tyrone and Ricardo not to bring up DeLuca's name in front of Alyssa. I'll just tell them it's because I don't want to scare her with the truth regarding who DeLuca is, so it's best we don't mention his name.

Tyrone will probably remind me that he's been completely honest with Shelby about everything, but I'll just tell him I'm not ready to do that with Alyssa.

He'll tell me I'm wrong, then we'll share another Doctor Phil moment...and it will be fine.

I hope.

As far as DeLuca himself goes...I'm going to ask Ricardo to set up a meeting with DeLuca for me next week. A face to face sit down.

I'm going to be honest with him and lay everything out on the line. I *was* going to tell him about Ford trying to recruit me to murder him...but after Alyssa told me that her dad trusted him, I don't think I should go that route.

Besides, if anything happened to Ford and Alyssa found out it was my fault...I know a small part of her would be upset.

I won't do that to her.

I'll just take my chances with DeLuca. I've still got the fact that I'm his best fighter as my bargaining chip.

I head into the kitchen and watch Alyssa sitting at the counter while Momma fixes her something to eat. She has her Finnley's t-shirt and a pair of jeans. Tyrone has a fight tonight, so we'll be heading to the club soon. He likes to get there a few hours early in order to center himself.

She gives me a smile when I enter the room. I walk over to her, bend down and kiss her soft lips. "Hey, baby. Going to work soon?"

She stretches her arms above her head and yawns. "Yeah. I'm exhausted but it's the least I can do. Shane's been great about me taking off."

Momma makes a face, and I know she thinks it's too soon for her to be going back.

I honestly hate the fact that she's going in tonight as well, but I can't stop her. I tuck a strand of hair behind her ear. "Drink plenty of juice, and don't leave your cup out anywhere. I'll be by the bar with the guys after Tyrone's fight ends. I can help you man it if you're still exhausted when I get there."

"I'll be fine, but thank you," she says while Momma hands her a sandwich. Alyssa looks up from her grilled cheese and her eyes open wide. "I almost forgot it was Saturday and there's a fight tonight."

Tyrone walks in the kitchen then, his expression tight. "Yup."

His demeanor is a little off right now and I'm not sure what to make of it. He's always a little nervous before a fight, but he usually gets a handle on it by using his sense of humor. Before I have time to call him on it, Alyssa hops off the stool and runs over to him. Then, surprising everyone, she flings her arms around his neck. "Please be careful," she whispers. "Please."

Jesus, watching my fight really did a number on her.

Momma fans her face and Tyrone closes his eyes. "I'll be okay, Alyssa."

The fact that he's not making a joke right now puts me on edge.

"And after I kick his ass, I'll be celebrating by getting another alpha male piercing," he says.

Momma covers her ears and I laugh, feeling the weight in my chest dissipate.

Alyssa smacks him on the chest and chuckles before walking away. "I just don't get it," she says to Momma while rummaging through her purse.

"Get what, sugar?"

"The fighting. It's scary, Momma. If you should be convincing *anyone* to quit their job—" She points at Tyrone and me. "It's *those* two. They're crazy for putting themselves through that."

Momma gives her a weird look. "Trust me, I would if I could. But you know it's all De—"

"Dinero," I shout, as everyone turns to face me. "Cause you know, it's all about the Benjamin's, baby."

Three sets of eyes stare at me like I've lost my mind. Luckily, Tyrone comes to my defense by putting an arm around my neck. "Come on, Biggie. It's almost 7, my fight starts at 9:45."

I give Alyssa a kiss and hug Momma goodbye since she won't be attending the fight tonight.

As soon as Tyrone and I walk out into the hallway his eyes are on me. "Either my music has really started rubbing off on you, or you're hiding something," he says.

"What's the matter?" I deflect. "You don't want to be the Puffy Daddy to my Biggie?"

He snorts. "Uh-uh. Nice try. Something's off with you. And you know I'm not gonna quit until you tell me, so you might as well save me the trouble and spill it."

"I can't."

"Jackson," he insists.

We walk out the apartment complex doors. "Look, I just need you to do me a favor and never mention DeLuca's name in front of Alyssa."

"What? Why? I mean, it's not like we talk about him all that much anyway, but he is the reason our lives are the way they are right now." He pauses. "Shit, she doesn't know you're involved with DeLuca...does she?"

I shake my head and avert my gaze.

"I thought you told her *everything* that night?"

I rub the back of my neck. "I told her that I was a murderer, yes. But I never told her that I'm tied up with DeLuca or that *he's* the reason I'm free."

He looks at me incredulously. "She never asked why or how you're free?"

Oh, she asked. Right before she fell asleep after making love that night. "I told her I got acquitted because of self-defense," I say. "Trust me, Tyrone. I have my reasons. I wish I didn't have to lie. It's just the way it has to be right now."

He thinks about this for a moment. "Can I ask you a few more questions?"

"You can ask, but I might not be able to answer them directly."

He rubs his chin. "First and foremost...does this have to do with *her* safety?"

"Yes."

"Does it have anything to do with the FBI?"

I'm about to ask how he knows that, but then he says, "The night you were drunk, you said something about her having an FBI sugar daddy. So, I assume he's got something to do with it?"

I shake my head. "No. He doesn't. And he was never her sugar daddy, I was just being a drunk ass."

"Oh, I know. I was there, remember? Okay, I have one more question."

"Shoot."

He gives me a look and I know he's about to crack the case. "If you were working for *any* other mob boss...would you tell her the truth about everything then?"

I give him a small nod.

"Shit," he says. "Alyssa's got one hell of a history, doesn't she?"

"I can't tell you, Tyrone. I wish I could. But it's for her own safety that she doesn't find out about DeLuca."

"You don't have to tell me, Jackson. I read you loud and clear, brother. I'm just worried now. I have no clue what her story is—" He pauses and starts listing things on his fingers. "But just knowing that her daddy was murdered, it's got something to do with the feds, and DeLuca himself is involved. Not to mention, the fact that she can't know about us working for him—"

"And he can't know about her," I interject.

"And the plot thickens," he whispers.

"You've got the most important pieces, Tyrone. I just can't be the one to put them together for you because it's not my place to."

He nods. "I understand."

"You still okay with her moving in?"

He waves a hand. "Yeah. She loves you, Jackson. And I know you love her." He closes his eyes. "Sometimes you do whatever you can for the woman you love."

We walk into the club and he looks around. His eyes zero in on the cage. "And to answer your question. I'd be Biggie." He snorts. "Especially tonight."

"Tonight? Why?"

He puts a hand on my shoulder and smiles. "See? Now if you really were a hip-hop fan and liked that song, you would get it."

I raise an eyebrow and he gives me a small laugh. "Don't give me that look, it's nothing. I was just making a crack about the album that song was featured on is all."

Then he pulls me in for a hug, which is rare for him to do here in the middle of the club. "You're my best friend, Jackson."

I hug him back and tell him the same, but an unsettling feeling washes over me. I'm about to question him about why he's acting so weird, but Ricardo shows up and they decide to do some last minute training.

Because apparently....they just got word that Tyrone's opponent for tonight got switched.

That only makes this feeling in the pit of my stomach worse.

One things for sure...I'm finding out the name of that album.

———

A little over two hours later, I'm standing in the middle of the crowd ready to punch someone.

Tyrone denied me access to the fucking dressing room. I spoke to Ricardo about it but he said that I know the rules before a fight, and since I'm not fighting tonight I have to respect them.

Then I told him that I thought something was wrong. I told him what Tyrone said earlier and I told him what the name of the album was- '*Ready to Die.*'

What the *fuck* is going on?

Ricardo looked spooked and tried calling DeLuca on his phone to figure out what the hell was going on with this new schedule change, but of course, he didn't answer.

Then he went in and tried talking to Tyrone, but he said he shut down and won't talk to anyone. He's in his own little world right now preparing for the fight.

When I see him walk out and into the cage, I know it's true.

He's not Tyrone right now. He's his own version of the Hulk.

But when I look at him and his eyes connect with mine. He gives me the look. "I got this," he mouths.

I nod my head and pat the space above my heart. To most people, we probably look like two sappy lovers. But fuck those people, I wouldn't have gotten through these past few years without him.

He's been the *only* good thing about making a deal with the Devil.

I look at Ricardo and he gives me the thumbs up sign. "Everything's okay," he mouths.

I breathe a sigh of relief.

Until I see his opponent walk out.

It's the same guy *I* fought last week.

Tyrone and I have a similar build for the most part. He's 6'2 to my 6'3, but unlike my 235lbs, he fluctuates between 230-245lbs, depending on when and how long Momma comes to visit.

I smile because I know he's on the upside of the scale due to Momma being at our apartment this entire week. Then I frown because I know that the extra weight won't make that much of a difference against a guy who weighs 388lbs and is 5 inches taller than him.

But I can't let myself think like that. Tyrone's one tough competitor. We both hold the title of being the best fighter in the club. Which is also why we train together.

He's never even lost a match. Hell, if I'm being honest, he's taken fewer hits than me now. He's only been hit twice, two separate matches.

His secret?

When he gets close to reaching his limit...he becomes fucking psychotic.

I'm not kidding, either. He turns into a full on psychiatric patient. To the point where he begins actually scaring his opponents. It's why his fans call him 'Hulk'. The guy just loses it up there.

In fact, I'd be willing to bet that Tyrone's fights bring in more money than *mine* do. He's way more entertaining to watch than me. If he's not scaring the audience to death with his antics, then he's making them laugh by taunting his opponent.

They announce Tyrone and the crowd goes wild and I join them. "Break bad on em', Hulk," I call out.

He hears me say this and blows me a kiss. Ricardo shakes his head and laughs and the crowd goes even crazier. The first time he did it, I wanted to pummel him, but he thought it was hysterical; and so did the crowd, so he kept doing it.

Then they introduce his shithead opponent. For whatever reason, his eyes lock with mine. I hardly ever do this, since it's not my fight...but this time, I issue my own stare down, letting him know that on a personal level if he plays dirty with Tyrone...he'll be dealing with *me*.

Instead of heeding my warning like I hoped he would. His lifts his pointer finger and traces it across his neck horizontally. Then he gives me a wink.

My stomach coils. Something's not right.

I look at Ricardo, but he's too busy whispering words of encouragement in Tyrone's ear to look at me.

When Lou-Lou walks out on stage, I try getting her attention, but she just gives me a weird look and shrugs before wishing Tyrone luck.

Fuck it. I'm walking up there myself. Maybe I can get Tyrone's attention *that* way. Since I'm standing in the middle of the large crowd, I begin shoving people out of the way.

The match begins but I'm still a good few rows back. That's when I start screaming my head off and pushing people out of the way. When they notice that it's *me* and see how angry I am, they start moving with no hesitation.

I've never acted like this before unless I'm in the cage so they know something's up.

I'm screaming Tyrone's name like a lunatic but I don't care. I look back up at the cage and what I see brings me to my knees.

Everything happens in slow motion.

The beast is sliding a knife down the middle of Tyrone's back. This was supposed to be a fucking fight, not a goddamned stabbing. Ricardo's going off like a motherfucker on the sidelines trying to get to him, but the beast's team of people start throwing punches and kicks, attacking him.

I start scaling the cage, not giving a fuck about anyone or anything, only Tyrone.

I hop on the beast's back and shove my fingers in his eyeballs so hard there's blood dripping down my fingers. He pulls the knife out of Tyrone, grunts and throws me off his back with enough force that I slam into the cage, but I don't care.

I get up, run right back up to him and headbutt him as hard as I can.

He looks woozy and backs up, but at the last second, he starts charging me with the same knife that he stabbed Tyrone with.

That's when Ricardo hops on his back and I hear a cracking sound.

The guy falls limp and I know what's been done...and I'd be lying if I said I wasn't happy about it.

But I have more important things to worry about.

I rush over to Tyrone. He's shaking, and his blood is pooling all around him. I take off my sweatshirt and tie it around his wound tight. He finally looks at me, but when he does, his eyes are glazed over, and I know he's out of it.

I scream his name and tell him to hold on. "I can't lose you, Tyrone," I scream. Hell, I'm probably sobbing, who knows.

I hear Ricardo on the phone calling for the mob doctor to get to the cage.

"Love you, J-man," he whispers.

"I love you, too," I say. "You're gonna be fine. The doctor's on his way."

"Tell Momma I love her and Shelby...tell Shelby I love her," he says. "I did this for her," he whispers.

"What the fuck do you mean?"

He begins nodding off but looks at me. "I made a deal with DeLuca. I asked to be out of the club. I wanted to end my contract." He gulps in a mouthful of air. "I wanted to start my life with Shelby. She didn't know I was doing this, though."

"And what did he say, Tyrone?" I scream, already fearing the answer.

"He told me I had to fight one last opponent...and then I was out."

I shake my head. "No. You had to know it wouldn't be that easy."

He begins nodding off again, but I force him to stay with me. "I know, Jackson. But he promised. His only stipulation was that I had to go a full 10 rounds with the guy you fought last week."

His eyes close but he keeps talking. "I knew it would be a tough fight. I mean, 10 rounds with *that* beast? You only went 3 with him. But DeLuca told me to drag it out to 10 rounds and take my hits and my punishment like a man. But, I never thought it would end up like this. I should have, though, Huh? I mean, it's fucking DeLuca. Still, I didn't anticipate being stabbed."

DeLuca was setting Tyrone up to be killed. There's no way he could have lasted 10 rounds with that guy without defending himself. I barely survived 3 and I did fight back. If Alyssa hadn't screamed, I never would have made it past that.

Weird thing is? That beast looked at me right before Tyrone's fight, like it was some kind of personal message.

Tyrone starts shaking again and I have to hold him down in order to make sure there's pressure on his wound. His eyes flutter and the feeling of dread washes over me. I lower my lips to his ear and whisper, "You're my brother and I love you. You better make it through this because I need you. Don't you fucking bail on me, Tyrone."

The doctor finally shows up, declares he needs to go to a hospital right away and they take him out on a stretcher.

I sit there in shock, my eyes are still wet and Tyrone's blood surrounds me. It feels like my heart just got crushed into dust.

But then venomous rage fills my blood.

And I know exactly who it's for.

The Devil himself.

Fuck sitting down to try and talk to him. *Fuck* laying it all out on the table for him. *Fuck* offering him an ounce of my loyalty in exchange for Alyssa's safety after he pulled this shit.

There's another way to ensure that she's safe.

There's another way to get payback for those I love.

This bastard has now hurt *two* people that I would do anything for.

Fuck this club, fuck his contract, and fuck *him*.

I stare into the camera and narrow my eyes. "I'm coming for you, DeLuca," I sneer, low enough so that only I can hear.

I see the camera move and I know he's watching me.

Good.

Chapter 34 (Alyssa)

L ast call ended 20 minutes ago.

Jackson, Tyrone, and Ricardo never showed up after the fight.

I've tried calling Jackson's cell multiple times but he still hasn't picked up or responded to any of my text messages.

I would call Momma, but she doesn't believe in cell phones.

It's obvious that something is *very* wrong. Which is why I locked up the bar and I'm currently standing in front of Jackson's apartment door, pounding on it as hard as I can.

I thought for sure that Momma would be here, but seeing as I'm still not getting a response, that only makes this bad feeling I have worse.

With no options left, I have no choice but to walk down the hall to Lou-Lou's front door.

She answers on the second knock. Her eyes are red and puffy, it's obvious that she's been crying and she's upset about something.

"Look, I'm sorry I'm interrupting whatever it is that you're going through right now, but I can't get a hold of Jackson, and no one is at the apartment—"

"You don't know what happened, do you?" she says, her voice raspy with emotion.

I swallow hard against the lump in my throat and tell myself to breathe before I shake my head.

"There was an accident at the club tonight. Tyrone got stabbed by his opponent when the match started."

My hand flies over my mouth and a sob escapes.

"Everyone's at the hospital because he's having emergency surgery. That's probably why you can't get a hold of anyone."

"Thank you."

I start running down the hall, but to my surprise, I hear Lou-Lou's footsteps behind me.

"It's after 2am, Alyssa. You'll never catch a cab because they're too busy picking up drunk idiots and it will take you an hour to get there on foot. Also, it's not exactly safe to go walking in the city by yourself this time of night. If you want, I can drive you," she offers.

I nod my head, too shaken up to form actual words. My heart is breaking for Jackson...and Momma. Oh, god, poor Momma.

I pray as hard as I can for Tyrone the entire ride to the hospital.

I give Lou-Lou a questioning look when she pulls up to the front of the hospital but makes no move to get out. "You're not coming in?"

She looks down. "I want to, but I don't think anyone really wants to see me."

"Look, don't take this the wrong way, but it's not about you right now. Tyrone needs all the positive thoughts he can get. Plus, I think Ricardo would appreciate you showing up and offering your support."

She gives me an odd look and I can tell she's ready to argue, but instead she gets out with me and hands her keys to a valet attendant. "Do you think they'll give us any information? We're not immediate family and we didn't come in with him. And you already said that Jackson wasn't picking up his phone."

Crap, I didn't really think about that.

I scan the emergency room. The look on both the security

guard's face and the nurse at the desk, tells me they're both going to be hard nuts to crack.

Out of the corner of my eye, I see my doppelganger's blonde ponytail and pink scrubs.

"Penelope," I call out, while taking Lou-Lou's hand and rushing over to her.

I quickly explain the situation. She looks sympathetic, and before I know it, she's leading us past the front desk and walking us toward a special section of the intensive care waiting room.

She tells us that Tyrone's still in surgery but she'll keep us updated if she finds out any information. I quickly thank her before Lou-Lou and I round the corner to the small waiting room.

That's where I see Jackson and Ricardo in some kind of stand-off, looking like they're about to rip each others faces off.

"You've gotta be kidding me," Lou-Lou mutters. "Stop it!" she screams.

It's no use. In the blink of an eye, Jackson advances toward Ricardo and holds him up against the wall by his throat. "You knew this was going to happen, didn't you?" he sneers.

"You're out of your mind, Jackson. For fucks sake, I snapped that guy's neck. You think I would ever let anything happen to either one of you?"

Jackson shakes his head. "You knew about them switching his opponent before the fight. You *had* to know something was up. You told me everything was okay right before the fight. But, it wasn't fucking okay. You knew about the meeting because he had to go through you to get one! You knew he wanted out and you never fucking told me. And now, my best friend is in surgery fighting for his life."

Jackson slams him up hard against the wall again, but I see Ricardo's eyes flash and that strange feeling washes over me. The very same one I had that night Jackson fought Dean in the bathroom and Ricardo showed up.

"I had no idea that any of this was gonna go down, Jackson. I got him a meeting, yeah. But I wasn't privy to their discussion. It was a closed meeting. Tyrone wouldn't tell me why he wanted the meeting either, he just said it was important. If I had known, I would have talked him out of it," he screams, his voice cracking with emotion.

"You guys are like my brothers. You both are the closest thing to a real family I've ever had. I would never be okay with someone taking either one of you out, ever. I don't care *who* might have issued the order."

Order? Taking them out? What is he talking about?

Jackson eases up on his grip and bangs the wall beside his head. "I swear to god, Ricardo; you better be telling me the truth. Because if I find out that you knew about this...we're fucking done in every way you can think of."

The dangerous intensity in Ricardo's eyes is replaced by sadness. "I didn't know. I swear. I'd let him take *me* out before I'd *ever* let him do it to either one of you."

What should be a somewhat comforting statement, instead forces the hairs on the back of my neck to stand up.

Jackson pulls him into a hug. "I don't know what I'm gonna do if he doesn't pull through this."

My eyes water because the thought of losing Tyrone is heart-wrenching, but the moment turns tense again when Jackson fixes himself and his eyes darken. "Actually, I do."

Ricardo shakes his head. "No, man. Get that thought out of your head right now. He didn't order it. It wasn't him. I'm telling you."

Jackson slams him up against the wall again, but Ricardo deflects it and now he's the one slamming Jackson up against the wall.

"It was. I know it was," Jackson screams. "And you can tell *him* I'm fucking done."

Ricardo's hand wraps around his throat. "Don't be stupid. You'll get yourself killed. You can't be done with him. That ain't the way it works and you know it."

Two thoughts hit me simultaneously at that moment—what else

is Jackson keeping from me? And more importantly...what kind of dangerous situation is he involved in?

Jackson lifts his arm and maneuvers out of the choke hold. They face one another again, but this time, it's clear it's not going to end in a hug. Jackson's fist flies out but Ricardo blocks it at the last possible second. Jackson jabs him again, though and gets him right between the eyes.

Lou-Lou and I start screaming our heads off, trying to get them to stop, but they ignore us completely.

"You're not out," Ricardo says before punching Jackson across the face. "I'm not gonna let you kill yourself," he screams before he throws another punch.

Jackson has that wild look in his eyes when he issues a kick straight to Ricardo's side. My hearts in my throat because I know that once Jackson gets started and he's in *this* mindset, the only one who can make him stop is Ricardo, but since he's fighting *Ricardo* right now—I'm terrified of how this is going to end.

Ricardo spits blood on the ground and motions for Jackson to come at him again. If Jackson's eyes are wild, Ricardo's are purely menacing and downright murderous.

My stomach drops and my hands shake because this time, I *know* I've seen that look and I'm not mistaken like before.

And I think I might just know what, or rather *who* Jackson is involved with. But my god, I *hope* I'm wrong.

Before I can focus on that, though, I have to stop this fight. My instincts are taking over and I surge toward them. Lou-Lou tries pulling me back but I twist away. She lets out an ear piercing whistle but it still doesn't stop me or them.

Both of their arms are pulled back and I know it's the last possible second that I have before they both strike each other again.

Lou-Lou screams my name when she sees what I'm about to do, but I do it anyway.

There's no way to describe how it feels to be punched full force by two massive men at the same time.

Well, except one. It really fucking hurts...a lot. Way more than I thought it would. Enough to almost make me regret doing it in the first place. It's literally the complete opposite of 'double your pleasure, double your fun.'

Jackson's fist lands on my cheek, and Ricardo's fist lands somewhere in my stomach region. Seeing as I'm 5'3 they were both obviously going for some low blows.

I let out a sound somewhere between a cry, a yelp, and a scream before hunching over and falling to the floor. That's when I hear Momma's voice. "Oh my god. Look what you boys did! How could you?" she screams.

Both Jackson and Ricardo drop down to the floor, their expressions horrified. "Alyssa? Fuck, baby. I'm sorry. I...god," Jackson says. He cups my face and I wince. "I'm *so* fucking sorry."

"Me too," Ricardo says. "I had no idea you were even here. What the hell were you thinking getting between us?"

"I just wanted you both to stop fighting. I didn't know how else to make you stop."

"*What* is going on here?" another voice calls out. I look up to find Penelope standing over us concern splashed across her pretty face.

"It was an accident," I say. When she raises an eyebrow, I stand up. "Honest, Penelope. I was the one who got in the middle. They didn't even see me."

She crosses her arms over her chest. "I'll get you a few ice packs." Then she looks at Jackson and Ricardo. "Gentlemen," she scoffs that word. "This is the intensive care unit of a *hospital*. This is not a zoo. Keep your hands to yourself. If it happens again I *will* have security escort you out," she snaps, before she turns on her heels and storms out.

"What were you boys thinking?" Momma whispers, her voice shaking.

She looks so heartbroken and devastated right now, I feel myself break.

Jackson and Ricardo stand up. "We're sorry, Momma," they say at the same time. "It will never happen again," they promise.

Then they walk over to her and wrap their arms around her.

I hear her sobbing softly and I lose it. I'm not the only one though, Lou-Lou's also weeping quietly in the corner. I don't miss the look Ricardo gives her. For a moment, I think he's going to walk over to her, but instead, he gives Momma and Jackson one last hug and leaves the waiting room altogether.

I look at Jackson and I want to confront him, but with everything else happening, I don't have the heart to just yet. I don't want to accuse him of lying to me and committing the ultimate betrayal until I have absolute proof and I know for a fact that it's DeLuca he's involved with. I'm going to need a little more to go on than just a gut feeling about Ricardo.

That doesn't mean I'm not still pissed to know that DeLuca or no DeLuca he's obviously been keeping something from me.

He walks over to me and holds out his arms. I take a deep breath and look down before he hugs me. He senses my hesitation and says, "I'm so sorry, Alyssa. I would never hurt you on purpose. Please forgive me."

The tears fall harder then...because if he's lying to me about DeLuca...I'm not sure that I can. Hell, for all I know, Jackson could be the one setting me up for DeLuca.

Oh, god. What if he is?

That thought sends a chill right through me and I have to push myself away from his embrace.

The look he gives me breaks my heart, but I can't stand the thought of being in his arms right now.

I slowly back away from him and he looks both crushed and stunned.

Luckily, Lou-Lou comes to my defense by taking my hand and saying, "I think she's in a lot of pain, Jackson. Probably not the best time to be hugging her. She did just get punched by two huge guys, remember?"

He winces and rubs his face. "I'm gonna go get those ice packs for you."

Momma looks at us. "I'm gonna go see if there's any news."

Before she leaves, I run over and throw my arms around her. "I'm so sorry, Momma. I know he'll make it through this. Because he's tough just like his Momma."

She hugs me tight and gives me a kiss on the cheek before leaving the room. That's when Jackson's eyes connect with mine. There are so many emotions in those eyes of his right now, I have to force myself to breathe.

He walks over to me and hands me two ice packs. "Here." Then he turns and walks out the door.

"I'm being a real bitch, aren't I?" I ask Lou-Lou, because let's face it, who would know better than her?

She considers this for a moment before saying, "It's probably not the best time to be so angry with him seeing as Tyrone's still in surgery and we don't know the outcome." She shrugs. "However, you can't really control how you feel when someone you love hurts you. And the fact that you can't even stand being touched by him combined with that look you gave him...tells me that whatever Jackson did to you was unforgivable."

I turn around and face her. "Like what Ricardo did to you?"

She closes her eyes in agony and I feel bad for even asking the question. "No," she says, opening her eyes which are now glassy. "Let's just say that I've been right where Jackson's standing. I know what it's like to be on the receiving end of that look and have the man you..." She pauses and wipes a tear. "The man you love, look at you like the thought of touching you is unbearable and he'd rather die."

She clears her throat. "I'm gonna go grab some coffee. You want anything?"

I *want* to know more about what happened between her and Ricardo, but I know she's not going to tell me. I sit down in one of the chairs. "No, I'm good. Thanks."

She leaves and I curl my arms around myself while saying another prayer for Tyrone.

A moment later, I look up to find one of the most gorgeous women I have ever seen in my life staring at me. Her eyes are bloodshot and there's a look of utter despair on her face, but that does nothing to diminish her beauty. Her skin is smooth and mocha colored, her dark hair falls around her shoulders in soft curls, and her bright green eyes are mesmerizing.

"I'm sorry. The nurse told me this was where everyone was waiting. But I must have been mistaken, seeing as there's hardly anyone in here," she says in a Southern accent.

The accent gives her away and I immediately know who she is. "Shelby?"

She blinks and looks surprised. "Why yes," she says. "I don't believe we've ever met before. I'm not from around these parts. How do you know my name?"

I stand up and hold out my hand. "I'm Alyssa. I'm Jackson's—" I don't have a chance to finish that statement because her arms are around me and she's hugging me so tight I have to force myself not to yelp.

"I've heard so much about you, Alyssa," she says. Then she starts sobbing. "Have you heard anything? Is he still in surgery?"

"The last I heard he was. I know a nurse who works here, she's my—" I pause because I'm not entirely sure what to refer to her as at this point. "Friend and she promised to update me as soon as she can."

"Thank you, tell her I appreciate it. I'm so scared, Alyssa," she sobs. "I won't be able to go on if I lose him."

"He's a fighter, Shelby. He's going to make it."

She pulls away and wipes at her tears with a tissue. "I can't believe this happened." Then her green eyes turn angry. So angry I become alarmed. "I swear, if that son-of-a-bitch DeLuca did this to him. I will raise hell."

My heart constricts and I'm pretty sure I make a choking sound from somewhere deep in my throat.

There's a world of a difference between suspecting something and having it outright confirmed.

Because now I have to face facts, I have no choice but to acknowledge what's happening.

I have no choice but to realize that DeLuca wants his revenge. I have no choice but to accept that Jackson was setting me up.

Somewhere in the back of my mind, I recall Jackson telling me not to go to the club. But before it can hit the surface of my thoughts, I stuff it down. He *has* to be setting me up, this is the only reason I can come up with for him lying to me. Why *else* would he be actively working and fighting for a man who he knows brutally killed my father?

The room spins and I'm struck with the feeling of wanting to call Ford for some kind of protection, but I force myself to stay strong. Despite my father, I already know that I can't trust Ford, he's already shown his true colors to me. There's no way in the world I would ever put myself at his mercy again.

"Alyssa?" Shelby calls out.

Her name sounds so far away now but I don't know why. It's only when Jackson's face appears right in front of me and I let out a scream that I realize I'm on the floor.

"Talk to me, baby. What happened?" Jackson says, searching my face.

I quickly crawl away from him and stand up. I look up just as Lou-Lou walks in the room.

The face Jackson's makes when I walk over to her and reach for *her* hand is unlike any I've seen.

As messed up as it sounds, it's my way of letting him know that I'm on to him. It's my way of telling him that I'd rather hold *Lou-Lou's* hand than ever touch him again, the traitorous motherfucker.

He steps closer to me, but to my surprise, Lou-Lou lifts her chin and glares at him. "Leave her alone, Jackson. I have no clue what you did but she doesn't want you near her for the time being. You need to respect that."

His eyes narrow and he opens his mouth, but the look I give him halts him and he looks taken back.

I thought I'd break down over his betrayal. But I'm not, far from it actually. I'm straight up seething. I'm so outraged I want to put my hands around his neck and strangle the shit out of him. I want to eliminate him and wipe his beautiful face off the planet.

They always say there's a thin line between love and hate and right now, I'm standing on it, planting my fucking flag, ready to build a goddamned house on my newfound land made out of pure wrath. "Touch me again and you'll be in a jail cell," I say deadpan while pointing to my cheek.

Shelby's eyes open wide and she gasps.

Jackson takes a step back and shakes his head. "That was an accident and you know it. I would never, *ever* hurt you on purpose. *You* stepped right in the middle of a full-on fight between two grown men, Alyssa. I didn't even *see* you until it was already too late. You *have* to know that I would never hurt you! I *love* you!" he screams, his voice thick with emotion.

He looks completely wrecked right now and part of me wants to take back what I've said, but then Momma and Ricardo walk into the room and announce that Tyrone's out of surgery and the doctor will be updating us on his condition momentarily.

Any altercation brewing between Jackson and I goes on the back burner as we wait for the doctor to enter the room.

When he finally does, we all hold our breath, until he says, "He made it through surgery."

There's tears, shouts of happiness and smiles.

Until the Doctor's face falls. "He's still not out of the woods quite yet, but we're hopeful about his recovery from the surgery." He pauses and looks at Momma. "But there was extensive damage inflicted to his spinal cord. Specifically his thoracic vertebrae region, and more specifically, his T11 and T12 thoracic nerves."

Momma shakes her head, confused. "I don't understand what that means, Doctor."

Beside me, Jackson closes his eyes. "It means he's paralyzed, Momma."

Momma gasps and Jackson walks over to her and envelopes her in his arms.

The Doctor nods sadly. "Yes. Although we won't know the full extent of the damage or his injury level until he wakes up, recovers from surgery and we can do further testing. And now that the surgery is over, I'll have to ask that only immediate family remain here to see him. The rest of you can come back tomorrow during scheduled visiting hours."

The Doctor leaves after that and no one says a word, but there are sniffles and sobs from both Momma and Shelby.

Jackson and Ricardo look like they're about to lose it but are trying to remain strong. Lou-Lou looks down and her lower lip trembles.

My heart just breaks for poor Tyrone. I'm so happy he's alive, but this is devastating in its own right.

A few moments later Momma and Shelby hug everyone good-bye. Jackson didn't want to leave but when he heard that I was going back to my own apartment and not his, he said he'd be back later.

The four of us walk down the hallways in a clusterfuck of awkwardness. Lou-Lou and I walk side by side huddled up together, the tension between her and Ricardo and Jackson and me is so visible that even the nurses stop and give our group strange looks.

"You need a ride back to your apartment, right?" Lou-Lou says after we walk out of the elevator and make our way toward the parking garage. Fortunately, Ricardo and Jackson went out a different way.

"Yeah, if you wouldn't mind. I'd really appreciate it."

"No problem."

Far behind us, I hear both Ricardo and Jackson's footsteps.

Lou-Lou and I exchange a glance wondering why they're still following us, but we soon find out when we look over our shoulders and Ricardo tosses his keys in the air before Jackson catches them.

"Don't wreck my baby," he warns.

"I won't. I appreciate the favor."

"You owe me," he says before he begins walking closer to Lou-Lou at the same time Jackson walks closer to me.

"Oh, shit," Lou-Lou whispers.

"What?"

"Alyssa, I suggest that if you don't want to be manhandled by Jackson—you start running, now."

She doesn't have to tell me twice. I start running like there's a fire up my ass. I have no idea *where* I'm running, I just know that I'm toast if Jackson gets his hands on me. Especially knowing what I know *now* about him.

I'm not in the least bit turned on like I was during our last cat and mouse game at the bar. My brain and my body are fully aware that this is for survival. I'm sprinting so fast I'm surprising myself.

However, I'm still no match against Jackson. In a flash, his arm wraps around my waist and his large hand covers my mouth so I can't scream as he drags me in the direction of some red Mustang.

In the distance, I see Ricardo doing the same thing to Lou-Lou; only he's shouting, "Give me your fucking keys," in a dark tone that makes me incredibly nervous for her.

Then I have that moment, that moment where I say to myself— 'Fuck this shit.'

I'm not letting him manhandle me. He's not taking me out of this parking garage without a fight.

I start kicking my legs and twisting as hard as I can against him. I even go as far as to bite his hand which causes him to curse.

Then I go limp and will my body to become a ferret. This way, I'll be able to slinky myself right out of his hold.

He seems to sense what I'm doing because he gives me a sinister laugh and says, "Nice try, Damsel."

The fact that he's using that name with me again makes me so mad I lift my head and spit in his face.

That's when he lifts me up and puts me right over his shoulder. "Why don't we save the exchange of bodily fluids for after we get home, baby?"

I grunt and smack my hand against his back. "I'm not going to your apartment, Jackson," I scream. "I know who's fight club you work at. I know how you betrayed me." I kick him. "And most of all, I already know that you're either going to kill me

325

yourself or you're handing me right over to DeLuca himself to do it."

At this, he stops moving entirely. "Jesus Christ, you're crazy. You know that!" he roars.

"Tell me, Jackson. How much are you getting paid to be his lackey? To do his dirty work for him?" Then I give him a sinister laugh of my own. "You really had me going with that whole Lilly story. How long did it take you to come up with that? Hell, there probably is *no* Lilly, is there?"

His entire body starts shaking and his hold on me tightens, but I keep going. "Or maybe there *was*. Who knows? Maybe she was a disgruntled ex-girlfriend of yours? Maybe *you* were the one who really killed her. Tell me, Jackson. Where did you bury Lilly's body right after you murdered her, huh!"

"Shut the *fuck* up! You have *no* idea what you're talking about!" he screams so loud I jump.

He opens the door to the Mustang and throws me in the passenger seat. The vein in his neck is bulging and there's sweat pouring down his face. I've never seen him this upset before, not even in the cage.

I open my mouth again, but he opens the dashboard and pulls out a roll of duct tape. Then he slams it across my mouth. I roll my eyes and proceed to peel it off but then he forces the seat all the way back, crawls on top of me and before I know it, both my wrists are being bound behind my back with the duct tape.

This action only further confirms my suspicions regarding his intentions with me.

I kick my feet up and try to kick out the windshield. He sighs and says, "Please, sit still. I know you know about my involvement with DeLuca. But there are some things that you don't know and I would like to explain them to you. Will you let me do that?"

I ignore him and kick the windshield again, until his hand slams down on my thigh and he gets close to my face. "I'm *not* going to hurt you. I'm *not* going to kill you. But I swear on all that is holy, if you don't cut this shit out, I *will* throw your ass in the goddamned trunk, Alyssa."

At this, I finally stop kicking and relax in my seat.

He starts the car but points a finger at me. "I'm warning you right now, do *not* try and do something that will run us off the road."

I want to tell him that since it's New York City, there really would be no point. At most, we'll be going 20 miles per hour before he has to slam on the breaks again. He should worry much more about me making a run for it during one of those stops.

Provided I ever get this duct tape off that is.

He starts driving in the direction of his apartment complex, which throws me for a loop. Doesn't he know that Momma could walk in at any time? Last time I checked, it's bad to have a witness when you commit a murder. It's just one more loose end that you'll be forced to take care of.

Oh god. Would Jackson *actually* kill Momma?

When we reach his apartment, he pulls in the back and parks in a hidden spot I've never seen before. All I can think is. *This* is where he's going to do it.

But to my surprise, he gets out of the car and opens my door. My eyes dart around contemplating where I can run to, but he anticipates this because he picks me up and it's back over his shoulder I go.

On the bright side, at least the surveillance footage will catch him carrying me into his apartment building like this.

My murder will be solved. I'll get my lifetime wish and be headlining the 6'o'clock news after all.

I lift my head as we begin walking and spot Lou-Lou's car parked across the street. Since her windows are tinted, I can't see them...but I definitely hear all sorts of shouting.

The door to the complex shuts behind us and Jackson begins making his way up the staircase.

When we get inside his apartment he heads for the kitchen and sits me on a stool by the counter. He cracks his knuckles and rolls his neck. I can't help but stare at him, that is totally a mob guy move. He notices my face and pinches the bridge of his nose before reaching for the tape across my mouth and tearing it off.

I don't waste the opportunity, I start screaming my head off. *Mariah Carey* has nothing on my vocal chords right now.

Jackson grunts and covers my mouth with tape again. "Fine, I guess I'll go first," he says. "First of all, I love you—despite how batshit crazy you're acting right now. Secondly, I would never hurt you or kill you. It kills *me* that you would ever think that. And lastly, *yes* I do technically work for DeLuca, but it's not because I want to...got it?"

I shrug because I'm not really sure what he means by that. New York is an 'at will' state, if you don't want to work for someone you don't. Not that the mob really adheres to bylaws and regulations, but still. If Jackson didn't want to work for him, he wouldn't. Besides, why would DeLuca want to keep an employee on the payroll that didn't even *want* to work for him in the first place? That's just bad business.

Unless DeLuca is holding something over his head? But what the hell could DeLuca use for leverage?

Jackson begins pacing the floors. "Every single thing I told you about me is the truth, Alyssa. I know a small part of you *has* to know that. I mean, I put it all on video tape for you for crying out loud. You think I would confess to a murder that I didn't commit?"

He has a point, I guess.

I shake my head and he walks back over to me and removes the tape. "Don't scream. Just let me explain. Okay?"

I nod my head because maybe things aren't what they seem after all.

Chapter 35 (Jackson)

I 've thought about having Alyssa bound and gagged quite a lot since I first met her.

I just never thought I'd be partaking in it to get her to stop screaming such god awful, vile things to me in the middle of a parking garage.

And the fact that she actually thinks I would hurt her? Or worse, *kill* her?

I just don't have the words to express what that does to me.

I wanted to bash my own head through a wall right after I saw what Ricardo and I did to her when she jumped in the middle of our fight. I've never felt like such an asshole but I didn't even see her. Hell, I didn't even know she was standing in the room because I was too worked up about Ricardo and his possible involvement.

And of course, the fact that my best friend was in the middle of surgery and the doctors had just told us there was a chance he wouldn't make it.

Then *that* shit happened.

Then she looked at me the way she did.

I figured she just needed space because of what happened but when I came back, she was different.

I saw her talking with Shelby and then she just collapsed.

I thought she was having a reoccurring symptom due to still being sick. Then she walked over to Lou-Lou and held her hand. Fucking Lou-Lou, the girl she basically hates. She'd rather hold *her* hand than *mine* while I'm going through all this shit.

I knew something wasn't right.

And when she gave me a different look—a look that could have killed me dead right where I stood and threatened to have me hauled off to jail over an accident...I knew I was fucked.

I knew that somehow...she had figured out the truth.

Then I heard the news about Tyrone and although I'm beyond relieved that he's alive...I know that when he wakes up and processes everything, he's going to be inconsolable. I'm inconsolable for him but I'll be there for him and whatever he needs.

The last thing I wanted to do was have it out with Alyssa, I wanted to stay by my best friend's side. Momma told me to go and said he'd probably be out of it until sometime tomorrow, but I still wanted to stay.

Then Alyssa mentioned going back to her own apartment and I knew this shit had to be dealt with tonight. She wasn't cutting me any kind of slack and I sure as hell wasn't losing her without a fight.

However, when she said those things to me in the parking garage? Spewing such *hurtful* things, things like *I* was the one who killed Lilly and she wanted to know where I buried her body. *That* was the closest I'd ever come to wanting to hit a female.

I settled for throwing her in the passenger seat and covering her vicious mouth with duct tape, instead.

Since she had no choice but to remain silent throughout the drive, I took the opportunity to put myself in her place.

That only made me feel like a shithead. Of course, she would think I was setting her up, regardless of the fact that *she* was the one who walked into his club. The fact is, DeLuca's been the metaphorical boogie man to her ever since she was a child. She knows first-hand what he's capable of.

No wonder she didn't push further after I said it wasn't his club.

She completely dropped it and never asked me again. A part of me thinks that she didn't *want* it to be his club, because he scares the absolute shit out of her, with good reason. I can't help but think that if she knew without a shadow of a doubt that it was his club, then a big part of her would feel like she'd have no choice but to avenge her father's death...even if it ended up in her murder.

Which let's face it...it most definitely would.

That's one hell of a demand to put on yourself, especially after going through everything that she already has. Not to mention Ford's own method of brainwashing that he did.

She was probably relieved when I told her that DeLuca wasn't the owner. Grateful that she had a few more minutes on the clock before her time was up.

Putting myself in her place puts it into perspective for me.

She's still trembling and I wish that I could hold her, but I know she needs to hear about my involvement with DeLuca before she'll let that happen.

If she'll ever let that happen.

"Everything I told you about Lilly is the truth. With the exception of me getting off on self-defense." She looks confused so I continue, "I was going down for both Mike and Lilly's murder," I say as her eyes open wide.

Maybe *now* she'll realize how much those things she said hurt me. "I didn't kill Lilly, Alyssa."

"I know," she whispers. "I know that now. I just don't know why you would lie to me, Jackson. I loved you. I trusted you. Why would you set me up?"

Her voice is so small and broken my chest squeezes.

"I'm not setting you up, baby. I would never do that to you."

"Tell me why you're working for him then. Tell me why you're continuing to work for him after you know what he did to me."

"Because he's the reason I'm out of jail."

"How?"

"He was my deliverance. He paid off the judge, planted evidence to ensure that I'd walk, and hired the best defense attorney on the East Coast. Hell, DeLuca did such a good job it didn't even make it to trial."

"What was the catch?"

"The catch is that I figured out that the devil doesn't offer you deal's, Alyssa. He only offers you an arrangement with a steep pay off. And he prefers his payment in blood."

She looks down and shivers. "Well, you know what they say— the devil was once an angel."

"I don't think this one ever was."

"What arrangement did you make with him?"

Time to tell her everything.

"Ten years in his *underground* fight club. Which is a load of bull if you ask me, because I've seen law enforcement officials there before. Hell, they place some of the highest bets. Anyway, the terms were one fight every two weeks, to ensure I could recover from any potential injuries."

I grab a stool to sit down on. "I'd be appointed a coach to ensure I never skipped town and to keep me on a leash."

"Ricardo," she whispers.

I nod. "Yup. I'd also have to win at least 99% of my fights."

Her mouth hangs open. "That's impossible. No one's *that* good."

"You are if it's your life on the line."

"You can't be that good for 10 years straight Jackson! Your body will start to deteriorate, it will break down from all the constant wear and tear. There's *no* way you can stay number one for 10 years straight. I've seen the guys you're up against, they're nothing but freak shows on steroids "

Her lower lip trembles and I can see the tears in her eyes. "Oh, god. DeLuca *knows* this. He knows that you'll most likely die in the cage before your contract is up. Hell, he'll probably make sure that it happens."

"Yeah, that's pretty much what happens. The only one who's ever made it through his 10 years alive is Ricardo. The reason Tyrone and I are the best right now is because there's no one else to compare us to. For the most part, guys usually die in the cage around the first year. If he senses you're weak, then he matches you up with an opponent he knows you can't take. If you prove to be worthy, well, then you usually get the honor of dying in the cage around the 7th or 8th year. DeLuca likes to up the stakes by then. Trust me, it's some real fucked up shit."

I look up to the ceiling because I can't look at her when I say this. "And by your 7th or 8th year, it's probably bittersweet because you're so close to being out. You can taste it. But, at the same time, the mentality of being nothing but a machine has gotten to you, so unless you have something on the outside that grounds you, something to go back to...there's really no point in fighting anymore. Sometimes I think the guys don't make it because they just give up. They get tired of feeling the pain that fuels them to survive. I know I am."

"Lilly's murder is how you survive, isn't it? That's the source of all your pain."

"I have to relive every second of it every time I'm in that cage. It's the only way."

I want to tell her that she was the one who grounded me, who made it better for me, and that she was my something to look forward to, but there's something more important that she needs to hear.

"I wanted to protect you, that's why I didn't tell you about DeLuca. I tried to let you go a few times, but I couldn't do it. I need you like I need my pain to win my fights."

"What are we gonna do, Jackson?" A single tear falls down her cheek. "How do we make it through this?"

I don't answer her, instead, I tear the tape off her wrists and hold her in my arms. She buries her face into my chest and sobs her heart out.

"I agree with Ricardo. Don't go after DeLuca. It's too risky and you'll end up dead. We'll have to find another way. There *has* to be another way. I can't and I *won't* lose another man that I love to him."

I stay silent because there *is* another way; the *only* way to stop him. I could care less about my own life, but I'm not letting him take hers.

She tilts her head up and I don't even hesitate to crush her mouth against mine.

There are so many emotions filtering the energy running through us, there's only one way to exert it right now.

I lift her up, place her on the counter and she wraps her legs around my waist. I wish I could be more gentle with her given the fact that I know she's probably feeling sore from what happened earlier, but when she sits up, takes off my shirt and scratches her nails down my back, I lose my composure.

I suck and bite on that plump bottom lip of hers, groaning when I taste the hint of copper because it reminds me that she's alive, that she's safe, and that she's here with me.

I make quick work of unbuttoning of her jeans and pulling them off. Her panties are next and I shred the delicate lace like it's paper while she lifts her t-shirt over her head.

The both of us are so worked up there's no need for foreplay, my own jeans fall at my feet and I'm entering her in a single thrust, pumping into her slickness like it's my salvation, because I know she is.

She falls back and I position her legs on my shoulders so I can get even deeper inside her. I'm so lost in her essence, there are no words. The only sounds are the moans of pleasure and the sounds of our frantic, hot-blooded bodies coming together.

After a moment, she begins to spasm and cries out my name like a lifeline. Her pussy grips me so hard it almost hurts as her come drips down my balls. Before I can stop myself, I'm quickly following her into the pits of euphoria and purging my own release deep inside of her.

I fall on top of her, loving the feeling of her body underneath me, where I can shelter her and see the rise and fall of her chest with every breath she takes.

She kisses me and it's clear that what just happened didn't diminish her feelings, if anything; it only charged them. She pushes her pelvis into mine, purposely enticing me into another round. Her tongue darts out and drags across her bottom lip slowly when she feels my cock twitch against her center. Since she's the puppet master of not only my heartstrings, but my desire—I'm rock hard and inside her again.

I flip her around so that I'm entering her from behind and watching that gorgeous ass of hers shake with my every thrust. I lean down and sink my teeth into her shoulder.

She looks over her shoulder and bites her lip. And fuck *me*, it's the hottest visual I've ever seen.

I don't have to worry about DeLuca killing me, because she's going to.

She moans and I start thrusting harder. The feeling is incredible and I know I won't be able to hold off much longer.

"Jackson, I'm...fuck," she says before she starts jerking and unintelligible screams rip out of her.

Wanting to make it even better for her, I circle her clit and watch as she grabs onto the counter and moans my name. She clenches around me and I get two more pumps in before I'm coming inside her.

"Thank you," she breathes. "You have no idea how much I needed that. How much I needed to lose myself in you."

I almost laugh because I'm pretty sure I should be thanking *her* for that experience. I pick her up and carry her into the bedroom. "You never have to thank me for that. Besides, I needed it just as much, maybe even more."

I pull back the covers and curl up beside her. "I love you," she whispers before she drifts off to sleep.

I kiss the spot over her heart. "I love you," I say before I stand up and reach for my cell phone.

I step out into the hallway and dial Ford's number. He answers on the third ring. "I want to talk about that deal."

Chapter 36 (Alyssa)

"Ford, it's me again. I need you to call me back, please. It's important," I say before I hang up.

I never thought I'd find myself in this position again. However, I know it's the only way. We can't beat DeLuca on our own and he's the only resource I have.

Despite how much of an asshole he is, I know that Ford wants to nail DeLuca. And now that I know for a fact that it's his club...I'm going to help him come up with a plan to do it.

I'm going to have him use me as bait like he originally intended. Then, Ford will take care of him and Jackson and I will be free.

Well, that's what I'm hoping will happen, but Ford has yet to call me back.

It's been almost a week since I first reached out to him. It's strange that he still hasn't contacted me.

I was hoping to see him and finalize a plan before Jackson has to fight again tomorrow night. There's no telling what will happen in that cage after Tyrone's last fight.

Since Jackson's currently at the hospital visiting Tyrone, I'm taking the opportunity to slip out and go to Ford's house myself.

It's too close to Jackson's fight and I can't take the chance of him getting hurt, I'll do whatever I have to in order to protect him.

The cab ride to Ford's is over an hour away, so I take the time to formulate the start of a good plan. I know that going to the club won't work since DeLuca never shows up there himself. Not to mention, setting up some kind of meeting there would harbor too many witnesses. There's no way Ford would take him out with that many people around.

I have to find a way to get DeLuca secluded and completely alone, but I don't know how to go about that.

My mind's on the verge of figuring out a way to do it, but every time I get closer, I hit a mental block and I can't work my way around it.

The cab finally pulls up to Ford's house and what I see causes me to freak the hell out.

There's a red Mustang parked in his driveway.

Ricardo's here.

What the hell is Ricardo doing here?

"Miss, are you getting out or not?" the cab driver grumbles.

"Not," I tell him. "Take me back home."

With a curse, he starts to drive away.

I'm more confused than ever now. It's obvious that Ford and Ricardo are doing business together, but what?

I sit up straight in my seat when I realize. They've got to be trying to take down DeLuca? That's the only tie those two have to one another.

My cell phone starts ringing and I almost want to ignore it because I don't want Shane to ask me to work tomorrow night. My life is hectic right now and there's no way I'm going to be able to focus on working at the bar while Jackson could be getting killed in the cage.

I rub my temples and answer the phone anyway. "Hey, Shane."

"Do you have a twin?"

Okay, that's not what I was expecting him to say.

"No, I'm an only child," I say, pushing down sad memories.

"I was joking, Alyssa." He laughs. "Besides, the chick I'm staring at is hot but she looks like an older, more sophisticated version of you, no offense."

"None taken." Then it dawns on me. "Does she have blonde hair?"

"Yup. And she just asked to speak to you. Hold on."

Why is Penelope sitting at Finnley's right now?

"Hey, Penelope. Is everything okay?"

"I don't know. You tell me?" she replies in a snarky tone.

"Um...you're the one sitting at *my* job. What's going on?"

"I thought you learned your lesson when it came to Ford?"

Shit...she must still be checking his phone records.

"I did. I only reached out to Ford because I'm having a personal problem that I need to involve the police with. I figured calling him would speed things along, but he still hasn't called me back."

I can practically smell the wood burning from her thinking so hard on the other line.

"Don't lie to me, Alyssa. Look, I'm not jealous. I don't want him back, but I am concerned about you going back to *him* because you and your current boyfriend are having problems."

I blow out a breath, trying my hardest not to go off on her for sticking her nose in my business. "Penelope, I'm never going back to Ford. I'm in love with Jackson."

"Then why the hell did I find plane tickets and passports with both your names on it?"

Say what?

"I'm sorry. I think I misheard you."

"No, you didn't. I went there to pick up my mail yesterday— since the asshole insisted on keeping the house that *he* bought in the settlement. He wasn't home so I used my key and out on the coffee table were two tickets to Mexico along with two passports. One for you and one for him."

"Oh my god. That's crazy."

"Exactly—" she starts to say.

"I'm *not* leaving the country with Ford. I have no idea what's going on or what he's planning. But I need you to promise me that you won't mention a word of this to him. Don't tell him that you know me and please don't tell him that we had this conversation, okay?"

"Shit, what's going on, Alyssa?"

"I don't know," I answer, before I hang up.

I breathe a sigh of relief when I look out the window and see city buildings.

I quickly take into account all the things I just found out— Ricardo and Ford have some kind of dealings going on together. My guess, is that it involves DeLuca. The only thing that *doesn't* make sense— is why the hell Ford's planning on whisking me off to freaking Mexico.

The only thing I can think of, is that Ford probably doesn't know that I'm with Jackson because we haven't had contact for months. He knows I've never kept boyfriends in the past and he probably just assumed I'm single.

On the plus side, Ricardo and Ford must be gearing up to take DeLuca down. And if my suspicions about Ricardo are correct, who better than *him* to help do it?

On the negative side, Ford's going to attempt to woo me and take me on vacation. Clearly he has another thing coming, but I'll gladly accept him getting rid of DeLuca for me and Jackson.

What I don't understand is why the heck he never picked up his phone for me if he's planning on doing all *this*? But then again, it's Ford. He's about as predictable as a tidal wave.

I pay the cab driver and walk into the apartment. Now that Jackson gave me a key, I don't have to knock on the door anymore.

"Hey," a deep voice says.

I turn around and practically have a heart attack when I see Ricardo standing before me.

How the hell did he make it back here so fast? Then again, he does drive a mustang.

He looks at me and makes a face. "Look, you've been acting a little strange around me ever since that fight. I hope you know that I really didn't mean to punch you. You don't have to be scared of me, Alyssa."

"Yeah," I squeak.

He scratches the back of his neck and it's only then that I notice he's wearing a sweat stained t-shirt and a pair of shorts. His hair is wet and his skin is glistening. He looks like he just finished working out, not driving back from Long Island.

"Where did you just come from?"

"The gym. Why?"

"Are you sure?"

He leans in and gives me a peculiar look. If he wasn't so fucking intimidating, he'd be *ridiculously* good looking. "Am I sure I got back from the gym?" He smirks. "Yeah, I'm positive. So, I'll ask you again. Why?"

"No r-reason." I turn around and attempt to get my key in the door as he walks across the hall to his own apartment.

Then it occurs to me. He could have let someone else borrow his car. Or, maybe it wasn't Ricardo's car in the driveway after all?

There's only one way to find out. "Hey, Ricardo? I was wondering if you would mind giving me a ride."

"I would, but I don't have my car."

Before I can question him further he says, "But you should already know that Jackson's borrowing my car until tomorrow morning because he's going to Boston." He shrugs. "Kind of surprised you didn't go with him actually."

"Going to Boston?" I whisper.

Jackson definitely never mentioned going to Boston this morning.

No. *This can't be fucking happening.*

I open my mouth to cover my fumble but Ricardo says, "He's going to Boston to visit Lilly's grave. Today's her birthday."

He takes a step forward and gives me an odd look. "Did he not tell you?"

"Of course, he did." I laugh nervously. "I just forgot is all." I give him a big smile. "I am naturally a blonde...we do have our moments."

He cocks an eyebrow. "Yeah. Okay, then. I'm gonna take a shower. Talk to you later."

I give him a wave before closing and locking the door behind me. Then I start hyperventilating.

Now it makes sense. It's *not* Ricardo and Ford working together. It's Jackson and Ford.

Which means that Ford *does* know I'm with Jackson.

But those plane tickets and passports...they can only mean one thing.

Ford is setting Jackson up to kill DeLuca and Jackson has no idea.

I wish he didn't shut me out when I tried to tell him everything that happened between Ford and I. Then he would already *know* not to trust him.

I pick up my phone and dial Jackson but it goes straight to voicemail. I leave the longest message I've ever left detailing everything that Ford did to me, including what happened that day in his office.

I also dial Ford, it rings a few times before going to voicemail. I close my eyes. In the back of my mind, I always knew this day would come. I used to be ashamed that I was so terrified about my date with DeLuca.

I mean, who doesn't want vengeance for the death of their father?

I thought I would cry and fall apart when it happened. But surprisingly, I feel like I'm finally thinking rationally.

It's time to have my dance with the Devil.

It's time to protect the man I love and inflict retribution on DeLuca for the one that I lost. Even if it's the last thing I do.

I walk into the bedroom and start going through the boxes that I moved in over the past week.

Covered in a pile of old clothes I find my lock box. I take it out, punch in the combination and open it. I eye my revolver and my semi-automatic pistol. The one good thing that came out of my relationship with Ford was him teaching me how to shoot a gun and taking me to the firing range when I was younger.

I make sure they're both loaded and ready to go before throwing a sweatshirt on and tucking both guns into the waistband of my jeans.

It's funny how a plan formulates itself when you find out the person you love is in danger.

I knock on Lou-Lou's door and wait for her to answer. I know her and Ricardo have some major problems and still haven't worked any of their shit out.

But quite frankly, I don't really give a fuck at this point. I just need someone to use as leverage against Ricardo and that someone is Lou-Lou.

She answers the door and although she looks surprised to see me, she invites me in.

As soon as the door is closed, I take out the revolver and put it to her head. "You crazy bitch!" she screams. "I thought we were friends now? What the fuck are you doing?"

"We are. This is nothing personal, Lou-Lou. I just need a hostage."

I pull her hair and position her in front of me. Given she's so tiny, it's easy to push her around. "However, feel free to think of this as payback for being such a bitch to me."

She starts screaming, but I dig the gun into her head. "Scream and I'll kill you. Trust me, you don't want to fuck with me right now."

She takes a deep breath. "Can you at least tell me why you're doing this?"

"Jackson's in trouble with a certain mob boss."

"Bruno," she whispers.

"Ah, I see you're on a first-name basis with the asshole. Good to know, that might come in handy." I shove her in front of me. "Now open the door and start walking down the hall to Ricardo's. If you run...I swear I'll kill him."

She opens the door with shaky hands and starts walking. She knocks on his door but he doesn't answer. That's when I remember. "Shit, he's in the shower."

"I have a key," Lou-Lou offers. "It's in my back pocket."

"I'm not falling for that."

"Then *you* can get it," she insists.

I dig the gun into her temple as I get her keys out of her back pocket and hand them to her. "You attack me with those and I'll shoot."

"I know."

Part of me is wondering why she's being so cooperative, but I don't have the time to question it.

We walk into Ricardo's apartment and I walk us to the bathroom, with Lou-Lou as my hostage.

Since there's no point in knocking on his bathroom door. I have Lou-Lou open it.

The look on Ricardo's face when he see's that I'm holding a gun up to Lou-Lou's head is one for the record books.

He reaches for a towel and quickly wraps it around his waist before he steps out of the shower.

That's when I silently pat myself on the back because the fact that he's naked as the day he was born means that he has no weapons on him.

However, what bewilders me is why he isn't more freaked out about this. I know he's worried about Lou-Lou, that's more than evident by the way he looks at her. But the fact that he's not puzzled by his current predicament is unnerving.

"How did you find out?" he says, his tone solemn.

I open my mouth, but Lou-Lou cuts me off by screaming, "I didn't tell this bitch shit, Ricky."

I whack her head with the gun. "No talking." I look at Ricardo. "You have his eyes. I'll never forget his eyes. They haunt me in my dreams."

He closes his eyes. "I'm not like my father, Alyssa."

"Doesn't matter. Your father took the most important person in my life from me and he's about to do it again. I want him to *feel* what it's like to lose the most important thing to him."

He sucks in a breath and glances at Lou-Lou. "Yeah. I get that, Alyssa."

His expression quickly changes to nervousness. "Wait, what do you mean he's about to do it again? Where the fuck is Jackson right now?"

"He's working with an FBI agent. An FBI agent that's going to set him up for the murder of your father. I have to get to him before that happens."

"Shit. Can't you just call him and warn him?" Lou-Lou asks, her voice cracking.

"He's not picking up his phone."

"Fuck. *No.* Oh, my god. Shit," she sputters, her breathing erratic.

I yank her hair. "As touched as I am about your sentiments regarding my boyfriend's current circumstance, can you kindly *shut up* so we can get on with the program."

She shakes her head. "I swear, I didn't mean to. I didn't know it was Jackson. Oh, my god," she squeaks.

Suffice it to say, she has both Ricardo's and my attention at this point.

I pull the other gun out of my waistband and put them both up to her head. "You better start making sense, Lou-Lou...or your brains are gonna be all over the carpet. What the fuck did you do?"

"There was this guy. This FBI agent. He started talking to me, you know flirting, all that."

"You talked to the fucking Feds?" Ricardo screams at the same time I scream, "Was his name Ford?"

"H-how did you know?"

"Cut to the chase, Lou-Lou. I know how Ford pulls the females in. Tell me what he wanted you to do. And how Jackson is involved."

"That's the thing. This Ford, guy. He seemed to know everything about me. Things that no one knows."

Ricardo lets out a curse and I scratch my head with one of my guns. "And you didn't find that a little suspicious? You can't be that dumb."

"I'm not dumb. *Of course*, I did. But then he offered me a deal."

"Goddammit, Lucianna! He's a fucking double agent. He's not legit, he works for us!" Ricardo screams at the same time I scream, "What kind of deal!"

I aim one of the guns for Ricardo's head and gasp. "What? What the actual *fuck* did you just say?"

It feels like all the air just got sucked out of the room. The only reason I'm not collapsing right now is because I still have to save Jackson.

Ricardo runs a hand down his face. "Shit," he says. "Look, Alyssa. Trust me when I say that you're better off not knowing the truth. I don't think you can take it and I'm not going to be the one to tell you."

I shoot the wall beside his head. "Tell me. Tell me the fucking truth."

"No. You can shoot me dead, but I will *not* be responsible for putting the same soul-crushing look on your face that my father did the day he killed your dad!" he roars. "My father's eyes haunt you in your dreams? Well, yours fucking haunt *mine!*"

"You—" I pause because my voice is wavering. "You were there that day? The day my father was killed?"

I look at him in disbelief. He's only 5 years older than Jackson. The only young people I remember seeing that day were the teenage gang members.

"I was 18," he says. "In fact, it was my 18th birthday. The day I officially became a man. My father wanted to celebrate by showing me what you do to rats. Or specifically, what you do when you find out that one of your men is an undercover agent."

His face contorts in agony. "You weren't the only one locked in a car that day, Alyssa," he says gruffly before his tone turns somber. "I'm so sorry. I liked your dad. We did some runs together and became close. I looked up to him. Wanted to be like him. He used to talk about how much he loved his little goblin— "

I shoot the wall beside his head again, much closer this time. "Shut the fuck up. You didn't know shit about my dad, you piece of shit! Your father killed him! He *killed* him and I watched every second of it and I saw the look in DeLuca's eyes when he did it. So don't you fucking try and stand there and offer me your condolences or sympathy. Like this is some kind of hallmark moment...when you're literally the spawn of fucking Satan himself!"

His eyes become glassy. "I didn't want to be. That day changed me. You have no idea what that day did to me."

"It will never compare to what it did to me."

"I know," he whispers.

In front of me, Lou-Lou's trembling and I hear her sobbing. "You're the little girl. The little girl in his nightmares."

"Stop, Lou-Lou," Ricardo warns.

Lou-Lou lifts her chin. "No. You need to know, Alyssa. He's not Bruno. Trust me, you don't know what Ricardo's been through. He's not the bad guy. Bruno is."

"I guess it's time to find out then, huh?"

Ricardo's eyes meet mine. "What do you mean?"

"Call your father and find out where he is right now. If you don't, I'll kill her in front of you and give you another nightmare."

Ricardo picks up his shorts off the floor but I click my tongue. "Are you armed?"

"Would it matter? I'm not going to kill you."

"A leopard doesn't change its spots."

"You know, bitch—you're not the only one who watched their parent get murdered by the hands of DeLuca."

"DeLuca killed your parents?" I question.

"Probably," she scoffs. "Who the fuck knows. However, I was referring to Ricardo."

"He killed your mother?" I ask in his direction.

Ricardo closes his eyes and nods. "Yeah. After I told him that I wanted nothing to do with him and said I would never be like him. He tracked my mother down and taught me another lesson."

This time, I see a tear fall down his face and I let mine fall with it. "How are you not more fucked up? How did you save yourself from becoming just like him?"

"Believe me, he's *plenty* fucked up," Lou-Lou whispers.

Ricardo turns around and I read the large tattoo on his back scrawled in black ink. *Sometimes there is absolutely no difference at all between salvation and damnation.*

"It's from the Green Mile," Lou-Lou offers.

I ignore her and wait for him to turn back around. "You going to call him?"

"I don't really have much of a choice. I'm not letting him kill Jackson."

"I swear I didn't know it was him," Lou-Lou whispers again.

I can't believe I almost forgot. "Lou-Lou finish telling me about your involvement with Ford."

She clears her throat. "Like I said, he tried to get in my pants and he knew all this stuff." Ricardo narrows his eyes and she quickly says, "Anyway, he offered me a deal. He said that he would set it up so that I could kill DeLuca. But seeing as he was FBI, *he* would make sure it wouldn't get pinned on me. He said there would be someone else there, someone with more motive than I had to take the fall. I didn't know it was going to be *Jackson* because he refused to tell me who this other person was. He said I wouldn't find out until I got there…but I didn't go through with it. I backed out at the last minute."

Ricardo starts pacing. "Fuck, he was playing you both."

I always knew Ford was manipulative, but even I didn't think he'd take it this far. "I guess that explains why he planned to take me to Mexico. There's really no doubt in my mind that he's setting Jackson up."

When they both look at me I say, "Ford and me…our relationship is…was…complicated. It's really fucked up."

Ricardo looks disgusted. "Trust me, sweetie. You really have no idea *just* how fucked up," he whispers.

My stomach knots with those words but I don't have time to concentrate on that. "Ricardo, I need you to talk to DeLuca. Find out where he is right now. Tell him it's an emergency and you need him to meet you at the docks near Jersey."

"You want to do this *there?*"

"Hell, yes." Not only do I like my revenge served cold too but I need to get him as far away from Jackson as possible and *still* manage to kill him in the next few hours.

I look down at Lou-Lou. "And after that, I need *you* to call Ford. Tell him the fucking jig is up and I'm holding both you and Ricardo hostage. Tell him to meet me at the docks, but *warn* him that if he brings Jackson it will be the last thing that he does."

Ricardo shakes his head. "That's not going to work. He's going to bring Jackson. Especially if he's already targeted him as the fall guy. Also, there's no telling what Jackson will do to Ford if he finds out he set him up. There could be a showdown between them."

Crap, he's right.

"Well then get a hold of Jackson and tell him that something happened to me. Say whatever you have to say to throw him off the course. Don't tell him about Ford just make sure he leaves."

"But you said he wasn't picking up his phone," Ricardo argues.

I smirk. "I'm sure he has a special company phone that you can get a hold of him on."

Chapter 37 (Jackson)

Ricardo: *Alyssa's gone crazy! She has a gun and is holding Lou-Lou and me hostage. Ford's a double agent, don't trust him. It's a set-up. Do not attack him just yet, he might be prepared for that. Get away from him and find a way to sneak to the docks near Jersey. We'll be in the small warehouse-sneak in through the back. Address is in my car gps listed under 10/29/01.*

Make sure you're armed—check the trunk. DeLuca will be there. Stay safe, brother. And when I call you—sound panicked and go with it. Alyssa's fine...well, physically anyway. Erase this text and do not respond to it.

I have to go into Ford's bathroom and read Ricardo's text message three times to make sense of it. Seeing as he texted the burner phone he gave Tyrone and me for emergencies, I know he means business. A minute later, the phone vibrates. "Yeah," I answer. I hear mumbling in the background and what sounds like Lou-Lou and Alyssa arguing.

How the hell did she figure everything out? But even more alarming than that, how the hell am I going to protect her *now* when she's pulling this shit?

"Alyssa's been shot. Come quick," Ricardo shouts before he hangs up.

My heart explodes in my chest, until I remember him telling me to just go with it. I erase his text and walk back out. Ford gives me an odd look. "Everything alright in there?"

"No. Something's come up. I'm leaving," I say, walking toward the door

He steps in front of me and it takes everything in me not to deck him. "What the fuck could ever be more important than *this*? Today's the day. I've set everything in motion."

I bet you did, you lying motherfucker.

I decide to see if his feelings for Alyssa were ever real or if he's been lying about those as well. "Alyssa's been shot." With that, I run out the door and head for the Mustang.

He runs after me. "What?" he shouts. "By who? Where is she?"

"I don't know. She's at the hospital. I have to go."

He's on my heels, but stops to answer his phone when it rings. I open my car door and see his face turn pale. He's so visibly shaken, he has to wipe the sweat from his brow as he whispers something into the phone.

Then he screams Alyssa's name in agony.

His feelings for her are obviously real. You can't fake *that* kind of emotion. However, whatever he feels for her, fails in comparison to what *I* feel for her.

Unfortunately for me...his pain will be cut short soon.

And unfortunately for *him*...it's because he'll be dead.

I peel out of his driveway and head for the docks.

Chapter 38 (Alyssa)

"Alyssa's been shot. Come quick," Ricardo shouts from the backseat of Lou-Lou's car before he hangs up the phone.

I point my gun at his chest. "Really, you couldn't have done better than *that?*"

"It got the message across. He won't be with Ford anymore."

I dig the gun into Lou-Lou's temple. "Now it's your turn."

She pulls up Ford's contact information and hits send. He picks up right away. "Lou-Lou?"

"Hi, Ford. Alyssa's holding me hostage and she knows what you're up to."

"I don't believe you," he snarls.

I grab the phone from her. "Hello, Ford. Or should I say—special *manipulating bastard* agent Ford?"

His breathing becomes uneasy but he stays silent.

"I'm going to make this real easy for you. Meet me down at the docks. Leave Jackson alone. This is between you, me, and DeLuca. If you bring Jackson, I swear on my father's death...it will be the *last* thing you ever do."

"Alyssa, no. Don't do this," he whispers. I don't respond.

"Alyssa," he screams.

That's when I hang up and look at Ricardo.

"You still have one more phone call to make."

I see his adam's apple bob and it's the first time I've ever seen Ricardo look nervous.

He puts the phone up to his ear. "Yeah, it's me."

I hear some murmuring on the other line.

"I know you're busy. But something's come up."

Just knowing that it's DeLuca on the other line makes me want to vomit. I have to force myself to breathe and not pass out.

"I'm being held hostage," Ricardo says before he adds, "I know you don't care."

Uh-oh. This is *not* the way I saw this going. I counted on Ricardo being my advantage.

"Tell him who's holding you hostage and tell him he better be unarmed when he shows up or I'll kill you."

I wish I could see the look on his face when he hears that it's me behind all this.

Ricardo looks at me before he says, "Listen, you need to meet us at the docks near Jersey. Alyssa Tanner's holding a gun to my fucking face."

There's more mumbling on the other line.

Ricardo closes his eyes and lets out a frustrated sigh. When he opens them, he gives me that murderous look before he screams, "I know you don't give a fuck about *me*, Babbo...but she's got Lucianna! And she *will* kill her. Make sure you come unarmed!"

There's silence on the other line and my stomach lurches. My plan is going downhill, fast.

"Okay. I'll be there...unarmed. Make sure that bitch doesn't touch a *hair* on Lucianna's head or I'll be bashing hers in just like her father's," DeLuca's gritty voice shouts before he hangs up.

I look over at Lou-Lou in shock. And to think, I *almost* didn't want to drag her into this. I was only holding her hostage as a way to get *Ricardo* to cooperate. I was going to have her drive us to the docks and let her go.

She's the *last* person I ever expected to be DeLuca's soft spot.

"Damn, Lou-Lou. I sure as fuck underestimated you."

She looks up and gives me a wink. "Yes you did, bitch. And if you want DeLuca brought to his knees, I'll be glad to help you do it. But if you hurt Ricardo; trust me—I'll make your life even more of a living hell than it already was."

I'm not sure if I have a newfound respect for her...or if she's just managed to scare the crap out of me.

"Noted, now start driving."

I adjust myself in the passenger seat of Lou-Lou's car. I have one gun pointed at her head and one gun pointed at Ricardo in the backseat. "Either one of you try and pull something, I'll be reenacting my own version of Romeo and Juliet, got it?

They both nod and I gesture between them with my guns. "So, what's the story between you two? I gotta hear this."

Ricardo lifts his chin and glares at me. "None of your fucking business," he grits through his teeth.

I crinkle my nose at him. "Well, seeing as I'm the one holding a gun to your face, call me crazy but I'd say it was."

"Oh, I'm calling you *crazy* alright," he mumbles.

"Seriously," Lou-Lou chimes in. "You got a set of cajones, Alyssa. I'm impressed."

"Thanks, I think. But I'm not crazy," I say softly. "I'm just protecting Jackson and getting my revenge."

We stay in silence for the better part of an hour. And all I can think is—what makes *Lou-Lou* so important to DeLuca? Even more important than his own son?

She *can't* be his daughter. That would make Ricardo and Lou-Lou's relationship beyond twisted, especially if it was mostly based on sex.

Unless? Well, I'll be damned.

"Are you guys like step-brother and step-sister or something?" I wiggle my eyebrows. "I'm not judging, that's kinda hot."

"Fuck off," Ricardo barks.

"He's not my step-brother," Lou-Lou whispers.

"Why are *you* so important to DeLuca?" I ask. She grips the steering wheel and winces. "Probably the same reason you're so important to Ford."

I have *no* idea what she means by that, but I have to put it on the back burner because we start pulling up to the docks.

My eyes automatically look at the spot where my father died and I start dry heaving. For a moment, I feel just like that little girl trapped in the car who watched it all happen.

Surprisingly, both Ricardo and Lou-Lou put a hand on my shoulder. "Breathe, Alyssa. DeLuca will be here any minute; if he's not here already and you'll make one hell of an easy target if you're passed out. Then all of this will be for nothing," Ricardo says.

"It's true," Lou-Lou whispers. "It's time to get your payback. DeLuca deserves everything that's coming to him," she says before she gets out of the car.

Ricardo looks in her direction before he closes his eyes and sighs. "Go big or go home, right?"

"I don't think I can do it out here. Not in the same place my father died. It just feels...wrong."

"I get it." He gestures his head to a small run-down building. "There's a warehouse over there."

When we get out of the car he says, "By the way, I'm not letting DeLuca kill you. So, just know that whatever happens, I got your back."

I guess Ricardo's been armed the whole time after all.

We begin walking toward the warehouse and I place both my guns to their heads again and have them walk in front of me.

Seeing as I didn't notice DeLuca's car anywhere, I almost piss my pants when I look down and see a pair of metal tipped shoes.

"Back the fuck up," I command in his direction, surprising myself.

He takes a few steps back and the look he gives me could burn through glass. I take in his jagged scar, which still hasn't faded much over the years and his evil eyes and my stomach recoils.

How can a single person be the source of every nightmare? I can't help it, I start sweating and breathing erratically.

Before I can say another word, he looks at Lou-Lou. "Are you okay, Bambina? Has she hurt you?"

Clearly, he really *doesn't* give a fuck about Ricardo.

"I'm fine," she replies icily.

"Don't take that tone with me," he barks, almost causing me to jump. "You know I worry about you, Lucianna."

Lou-Lou looks up at him and it's like she transforms into a servant right before my very eyes. "I'm so sorry, mio amore. It's been a long day."

I see Ricardo's entire body tense in front of me and I gotta say, my heart goes out to him.

I haven't taken much Italian...but I do know what '*mio amore*' means- 'my love.'

It's obvious DeLuca and Lou-Lou are in a relationship of some kind.

Wow. That's just...holy shit balls.

Not to mention...odd and kinda gross.

Lou-Lou's *my* age. DeLuca's in his late 50's, at *least*. Not that *I* should really be one to judge. But now her statement about me and Ford makes perfect sense.

Poor Ricardo.

I can't focus on that right now, though. I have a bastard to kill first.

"Sit over there," I tell them, motioning to the wall.

They do as I say, but I don't miss the look in Ricardo's eye, telling me to get this over with.

I have to take a long deep breath when I realize that it's just DeLuca and I facing one another.

It's surreal. I don't know whether to pinch myself because it's finally happening or scream because a part of me is petrified.

"Alyssa," he says.

I internally shiver because hearing him say my name sounds like nails on a chalkboard. "So we meet again."

He gives me an evil smirk. "Only much closer this time."

"I'm not afraid of you," I say, my voice surprisingly strong.

He puts his hand in his pocket but I point the gun toward Lou-Lou and he pauses.

Dammit, I should have done this earlier. Stupid fucker already showed his cards. "Stand by me, Lou-Lou," I order.

"No!" DeLuca shouts. Ricardo narrows his eyes at me, but I ignore him.

Lou-Lou ignores DeLuca, stands up and walks over to me—staying true to her word. I don't miss the look DeLuca gives her. He's *pissed*.

I pull her in front of me. "It's safe to say that you might not want to make any sudden movements again. I specifically told you to come unarmed."

I glare at him. "Granted, it's not a crowbar, but I swear you'll feel every second of the impact when I kill her."

Lou-Lou's lower lip trembles and I don't know if it's an act or the truth, but either way, it makes DeLuca remove his hand from his pocket.

"You'll never get away with this," he says.

I laugh at him. "I beg to differ."

That's when I hear the sound of someone's footsteps and see a large shadow walking through the back entrance of the warehouse. My heart and my stomach reel when I see a gray suit come into focus and I look up into a pair of blue eyes.

Then I notice the barrel of his gun is pointed at me. "Drop the gun, Alyssa," Ford sneers.

My 10-year old heart breaks all over again. "You gonna kill me, Ford? That's what it's come down to?"

I hate that there's a small part of me that can't kill him because he's the tie to my dad and my dad loved him.

His eyes waver and he sighs. "You know I could never do that. But I can't let you kill DeLuca, either."

"Why not?"

"Because then how would you find out the truth, Alyssa?" DeLuca sneers behind him.

I hear a gun cock and DeLuca laughs and says, "I appreciate you volunteering to be my bodyguard, Ford."

Ford curses under his breath and closes his eyes.

"However, I suggest you stay right where you are, special agent. There's something I've been meaning to tell Alyssa."

Ford moves the gun toward Lou-Lou. "If you do, then I'll take out Lou-Lou."

That's when Ricardo stands up. I breathe easy because I know he's on my side.

Or at least, I *thought* he was.

Ricardo cocks his gun and stands behind me. "And I'll take out Alyssa," he says to Ford.

Over Ford's shoulder, I see DeLuca smile. "Good job, son. I'm proud of you."

"Shit," I mutter as Ricardo jabs the gun into my lower back.

"Sorry, Alyssa," Ricardo says. "But I'm not letting him kill Lou-Lou."

It's safe to say, my plan has officially gone to hell in a hand-basket. Everyone has a gun pointed at them *except* for fucking DeLuca. Everyone's going to die, except the *one* person who should. This situation is completely fucked.

DeLuca claps his hands. "Good. Now that we've got that all sorted out and everyone knows where the other stands. Alyssa, I would like your attention."

Ford's eyes meet mine. "Don't, Alyssa. Whatever he says isn't true. You have to trust me. I love you. I have always loved you."

Behind me, Ricardo coughs. "You are one fucked up person, Ford. And I've seen some shit, but this right here...this takes the cake."

Against my better judgment, I look at DeLuca.

"Please, DeLuca," Ford pleads. "I've never asked you for a single thing, other than sparing her life. If you tell her everything. It will kill her."

"I'm counting on it," DeLuca sneers.

I look back to Ford. "Do you or do you not *work* for DeLuca?"

"Technically, yes. But I didn't always. I am a member of the FBI first and foremost."

Behind me, Ricardo says, "Yeah, he's what we like to call a flipper-flopper. You know, when it suits him."

"Why, Ford? How could you do that after you saw what he did to my father?"

"Because I became too powerful for him to keep trying to take down," DeLuca interjects.

Ford's face pales. "I couldn't beat DeLuca. So, I had to join him. There was no other way."

DeLuca takes a step forward and his face hardens. "Go ahead, Alyssa. Ask him what his *first* job for me was."

Ford's face contorts in pain and I feel so lightheaded white spots form in front of my eyes.

I shake my head and point my gun at him. All thoughts of Lou-Lou as my leverage forgotten. "No," I shout. "You wouldn't do that to my dad. He was your best friend. You grew up together. He loved you. You wouldn't set him up to get killed."

"I'm so sorry," Ford whispers. "I had no choice."

"There's always a choice!"

DeLuca grins and it looks so sickening I have to look away. "And what a choice it was. He obviously chose to save his own ass. He came to me, worked out a deal and gave up your dear old dad in the exchange. You know, he was the one who suggested we do it right here, too. He said your dad liked the water." DeLuca chuckles. "He even set up the two gang members to take the fall for it. I'll admit that was brilliant."

I look at Ford, not even trying to hold back my tears. "You're fucking sick."

Behind me, Ricardo whispers, "Yup."

"I won't deny that," Ford says. "But I love you, Alyssa. You know that I do."

I'm more certain than ever that what he felt for me wasn't love, it was some gruesome combination of guilt, fixation, and control. I look Ford right in the eyes. "No, what I know...is that you were on the phone with me when it happened. You heard me cry my heart out. You heard my screams as DeLuca took my father from me."

I have to put my hand to my chest just to make sure my heart's still beating and it didn't physically crack into a million pieces. "You picked up that scared and destroyed little girl and held her in your arms like she was your own. You held her like you would protect her...all while knowing *you* did this to me. To *him*! How could you?"

A guttural cry rips from my throat and DeLuca laughs like it's the funniest thing in the world. "And that's not even all of it."

"What *else* could there possibly be?" Lou-Lou whispers. Then she gasps.

DeLuca gives me a sinister smirk. "Alyssa? Besides your father dying, can you think of anything *else* that might have ruined your life?"

"Shit," Ricardo mutters.

"*You* were behind the sex tape, Ford?"

He stays silent.

"Answer her, Ford." DeLuca directs. He shakes his head.

"You tell her the truth now. It's the *least* you can do, you fucking scumbag," Ricardo says, low and deadly.

"DeLuca promised Gaffney that he would win the run for mayor if his son Dean did it," Ford says. "However, it was my idea in the first place. I paid the Gaffney's off and promised that Dean would never get busted on a DUI charge if he fucked you and filmed it."

"What the fuck is wrong with you? Why would you do that to me?"

"I needed to do something to—" he pauses like he can't even say it.

DeLuca gives me a shit-eating grin. "To make sure your pretty face would never end up on the evening news. Where you could slip up and tell the whole world what I did to your daddy. Live from New York. You know, you really should have chosen a different major at NYU." His eyes blacken and I take a step back, not even caring that Ricardo's gun is still digging into me.

"I run this city," DeLuca shouts while taking a step forward. "It's *mine*. My greed, my hunger, my money...but most of all *my* control and power. I let you live as a courtesy to Ford; after certain assurances were put in place, of course. But, I *wasn't* going to have your stupid fucking ass mess up what I worked so hard to build. I couldn't take that chance." His lips turn up in a snarl and he winks. "However, I *would* like to thank you for being such a willing participant. Nice tits by the way."

I blink back impending tears...but there aren't *any* left. There's only darkness and pain.

I look at Ford again. "The way you treated me after it happened. I went to you for help and you—"

"Made her believe she was nothing but a whore. Broke her trust in everyone and everything. Hurt her beyond *all* repair. And this was all *after* you had already ripped her heart out. You really are one *despicable* motherfucker," Jackson's voice booms from somewhere in the distance.

"No," I say with my hand on the trigger. "He's one despicable *dead* motherfucker."

"No!" Jackson shouts, coming into view and halting me at the last possible second. "Don't do it, Alyssa."

In my peripheral vision, I see Ricardo aim his gun at DeLuca.

"He deserves it," I argue as Ford's eyes close and he clutches his stomach.

"He does, baby. I know he does," Jackson says. "But you need to let me do it."

"What? No."

"Yes," he insists. "You're not a killer, baby. I am. Your soul is still untarnished and I want it to stay that way. You don't know what it's like to take a life, Alyssa. Mike deserved everything I did to him and I would take his life again in a heartbeat. But, murder is a burden that I never want *you* to bear. I won't let you destroy yourself again because I love you."

He walks behind Ford and lowers his gun to his head. "And you need to let me do this for you. And after this, I'm going to take out

DeLuca. I'm going to take every single nightmare away, baby. I promise."

"No," Ricardo barks in DeLuca's direction.

Ricardo moves closer to DeLuca and grabs Lou-Lou right before DeLuca has a chance to shoot Jackson. "Don't you even think about it, Babbo," he says before he puts the gun to her head.

Everyone's attention turns to DeLuca and Ricardo at that moment.

As thankful as I am to Ricardo for not letting DeLuca shoot Jackson, I'm equally petrified for Lou-Lou. I never thought Ricardo would kill *her*. I regret ever bringing her here now.

Then, before anyone's brain can catch up to what's happening, Ricardo leans down and kisses Lou-Lou's tear-stained cheek. "Ti amo. Sii libero," he whispers in her ear.

Lou-Lou reaches behind her and pulls a gun out of her waistband.

She lifts her chin and aims the gun directly at DeLuca's head. He's so caught off guard, he doesn't even have time to aim his gun at her. "Brucia all'inferno. Burn in hell, Bruno," she says as she pulls the trigger, four times.

In slow motion we watch DeLuca's brain splatter all over the warehouse, his body falling to the floor with a heavy thud.

I can't contain the smile on my face. I think it's the brightest it's ever been. I barely even hear the sirens in the distance.

I open my mouth to thank Lou-Lou but she runs out the back door in the blink of an eye.

The sirens get louder and blue and red lights illuminate the warehouse.

"Jackson Reid, put your hands behind your head. You are under arrest," a voice says over a megaphone as the doors burst open.

My heart shatters like glass and I drop to my knees.

That's when Ford lifts his head and smiles at me.

Three weeks later...

Chapter 39 (Alyssa)

I learned the world was unfair at an early age. I knew that the bad guys sometimes won and that the good usually paid the price for their sins.

What I don't understand, is why I was forced to learn the harsh lesson twice in my life and why it had to involve the two men I loved the most.

Ford's living his life free as can be while Jackson's sitting in a jail cell.

For murdering Lilly's killer.

Ford attempted to get him for the murder of DeLuca but Ricardo and I vehemently fought those accusations without incriminating Lou-Lou.

Besides, it's not like anyone would be able to find her even if we did give her up. She skipped town right after killing DeLuca and no one's heard from her since. Not even Ricardo.

I have no idea *what* the story is between the three of them, but something tells me that Lou-Lou needed to kill DeLuca way more than I ever did...and that's saying something.

As fucked up luck would have it, the secret wire Ford was

wearing in the warehouse didn't support his claims that Jackson killed DeLuca, either.

Ford couldn't pin that on him no matter how hard he tried.

Unfortunately, the tape didn't get any incriminating evidence on Ford himself, the tape just magically happened to 'pick up' right when Jackson walked in and admitted to being a killer. Then it cut off.

And since Ford played both sides of the fence, he claims that he was working undercover at the warehouse. And since he did call for backup he's not being investigated.

But little did Ford know...I have my own brand of justice that I want to personally serve him.

After tracking down and talking to a few of my dad's old friends who are still members of the FBI, it was finally going to happen.

Jackson was right...I'm not a killer. My soul isn't tarnished, but my childhood was.

I make sure that I have everything in place before I walk into Ford's office. I'm surprisingly feeling calm. The look on his face tells me that he most definitely wasn't expecting me, but he's pleased nonetheless.

"Alyssa," he says.

He stands up from his desk and it's so reminiscent of that day, nausea overwhelms me.

I fight through it, though and take a deep breath.

He walks around his desk and smiles at me. "I knew you would come to your senses. I knew you would realize that I was only protecting you and I *knew* you would forgive me sooner or later. I love you, Alyssa. Everything I did was for you."

I just stare at him, dumbfounded. It's never occurred to me before that Ford might be downright delusional.

Or maybe, he's lied so much that he just can't tell the truth from all of the different worlds he's created.

When I don't say anything, he takes a step closer to me.

I stand there silently urging him to dig his own hole. "I couldn't let you be with Jackson, sweetheart. I had to make him go away. You belong to me, you always have."

He reaches for my hand. "I divorced Penelope for you a few months ago. I wanted to take you on vacation after I got rid of DeLuca and surprise you. We can get married now just like you always wanted. I'm choosing you this time."

I try my hardest not to grin. This is turning out even better than expected.

"You were really going to get rid of him for me?"

He kisses my wrist. "I'd do anything for you."

I reach up and touch his cheek. "I have a question."

"Yes?"

"At what age did I *first* belong to you, Ford?"

He blinks and makes a face. "Come on, Alyssa. Don't be stupid. You remember that night in my car by the docks. You promised to be mine forever."

I lean into him and nuzzle his neck, my nausea getting worse the closer I get to him. "I know it was around my birthday, but I'm having trouble with my exact age. I was hoping you could refresh my memory."

The look on his face is priceless as he pushes me away. "Nice try, sweetheart. Are you really *that* dumb that you don't know the law?"

He walks back to his desk. "Bit of advice, never try to school a federal agent on the law." He crosses his arms over his chest and gives me that movie star smile that makes me want to hurl. "The age of consent in New York is 17."

He sits down and props his elbows on the desk. "And I hate to break it to you, but even if that night was illegal; New York's statute of limitations is only 5 years from the time you turn 18. You're 24, Alyssa. Your time has run out."

He props his feet up on his desk. "In other words, you're screwed. Besides, we never had intercourse when you were 17, anyway. You were 21 the first and only time I fucked you."

I don't know which is worse, how much thought he's obviously put into this, or the smug smirk plastered on his face.

A smirk that I can't wait to wipe off.

I take a step forward and smile sweetly at him. "Hmm. You know what? You're right. I'm sorry, Ford."

He opens his mouth to say something, but I cut him off. "I'm sorry the night you put your hand down my panties and touched me in your car, that I was only 17." I put my finger to my lips. "Or maybe even 16 depending on the exact time."

I take another step forward. "On second thought, No. I'm not sorry. Because I was too young to be making the adult decision to let you touch me like that. And we both know, that as the only *adult* in the car; you should have known better than to touch me like that."

He stabs his finger in the air. "Save your breath because it doesn't matter. You've got *nothing* on me."

He sits up in his chair and snickers. "It doesn't matter that I was the first man to see and stick my fingers in that innocent, virginal, tight little pussy of yours before you became a whore. It doesn't matter, Alyssa...because you're too fucking *late*."

I sharpen my eyes in his direction and reach for the goblin on my necklace. "Does it matter that it was in Jersey, Ford?"

I can see the wheels spinning in his head and I continue, "Because those docks were technically in Jersey territory."

I open my arms wide. "And you know the great thing about Jersey?"

When he doesn't answer I proclaim, "There *is* no statute of limitations for sexual assault. And there is no *deadline* for filing sexual assault charges."

His jaw practically hits the floor. "And just so we're clear here, Special Agent. You did just fully admit to sexually assaulting me and penetrating me with your fingers when I was a teenager. And given your position of power and authority as an officer and the fact that you had a gun on you...do you know what that means?"

He slams the desk with his hand. "Knock this shit *off*, Alyssa. You *wanted* it. You dressed like a little whore and you begged for me that night. It was all *you*."

I ignore him. "It means that it's technically aggravated sexual assault. And do you know what that's punishable by?"

I look up to the heavens and smile. "Up to 20 years in prison."

I start unbuttoning my shirt. "And there's plenty of proof, including phone records. And let's not forget that you gave me a car when I was 17. In addition to your ex-wife who's willing to testify."

I undo the first 3 buttons and I open my shirt. "And there's the fact that I'm wearing a wire and just caught every disgusting thing you said."

He charges after me, but the door opens and in walk a few men in uniform. I wave to my dad's former friend who now lives in Jersey and is an officer there.

"Ford Baker you are under arrest. You have the right to remain silent..." the officer's start to say as they handcuff him.

I walk over to him and put my hands on his cheeks.

"How could you do this to me?" he whispers.

I look at him hard and say, "You only did it to yourself, Ford."

"But why?"

My grip tightens around his cheeks. "Because sometimes in life, sweetheart. The *good* guys win."

I let go of him but he leans his forehead against mine. "Do you know what they do to cops in jail, Alyssa?"

I grab his face again and stare into his eyes. "I'm not sure. I imagine it will be harsh, though. Given they don't take kindly to cops who commit sexual assault on children." I wrap one hand around the back of his neck. "And with that handsome face of yours...you're probably going to be passed around like a little *whore*." I lower my voice and whisper in his ear, "But if I were you, I'd be even more worried...because I hear that you're going to be sharing a cell with Jackson."

When I back away his face pales and he starts trembling.

I kiss the goblin and look at him one last time. "I think my father would be really proud of me right now."

And then I slam the door.

"I knew you could do it, sugar," Momma says as she wraps her arms around me.

I hug her back. "I almost tossed my cookies like five different times in there because he made me so sick."

She gives me a peculiar look but I shift my attention to Tyrone.

It pains me to see him in his wheelchair. Although the damage wasn't as extensive as the doctor's initially thought, he did lose the ability to move his legs. With time, they say he'll be able to drive a car and possibly even walk with special equipment one day. He's adjusting much better than the doctors expected him to...but then again, they don't know Tyrone's perseverance and inner strength.

Shelby's been by his side the whole time and I know that's exactly where she'll always be.

I just wish I was able to get Jackson out of jail so he could be here for him too.

"I know you do," Tyrone says, while looking at me. "And I'd be lying if I said I didn't feel the same way."

I didn't realize that I had spoken my last thought out loud.

I sit down next to him. "I'm worried about the trial. His lawyer's good, but he's not the best. Especially since he refuses to spend any of the money in his bank account because he wants me to have it."

Which of course, I adamantly declined.

Tyrone closes his eyes. "Too bad people's perceptions of killers is so black and white. I mean, yeah—he murdered someone...but he's not a bad person. And if everyone knew what actually happened, they would realize that. But even if they did; who knows if the jury or the rest of the world is going to really believe it. They'll probably think it's all some kind of act."

I thumb the goblin on my necklace and think about this for a moment. "I know, I just wish everyone could see the real him."

The idea hits me like a semi-truck.

I stand up and look at Tyrone. "I know how to do that. I think I figured out a way to help Jackson. It's a long shot but it's—" I start to say before everything fades to black.

———

I wake up to four sets of eyes staring at me: Momma's, Tyrone's, Shelby's, and a man wearing a white lab coat that I vaguely recall seeing once before.

Never mind that though, I have to finish telling them my plan.

I quickly sit up in bed. "We all know how the media affects people's perceptions of things, right?"

They all stare at me like I'm bonkers.

"I think she might have a neurological issue of some kind," Tyrone says while looking up at the doctor.

Momma pats my head. "You do know you're in a hospital, right?"

I roll my eyes. "Yeah, I know; I probably passed out again or something. Maybe I'm sick again. Whatever. This is more important—"

The doctor approaches me and cuts me off. "Young lady, I have *important* rounds to make. So, if you don't mind I'd like to speak with you."

I hold out my hand. "Just fork over the prescription for my antibiotics and I'll be on my way, Doctor. I have important stuff to do."

He sighs "I think we should probably speak in private, this time."

"No. I'm fine," I insist. "I really need to go back home so I can save my boyfriend who's currently in jail."

His eyebrows shoot up. "In that case, I really must *insist* that we speak in private."

He looks at Momma but she shrugs. "I ain't leaving if she doesn't want me to."

I hold out my hand again. "Put it here, Doc."

He pinches the bridge of his nose before he reaches inside his lab coat and hands me a large bottle of pills.

I stare at the bottle of prenatal vitamins and blink while Momma gasps with tears in her eyes. I try handing them back to him. "I think this is a mistake."

He focuses his attention to his tablet. "No mistake. Your HCG levels are consistent with being around 4, maybe 5 weeks pregnant. You'll need to have an ultrasound to confirm this, of course." He moves his glasses up his face and looks at me. "By the way, you're anemic so you really need to start eating more meat in addition to the iron pills I'll be prescribing you. I think that's why you fainted. Either that, or you stood up too quickly and your blood pressure plummeted."

I jump up from the bed, horrified. "I'm not pregnant, Doctor. I'm telling you, there's been a mistake." I lower my voice. "I'm on birth control."

Out of the corner of my eye, I notice that Tyrone appears to be in deep thought before he says, "Did you use a backup method while you were on those antibiotics?"

My hand flies up to my face and I sit back down on the bed.

Fuck a duck. That was an entire two week period of unsafe sex. How could I be so careless?

I look at Tyrone and he smiles. I've never wanted to strangle someone for being so goddamned smart and perceptive. Momma starts jumping around the room acting like she won the lottery. "I'm gonna have a grandbaby."

I can't share in her glee, though. Shelby's eyes meet mine and she gives me a sympathetic look.

At least she understands.

Maybe it's the hormones, but the dark cloud is over my head with a vengeance and I bury my head in my hands and cry. I miss Jackson *so* much. He should be here with me right now.

"Everyone out. Now," Tyrone shouts, causing everyone to startle.

Open mouthed, everyone, including the doctor, leave the room.

He rolls his wheelchair by my bed and reaches for my hand. "I'm not going to sit here and tell you to keep this baby or to get rid of it, Alyssa."

I squeeze his hand. "Thank you. Because right now, I have no idea what to do."

"What I'm going to tell you, is what Jackson would tell you."

"What do you mean?"

"He'd tell you that he'd hold your hand the entire time. And he'd remind you that you're stronger than you think. He'd tell you that he'd respect whatever decision you end up making. He'd also tell you that he loves you." He puts his hand over his heart. "And that's what I'm gonna do, Alyssa. Because no matter what happens...you're not alone and you have me. If you want to cry, if you want to shout, if you want to punch my face in so you feel better. Whether you want to keep this baby or not, I'll still be there."

"Me too."

I look up as Ricardo enters the room.

He looks at Tyrone then back at me. "Tyrone told me you were here. I know I haven't been around much in the last few weeks. I've had to take care of some business. But, I have good news."

"I'd love some good news right about now."

Ricardo smiles. "I've just hired the best lawyer on the East Coast to take Jackson's case."

"How can you afford that?"

"You probably don't want to know. But, I'm going up to the jail this weekend to see Jackson and tell him. I wanted to see if you wanted to go with me but—" his voice drifts off and he looks uncomfortable.

I look down. "Should I tell him?"

Tyrone considers this for a moment before saying, "It's up to you. You don't have to make any decisions right this second. You still have time."

"How good is this lawyer?"

"Excellent."

"I hope so, because I want to put Jackson's video confession out into the world. I want the world to know who Jackson really is."

Tyrone's eyes open wide. "You still *have* that?"

"Yeah. I never intended to use it against him. I just...the video made me fall more in love with him. When he talks about Lilly and how they grew up, how much he loved her and what happened when he found her, you just know that it was raw and honest. Every single word he uttered in that video showed Jackson's soul. He spoke straight from the heart."

Tyrone's eyes are gleaming. "I never thought I'd say this, but we need to use that video. Influence the media, get people to hear what happened. It might not change their minds completely and there will still be people out there wanting him to serve time, but I think a majority will agree that he was justified."

Ricardo snaps his fingers. "I agree. Upload that sucker on youtube right now."

Chapter 40 (Jackson)

You would think I'd be upset to find myself back in jail again, but I'm not.

I've accepted it.

But it doesn't mean that my heart doesn't ache for Alyssa every second...or Momma, Tyrone, and Ricardo for that matter.

It was ironic that I ended up back here on Lilly's birthday. I chose to kill DeLuca on that day because I thought it would bring me luck. Obviously, fate thought otherwise.

I took it as a sign that Lilly herself obviously wanted me to pay.

But I still don't regret it. Even now.

Just like I wouldn't have regretted taking Ford's life or DeLuca's. Although, after Ricardo visited me and explained what really happened between Lou-Lou, him, and DeLuca; I know that the right to kill DeLuca definitely belonged to Lou-Lou, and I hope that wherever she is now—she's happy.

I was beyond pissed at him for having a gun to my girl's back, though, but I couldn't really argue when he explained that if the roles were reversed I would have done the same.

You see, he trusted Alyssa not to kill Lou-Lou. Hell, he even trusted DeLuca not to kill Lou-Lou due to his sick obsession with

377

her. But he just couldn't trust that Ford wouldn't kill Lou-Lou...because he's a manipulating fucktard.

Those were his exact words.

However, I fully agree.

Especially looking at him right now from across the cafeteria in his orange jumpsuit.

The sight is so spectacular, I wish I could snap a picture and send it to Alyssa.

I thought I needed to protect her and make those who hurt her pay, but as it turns out; she got something even better than payback all on her own.

She got her own brand of *justice*...the way *she* needed to do it. I'm even more in awe of her and the woman she is.

And I know the man who gets the honor and privilege of spending the rest of his life with her, *will* be the luckiest man in the world.

I just wish it could have been me.

But for now, there's one more thing I have to do to settle the score with Ford.

Not only is he serving time for what he did to Alyssa, but he's also the main suspect in the murder of DeLuca now. He, of course, tried to tell them about Lou-Lou, but Alyssa and Ricardo along with me, are refuting his claims.

Which leaves all fingers pointing to him. The fact that he told Alyssa that he was planning on vacationing after taking DeLuca down and she got it on tape, doesn't look good for him.

He keeps insisting that he called for backup and was acting as a member of the FBI, though; so I guess we'll have to see how his defense will pan out in the long run.

And although he could be facing up to 20 years for what he did to Alyssa, the reality is that he most likely won't serve that much time.

For all we know, he could be out in a few months depending on his trial. The only reason he's sitting in jail now is because he's a flight risk and the judge ended up being a friend of Alyssa's dad.

Oddly enough, that's the saddest fact of all to come out in all this.

Alyssa's father really was a stand-up guy...but his worst quality was having Ford as a best friend and partner.

And had Ford not sunk his hooks into Alyssa right after his murder and coerced and scared her into lying about DeLuca...she would have been responsible for bringing him down a long time ago.

That's the way the world works, though, the bad guys win far more often than the good guys do.

But there's days like today. The rare exceptions to the rule.

And that exception is staring at me from across the cafeteria looking like he's about to piss himself.

My guess, would be because rumor amongst us jailers is...that 14 years ago, he pinned the murder of a prestigious officer on two rival gang members.

I look at him and give him a great big smile and he flinches. He was so freaked out about sharing a cell with me, he purposely hit his head against the sink and has been hauled up in the infirmary for the past few days.

But he's out today.

And no matter where Ford turns, he's up shits creek without a paddle.

The rival gangs want a piece of him. Any man with a teenage daughter wants a piece of him. Even DeLuca's inside people want a piece of him, now that Ricardo's taken over.

And then there's the guards.

The guards who heard the latest rumor. The guards who despise the dirty cop who backstabbed their own partner and set up his death. The guards who despise the dirty cop who's in here for sexually assaulting their dead partner's teenage daughter.

That's the funny thing about perception...sometimes, it really is everything.

He's as skittish as a kitten when he makes his way over to me.

I manage to keep my joy in check. "Hi, Ford. How are you doing on this beautiful day here at Rikers?"

"Look, Jackson. I'm going, to be honest with you," he says and I try not to laugh in his face. "I was hoping to bury the hatchet. We're cellmates and—"

"You set me up." I turn to face him. "Why in the world would I ever help you?"

His shoulders slump. "I was only trying to do the right thing for her. You can't blame me for loving her. I know you do, too. And face it, Jackson. You and I aren't really all that different. You're a murderer. And I'm—"

"You're what, Ford?"

He looks away. "I set people up for murders. The point is that we're not good people. So don't act like you're so much better than me. But I think if we work together in here, we might stand a chance."

I almost choke on my barely edible food. "I'm doing just fine on my own."

He makes a sweeping motion with his hands. "Yeah, right *now*. But sooner or later, you're going to need a favor. You're going to need to—"

I stab my food with my fork. "Make a deal?"

He sits closer to me and it takes everything in me not to throw him off his chair. "Yes. You're going to need someone in here who has your back. You're going to need someone in here who will take care of you."

That's when I laugh. "Are you offering to be my boyfriend, Ford?"

He makes a face. "What? No."

"Too bad, that's the way it works in here."

He looks horrified. "You can't be *serious*. For Christ's sake, we were both in love with the same girl. "

"A girl that I'm no longer going to see...thanks to you."

He swallows hard. "So, are you saying that you want *me* to—"

I give him a smirk. "Be my bitch. Yeah. That's *exactly* what I'm saying."

He stays silent. I can see him mulling his options and I'm loving every second of this. I push my tray away. "You know, I'm still having trouble figuring out why you're here talking to me. What exactly is it that you want?"

The funny thing is I already know exactly what he wants. He has no control, no power, he's helpless.

Just like how he made Alyssa feel.

He looks around the cafeteria. "I need protection. You know what they'll do to me in here. I need your help, Jackson."

That's when I stand up. "What are you willing to do for it?" I whisper.

He looks up at me and panic flashes across his face. "I'll do a-anything. Just help me. Please."

I adjust myself in front of him and raise an eyebrow. "Then get on your knees."

He looks around the cafeteria again. "Right *here*? Now?" he croaks.

"Yup. I want everyone to know that you're my bitch."

To my absolute delight. He slinks down in his chair until he's on his knees. "Now close your eyes."

After he closes them I back up and another inmate hands me a crowbar. I'll have to thank Ricardo for paying off the guard for me.

"Open your mouth for me, whore."

He winces and opens his mouth.

That's when I thrust the crowbar in his mouth.

His eyes fly open and the look is priceless. Pure fear. I'm pretty sure there's a puddle of his urine on the ground.

He starts choking and trembling. "Yeah, you like that? Of course, you do, you little slut."

He tries to move his mouth away but I don't let up. "Yeah, you heard me. You worthless slut."

There's cheering around the cafeteria and I give him a megawatt smile. "Figure your own way out of this mess, Ford. I suggest you whore yourself around because that's all you're good for. Now, get the fuck away from me."

I take the crowbar out of his mouth and hold it above his head because I want him to know what *that* feels like, too.

He scampers away and cowers.

Just like the vermin he is.

"Y ou have visitors, Reid."

I walk into the visiting room and my eyes immediately connect with Alyssa's.

As happy as I am to see her, I already told her that I didn't want her to visit. Visitation at Rikers is practically an all day event and it's not always safe.

Especially when she comes here looking like that. She's wearing one of my t-shirts and a pair of jeans. Her still dark glossy hair is hanging loose and she's glowing.

She looks so beautiful it hurts to breathe. I'm actually thankful that Ricardo and Tyrone came here with her.

My heart sinks when I look at Tyrone. I can't believe he came all the way here to see me. He has enough of his own problems right now.

Ricardo's the first one to give me a hug. I didn't think it was possible but we've grown even closer after what happened.

In part, due to the three-hour visit that we had when I first got here. He opened up to me and told me the truth about everything. When he left, we both practically had tears in our eyes. He also offered to do what DeLuca did for me. He offered to pay off the judge and have evidence planted again, but I declined.

He said he would figure something else out, but I told him that unless it was legit, I wasn't interested.

I want to be free on my own merits, even though a big part of me knows that won't ever happen.

I hug Tyrone next and seeing him in his wheelchair kills me. He gives me that look that tells me he's doing okay and follows it up with a smile. I smile back because I know that he's going to pull through this.

Finally, I turn and face Alyssa.

Then I force myself to back away. She looks hurt, and I hate myself for doing that to her. But I can't kiss her. I can't hug her. I can't *touch* her because if I do I'm afraid I won't ever stop. I'll unravel and I won't make it through prison if that happens.

We all sit down at the table and Ricardo's the first to speak. "I hired a lawyer for you. He's the best on the East Coast."

My ears start ringing because this whole thing is all too familiar. "I told you I wanted everything to be legit."

"It is," he assures me.

"I wish you wouldn't waste your money. I'm not getting out of here. The prosecutor's going to have a field day with me because they know that I don't regret it. They know that I'm going to accept whatever happens. There's no point in fighting this."

Ricardo lets out a frustrated sigh.

Tyrone looks pissed and opens his mouth to argue, but Alyssa stands up and puts her hands on her hips. "Ricardo, do you think you can distract the guards for a little? I need to speak to Jackson alone."

"You got it," Ricardo says before him and Tyrone leave.

The slap across my face knocks me for a loop. "Snap out of it, Jackson!" Alyssa screams.

I stare at her wide-eyed. "There's nothing to snap out of. I love you but I need you to come to terms with this. I need you to find someone else. Someone who's good. Someone who can take care of you an—"

She sits back down and points a finger at me. "Shut up. There is no one else, there will never be anyone else. I know you're scared because of the first time you were in prison. I get it. I know you've given up all hope of the system working in your favor but you can't. I still believe that good things can happen. I haven't in awhile, but I do now, Jackson."

"I wish you wouldn't because it will only hurt you in the end. And I don't want to hurt you, Alyssa."

She leans forward. "There's still some good in the world." Her brow crinkles. "Now can you do something for me? Please?"

"You know I will."

"I just need you to believe. Believe in me. Believe in yourself."

She stands up and reaches for my hand before placing it over her stomach. "Believe in us. Because I do."

Her stomach feels just like it always has, but for some reason, my heart rate skyrockets and I've never felt more nauseous in my life. "Alyssa, why did you put my hand on your stomach?"

She plays with her necklace. "Because I know deep down that you're scared. And I think you need some extra strength. But I know you can do it. I know you can get through this." She places her hand over mine. "You're not getting rid of us. We're going to be a team for life."

Tears sting my eyes as I remember everything she told me about the last conversation with her father.

And that's when I realize.

She said *us*.

"How? Not that I'm not—" I pause because I really don't know what I am.

Actually, I do. I'm fucking scared out of my mind. This is a different kind of scared that I've never experienced before.

But I'm strangely happy, too. Christ, does that even make any sense?

"I didn't think to use a backup when I was sick and on antibiotics. I'm sorry. I know it's not ideal. I know our situation is completely—" she pauses and exhales.

I place my hands on her hips and move her closer to me. "Scary?" I offer.

She blinks away tears. "Yeah. It is...but I know we can do this. No matter *what* happens. We'll get through this somehow. I don't give a fuck what the rest of the world thinks about you. Our baby will know their daddy is a good man, because they *will* know you."

She runs her hand through my hair and I place a kiss on her belly. "Okay." A sense of calm washes over me. "No matter what happens, I'll still believe in us."

I stand up and give her a hug. Ricardo and Tyrone's eyes meet mine. They both pat the spot over their heart and I smile.

Our visit ends after that but Ricardo walks over to me right before the guards take me away.

"Make sure you go to the recreation room tonight."

"Why?"

He starts walking. "Because there's a television in there."

"And by the way, you have a meeting with your new lawyer tomorrow," he calls out before he walks out the door.

Chapter 41 (Jackson)

I walk into the recreation room and find a seat. I have no idea what's going on, but Ricardo insisted I come here.

Since there's nothing better to do, I decide to start playing cards with another inmate.

"Hit or Stay?"

I eye my cards. "Hit."

Dammit. I lost. Story of my life.

"Yo, man. That dude on T.V looks just like you," some guy calls out.

I pick the cards up and begin to shuffle them.

"Yo, man," the guy shouts.

My card-mate tilts his head. "I think he's talking to you." I turn my head but get distracted by my image on the screen.

Then I hear the words that I'll never forget. "*My name is Jackson Reid. There are two things you need to know about me. The first—is that I'm in love with Alyssa Tanner. The second—is that I'm a murderer.*"

"That *is* me," I tell the guy.

Me and my entire confession. On the fucking news.

What was Alyssa *thinking*? I didn't even realize she still had that.

"A new video has gone viral," the newscaster says after my video ends. "It's sweeping across the nation and has garnered the attention of all social media sites."

My chest tightens. I don't know if this is a good thing or bad.

Every inmate in the room and a few of the guards start watching the television with earnest.

The newscaster's face becomes serious. "We at WKWNY decided to take it to the streets of N.Y with our news correspondent Anne Walley to find out what your opinion is regarding Jackson Reid's leaked confessional tape. Do you think he should stay in prison, America?"

"Shit, man," the inmate across from me says. "If that was my baby sis. You best believe I would have done the same damn thing."

There are a few nods of agreement around the room, but I don't get my hopes up. These are my fellow inmates, after all.

Anne Walley holds the microphone up to a woman with short blonde hair carrying her puppy in one of those big designer purses. She looks nice, maybe this won't be so bad.

"Jackson Reid should spend the rest of his life in a prison cell. What is *wrong* with you people! He's a killer. He shouldn't be allowed to roam free. You don't take the law into your own hands. You do the crime, you do the time," she bellows, before she pets her puppy.

I close my eyes. This is worse than torture. At least, I'll be well prepared for court. I told Ricardo not to waste his money.

I open my eyes as Anne Walley approaches another person and asks their opinion. A male this time. He's about 17 or 18 and he's wearing a baseball cap backwards on his head. "I don't know," he says appearing to be lost in thought. "I mean, I don't really like my little sister all that much." He looks down. "But, if someone ever hurt her or worse, killed her. I can't say that I wouldn't do the same, you know? I guess I can understand where he's coming from."

Anne approaches another bystander. It's another woman. She's in her late 30s and she's holding a crying toddler in her arms. "I'm a Jackson Reid supporter. We need more men like him in the world." She looks down at her child. "I don't want my little girl to live in a world where domestic abusers can get away with hurting or killing others. I want her to live in a world where there's men like Jackson Reid who aren't afraid stand up and get revenge for women like his sister."

Anne approaches another woman. She's in her mid-20's and has a few shopping bags in her hand. "Well, I have a few ex-boyfriends that I'd like Jackson Reid to take care of."

Her face turns sad. "But in all seriousness. Have you seen that video? Ignore the fact that he's good looking and actually listen to the pain he's in, people. The guy lost his sister. She was killed by his best friend. Beaten to *death*. Can you really blame the guy, Anne? I don't think he should be serving any time. It's obvious that he's already suffered enough."

Anne approaches another person. A man in his late 40's this time. He has a beard and a few tattoos. "I don't have a sister," he pauses. "But I *do* have a daughter. And if any—" There's a beep. And another beep. "Put his—" another beep. "Hands on her or *killed* her, you'd better believe I'd find his—" another beep. "and kill him with my bare hands!" he screams into the camera before he briskly walks away.

The recreation room erupts in applause. But then Anne approaches another woman.

Oh, god. It's Momma.

"Jackson Reid is my son," she says in her Southern twang.

Anne Walley looks skeptical. "I'm sorry ma'am, did you say your *son?*" Momma gives her a look and grabs the mic. "That's right. He's my boy. And this—" The camera moves and I see Tyrone, Shelby, Ricardo and Alyssa. My heart squeezes.

"Is his family," Momma continues as they all nod in unison. "We love him. He's a good man, America. He's not perfect, but he's got a heart like no one else and a good soul. Judge not, lest you be judged is all I'm sayin'."

The camera focuses back on Anne. "Well, there you have it, folks."

I walk into the room and I immediately want to turn right back around. This can't be my new lawyer.

She's too young. Younger than me. Maybe even younger than Alyssa, who knows.

The one thing I do know is...there's no way she's the best lawyer on the East Coast.

"I'm sorry. I think there's been a mistake," I say before turning around.

"There's no mistake, Jackson. My name is Michelle. I know you were probably expecting my father."

Needless to say, she's got my attention. "I didn't mean to be rude. I'm just—"

She holds out her hand. "Worried? Scared? Nervous?"

I shake her hand. "All of the above."

She sits down. "My dad is the big wig in the family. The one Ricardo spoke to and hired, actually."

I take a seat, although, I'm not sure why, but for some reason I feel compelled to. "No offense, Michelle. But if your dad is the lawyer. Then why are you here?"

She smiles and tucks a strand of hair behind her ear. "Well, I'm a lawyer too, actually."

"Oh, so I guess you're just taking care of some of the paper-work for him?"

She pulls out a briefcase. "No. I actually asked my father if it would be okay to take on this case myself."

I shift in my seat, trying to think of a polite way to decline and tell her that I need her father. "Look, you seem really nice and—"

"I went to school with Lilly."

I feel the gravitational tug on my heart from hearing her name. *Well, that would explain why she looks so young.*

She folds her hands on the table. "We had a few classes together at Harvard. I'd like to think we were friends. Your sister was an amazing person."

"I know."

"I saw the subtle change in her, Jackson. She went from being happy-go-lucky and so full of life and happiness to being miserable."

I put my head in my hands. "I should have noticed the signs. I should have—"

"She would have denied it," she says. "I tried talking to her a few times and it was like talking to a brick wall. The only thing that confronting her did was make her distance herself more." She holds my gaze. "Abuse victims leave their abusers on average seven times before they leave for good. It wasn't her fault, but she would have stayed until she found the strength within herself to leave."

I look down. "But if I knew...I could have saved her life."

"No," she says. "And you know why? Because Lilly *already* knew she could go to you, Jackson. She knew how much you loved her. She knew that if she called you and said that she needed you that you would have been right there. She knew that."

I look up. "Why didn't she?"

That's the question that will always haunt me. *Why didn't she?* I would have done anything for her, *anything.*

"Because she blamed herself for the pain," she whispers. "Because he made her. That's what abusers do. They tear you down piece by piece and bit by bit. Until there's nothing left anymore."

She wipes her eyes. "But make no mistake about it. None of this was her fault. It was all him."

"I know." I sit up and look at her. "You know a lot about this."

She nods. "I do."

There's a moment of silence between us before she takes out a manila folder. "It's why I asked my dad if I could take on this case." She bites the cap of her pen nervously. "But you'd really be taking a huge risk with me."

"What do you mean?"

"This would be my very first case by myself."

Oh, *that's* what she means.

I sit back and cross my arms. "Okay, Let's say I hire you. What's the argument?"

"I don't have one."

"Look, I didn't go to law school. And I'm not nearly as smart as Lilly was...but I do know that defense attorneys should present an argument. You know, like self-defense, insanity, or an accidental killing."

She crosses her arms, stares me down and I immediately feel it. "He wasn't attacking you, he attacked Lilly. You're not insane. And you don't regret it, so I'm not sure that going with an accidental killing defense would be the best way to go. So, the way I see it...that only leaves me with one choice."

"Which is?"

"Telling the truth."

I stand up and shake her hand. "You're hired."

She jumps to her feet. "What? Really? You mean it?"

"Yup. That's the only way I want to win this case. And I can't help but think that if it was Lilly herself defending me, she would want the same."

Chapter 42 (Jackson)

$\mathbf{F}$our months later, I'm sitting in a courtroom watching my lawyer, Michelle stand before the jury for her closing argument.

As far as juries go, this one is as versatile as it gets.

Out of the 12 jurors made up of my peers...six are female and six are male. They're all difference races, ages, occupations, and they all come from different backgrounds.

But only two of them have sisters.

Seven of them are only children. And the remaining three males have brothers.

Michelle told me not to let it get me down and to let her worry about that.

I turn around and look at my family. Tyrone and Ricardo's eyes find mine. They don't say a word, they just put their hands over their hearts and nod their heads. I look at Momma next. She mouths the words 'I love you,' and I mouth them back to her.

Then I scan the courtroom for Alyssa...but I can't find her.

She's been here every step of the way, so it's disheartening that she wouldn't be here today of all days.

Then it hits me. She won't be able to watch them find me guilty. Her heart won't be able to take it.

Suddenly, I'm glad she didn't come. It would put way too much emotional stress on both her and the baby. I would never forgive myself if something happened to them because of me.

I feel guilty enough for putting her in the position that she's in.

But that's the only regret I feel, still to this day. And the jury knows it because I was honest with them and told them.

Right after Michelle played the video of my confession in court.

That was the only thing that Alyssa and her fought about. Professionally, Michelle was upset because it was going to make finding potential juror's that hadn't seen or watched the video that much harder.

However, personally, she understood why Alyssa did it.

I turn back around in my seat. I don't know whether to face the jury myself or not.

Michelle's not going to like it, but I decide not to. Even though I know that she wants to get their sympathy and she wants them to witness my pain.

But I don't want to look at the jurors because I don't want them to think that I'm purposely trying to intimidate or influence them somehow. And mostly, I don't want them to lose focus on Michelle during her closing speech.

So no, I won't look at the jury. Instead, I close my eyes and feel Lilly's presence around me. I silently tell her that I love her and I tell her that no matter what happens, none of it was ever her fault...because I think *she* needs to hear it much more than *I* ever did.

That's when I hear Michelle start to speak.

"Thank you for your attention ladies and gentlemen of the jury. By now, you've formulated your own personal opinion regarding my client, Mr. Jackson Reid. I know there's nothing that I could say to sway you in either direction at this point."

She pauses. "You also know that by now, my argument has never been about self-defense. Because let's be honest; Mr. Reid was never defending himself against his own abuser. So, I'm not going to stand here and claim self-defense for Mr. Reid. Instead, I'll claim *Lilly's* defense.

"I'll also educate you on some facts regarding the law. To adequately determine the justification of deadly force in defense of a person, in a court of law, one must establish the existence of two main facts, first and foremost. One—you need to determine whether or not my client's use of deadly force was necessary to defend himself or rather, Lilly. Two— you need to determine if Mr. Reid did something that a 'reasonable person' would do in his position.

"And that's where you come in, ladies and gentlemen. You watched the video, you know the facts, you've heard from Jackson Reid yourself. So, knowing what my client knew and being in the same circumstance, would you yourself have had those same beliefs that he did?"

She clears her throat. "But forget all that. I didn't even need to tell you those things in the first place. That's not my real argument, here. Because the only thing I needed to do for this case was let the prosecutor's do their job and let you hear their arguments. The prosecution is required to prove beyond a reasonable doubt that Mr. Reid was not justified in doing what he did. And just so we're clear— *justified* means having done something for a legitimate reason. It's an exception to committing the offense. If the prosecution has failed to prove beyond a reasonable doubt that the defendant was justified, then you the jury must find Mr. Reid not guilty."

She takes a deep breath. "In closing, I just want to leave you with this. If Lilly was someone that you loved. And you found her beaten and murdered like Mr. Reid did. Would you feel justified doing what he did?"

The bailiffs take me away while the jury deliberates. I was told it would be anywhere from a few hours to a few weeks.

To say I was surprised to be called back as soon as I stepped foot outside the courthouse in my shackles would be an understatement.

After we rise for the judge, he calls the court in session and he collects a piece of paper from a member of the jury.

A piece of paper that will determine the rest of my life.

A piece of paper that will determine whether or not I get to spend the rest of my life with Alyssa, my future child, and the rest of my family.

The jury's faces give nothing away.

I wish I could see Alyssa's face *one* more time, I wish I could see my *child* growing in her belly. The thought causes blood to rush in my ears and vertigo plagues me, I want to sit back down because I'm not sure I can stand anymore.

I don't know why Michelle's arms are wrapped around me and she's telling me goodbye, because I'm too distracted by the sound of Momma shouting at the top of her lungs.

Oh, boy. I really hope Momma doesn't try to put a hurtin' on those jurors. Or the judge for that matter, poor guys already frail and old. I turn around to tell her it will be okay, but both Ricardo and Tyrone's arms are around me next. Their hugging me so tight I almost fall over.

"It's okay, guys," I tell them. "I'll be okay. Just promise me that you'll take care of Alyssa and the baby for me. Please."

They pull away and exchange a glance with one another. "Why?" Ricardo says. "You'll be able to do that yourself."

"What—" I start to say, but my breath leaves my lungs as Momma herself plows into me.

I close my eyes and hug her back. "I knew it would all work out in the end," she says.

That's when it hits me.

I look at Tyrone for confirmation. I don't even have to get the words out because he looks at me and says, "Not guilty, brother."

I'm not ashamed to admit, I'm barely holding back tears.

I'm going to be a father to my baby. I'm going to spend my life with Alyssa. I'm going to see my family.

I look at the jury again. And this time, they look at me. "Thank you," I whisper. I get a few small smiles before they start to clear out.

The bailiffs unchain me, and Michelle informs me that I'll need to sign off on some paperwork before I'm free to leave.

This time, I'm the one hugging her because I know what's happening. "Thank you and congratulations on winning your first case."

"You don't need to thank me, Jackson," she says with a grin. "But thank you for being the most memorable client I'll ever have. Thank you for reminding me why I became a defense attorney in the first place."

After I sign the paperwork we walk out to the car. It almost feels unreal. The air is fresher, the grass is greener, and I have a sense of peace.

A light breeze flows through the air and I feel Lilly's presence again. I look up to the sky and blow her a kiss.

Then a bird shits on my head.

Tyrone and Jackson burst out laughing. "Yup, that was definitely Lilly. Totally a little sister move."

I start laughing with them and it's the greatest feeling because I *know* that Lilly would find this highly amusing right now.

Momma hands me a napkin and I clean up before I get in the car.

We head back to the apartment complex and I can't get in the door fast enough.

Apparently, Tyrone and Shelby moved into Lou-Lou's old apartment so that Alyssa and the baby could have this one. Tyrone wanted his little niece or nephew to have his own room.

I'm surprised Alyssa didn't want to move to the suburbs to raise the baby but Ricardo said she wanted to be by her family.

I'm running around the apartment looking for her and my anxiety's through the roof when I can't find her. Then I notice that the door to the balcony is partially open.

I step outside into the warm July evening air.

I find Alyssa standing there with a mug and she gives me her gorgeous smile, complete with her adorable dimple. I don't hesitate to cup her face in my hands and kiss her like it's my last breath.

When I pull away her eyes are still closed and she sighs. "God, I missed that."

"I missed you." I place a kiss on her belly. "The both of you."

She hands me the mug, I take it with one hand and she grabs my other hand. "Come on, you're just in time to watch the sunset."

It's only then that I take a look at the two rocking chairs she has set up on the balcony.

Along with some bingo boards on the table.

"I didn't show up at court today because I knew you'd come home to me," she whispers.

I take a sip of my hot chocolate before I press her hand to my lips and kiss it. "I love you."

She takes a sip of her own hot chocolate. " And I love you."

It's then that I realize.

Without pain, you wouldn't know happiness. If you let the pain take over, you miss out on the good things, the things that really matter...like love and family.

If you don't find a way to make it through the pain...you miss out on the best parts of your life.

Epilogue

P ain. It hurts us. It pushes us. It punishes us.

Or, for the few poor souls out there like me...it defines us.

Yes, I've taken a life...and I would do it again in a heartbeat.

And one day, I will explain to my son the way the world works.

I will tell him, that the bad guys win far more often than the good guys do.

But I will raise him to know that in a world full of bad...he should do good anyway.

I will tell him that I don't think I'm necessarily a good person, but I'm not a bad person, either.

I will tell him the truth.

I'm flawed. I'm human. I lead with my heart.

And that's okay, because I have a good one.

About the Author

_____

If you liked the book, it would mean the absolute *world* to me if you left a *review*. It's so hard for indie author's to receive acknowledgment and reviews *really* make a difference for us.

But even *more* than that...I *urge* you to read the message on the next page.

Want to be notified about my upcoming releases? https://goo.gl/n5Azwv

Oh, and if you're wondering if Lou-Lou and Ricardo will have their own story? You bet they will. I'll be releasing a special 'series' titled- **'Blame It on the Shame'.** Follow me on Facebook for more details.

Ashley Jade craves tackling different genres and tropes within romance. Her first loves are New Adult Romance and Romantic Suspense, but she also writes everything in between including: contemporary romance, erotica, and dark romance.

Her characters are flawed and complex, and chances are you will hate them before you fall head over heels in love with them.

She's a die-hard lover of oxford commas, em dashes, music, coffee, and anything thought provoking...except for math.

Books make her heart beat faster and writing makes her soul come alive. She's always read books growing up and scribbled stories in her journal, and after having a strange dream one night; she decided to just go for it and publish her first series.

It was the best decision she ever made.

If she's not paying off student loan debt, working, or writing a novel—you can usually find her listening to music, hanging out with her readers online, and pondering the meaning of life.

Check out her amazon page and Facebook page for future novels.

She recently became hip and joined Twitter, so you can find her there, too.

She loves connecting with her readers—they make her world go round'.

~Happy Reading~

Feel free to email her with any questions / comments: ashleyjadeauthor@gmail.com

For more news about what I'm working on next: Follow me on my Facebook page: https://www.facebook.com/pages/Ashley-Jade/788137781302982

Other Books Written By Ashley Jade
Blame It on the Pain
Blame It on the Shame - (Parts 1-3)
Complicated Hearts - Book 1
Complicated Hearts - Book 2
Complicated Parts - Book 1
Complicated Parts - Book 2

Older Titles
Twisted Fate series (Books 1-4)
The Best Deception
What Happens in the Dark (Books 1-3)

1-800-799-SAFE (7233), or 1-800-787-3224 (TTY).

The National Domestic Violence Hotline

1-800-799-SAFE (7233), or 1-800-787-3224 (TTY).

If you or anyone you know is a victim of ***domestic violence***, I urge and I *beg* you to reach out.

You're *not* alone…and I will pray for you every single day of my life.

Please, don't blame yourself.

And just in case you never hear this…it's *not* your fault. It's **NEVER** your fault!

If you or anyone you know is a victim of ***sexual assault***, again; I urge and I *beg* you to reach out.

It's *not* your fault. It's **NEVER** your fault! Please don't ever blame yourself.

National Sexual Assault Hotline 800-656-HOPE (4673)

National Child Sexual Abuse Helpline (*Darkness to Light*) 1-866-FOR-LIGHT (866-367-5444)

For rape & sexual assault victims call: 212-227-3000

or **email** : help@safehorizon.org

All calls are kept completely confidential.

And if you still can't pick up that phone, you can always email ashley-jadeauthor@gmail.com I'll never judge you, I'll just listen <3

Acknowledgments

I like to keep these short and sweet.

First and foremost: *Thank you* my amazing fans...seriously, you rock! You'll never know how much you all mean to me.

I can never thank you enough for sticking it out with me and hopefully *now*, I'm starting to make it worth your while and delivering the goods.

Either way, I'll keep trying and giving you everything I've got.

Check out my Facebook page, Twitter account, and page for more updates and new series/more novels. I *love* connecting with my fans! You guys give me that extra 'push' whenever I feel defeated. (*I also like to give out arcs from time to time.*)

A special thank you to my **Hammie**: You are my love, my muse, my everything. I couldn't have done this without you.

Made in the USA
Middletown, DE
10 August 2021